Fortune

By

Katie Godman

Copyright © 2022 Katie Godman All rights reserved.

Acknowledgments:

To my fiancé Mark for his support. To Mum, Dad, Michael, Charlotte, Noah, Danielle, Tom, Ana, Leo. To the various and extended O'Donoghues, and Godmans. For Sharona for being an amazing proof reader and cheer leader. For the Paper Dolls writing group, especially Jo, Llew and Wenna. For the Next Chapter Writing Group, Lesley, Louise and Cler. Apologies if I have missed everyone – thank you to everyone who has helped!

1800

Chapter 1

Jessica
With a smile I poured myself some steaming coffee and sat down to savour its heady dark flavours. There was the calf's head to boil, pastry to make and countless fruits and vegetables to pit and peel but there was plenty of time for that. For a few moments, I rested in silence, enjoying Amelia playing an aria on the piano in the empty dining room.

Amelia's playing would have pleased my mother enormously - not that she was a lover of music, it was the owning of the piano that she would have derived pleasure from. For myself, I am pleased that Amelia has a hobby which makes her happy.

As I took a second sip of coffee familiar guilt crept up on me. She had been dead ten years, but I could still hear my mother's voice telling me I had been idle long enough. There was work to be done. Maybe I wasn't grateful enough for the business she helped me establish. And what about Peter, she would always demand. Was Peter happy? Peter was always happy. She used to say I must keep it that way for I had more to lose if his attentions wandered. That was true enough. Over and over again she would remind me, I should count myself lucky that he had chosen me.

I shifted in my chair. Maybe that was true enough once, twenty years ago, when we married...when he was a handsome man in his mid-thirties and I was fifteen. Without him, I would have gone into service as my mother had done, but with him I had servants of my own, a fine, flourishing inn and two lovely daughters. I breathed through my nose, trying not to get lost in my thoughts.

As Amelia's playing continued the clock in the hall struck midday. Lydia was still at Mr Syrett's, Peter was upstairs in his study. As for the staff, after the breakfast rush, the cook Laurence Wrenthorpe was at home, tending his sickly wife and the housekeeper Nan Forrester had finished cleaning the bedrooms, and gone out. Both would return later in the afternoon as we prepared for dinner, along with the waiters Billy and John, as well as Alice who cleaned up and washed dishes. Valancourt snoozed underneath his spit wheel, his furry legs twitching. The bell above the door chimed announcing guests.

I was on my feet, hair and dress smoothed, then out into the hall. Two gentlemen stood waiting for me, both naval officers, both *almost* handsome; one's appearance was too fussy and the other had a prominent Roman nose. The fussy one had already set down a large trunk, whilst the other held a modest sized bag.

'Good morning gentlemen, are you looking for rooms?'

The taller one, with the smaller bag and Roman nose, nodded. 'Yes madam, but we have no booking.'

From what I knew about naval uniforms, his meant he was a captain and I would guess he was in his mid-thirties, about the same age as me. His olive skin and black hair gave him a continental look.

'That shouldn't be a problem,' I smiled, opening the guest book. 'Is it just the two of you?'

'Yes,' said the shorter, younger one. He was a dandy with an Irish accent and a lieutenant's uniform. 'Two single rooms if you have them.'

'How long will your stay be?'

'A week for me,' said the dandy lieutenant.

'I may stay a little longer,' the captain said. 'Depending when my business concludes.'

'We have two single rooms free, though one is without a window.'

'As long as it has a looking glass,' the captain said. 'Lt. Driscoll will be very happy with it.'

'You see this cruel treatment I must put up with from my superior officers, madam?' The dandy chuckled with a wink.

'The one without the window is cheaper,' I said and told them the prices for rooms and additional prices if meals were required.

'Aha, then I shall be happy to take it. You see, Captain? I shall not be kept down for long.'

'If I could just take your names…'

'I am Captain James Parnell.'

'And I am Lieutenant Dara Driscoll, at your service Mrs-?'

'Mrs Fitzwilliam.'

'Ah,' Lieutenant Driscoll looked around with a grin. 'So, you must be the owner of this fine establishment?'

'Yes Lieutenant, along with my husband. We have owned The Fitzwilliam nearly twenty years. If you'd like to follow me,' I unlocked the cupboard and retrieved their keys. 'I will show you to your rooms. I will have your bags sent up shortly.'

'We can manage, Mrs Fitzwilliam,' said Captain Parnell shooting a look at Lieutenant Driscoll, who none too subtly rolled his eyes and heaved his bag up. He brightened considerably as the piano music stopped and Amelia stepped into the hall.

'Good morning,' she smiled. 'New guests, Mama?'

'Yes, Captain Parnell, Lieutenant Driscoll, this is my youngest daughter Miss Amelia Fitzwilliam.'

'A pleasure,' said Lieutenant Driscoll, while Captain Parnell nodded. I started up the stairs and the captain followed me.

'Where have you sailed from?' Amelia asked the lieutenant.

'We have been patrolling the Channel, but in ninety-eight we were part of the battle on the Nile-'

'Driscoll, you can tell Miss Fitzwilliam all about it later. For now, Mrs Fitzwilliam is waiting to show us to our rooms.'

The lieutenant sighed and followed us upstairs. Amelia shrugged and went back to the piano. I threw the captain a grateful look and he gave me a small smile. At fifteen Amelia, always a pretty girl, was turning into quite a beauty and many of our male guests were noticing. She had blonde hair from me, (what Peter called 'Sommers' Gold' in a pun on my maiden name), but Peter's curls as well as Peter's blue eyes and my cupid bow lips. She had been plump like Peter, but now her roundness had turned to ample curves. Like me, she had an appreciation for fashion, and while she did not dress like a slattern, knew how to use clothes to her advantage - many of which she made and altered herself in whites, pale pinks and floral prints. I was starting to wish her married sooner rather than later as her good looks could attract the wrong sort of man, especially in our line of business.

I opened the door to Lieutenant Driscoll's room and he was all smiles, for despite there being no window I had worked hard to ensure it a very pleasant place, looking glass and all. Decorating the rooms was something I enjoyed immensely. Each one was different, for it all depended on which colours looked best in different lights, and which furniture suited different shaped rooms. It vexed Peter but over the course of nineteen years I had decorated all the rooms twice, trying to balance between having them not too fashionable as to make people feel uncomfortable, while making sure they did not look dated.

I showed the captain to his larger room, with its view of King's Street.

'I hope the noise from the road won't trouble you, sir.'

'No, indeed, I am used to it.'

'Are you from a city yourself?'

'From Liverpool,' he allowed himself a smile. 'My accent has gotten lost on my travels.'

Apart from when he said *Liverpool,* I thought with an inward smile. 'I suppose as a navy man, this isn't your first time in Bristol?'

'Quite right. Last time I noticed this place, but a sign in your window said you were fully booked. I resolved to try again this time, having heard some favourable reviews from other officers.' He set down his bag. 'May I ask if you are you born and bred in Bristol?'

'Originally, I am from Glastonbury, as is my husband. My mother was a cook, and it was her idea we start a hotel an idea of which I approved.'

'Indeed. This does seem a very comfortable place.'

'Thank you, sir. Good day to you.' I left him and ascended the stairs to the family floor and went to Peter's study. The cards from his morning game of cribbage with Lydia were still out. As I expected he was dozing, newspaper open before him, a story about The British Museum on the page. Lydia would like to visit British Museum. It would be nice to take her, if I could get away. Both she and Amelia would love a trip to London, as would I. I was ashamed never to have been. Amelia would love the fashion, Lydia the culture and I would like to visit some of the restaurants – places which I had read were better than mere taverns and sold all sorts of fine foods. I wondered how the food I cooked for our guests compared. As much as pride was a sin, it was a fact that my food received the many compliments in this inn.

I kissed my husband's forehead. His eyes fluttered open.

'Hello, my love,' he said, kissing me on the cheek.

I pressed his hand. 'Hello dear,' I said. 'I just came to let you know the last two rooms have been taken by navy officers. Lt. Driscoll and Captain Parnell.'

Peter grunted. 'Irish, eh? They get everywhere these days.'

'Captain Parnell is from Liverpool,' I said, knowing it best not to make a comment about the Catholic Relief laws being years old and that my husband ought move with the times. He didn't like to be reminded he was twenty years my senior.

'Even worse,' Peter laughed. 'A northerner!'

I jokingly rolled my eyes. He pulled me onto his lap and kissed me again.

'How go the accounts?' I asked, my eyes drifting to the large open ledger. Peter reached over and snapped it shut.

'Dull as ever,' he said. 'You just concentrate on keeping this place pretty and our guests well fed.'

'I still think you ought to teach Lydia how to manage the accounts. She has such a sensible head on her shoulders and she already knows a little of it, as Mr Syrett has taught her-'

'Mrs Fitzwilliam, I will say again, no man will want our eldest daughter if you keep encouraging her in this fashion! That will then blight Amelia's chances, and with all her charm that would be very unfair.'

'Some men might want a wife with book learning to help with their trade and engage in conversation with, like a doctor or a lawyer-'

'Careful or you shall make her a bluestocking only fit to marry a dissenter!'

Peter seemed to treat it all a joke, but I did not think that would be such a bad thing. Lydia would probably go mad married to a man who expected her to be idle. Though Peter can't see it, I would have as well. It is his relaxed nature which has allowed me free reign over The Fitzwilliam, something my mother had happily and correctly predicted.

I stood. 'Should you like me to bring you up a tongue sandwich?'

'Yes please, you know that sandwiches are my one indulgence,' he patted his rounded stomach, then looked up at me with tenderness in his eyes. 'May I just say, you are looking very beautiful today. Worth your weight in Sommers' gold.'

Peter never ceased complimenting me; which was amusing when I remembered what a distant figure he had seemed when I was growing up. I had always been aware of him, the youngest son from The Fitzwilliam farm; strong looking with blue eyes and brown curls. He was seen with his brothers and the other gentleman farmers and landowners at church and about the village. Aside from being a Fitzwilliam boy, he was most famous for having won two cows in a card game from the Roberts' oldest son. The Roberts were my parents' employers.

It was only when his oldest brother Henry married Miss Jane Roberts that Peter noticed me. I was the same age as Amelia is now. He told me later he had seen me on the Roberts' grounds and at first mistook me for a visiting cousin. He was surprised to learn I was actually the only surviving child of the deceased gardener and the cook. His mother had encouraged the union however, partly wanting to get her last bachelor son wed and also, as she told me herself after the marriage, as a youngest son it was less important if he married 'down' so long as he had a practical wife who wouldn't be afraid to support his venture into trade, or at least manage a household on a limited budget, because he would not inherit the farm. It was her way of giving me a compliment, but it just served to remind me how lowly Peter's family thought me, and reinforced my own mother's words that I should be more grateful than I felt.

My own mother had jumped at the match, and it seemed the whole thing was in motion before anyone had spoken to me on the subject and before I had exchanged little more than pleasantries with Peter. I did as I was told. It made my mother exceptionally happy, especially when Mrs Fitzwilliam called on her. It made me happy that my mother was happy, and while most of my friends were being courted by penniless boys it was as if I had been chosen for something special. Everyone said how lucky I was, how happy I must be and I supposed I was, or at least I did my best to be knowing that to be confused and frightened was not the expected reaction, and that if I did even question anything about the situation, I could risk losing Peter's favour which my mother thought was much worse than marrying an older man I barely knew.

As it turned out well, what reason do I have to complain? But it is not as if marrying Peter immediately bought wealth, as everyone assumed it would. He was not the sole reason for our good fortune. It was my mother and I who worked on the hotel. He gave us the means to create something, we did most of the work.

If a man wealthier than us came into the hotel and decided, after limited acquaintance, that he wanted to marry Amelia, what would I say? Peter would agree to it, my mother would have, but what would I do? I think I would not. I would insist upon a prolonged courtship; I would like to think my daughters might be married for more than their good looks and assumed subservient natures – which I am very pleased to say, while they do have good looks, their natures are anything but subservient. I swallowed. But then, my mother's disappointed voice sounded in my head, asking what did Peter ever give me to complain about?

For his part, he has never reproached me that I have only born two daughters and had a miscarriage either side. Indeed, for the past few years he has shown not even the slightest inclination for more children, perhaps a benefit of an older husband. Now his hair has thinned, his eyes grown watery and his strong looks softened to plumpness – though that was probably the fault of my cooking. I thanked him for his compliment, then hurried downstairs to make him a sandwich.

*

'Amelia, it's time to start on dinner.'

Her groan carried from the dining room. 'Very well, I will go and change.'

'Be quick about it.'

As I started on the pastry the back door opened and Lydia came in, bringing the warm spring air with her. The cats, Ellena and Desdemona, circled around her ankles.

I kissed her cheek as she set her basket on the table.

'How was the shop?'

'Fine,' Lydia said. 'I borrowed some more romances for Amelia as Mr Syrett just bought a load from the estate of an old widow. There were no new cookery or scientific books though.' I peered over her shoulder, disappointed that there had been no cookery and worried that there was yet more romance for Amelia. She read them avidly and would not read much else; whilst I was pleased that both the girls were keen readers I wondered if too much of the romance might giddy Amelia's already impressionable mind.

Lydia carried on talking as she unpacked the books. 'We had a group of medical students who refused to be served by me and insisted on speaking only to Mr Syrett. He knows nothing of the medical books, only the poetry.'

'Well it is their own fault if he gave them useless books.'

'True,' Lydia paused. 'Is that calf's head waiting for me?'

'It most certainly is.'

'Marvellous.' Lydia removed her spencer and bonnet, tied on her apron and rolled up her blue sleeves. Ever since she was a child, she enjoyed butchery. Peter thought it a ghastly hobby, but I was proud of her, she was good at it and knew the names for most organs in English and Latin. Amelia swept in, as Lydia started to peel the skin from the already boiled head.

'This one's got quite a thick layer of fat on it, more so than usual.'

'Lord, must you Dia?' Amelia raised her eyebrows.

'You might learn something if you heed me, Millie.'

'About cow's heads? I'd rather not.'

'Did you notice this one has one eye bigger than the last one, Mother?'

'No-'

'Are these books for me?' Amelia asked, picking them up.

'Yes, but they are only loans. I've to take them back to the shop to be sold.'

'Amelia, could you make a start on the chicken please?'

Amelia sighed, set down the books and started plucking the chickens.

'Is that a new pattern on your sleeve?' I asked.

Amelia nodded, extending her arms. She had gone upstairs to change from her pretty day dress to her work dress. She used her work dress to practice embroidery on, so the faded blue gown was awash with various flowers and shapes, in all different colours. Sometimes, she embroidered while wearing it if she thought she could shy away from work for a few moments, especially when she was supposed to be tidying the bedrooms. I would much rather that she used her sewing skills for some practical purpose instead of idling them away. 'I intended it to be daffodils but it didn't come out right.'

'Daffodils aren't red for a start,' Lydia looked over. 'They look more like French horns, which is hardly patriotic.'

I smiled.

'Oh dear, those navy officers will think me very terrible,' Amelia giggled, and started to unpick the pattern. 'Maybe I should embroider oak leaves instead.'

'What navy officers?' Lydia asked. 'Are they so fine to warrant you embroidering oak leaves in their honour?'

'They took the last two rooms this morning,' I said.

'One of them has a large nose and looks like a villain from an Ann Radcliffe novel-'

'Amelia!' Foolishly I threw a look to the kitchen door, half worried she would be overheard. She could be too much like Peter at times.

'I didn't say looking like an Ann Radcliffe villain was a bad thing, did I? Anyway, he is about as old as you Mama, so the oak leaves aren't for him. The lieutenant however was very handsome and well dressed.'

'I think he was vain, Amelia. I'd rather you didn't embroider oak leaves for him. Perhaps you are better off embroidering daises.'

'I've done daisies a thousand times. Besides, I was not serious. A navy officer hardly has any money at all and one must spend all one's time moping around, waiting them to come home from sea.'

We carried on in silence, but for Amelia humming and a calmness came over me, as it often did when just in the presence of my daughters. Maybe it was the knowledge that at least so far, neither of them thought me beneath them or ungrateful or perhaps it was simply the happy knowledge that we all worked well together.

Amelia kept most of the feathers she plucked in a bag; we would reuse them to replenish pillows, quilts and cushions. She let a few strays fall for the cats to chase ('Get it Mona! Get it Ellie!') and I pretended not to notice. With Amelia, it was easier to pick my battles and wasting the odd feather did not seem enough to send her into a sulk over. Peter would say I was too hard on her, my mother would say I was too soft on her but as for myself it was simpler easier to keep Amelia in a good mood while we readied for dinner.

Lydia stuffed the pie I had made with meat from the calf's head. She worked with quick precision and I gave her a smile of thanks which she returned. Amelia brought over the plucked chickens which Lydia prepared, then mounted on the spit and clicked at Valancourt to hop in the wheel, which he did so with an excited bark.

Lydia held the stripped calf's skull aloft. 'I think this will be an excellent subject to draw. Look at his teeth, one has cracked—'

'No Mama, don't let her! She already has enough gruesome skull drawings as it is. I can't sleep at night with them looking at me.'

'Lydia, I told you not to put them on the bedroom walls.' I tried to keep the smile from my face for Amelia would say I was siding with Lydia, but I did not wish that Lydia stop drawing the carcasses. She was developing a skill for them, where that skill would lead I did not know but I saw no point in stifling it. The farm girl in me wanted to tell Amelia not to be so squeamish, but as the mother it was up to me to mediate the middle ground. 'Lydia may draw this one but keep it away from your sister, and I shall want it tomorrow to make broth with.'

'You shan't make the broth tomorrow, Mama,' Amelia smiled. 'Laurence shall!'

'She will have to start it in the morning, ball or not.'

'Lydia, where is your sense of fun? Which reminds me, are you sure you don't want a train on your gown? Even a small one?'

'Quite sure.'

'Very well, but then you mustn't be jealous of me at the ball.'

'I'm sure I won't be.'

'Are the Webster brothers going?'

'The ones not at sea are,' I said. 'But even though the Websters are our friends I would rather you be careful the boys, they have quite a reputation.'

'I don't want to marry them, Mama. Lord, they are butchers' sons and navy men-'

'Edward is a lawyer,' Lydia interjected. I glanced at her but she did not meet my eyes. Was she starting to wonder, as I was, if Edward Webster had feelings for her? Were her feelings of friendship for him starting to develop into something else? I would not be against the match for he is far and away the most sensible of the hoard of Webster boys but it would sadden me, selfish though it was, to lose her company to marriage so soon.

'But he is the dullest,' Amelia said. 'I just want to dance with the others for they are such fun.'

'As long as it is just dancing and you don't make a show of yourself.'

Amelia glared at me. 'I do not mean to make a show, merely to enjoy myself.'

'There is a fine line between the two.' I spoke more harshly than I felt, knowing that it was better for her to be warned now than judged in public. It was not fair, but it was the way of the world.

'I suppose you would rather I danced with some bore like Joshua Hughes?'

'Not really, that poor boy can't dance at all and you'd make an altogether different show of yourself.'

As I thought, my comments appeased Amelia. She snorted with laughter. 'Abigail and Ruth told me he was getting engaged to Beth Walker anyway.'

'Maybe Joshua Hughes is not quite such a bore as we all thought,' Lydia said. 'Any how, what of Abigail and whats-his-name, the coffee shop boy?'

'*Well-*'

As we gossiped, the girls got on with their tasks, Lydia checking on the wine and beer she had brewed, as well as making a start on the syllabubs whilst I made the cakes and Amelia got on with the vegetables and ketchups. The kitchen became filled with a mixture of warm aromas of fresh carrots and parsnips, sweet honey and sharp lemon. In my head I went through my conversations with the guests, adjusting some of the recipes to suit different palates and requests. It was a pleasure to personalise the food, and to anticipate their happy responses.

'Aha,' Peter entered, took a spoon and tried some of Lydia's syllabub.

'Very good,' he smiled. 'Sweets from my savoury and savoury from my sweet.'

The girls rolled their eyes at his old joke. He found it very amusing that Amelia was better at savoury and Lydia better at sweets, (aside from the butchery) thinking this the opposite to their natures. However, the reality of cooking is often that sweet food needs more exact measurements and patience whereas savoury can be freer; altered and changed as it goes along, which meant what the girls were good at was no surprise to me.

'Good evening all,' said Laurence as he came through the back door.

Amelia threw me a look.

'Good evening, Mr Wrenthorpe. Yes, Amelia you may go and finish your ball gown.'

Amelia bolted from the kitchen, the cats chasing her. Lydia rolled her eyes and presented Laurence, Peter and I each with a glass of her elderflower wine.

'What do you think of this?' she asked.

'Delicious,' I proudly smiled, savouring the floral notes.

'Very good,' enthused Laurence.

Peter nodded. 'This could become my one indulgence, dear.'

He poured himself a bit more, raised it as if to toast and went up the stairs after Amelia.

Chapter 2

Amelia

My fingers softly played the notes of Bach's Aria while the guests breakfasted. There was a skinny abolitionist, two gnarled merchants, a family awaiting their ship to America, a very old Major and no sign yet of the navy officers.

As the waiters weaved between the tables, Mama spoke with the family bound for America and the father enthused a great deal about liberty. His wife looked less convinced. Papa was sitting with the merchants and the abolitionist, having his second breakfast of the day - and he has the cheek to say I must marry well to keep me living in the way I am 'accustomed'! He wanted to have words with that abolitionist for giving Lydia a leaflet about the true cost of sugar, but it was hardly the abolitionist that set her on that path, more like old Mr Syrett. By the expression on Papa's face it looked as though he was getting quite the earful about the suffering of Negroes.

The two gnarled merchants rose, and one turned to me.

'What a fine talent you have for music, Miss,' he lisped, his gaze pointed below my face.

'Thank you, sir,' I said tersely, not wanting him and his gaze to linger.

'That is a very fine instrument,' his friend said, apparently genuinely interested in the piano.

'Yes, my father obtained it for me,' I said. 'He is a most attentive parent.'

That caused the gazer to glance over to my father, who frowned at him. They nodded and went on their way, and I smiled gratefully at Papa, who smiled back, rolling his eyes at the abolitionist who was still going on. I suppressed a giggle and returned my concentration to the Aria.

The merchant had been right; my piano was particularly fine. Papa had won it at cards some years ago. At first Mama had been shocked, 'But what will we do with it?'

'One of girls can learn to play of course!' Papa chuckled. 'Amelia is always singing, why not let her?'

I was immediately taken with the idea and Papa, who had played a little in his youth, would sit with me and teach me. It seemed magical to watch his stout fingers glide over the keys, producing such beautiful, delicate sounds.

Lydia walked in with the post. She gave a letter to Papa, but threw Mama a look. What could that mean? Lydia was much better than I at guessing handwriting, so it might well be from our Glastonbury relations given her warning look. I supposed I would find out soon enough.

As Lydia went around the tables giving out letters to the guests, the navy officers entered. The young, handsome one smiled at me and I smiled back. I saw no harm in it. It was true that I should not wish to marry a navy man, but there is surely no harm in looking upon a handsome face, is there?

I carried on playing until the end of breakfast, when the navy officers were the only guests left. As Tawny Alice came to clear away their plates, the younger one looked at me again.

'What lovely music to accompany our breakfast,' he said in his charming Irish accent as he stood.

'Thank you.'

He made his way to the piano as the captain went to leave the room.

'Perhaps you could help us out, Miss Amelia?'

'Do not trouble the young lady, Driscoll.'

'I was wondering if you could tell me...'

He paused and I waited.

'...where I could get my boots fixed?'

'Oh,' I said, a little disappointed. 'You could try the Hughes, near St. Nicolas' Market. They are friends of the family so if you mention you are staying with us, they might treat you favourably.'

'Wonderful, thank you.' He grinned as if something had just occurred to him. 'I wonder which amusements you would recommend in this fair city? We went to the theatre last night and saw Beggar's Opera. What else do you think is worth our attention?'

'There is the spring ball tonight,' I said. 'It is a public ball. There are lots of good people going and I am sure you would be most welcome, so long as you buy a ticket. Officers from the army and navy will be in attendance.'

'Did you hear that, Captain Parnell? From the army *and* navy? We don't want to be out-swaggered by the army now, do we? I think we might have to put in an appearance, especially if Miss Amelia will be there.'

'Oh, I shall be.'

'I must request the honour of your first dance then,' Lt Driscoll said with wink, which the captain rolled his eyes at, nodded at me and together they left the room. I waited until I heard them close the front door before running up the stairs to fetch my dance card.

I studied my reflection in the mirror as Mama inserted the last pin into my hair.

'Very beautiful,' she said.

I turned my head so I could see myself from a different angle. Satisfied, I nodded.

'It won't fall out when dancing will it?'

'No, there are plenty of pins.'

'But my hair is thicker than yours and Dia's.'

'I am well aware, but I've been doing your hair for fifteen years.'

That was true enough. 'And my dress?' I asked, stroking the floral embroidery.

'Very pretty.'

I stood, my shoes pinching my toes, but hopefully I would get used to them. We went to the parlour where Papa and Lydia were waiting.

'All hail Princess Amelia,' Papa said. 'Goodness me, Mrs Fitzwilliam, can you believe this beautiful lady is our youngest daughter!'

Mama smiled. 'Both the girls look lovely.'

'I have a treat for Mama and Lydia,' I said. I had made us each a fan; Lydia's had Athena on it, and Mama's had a likeness of her as Hera and Papa as Zeus. Papa was especially flattered by this depiction, Mama said it was lovely and even Lydia looked pleased. For my own scene I had painted Aphrodite. Perhaps the goddess of love would smile upon me at the ball!

Lydia stood. Her dress plainer than mine, for that was what she had requested, save for the small amount of embroidery on the bust. She stood next to Mama. They looked so much alike, apart from Mama's hair was Sommers' gold and Lydia's was Fitzwilliam brown. Lydia did not realise how much she looked like Mama, nor how beautiful she truly was. Men don't always notice her, but when they do they can't take their eyes off her, though she ruins it by talking about anatomy, politics or being sharp.

'Are we finally ready then?' she asked, proving me right.

The ballroom was already full when we arrived but luckily the dancing had not started. Abigail and Ruth Hughes waved over Lydia and I.

'What do you suppose?' Abigail asked before even greeting us. 'Will Webster has asked me to dance and Tom Webster asked Ruthie.'

They were the handsomest of the Webster brothers! But still, I fancied Lt Driscoll was handsomer.

'I have a lieutenant who has promised to dance with me.'

'In the cavalry?'

'Alas, no.'

'The infantry?'

'No-'

'Not the navy? Oh poor Amelia!'

'He is very handsome, is he not Lydia?'

'Yes,' Lydia nodded and did not say a word about him being a dandy. 'Very dashing indeed.'

'And what of you, Lydia? Who will dance with you?'

'I-'

As if on cue, Edward Webster, the-dull-but-not-ugly-lawyer, stepped into our midst. 'Miss Fitzwilliam, I wasn't sure if you were coming.'

'Well, here I am,' Lydia said.

'I suppose you have someone for your first dance?'

'No.'

'Well, would you dance with me?'

Lydia gave a quick curtsy. 'Yes sir.'

Lord, I hope they do not form an attachment for he would be a very dreary brother-in-law, although Papa and the Websters seem set on either Lydia or I becoming a future Mrs Webster, and I must say, as merry as the Websters are I would rather it wasn't me. Indeed, I fancy we could both do better. Tom and Will Webster appeared and whisked the Hughes sisters away. I looked about, worry fluttering in my chest. Was I to be jilted at the first dance? What could be more humiliating?

As heat crept up my spine and the music started all I could think was how everyone must be staring at me. What an over done fool I must look, standing on the edge of the dance floor alone. All the handsome young men were lining up with partners, leaving only the hideous ones loitering around the dance floor - but now I was among them, so I must look hideous…

'Miss Amelia, a thousand apologies!'

I spun around to see Lt. Driscoll, out of breath but still handsome in his dress uniform. He extended his arm to me. Deciding not to seem desperate or shrewish I took it without comment. We joined Lydia's set and were soon prancing about the dance floor.

He chatted so amiably about his pleasant day and his boot repairs, his stroll on the downs and visit to the tailors that my mood softened.

'And listen to me, going on. What of your day, Miss Amelia?'

'Why, I was getting ready of course,' It was out of my mouth before I realised how vain it sounded but he only laughed.

'That is half the fun is it? Well, perhaps not quite so much as half but the anticipation is rather thrilling. And the effort was well worth it, you look quite divine-'

He leant in close as we came together. 'Far out-shine the other girls, I'd say.'

I laughed at this. 'You know how to please me,' I said as the dance ended. It all seemed over far too quickly.

'May I beg another dance?'

I nodded and we set off again. 'Do you dance often?'

'I practise regularly with my sister. This is only my fourth ball.'

'Only your fourth? You are very confident of the steps I must say-'

We parted and met up again. 'My captain is talking with your Mother and an older gentleman.'

I glanced to where he was looking. 'Oh, that's my father.'

'Ah yes, I saw him at breakfast this morning. What do you suppose they speak of?'

I shrugged. 'Pleasantries, I hope. Or my father might be trying to engage your captain in cards. Papa does love cards.'

'I do also, though my captain does not. Maybe I should play your father later.'

'It may not be wise. Papa is excellent at cards and does not always approve of Catholics in the navy you know, so he would try very hard to beat you. That could be what he's talking to your captain about.' I grinned wickedly.

'How do you know the captain and I are Catholics?'

'I was assuming on your names. Am I correct?'

He nodded. 'You are. Though I fancy neither my captain nor I are particularly good Catholics.'

I laughed.

'I think they only let us be officers in the navy these days because they know they need a proper big old god to control the sea, not your genteel protestant one.'

'Lt Driscoll!'

He chuckled.

'So the protestant God for the land, the Catholic god for the sea?'

'That's right. Those army men have it easy.'

An infantry captain in the next set threw us an annoyed look, and we both guffawed.

'They've just to fight the enemy, we've to fight the enemy and control the ocean.'

'How very brave of you,' I said, not sure if I was bored by his boasting or impressed by his irreverence. Before I had chance to decide the dance was at an end, and Will Webster appeared before me and asked me to dance. Lt Driscoll winked at me and offered himself to Lydia, who accepted looking perplexed. They did make quite a funny pair, him more over-preened than she.

When the dance was ended Tom Webster asked me, but I told him he could have the one after, I was quite breathless and in need of punch. As I came back, I neared Mama and Papa. He was sitting and she was standing. Captain Parnell was still with them.

'Are you a gambling man, Captain?' Papa said. 'There is some fine boxing near the docks. I suppose a navy man like yourself might like such a sport?'

'Not so much, I'm afraid sir.'

'I could never understand it myself,' Mama said. 'Two men beating each other to a pulp.'

'It's the skill of it, don't tell me you don't appreciate that?'

'I do *appreciate* it,' Captain Parnell smiled wryly. 'But I'd rather not stake money on it.'

'How very genteel of you.'

Mama sighed, and turned to sway to the music.

'You see my lovely wife would rather dance than talk about boxing, Captain Parnell.'

'I do not mind-' Mama started.

Papa waved her complaints away and looked at her in the very tender way he does. I had never seen him look like that at any one else. That was love I supposed. It must be quite feeling to be looked at so.

Chapter 3

Lydia

Father still hadn't mentioned to Mother that he received a letter from Uncle Henry yesterday morning, which must mean that either Henry wanted Father to go out to Glastonbury to visit him, or worse, Uncle Henry wanted to visit us.

I stopped outside Father's study and knocked on the door, hoping I could broach it over our morning game of cribbage. When there was no reply, I entered. Father was nowhere to be seen but the letter was on the desk, so I read it.

In his brisk way, Henry told Father he was coming to visit on a matter of business next week, to meet with one of the millers who bought his wheat. He also said he would like to discuss payments of the debt. What debt? Had Father loaned Henry money? Henry was always moaning about how lazy his farmhands were and how bad the harvests were…

Would details of the debt be in the ledger? I looked at the thick leather-bound tome. Father never let anyone else do the accounts, even though thanks to Mr Syrett I had a good understanding of such matters. With a quick glance over my shoulder, I pulled the book close to me and opened it. Father's neat handwriting detailed the money the guests paid, as well as the money we paid out to staff and to the suppliers of food; Mr Webster for meat, Mr Thomas for vegetables and so on. There was no column for mortgage since that had been repaid a few years ago, and the rest of the hotel had been bought outright twenty years ago with money from Father's family and his gambling winnings, as well as money Mother's parents had saved. But then there was another outgoing column, it said simply 'Debt – Henry'.

I frowned. Henry wasn't paying Father but the other way around. Why on earth would Father owe Henry money? The amount was in the tens, and increasing every month. A creak on the stairs told me Father was coming back so I shut the book and fled the room. I cursed myself for a foolish child, but I did not want to be caught prying and I wasn't ready yet to face father over cribbage, with the knowledge of the debt and the uncertainty its nature hanging between us.

I hurried off, early to work. If I confronted Father, it might turn into a row and then he might stop me working at the shop, though if he was in debt, I could understand why he'd changed his mind about me working.

Mama had always taken Amelia and I to buy books from Mr Syrett's. His second-hand books were reasonably priced and because he often bought books from estates selling items off, it wasn't unusual for him to have the cookery books which Mother enjoyed.

Mr Syrett's wife and children used to help but his wife died a few years back and while his daughter went to America with her husband, his sons took up careers as school masters and clerks in Bath, Cambridge and London. Whilst he was proud of them, it has left him alone to run the business. I'd been visiting one day when he'd been busy and I found myself helping out, which soon became a regular arrangement with him letting Amelia and I read books before they went on the shelf; then six months ago he offered to pay me for my trouble.

At first Father had been cross, saying we'd look impoverished, but Mother liked the idea. He seemed to come around to it until Mother said I was to keep my pay, not to give it to Father. He was never really furious, especially at her, but he had screamed and shouted then, asking if she didn't trust him. She had stood her ground and said while she did trust him, we had no need of the money as business was going well and I should save the money for a 'rainy day'.

If he was in debt to Uncle Henry, I could see now why he was angry. He probably hadn't told Mother as Henry made his distain of her quite clear, but she should know. The repayments had been quite large. Perhaps that was why she didn't trust him with my money, so maybe she did already know but then surely they'd tell me and Amelia? We were old enough and if sacrifices needed to be made, we could help.

Maybe I should offer Father the money but if I didn't know the nature of that debt was that fair? I shook my head. He was my Father-

'Good Morning,' Mr Syrett smiled as I entered the shop, a cup of tea waiting me for on the counter. 'How was the ball?'

'Oh,' I forced a smile. 'It was good, thank you.'

He chuckled. 'I'm just going out the back to sort through the new delivery, you hold the fort here.'

I nodded, and after removing my bonnet and spencer, settled behind the desk, plucking a copy of Lavoisier's Elementary Treatise of Chemistry to read. I hadn't got very far when the bell rang, announcing the opening of the door.

'Miss Fitzwilliam I am glad you are at work today, that's why we've come. We are in want of a friendly face.'

I looked up to see Mr Amos Thomas, the fruit and vegetable supplier to The Fitzwilliam. He was a middle aged, plump, negro gentleman. The bell rang again, and a tall youth stepped in behind him. He had wavy black hair, green eyes, olive skin and if he hadn't smiled in the same way as Mr Thomas, I would never have guessed they were related.

'This is my son, George Thomas. He has just been accepted to study medicine in Edinburgh.'

I hid my surprise with a smile. Now I thought on it, Mr Thomas had told Nan Forrester that he was a Sambo, but I assumed he'd just said that to curb her snide comments about Mrs Thomas being a white woman. Looking at his son though, it was much easier to believe.

'Oh, how wonderful! I must admit to being very jealous of you.'

'Yes,' Mr Thomas enthused. 'We are very pleased. He has this list of books he ought read, do you have any here?'

Mr Thomas nodded at George, who passed me the list.

'When will you start?'

'Not until September,' George said. 'But father insists I am fully prepared.'

'Well, it won't hurt will it?' I said, leading the way to the medical section.

'And you know, you'll have to work twice as hard as any of them-'

George flushed. 'They might not know,' he said quietly.

Uneasiness crept over me as I realised what he meant. He could pass as white and intended to do so. I didn't blame him, but still busied myself with the books, embarrassed. However Mr Thomas seemed to take it in good grace.

'You'll still be from trade, won't you? You can't pass as a Lordling, eh?' He chuckled and ruffled his son's hair and I supposed the difference in their skin tone, and the advantages this would bring to George, had been long accepted between them.

'True enough.'

'So, we have these titles-'

I was glad to have the medical books and discussions about Edinburgh to take my mind off the mysterious debt. While we didn't have all the books, I said I'd hold anymore if they came in and George said he'd call back in a few weeks. The rest of the day passed in its usual pattern, and when I got home, I saw little of Father. While I worked with Mother in the kitchen my mind whirled as she gossiped with Amelia about the ball. What did she know of the debt? Was it my place to tell her?

That evening, after they had bid us good night Father beckoned Mother back to the parlour to talk a little while. I left with Amelia, and then waved her on. She rolled her eyes.

'Eavesdropper,' she whispered, but she'd want to know what I learnt.

In the cupboard in the hall was a set of drinking glasses. I had long used them to amplify conversations held on the other side of the parlour door.

'Why didn't you mention it earlier?' Mother said.

'I knew it would only worry you.'

'But Henry will be here next week-'

'Well, he didn't give me much notice either but luckily one of the bedrooms will be free.'

'Yes, but then that means we can't have any passing trade.'

'I can hardly turn my brother away.'

'I know, I just wish I had more time to prepare.'

'Darling, there is nothing to prepare, I run a fine hotel. What more could he possibly want?'

She started to plan changes to the menus to accommodate Uncle Henry and Father gently agreed with her. It didn't seem like he was going to tell her about the debt tonight. I put the glass back and crept to bed.

'So,' Amelia asked as she twisted rags into her hair. 'What did they speak of?'

'Uncle Henry is coming to visit.'

Amelia frowned. 'When?'

'Next week.'

When Mother told us over our breakfast in the kitchen that Henry was expected next week we both pretended to be shocked, Amelia perhaps pretended a bit too much, though Mother was so busy cleaning the kitchen she barely noticed.

'Come now, sweetheart,' Father said. 'It's not as if he'll come in here.'

She nodded distractedly. 'Girls, can you wear best day dresses when your uncle is here? Actually no, not your best for he'll say you are vain, but nice ones please.'

'When do the girls not wear nice dresses?' Father said and Amelia smiled at him. 'But Lydia, you'll have to take time off work. It won't do while your uncle is here.'

I knew why. Henry would think me working in a shop was beneath him and he wouldn't be able to fathom a woman in a bookshop. But what was more, I'd bet Father didn't want Henry to know about our family's, albeit small, other source of income. Henry might request it towards the repayment. Instead of arguing I said, 'You ought have given me more notice, now I shall leave Mr Syrett in the lurch. You wouldn't like it if Laurence did that to you.'

'That's hardly the same.'

His words, tossed off casually as if I was a silly little girl, hurt. I was as important to Mr Syrett's shop as Laurence was too our kitchen, but apparently it was hardly the same. Father saw Laurence as a man with a good job; I was little more than a girl with a hobby.

Chapter 4

Jessica

Mr Thomas, our grocer, arrived while I had been overseeing the clear up in the kitchen after breakfast. It was time to pay our monthly bill.

'Good morning,' he smiled.

'Good morning,' I replied as I poured him a cup of tea. 'Lydia mentioned you came into the shop yesterday.'

'I did. She was very helpful. We were choosing books for my son. He is going to Edinburgh to study medicine.'

'My congratulations!'

'Truly?' Peter asked, looking dumbfounded.

Mr Thomas nodded proudly.

'I didn't think…' Peter trailed off as Mr Thomas raised his eyebrows. 'What I mean to say, I've heard the boy takes after his mother.'

'His mother is not a doctor, Mr Fitzwilliam,' Mr Thomas chuckled, but his mirth didn't reach his eyes.

'No, no. Of course not. What I meant was…Oh, never mind.' He gave me a look, but I wasn't going to dig him out. 'Come then, Mr Thomas. Let us settle my bill.'

Peter took him up to his office. I went upstairs sometime after, to fetch fresh tablecloths. As I half expected, Lydia was listening at the study door with one of the glasses we'd inherited from Peter's mother. She beckoned me and I crept over to her. Ever since childhood, Lydia had been extremely curious. She'd always watched guests, asking 'hows' 'whys' and 'whats'. To begin with, many of the men found this endearing, mistaking her for a boy yet to be breached, and answered her questions. However, when they realised she was a girl, many of them dismissed her questions, which were starting to develop in their nature to genuine queries about the men's profession involving law, medicine or the church. I think this was when she started listening at doors.

It meant that for a while she drew bizarre conclusions about various things, which was I why started taking her to Syrett's bookshop. Even with books to read, she carried on eavesdropping and I never discouraged it, finding it useful to learn about our guests - and at times my husband and his family. I was aware this meant that occasionally she eavesdropped on me, but that was a price I was willing to pay.

'Well?' I whispered. Lydia took my hand and lead me into her bedroom, a worried frown on her brow. Normally when she listened to Peter's meetings there was none of this concern. He paid the bills on time and tended to get on well with our suppliers.

'What is it?'

She swallowed. 'I think Father is in debt.'

My insides clenched. 'How do you mean, in debt?'

Lydia shrugged. 'I read his ledger, and there was a column repaying a debt to Henry. He was sending large, regular payments.'

'But we don't owe Henry money. Your father's winnings, his parents and my parents gave us money to buy this place. It wasn't a loan and he told me we paid off our mortgage a few years ago.'

'I know,' Lydia chewed her lip. 'What else could Father spend money on?'

Lydia's eyes searched mine and my heart sunk. What did men like to keep from their wives? I had a horrible inkling I knew. He didn't have the energy for a mistress, he liked a drink though wasn't a drunk... but gambling was different story. He played cards at every party, lamented that Lydia wasn't a boy – not so she could pursue a good profession but because he thought she was an excellent card player. He wasn't out often, but when he did go out alone it was to watch dog fighting, horse racing and boxing, all of which involved placing bets.

But he was good at it. He'd won Amelia's piano, hadn't he? He won some of the money that had paid for The Fitzwilliam. I would know if he'd made a big loss, wouldn't I? I thought of how he'd snapped the account book closed the other day. Maybe he thought there was a difference between lying and simply not telling me. I was so wrapped up with the hotel I never really enquired about his gambling as he didn't seem to lose...when he won, he won - a great deal. Which must have meant he bet a great deal.

'Are you sure you read it right?'

Lydia raised her eyebrows. 'Yes, but how can we know unless we ask him?'

I swallowed. 'I will ask him, but I will need time to think on how to do it.'

This could upset the balance of our business if he felt I had been spying on him and that I didn't trust him. Lydia had been snooping not I, but saying so would appear as if I was shifting the blame onto my daughter and I didn't want him to be angry with her.

I paced, hoping she had made a mistake but that seemed unlikely, but then so did the idea that we could be in debt and Peter was concealing it from me.

From the hall came the sound of Peter's study door opening and Mr Thomas leaving.

'Good day, Mr Fitzwilliam.'

'Good day to you, and pass my best wishes to your son.'

Lydia looked at me so I stepped out and nearly bumped into Peter in the corridor.

'Ah, there you are, my darling. Could you bring me a sandwich? And maybe a slice of last night's cake?' His eyes twinkled.

'Of course,' I nodded, trying to gather myself. He went back to his study and I followed him, trying to steel myself. Peter didn't usually get angry with me, but I knew this was different. Lydia had pried into what he considered his affairs. Maybe, I could still get the truth without being direct but by giving him the chance to confess. He sat down and looked at me.

'Yes?' he looked puzzled. I closed the door, knowing Lydia would listen anyway.

'I was just wondering,' I sighed. 'You seem a little anxious of late-'

'I do?'

'Yes.' Was that true? Not really, and though he had been angry about Lydia's job that had been months ago. 'I was just wondering if you would tell me if there was anything troubling you?'

He blinked. Did that mean something or was it just a blink?

'Of course, I would my dear. How kind of you to ask.'

I lay my hand on his arm. 'Truthfully Peter, are you sure nothing troubles or ails you?'

'No,' he chuckled. 'Well, no more than usual for an old man with two pretty daughters close to marrying age.'

I had to push a little harder. 'And there is nothing wrong with the business, the finances, then?'

'No, not at all.'

'You would tell me, wouldn't you?'

'Of course,' his face became serious. 'Though I wouldn't want to worry you. You have enough to think of running this place. Leave the finances to me.'

'It would worry me more to think you carried a burden alone.'

'Is that so?'

'Yes.' He drew me into an embrace. We held each other tightly and for a moment he pressed me so hard it hurt. As we pulled back, I braced myself, feeling now he would reveal the debt.

'That is reassuring to know dear, but there is nothing for you to worry over,' he kissed my cheek. 'I have everything in hand.' For a moment it seemed his eyes were sad or maybe I'd just imagined it, because then they were bright with happiness as he said, 'Now, where is my sandwich, eh?'

*

I decided to let him think it over for a while. I had given him the opportunity to tell me, and whilst he had not, if he was hiding something it would give him a chance to mull it over. I would give him a few days before broaching the subject again, while keeping a close eye on him. It could be that he wasn't concealing anything at all, and that Lydia was mistaken. It could be that I needed to be more direct.

The next morning, after his usual routine of having breakfast with me and girls before the morning rush, then his second breakfast with the guests followed by a quick game of cards with Lydia, he headed through the kitchen towards the back door.

'Where are you going?' I asked, my imagination suddenly leaping to dark gambling dens or sinister money lenders.

'To see Mr Hughes. He sent me a note with his apprentice over breakfast to tell me he has finished his repairs on my boots. I would send Lydia, but it's best I try them on lest he has made a mistake.'

I nodded, relaxing and kissed his cheek. 'Very well.'

I watched him go then slipped upstairs into his study, drawn by curiosity. The ledger was on the desk. Taking a deep breath, I carefully opened it. For a few moments my head swam looking at the numbers but then my eyes settled on the titles for the columns. There were out goings, prices paid for rooms and then there, very clearly was 'Henry – debt'. Drawing my finger down the column I saw that there were hundreds of pounds which had been paid to Henry since last summer. I sat down, winded. It had to be wrong. I had to be a miss understanding. Such a sum! How much more was owed? I dreaded to think. Setting the ledger back where it was, I stole from the room. Lydia was waiting the hall. She raised her eyebrows.

'I think you are right. When he returns…I don't know what I will say.'

Lydia took a deep breath. 'Ought we tell Amelia?'

I shook my head. 'Not yet,' I said. 'Only when we have spoken to your father and know the full truth of this matter. I wouldn't want to worry her.'

Maybe that was why Peter had never told me. He didn't want to worry me, but I was not a child! Goodness, how would I broach it with him? His pride would be deeply wounded to think I had spied on him. Maybe I could say I dropped his ledger while I cleaned his study?

'Maybe,' I said, 'the debt has nearly been repaid.'

'Maybe,' Lydia said. 'But surely half the riddle is how it came about in the first place.'

'Come,' I said. 'Let us go and have a cup of tea and think it over.'

Lydia shook her head. 'I must get ready for work.'

I descended the stairs alone, to the sounds of Amelia playing the piano. I hated to think of that instrument now, a reminder not of my daughter's skill but Peter's gambling and the debt.

Once in the kitchen, I set to making tea. The bell above the front door sounded

and I stepped out to see Captain Parnell not in uniform, but dressed very stylishly none-the-less, shaking rain from his hat.

'I didn't realise it was raining,' I said.

'It only just started.'

'Would you like a cup of tea?'

He paused as if to refuse but then said, 'Thank you, Ma'am.'

I was going to bring it through to the dining room, but then thought we had had a friendly conversation at the ball with Peter so why not invite him into the kitchen? Also, a conversation would distract me from worrying about the debt. He stepped in after me and I poured him a cup from the old cast-iron tea pot, which I had brewed earlier.

'You were out and about early this morning,' I said.

He nodded. 'Yes. I was concluding my business which I had expected would take much longer.'

'Can I ask the nature of your business?'

'Of course. In fact, you shall be the first person to hear its outcome. I have bought a house.'

'Oh, my congratulations!'

'Thank you.'

'Are you to settle in Bristol then?'

'I have bought the house as an investment. I think the navy will keep me from settling anywhere for a while yet. I intend to rent the house out.'

'An excellent idea. We ought toast to your success with more than tea!'

He laughed. 'Well, I shall take that as a hint that you wish me to buy a bottle of fine wine.'

'Nonsense. I have a whole cupboard of fine wine. I-'

The front door was flung open with a thud. 'Mrs Fitzwilliam!'

Captain Parnell and I exchanged an alarmed look and I hastened to the hallway. Amelia sprung from the dining room and Lydia ran down the stairs. Lt Driscoll stood there, looked between us all with a horrified expression and hurried over to me. 'Madam, I do not know how to begin.'

'Driscoll,' the Captain was at my shoulder. 'What is it?'

'Madam, you might what to sit down.'

'What is it?'

'I was in the marketplace, and there was a commotion. A horse had gone wild and escaped its cart. It kicked Mr Fitzwilliam.'

I went cold. 'He's injured?'

There was an awful pause.

'I'm sorry, Mrs Fitzwilliam. It is worse than that,' Lt Driscoll swallowed and lowered his voice. 'He has died.'

For a moment I heard, saw, felt nothing. My legs went weak. I grabbed the door frame to settle myself. Captain Parnell's hand was on my elbow. 'Come, sit down.'

I allowed myself to be led to the chair in the hallway. 'Can you...repeat your words, Lt. Driscoll?'

'I am sorry, Mr Fitzwilliam is dead. Some men are carrying him back now.'

I looked to where the girls stood frozen, I beckoned them to me, pushing my own pain and confusion to one side. Amelia rushed to bury her head on my shoulder. Lydia sat on the chair next to me, pressing my hand. She didn't shed any tears, but my bones crunched as she gripped my hand.

Lt Driscoll looked at me. 'Where ought the men put him?'

What a question! Though he looked ashamed to have asked it.

'I – our bedroom I suppose,' I went to stand.

'Do not stir, Mrs Fitzwilliam,' Captain Parnell said. 'We can direct them. Your quarters are on the top floor, are they not?'

'Yes, our bedroom is the first door on the right.'

'Very well, you see to your girls.'

I held Amelia's head close as four downcast looking men carried in a male figure shrouded with a bloody sheet.

'You are sure it is him?'

'Yes, I am afraid to say,' Lt Driscoll said as Captain Parnell led the way upstairs.

I watched them carry my husband up, while Amelia wept. Tears wet my cheeks. Peter was dead? But he was just going to get his boots fixed. We were going talk later. How could he be dead? I rose, supporting Amelia and holding Lydia's hand. Together, we ascended the stairs and made it to the parlour. We passed men on the hall, and somehow that gave me focus. I left the girls in the parlour stepped out into the hall, where Captain Parnell and Lt Driscoll were showing the men down the stairs.

'Thank you, gentleman,' I managed.

They looked at me, faces wrung with pity. 'Would you like any refreshments?' I spoke almost on instinct. There was a dreadful pause.

'They are perfectly all right,' said Captain Parnell.

'Yes, we're fine,' a few of them chorused. Once they'd left, Captain Parnell turned to me.

'What can we do?'

I blinked, he was a relative stranger. I had no idea. He seemed to realise this as well.

'Give me a list of some of your friends and your priest. Lt Driscoll and I can summon them while you tend to your daughters.'

I nodded and hurried to do so. After they had gone, I stood outside my bedroom door instead of going back to the girls. I needed to see Peter for myself before anything else, but I dreaded doing so. It seemed an age that I waited with my hand on that familiar handle, which now seemed so alien. It was the sound of Amelia's sobs that made me push on.

I stepped into our bedroom, the first thing that hit me was the metallic tang in the air. The sheet which covered Peter was shining with blood and as I neared, I saw some had stained the bedsheets around his head, like a strange halo. There was no sound of breath from him, no rising of his chest. I took a corner of the sheet and tensely pulled it back.

   Closed eyes stared up at me. A face that was surprisingly peaceful, but already pale and waxy. The blood had come from his chest, where he must've been kicked. The rest of the blood pooled behind him where he had clearly hit his head. He looked like Peter, he was Peter, but something was missing. I swallowed, my skin clammy. He was gone.

   Now it was confirmed for my own eyes, I was more tense than before. With each passing second, I could feel with heavy sadness this was not a dream, not a mistake or a misunderstanding. Replacing the sheet, I left the room and went to comfort my daughters.

Chapter 5

Lydia

I walked. The air was fresh and cool after the rain. Mother had urged me to stay inside but I told her I had to be out, if only for a moment. I had gone into the bedroom to see him; Amelia could not, and Mother nodded at me like she knew I would want to.

I had seen corpses before. We had an old man pass away once in the night. I have seen corpses go past on wagons, and a couple of times slave corpses from the boats. I have seen drawings of corpses cut up in medical books at work.

My father was, of course, different. I had never seen a corpse that I had known well before. A number of our countryside cousins had died, but I had not seen their bodies. Same with friends and people in our circle. Now, I looked down at a corpse that I had known in life; it looked so different. He did not look like father at all, there was nothing to animate, to give him expression or feelings, to give him soul.

Had I questioned the existence of such a thing before? Maybe, unknowingly. Mr Syrett sold all kinds of books and pamphlets, so I had read about such topics, but I hadn't thought about them too deeply. I thought such ideas were for men who had the luxury to worry about inconsequential matters. The rest of us still had to struggle through life enough, to be concerned with the existence of God, so I read Mary Wollstonecraft and my medical books, and didn't dwell upon my soul. But there, staring at my father's lifeless body, it made me realise that I did believe in God, or souls at least. For that was the only way to describe what was lacking in my father, to describe the difference between the living and the dead.

I walked, circling the mud dock, pacing the busy streets, avoiding St Nicolas' Market until I eventually ended up at Mr Syrett's.

'Miss Fitzwilliam! Are you well? You look quite fatigued.'

'Yes, I came to tell you, I came to say-'

'Please sit down, let me fetch us some tea.'

'Mr Syrett, I cannot come to work this week I must help my mother-'

'Why of course. Are some of the staff of sick?'

'No.' A great sob suddenly welled up in me. His soul was gone.

'Miss Fitzwilliam?'

'My father is dead.'

And then I started to cry.

Amelia

I couldn't recall how I came to be in bed. Mama was applying a cool flannel to my brow, and Lydia stood in the doorway, eyes red, dress and hair wet, gnawing on her nails.

Mama turned to her. 'Lydia dear, please change out of those rain-soaked things.'

Lydia nodded and stalked over to the wardrobe. Mama looked back at me.

'It is true then?' I asked. 'About Papa?'

'Yes darling,' she nodded.

The great panicking and whirling which had arisen in my chest at the news was not as strong, but I still felt as if a great storm had stripped out all of my insides and left me hollow. My father was dead. I had barely paid him any attention this past year, and yet when I was a little girl I was always at his knee.

I sank back among my pillows. Tears rose up, and it was the same for Mama. Lydia sat on the bed, wrapped in her dressing gown, weeping as well. I wasn't sure how long we stayed like that, first holding hands, then holding each other.

When I awoke, alone but for the cats, sunlight streamed in through curtains and for a few moments my only concern was what the time was, then the memories of all that had happened came crashing down. It was not a dream. The bedroom door opened, and Lydia came in. She was holding a bouquet of lilies.

'These are from Lt. Driscoll, for you.' She set them down on the table, with force, like she was accusing me of flirting instead of mourning.

'Do you want to see him?'

I shook my head, the smell of the flowers filling the air. She left me and I wished she'd taken the flowers with her. They were a large, vivid bunch and I knew I normally would have loved them, but today they seemed in bad taste and almost offensive to me, so bright, big and *alive* that they were. I turned away from them, not wanting to leave my bed, to walk along the corridor past father's office which was now empty. Was his body still in the bedroom? I shuddered at thought, before guilt welled up in me.

'Amelia? Millie darling?'

It was Mama. She backed into the bedroom carrying old gowns and folded black poplin.

'You can stay in bed today,' she said. 'I'll bring some food up.'

I nodded as she spread the fabrics and old dresses out on to the bed.

'I'm going to dye these, and alter some of my old mourning clothes-'

'You can't re-wear mourning clothes,' I remembered, strangely. 'Nan Forrester said it's bad luck.'

Mama tsked. 'It doesn't do to be superstitious, though you won't be wearing old mourning clothes. You can wear new ones out of these, if you will make them.'

I nodded, since I could hardly refuse, and it gave me an excuse for not leaving the room. We got to work in silence, and I cut simple patterns. Now I had started I just wanted to get the hateful task over with, the quicker the better.

Fancy variations might usually have occupied my mind, but despite all my sleep I felt exhausted and I fumbled with the scissors, needle and thread, making silly mistakes. My mind kept tumbling back to Papa, expecting to hear his footsteps on the hall, or thinking of his smiling delight the day the piano he won was delivered, how he scooped me up and spun me around, how he had praised my sewing saying he could not fathom how I picked up the skills so easily - but then I remembered with a jolt the shrouded figure carried up the stairs. A cold fist pulled at my heart.

Jessica

The next week passed as if a blur, as if I were acting out a part, not really thinking or feeling anything. I kept the hotel open, though mostly

Nan and Laurence ran it. My mind was in a fog, my body gripped by a tense, physical pain, my hands fumbled at tasks, dropped plates and my mind forgot the simplest thing, only able to keep reminding me Peter was dead, Peter had been killed, painfully and publicly. Alone, but surrounded by strangers he had bled out in the market while I had brewed tea and pried into his accounts.

Peter's body was taken away and though I striped the bed and burnt the sheets, I didn't sleep there again. I left his study closed. Amelia kept mostly to her bed. Lydia stayed mostly at my side as friends and acquaintances streamed through our parlour, with food and sympathy. None of it seemed real. I had always expected to outlive Peter, but I had not expected his death to be anything like this. Hanging over it all was the mysterious nature of his debt.

I sent word to Peter's family and they arrived, en masse, the day before the funeral. The middle brothers, Joseph and Jeremy, came first with their wives, Martha and Eliza. They jointly owned a farm on the other side of Glastonbury to the Fitzwilliam farm. It was the family farm of Eliza and Martha, who were sisters. Between them they had twelve living children, who did not accompany them.

'Jessica! Where are girls?' Eliza demanded. 'Ah, here is Lydia - how drawn she looks!'

'Yes indeed, poor dear girls,' Martha tutted. 'The city is no good for them.'

'I rather think it was my father's death that did me ill, rather than the city,' Lydia said icily.

'Poor child,' Eliza breezed over Lydia's abruptness which had momentarily stumped Martha. 'Where is Amelia?'

'She keeps to her bed-'

'Ah, we shall go and cheer her. Amelia! Amy!'

I winced. We never shortened Amelia to Amy, she hated it.

They bustled off, leaving Lydia and I with their husbands who looked awkwardly at me.

'Tea? Coffee? Ale?'

They visibly relaxed. 'Ale please.'

Our upstairs quarters felt very crowded very quickly, but luckily some of our guest rooms became free, Captain Parnell's and Lt Driscoll's among them. I only realised they had gone when my day was not interrupted by Lt Driscoll's enquiries into Amelia's welfare. Nan Forrester told me they had left their best wishes and condolences.

Eliza and Martha buzzed around as if they were helping but made more mess as we prepared for Henry, the eldest brother. He arrived late at night and was shown up to the parlour by Laurence. A widower himself, he was accompanied by his eldest son Harry, who was the same age as me. Harry had the round, cherub like look of the Fitzwilliams. Henry had never looked much like his brothers. He was taller, with angular features which when he was younger had made him handsome, but now they made him look gaunt. His hair was streaked with grey and he still favoured the bigger frock coats of decades past.

He surveyed the room with obvious distain.

'My condolences for your loss, Jessica.' He never called me Mrs Fitzwilliam or even Mrs Peter, which was the polite and acceptable alternative with multiple sisters-in-law under one roof. 'And Miss Fitzwilliam. Where is Miss Amelia?'

'She keeps to her bed,' I said. 'Can I offer you any refreshments?'

'Nonsense, we can do that-' Eliza started.

'No,' Henry said. 'The journey was long. We will retire to our beds.'

Laurence moved to show them the way and I stepped out into the hallway after them. 'Before you retire, may I have a word Mr Fitzwilliam?'

He nodded, as Laurence led his son away. 'In my husband's accounts there is a record of a debt to you-'

'You mean, you didn't know?'

'I did not know. What is the nature of the debt? How long until I repay it?'

Henry raised his eyebrows. 'That depends what he did with his will. If he'd done as we'd discussed it won't take you very long to pay off at all.'

The words ought to have been reassuring but Henry's tone was smug. 'How do you mean? Why was there a debt in the first place?'

'You knew Peter liked to gamble,' he spoke slowly, as if to a child. 'Didn't you?'

I nodded, fear inching up me. 'I know he did in his youth, before our marriage. He said he was good at it. He carried on a little bit, and he often won.'

'Well two years ago he must've lost the knack.'

I felt sick. 'How do you mean?' I could sell the piano, couldn't I? Some of the more expensive kitchen wares, my jewellery...

'He lost everything, he bet your business.'

It was as if the ground had fallen out from under me, as if Henry had struck me. I was winded, giddy, nauseous. 'It was days away from being taken, did you know that? We helped him, his brothers, but I did the most. I had to re-mortgage part of the Fitzwilliam farm, that was how bad it was.'

As he spoke spittle formed on his lips and his temple throbbed.

'You had to re-mortgage the farm?'

He nodded. 'Yes. He said until he paid the debt off, I would inherit this place if he died before it was settled.'

I swallowed. 'Had he paid off much?'

'No, not so much as a quarter. I suggest you summon your lawyer and we shall read the will tomorrow afternoon.'

He headed off and I stood, stunned, before running into my bedroom to vomit into the chamber pot.

Chapter 6

Amelia

Mama burst into the room. I blinked at her. 'I do not know if I am able to entertain the Glastonbury Fitzwilliams.'

She waved a hand. 'I quite understand. I just wanted some calm.'

I sunk back among the pillows.

'You will get out of bed tomorrow though, and sit with me while the funeral takes place?'

I nodded, glad we were not men and didn't have to go. I didn't think I could bear it. She came to sit on the bed and took my head in her lap, stroked my hair as if I was little again.

'The will shall be read tomorrow afternoon,' she said, sounding far away.

'Father left this place to you, didn't he? The Fitzwilliam is hardly important enough to be entailed away.'

'That is what I thought.'

'What do you mean?'

She sighed. 'I am not sure, darling. It seems your father may have had debts.'

'What sort of debts?' I sat up. 'Serious ones?'

She was about to answer when the door opened and Lydia came in, shutting it firmly behind her. 'Lord, can they never be quiet? Gossiping about everyone in their village. How are my uncles allowed to attend father's funeral but I am not? Is that not unfair, that we, his children must sit at home? Cousin Harry may go, and who is he to father?'

Mama and I blinked at her outburst, then Mama sighed. 'I suppose you are quite right, dear.'

'Urgh,' Lydia scowled. 'If only I were a boy!'

She used to say that all the time when we were younger. Mama and Papa never paid it any heed, but now Mama stopped stroking my hair. 'It would certainly make things different. Maybe easier, less uncertain. I am sure you'd be well on your way to becoming a doctor, a lawyer…some stable profession.'

'I know,' Lydia paced. 'And I would be a doctor, obviously.' Then she stopped and that look that she gets when butchering or if she has found a really gruesome medical book came over her.

'What?'

'Tomorrow morning I will go to the reach down shop,' she said.

'Tomorrow morning I would wish you in the parlour with me and you sister,' Mama said. 'While the men go to the funeral. Why in heaven's name would you go shopping?'

'I will go first thing. I will buy boy's clothes.'

Her face was set, like it had been when she decided she was going to work at Syrett's. 'Mama, she can't do that! Dress like a boy and sneak into church!'

Mama stopped stroking my hair. 'Oh, why not? Why shouldn't one of us be at his funeral? Mr Webster, Mr Hughes, Mr Thomas and Mr Syrett are going, as well as Laurence and probably some of his wretched gambling friends. Why can't Lydia go? As long as you are back and presentable for the reading of the will and the wake. I fear there will not be good news.'

Lydia sat on the bed. 'Because of the debt?'

I was about to ask how Lydia knew about the debt when I did not, but I already knew both possible answers; she was older and she eavesdropped like a spy.

'Yes. I think it may end up with Henry having a stake in the hotel.'

A weight settled in my stomach. I wasn't sure what that would mean but it wouldn't be good.

Lydia

Mama and Amelia helped me dress in the kitchen. Because of the funeral it was closed for the day, and we thought if anyone saw a young man leaving mine and Amelia's bedroom, a scandal would ensue. If I hadn't found a suit in black and a hat I wouldn't have gone through with it, but as it was they were the first things I saw and they fitted well. I wasn't normally one for believing in fate, but there it was.

It was strange to have one's legs separated by trousers, almost lewd to have one's posterior so tightly fitted. I didn't have a big bosom like Amelia, but none the less my breast had been bound more tightly than my stays. My hat felt as if it would blow off without a ribbon or pin to secure it, but Mother pushed it down hard then tied my hair back with a ribbon. Most fashionable young men cut their hair short these days, but a low ponytail would not look so out of place. No one had ever seen me with such a style as I always wore my hair up.

'There.' Amelia lifted up a polished metal tray and a young man stared back at me.

'Very dashing!' said Amelia, managing to smile. Mama nodded. 'Yes, you'll pass. What will you say I anyone asks you how you knew your Father?'

'That my father was his friend.'

Mother nodded. 'That'll do.'

She kissed me on the cheek and let me out the back door.

I headed to St John's church. I hadn't anticipated the freedom walking in trousers could bring, I could stride. People looked at me differently; or rather men barely looked at me at all and a few young women smiled. Without the men looking at me I felt safer, which surprised me. I hadn't realised how guarded I always was. When I reached the church, I sat alone. The reverend, who had baptised me and spoke with Mama every Sunday, didn't look at me twice. I was glad of it. After my strange morning I wanted to reflect upon my father.

My grief rose up, a lump in my throat, but I knew it wouldn't do for a young man only on friendly terms with my father to be weeping, so I swallowed it back. I would cry later. I knew I had been lucky, many other fathers would have reprimanded me for my boyish ways, not allowed me to work at Mr Syrett's; he could have checked up on my reading and forbade most of it like many men would have done at the first whiff of Wollstonecraft or the medical journals.

I remembered his warmth. He had loved mother, there had been no doubt of that. He got a look of pure happiness on his face when she walked into a room. He had been proud at how well I'd picked up whist, cribbage and other card games. He'd said I was like him after all. I had sat on his lap when young as he'd played games against family friends at parties. We'd always win. There was a tightening in my guts. But now the debt. A gambling debt, Ma said Henry had told her. But Henry could be lying. But where else could he have incurred such a debt? I shifted. We'd only know how big the debt was this afternoon.

'Excuse me.'

Lost in my thoughts I had barely noticed the church filing up. The smell of men had permeated the cold air of the church; their starched linen, boot polish, tobacco, ale and sweat. I saw Mr Webster and a selection of his sons, as well as Mr and Josh Hughes, Mr Thomas but not George, Mr Syrett, who I bowed my head from and surprisingly, Captain Parnell though not Lieutenant Driscoll. An older man wanted to get by me so I made room. How did he know Father?

I asked him, suddenly desperate for any crumbs of my father's memory.

'We used to watch the boxing together,' he said. 'He always knew which way to bet. That is, until he didn't…'

'What do you mean?'

'Lost quite a bit a few years ago,' he said. 'I can't remember the particulars, but I suppose it can't have been as bad as it seemed. He kept that hotel and pretty wife, after all didn't he?'

I nodded.

'How do you know him?'

'My father was an old acquaintance.'

A silence descended as my uncles and cousin Harry entered, carrying the coffin. Men removed their hats, so I followed suit dreading someone would see through my disguise but no one spared me a glance. All eyes followed the coffin. My heart lurched in my chest. Oh God. The priest began to speak. It had really happened. He was dead.

*

I left the churchyard, giddy, numb after sitting through the service in church, and then watching the box which contained my father place in a cart – it was to be taken to Glastonbury to be buried at Fitzwilliam family plot. My insides twisted and I felt a stupid mockery to come here, dressed as a boy as if a game. But I hadn't wanted him to be alone. I stopped to steady myself, then sat on a bench as the small crowd went by, no one looking at me. A pair of well-polished boots stopped in front of me. I looked up to see Captain Parnell.

'Are you well?' he asked.

I nodded.

'Would you like me to fetch someone?'

I shook my head. 'No thank you, sir, I am well. I must be getting home.'

I stood and we walked together. I was relieved he didn't ask me how I knew the deceased or any such thing as I didn't think I could lie.

'Will you go back to The Fitzwilliam for the wake?' I asked.

'I didn't know there was one,' he said. 'I only wanted to pay my respects. I was at The Fitzwilliam when he died.'

I nodded, remembering how he had fetched our friends.

'You ought to come back,' I said. 'You did a good thing that day. You've more right to be there then some of those Glastonbury relations.'

He raised his eyebrow but didn't say anything. We walked back in silence. When we reached The Fitzwilliam, I pointed him to the dining room. 'It is closed to guests, for mourners only.'

He nodded.

I was so tired with my pretence that I made no excuse as I hurried up the stairs, and he did not call after me.

Jessica

Laurence cooked some of the food and I prepared the rest while I was supposed to be sleeping last night. People wouldn't expect a lot, Nan Forrester said, but I wanted to cook, I needed to cook. There were sweet plum cakes, soft, fresh bread, chickens roasted on the spit smeared fat and thyme, their aromas flooding the hotel, all of Peter's 'one indulgences'.

Everything was like a dream – not a nightmare, just a very disconnected dream, as if it were all happening to someone else. If I prepared the food, I could focus on something; weighing, mixing, tasting, stirring. My sisters-in-law gave up on trying to coax Amelia and I back upstairs and came down to help us set up, but only succeeded in getting Nan Forrester's way. There was a swarm of men which meant the funeral was finished. I shivered.

People spoke to me but I barely heard. I was exhausted, I wanted them all gone and to sit down and cry. Peter was dead and he was not coming back. Why did I have to put up with all these people?

'-the will,' Lydia hissed at my side, dressed like a girl again only not looking like herself for she, Amelia and I were in black. The girls did not suit black, Amelia especially.

'Mr Brock is here now,' Lydia said. 'Uncle Henry wants to go upstairs to read the will.'

Amelia and Lydia linked arms with me. We left the guests feasting and talking, my sisters-in-law cornering Captain Parnell and Mr Thomas.

'Where are you from? Truly?'

We reached the parlour where Mr Brock sat down. I sat between my girls and my head swum as a dizzying headache locked itself around my temples. I could barely hear, let alone take words in. Both my hands were pressed sharply and Amelia gasped.

'No sir, that cannot be so,' Lydia said, standing. 'You must read it again.'

'I have read and re-read it to myself all week as I prepared for this,' Mr Brock said. 'I tried to find loopholes, believe me, but this is how your father left things. He meant to make a provision for you but he never got the chance—'

'Make a provision?' I said, fighting through the fog. 'What has happened?'

Henry frowned. Mr Brock looked at me kindly. 'I am sorry Mrs Fitzwilliam, but your husband's gambling debt was substantial. He was only saved from ruin when Mr Henry Fitzwilliam re-mortgaged some of his farm. During that time, he came to me with his brothers. The will was changed, if Peter died without at least half the debt paid, the hotel would have to be sold to cover it. Your husband hadn't even paid a quarter.'

I blinked at him. 'But it's my hotel, mine and Peter's. My parents gave money towards it. I have worked for it. There is not an entail and I am his widow.'

'I know, but these are special circumstances. Legally, the hotel was your husband's. A married woman cannot own property. Mr Henry Fitzwilliam insisted on the agreement before he gave your husband the loan. I didn't know you weren't aware.'

'I was not,' I said numbly. My life's work was not mine. I had nothing.

'You can't be so surprised, Jessica,' Henry said. 'Why do you think he married so late? He ran up such large debts in his youth, most respectable fathers wouldn't let their daughters near him. Why do you think my mother was pleased he was marrying you? She knew she had some to pass him off to who'd be grateful, someone who'd work for a living to support his gambling.'

'But he won…'

'More often than he lost, but when he lost, he always lost big.'

There was a horrible, hollow silence as I realised something. Henry had never hated me for myself or my class, not really. He hated Peter, and hated me simply because I was his wife.

'You've resented him all these years, why? What did he gamble of yours?'

Henry frowned, and looked towards the fireplace. 'My first fiancé, Miss Lidcombe was forbidden to marry me because of Peter's history of gambling.'

I nodded. 'So, you will sell this place and evict us? Are we not just victims as you? More so as we have less power to help ourselves?'

For a moment Henry's face flickered. 'I want to pay off the land I had to re-mortgage.'

'We could come to some arrangement.'

'It will take years to pay off, I probably won't live that long. I don't want to give my son mortgaged land. That was why I had the clause wrote in. It might not be so bad, Jessica. We could help you find work as a cook. Maybe your girls could become governesses or housemaids.' I had worked hard so my daughters would not have to go into service as all the women in my family before me had done. Was that worthless now?

Henry shrugged. 'But I can and will pay off my mortgage.'

With that, he stood and left us, Mr Brock scurrying after him, wringing his hands and apologising.

Amelia wept, Lydia shouted, Eliza and Martha appeared to tell us Henry had 'kindly' given us a few weeks to move out and that they could help find us positions in households back in Glastonbury.

'She has friends in Bristol, right enough,' Mrs Webster barged into the parlour, and I was glad of her matronly presence. 'We shall help her.'

'I am so sorry,' Mrs Webster said, after my sisters-in-laws left the room. 'The boys saw him betting at the boxing often. If I'd have thought he'd done this, I would have told you.'

I nodded, would it have made a difference if she had told me? I'd known he liked the boxing and playing cards. I had never tried to curb his interests.

'You can stay with us,' Mrs Webster said. 'Come tomorrow and I'll do one of the older boys' rooms for you. It's not as if they live at home now. It's yours until you decide what you want to do.'

Chapter 7

Jessica

Henry told me to close the hotel, so I wrote to tell forth-coming guests and notify the new ones. 'We have bookings for the week. Let them stay out.'

He agreed. The rest of the Glastonbury Fitzwilliams left the night of the funeral, and Henry sat up in the parlour already acting as if he had free run of my home, which of course he did. I went to the girls' room and slept deeply.

The next morning while everyone slept, I slipped down to the kitchen and packed up plates, cutlery, utensils - not all of it but enough for us and some to sell. Henry said he'd be doing an inventory so I couldn't take too much or it would look suspicious but in the kitchen were some of my most valuable items and Henry wouldn't know the first thing about them. I packed them into bags with the girls' clothes and told them to go straight to the Websters when they awoke.

'But Mama-'

'I will follow in the next few days,' I said, then leaned into whisper. 'You have important cargo in your bags. Keep it safe.'

Lydia took my hands. 'It isn't much but we can use my savings, maybe help us rent somewhere for a month or so.'

I held her, and nodded, hating myself for having to use my daughter's money but knowing I had no choice.

'Let us weather the storm at the Websters' and then we can start looking for somewhere. It is very good of you to let us use your money.'

'What else is it for, if not this?'

They finished packing their books, took a cat each and set off. I scoured the empty guest rooms, taking what could fit in my bags, candlesticks, bed linens- all things I had bought for this place with care and consideration, meant to make it comfortable and welcoming, now would help keep me and the girls above water when I sold them all. A few weeks ago that idea would have mortified me but, with faced with no alternative it was not such a sacrifice.

Lydia

Amelia and I arrived at the Websters' early in the morning, hastening past the unsavoury types at the dockside with our heads down and cloaks clutched tightly about ourselves.

'We look like a pair of vagabonds,' Amelia said.

'It's not as bad as that,' I sighed.

'What do you suppose she's loaded our bags with? They are so heavy.'

'Kitchen wares,' I said, and she looked disappointed, obviously hoping for a stash of secret jewels.

'Girls, good morning! Do come in!'

Mrs Webster opened the door and ushered us in. Her husband bustled out to work, along with John, Will and Tom, all touching their hats to us.

'Come and sit in the kitchen, have you eaten?'

'No,' I said, though I wasn't hungry. Edward Webster was finishing his breakfast. He was dressed more smartly than his brothers and father, ready for his day's work as a lawyer. He greeted us, giving me a brief smile, before heading out. Mrs Webster set down two large sausage sandwiches before us with full mugs of small beer.

'Those sausages are fresh, Mr Webster made them this morning,' she said proudly. 'Goodness, I am so used to feeding my boys! That isn't too much, for you is it?'

Amelia was already eating as if famished, and my own stomach rumbled. There had been so much food at the wake yesterday, but I couldn't remember eating any of it. I'd had no appetite. Much to Mrs Webster's pleasure, we both wolfed down our breakfasts as she bustled around, cleaning up with her maid Bertha, and fussing over our cats.

'Come then girls, let me show you your room. And don't worry, I had Mr Webster put a bolt on the door for modesty's sake. Don't want my boys wandering in after a few drinks!'

Amelia's eyebrows shot up and I was so surprised at her frankness, I must've given her an angry look for she said, 'Oh heavens no! Not like that!'

Behind her mistress' back, Bertha rolled her eyes.

'Just because they would be confused! No, no nothing like that. You are quite safe here!'

We followed Mrs Webster up the stairs to a large, clean room with a double bed and empty wardrobe. There were a few crates in the corner, which she said contained the belongings of Richard and Philip, her sons in the navy. She hoped we didn't mind, and I said of course we did not. She said once we had settled in, we were welcome to join her in the parlour. She had a mound of mending to do, ('Boys will be boys!') and would be glad of our company.

Once she left Amelia sunk on the bed, looking around the plain room with an annoyed expression.

'What's wrong with it?'

'Nothing, it's just...a bit simple isn't it?'

'It's clean and warm,' I snapped. 'After the mess father left us in, we are lucky to say that.'

'Don't speak ill of father!'

'I was speaking truthfully.'

She swallowed. 'Why should he not be allowed to gamble? He won nice things, like the piano. He intended to pay everything back and settle it all, it's hardly his fault about...'

I folded my arms, too tired to argue. 'He shouldn't have gambled. We never needed those things he won, nice though they were. Him winning a piano isn't worth losing the hotel, is it?'

She slumped back. 'He meant to pay it back.'

'Yes, but he didn't, did he? And he made no provision for that. He wasn't a young man, there were plenty of ways he could have died.'

Amelia looked aghast. 'I can't believe you can be so cold.'

'I can't believe you can complain about our lodgings but still make excuses for the man who put us here!'

Tears welled in Amelia's eyes. 'He didn't mean it to be like this!'

I sighed. 'No, obviously not, but that's the problem. He didn't think. Now come, we must go downstairs to sit with Mrs Webster or she may worry.'

We sat with Mrs Webster most of the day, taking it in turn to read to her from the romances which she and Amelia favoured and helping her with her sewing. Her conversation and company were gentle; I could see she wanted us to feel relaxed in her home.

I found the sewing and reading hard going though; I made stupid stitches, stumbled over words, lost track of what I was reading or sewing. All the time my insides twisted and my back grew increasingly knotted. What was to become of us? My chest felt a great weight pressing on it and I knew why; it was for father's loss and I couldn't think of a time when it would not be there. It was made heavier with my anger at him that I couldn't shake. How could he have been so thoughtless regarding our welfare and so cowardly as to not tell us?

Jessica

When Henry awoke, I asked if I could stay until the last guest left. He said that was fine, he would also be staying. I wrote good references for all of my staff. Laurence told me he had found work at a big house in Clifton and offered to take the spit dog with him. Nan went to live with her daughter and son-in-law, to keep house for them while her daughter was with child. The waiters and cleaners also found work quickly enough; they were all young, friendly and hard working. It was why I'd hired them in the first place.

I worked downstairs and slept in the girls' room. Henry had the parlour, Peter's study, our bedroom. Who knew *that* morning, I would never sleep in my own bed again? It did not take long for me to feel lonely and I knew I was at the bottom of a deep, dark pit with no way out, but I had no choice to carry on as best as I could, and to try and find a new way for myself and my daughters to live.

I visited the Websters most days for dinner. They had been the first friends we'd made on arriving in Bristol; we met them at a traders' ball. Peter got on well with Mr Webster, my mother with Mrs Webster, I was busy with the hotel and carrying Lydia. At time, the new friendship had made me feel like a child, the Websters were older than Peter, but younger than my mother. I was closer in age to their eldest son John than to them, but as the years went on I grew to enjoy their jovial friendship even if at times they still treated me like a green girl just arrived in Bristol.

Mrs Webster said it was a joy to have some female company in the house with my daughters staying. Amelia told me she had seen Abigail and Ruth Hughes. Abigail Hughes had announced her engagement to the son of a coffee shop owner, and Amelia had been asked to make a dress. Abigail had offered to pay, not as much as for a proper dressmaker but it was better than nothing, and if other girls saw Abigail's dress that may bring more work to Amelia.

Lydia had taken more hours at the bookshop and Mrs Webster said her husband would like me to make meat pies for him to sell in his butchers' shops and to the other businesses they supplied. They didn't offer me a huge amount of money but they gave me a fair price and I saw it was a good start for me. What I needed was my own kitchen so I could perhaps sell to more places, but I knew I would be living with the Websters for a few months yet.

My friend, Mrs Hughes, ceased to call after the funeral. Mr Syrett called, as did Mr Thomas. When I asked Mr Thomas if he would be interested in selling my fruit pies to other businesses he supplied, he enthused that he would, and even insisted that the girls and I dine with his wife and son next month. I thanked him. Penniless, I was finding out who my true friends were.

Lydia

Mother came to join us for dinner, as Laurence was overseeing dinner at the hotel. She looked drawn and as if she had aged a decade in day. She bought a bag with more items from the house; things that had decorated the guest rooms and more kitchen wares. We had dined with the Websters many times before and usually it was a rowdy affair with all the boys jostling with tall tales and jokes, but today they were all very sombre and quiet.

Edward Webster sat next to me. He had been my playmate in childhood, and had sometimes lent me books from his grammar school library. Amelia noticed he often asked me to dance at balls; but that must only be because we were both more bookish and felt comfortable standing up with a friend.

'How do you fair?' he asked quietly, while Mrs Webster spoke to Mama and Amelia pushed her food around the plate.

'Well enough, thank you. Your family has been most generous.'

He gave me an encouraging smile, then passed me the plate of dumplings with his inky fingers. I only took a couple, for I had no desire to eat but did not want to appear ungrateful to Mrs Webster.

Mama left, giving each of us a tight embrace. She told us she was to stay at The Fitzwilliam for its last weeks.

'But why?' Amelia asked, tears in her eyes.

'I want to see the job done, I suppose,' she said. I understood.

After Mother had gone, Amelia and I were alone in the hall. 'I'm going to bed,' Amelia said. 'Make my excuses.'

She flounced up the stairs. I watched her go and walked quietly towards the parlour. Mrs Webster's voice carried, and I stopped to listen.

'She is still a very nice girl, but it's different now.'

I stepped closer and craned my neck to hear Edward's much quieter voice. 'But I think it could be a good match for me. We know each other, our temperaments match. I think I would do well with a clever wife.'

'That's all true of course, but be practical. Lydia has nothing at all to her name.'

Edward was considering a match with me? My head spun. He was nice enough, but I did not see him in that way at all.

'Before, I'd have thought she would have come with a good few hundred and a stake in the hotel. That would have been perfect. But now? How will you support yourselves? You have your work, but you know John will get the business and the rest won't go far, split between you and your brothers. It is a shame, but I am urging you to be practical. Look to a daughter or sister of one your colleagues, or how about your friend from Oxford? He is landed gentry with three sisters, is he not? They would come with a good amount of money.'

There was a long pause and I waited, not sure of what I wanted him to say. It was strange to see how Mrs Webster viewed me now; assumedly a friend, someone who needed charity, but I was no longer good enough for her son. She was just being practical, I supposed. I ought get used to be viewed as such.

'You are right, Mother,' Edward sighed. 'I do like her, but not enough for a life of poverty.'

I stepped away and headed upstairs, an odd mixture of relief and annoyance. The relief was the stronger of the emotions and I realised that must mean my feelings for Edward Webster amounted to no more friendship. The annoyance was hurt pride. I had learnt quickly that he liked me - and if I had money, he would have tried to court me, but without money I was not worth the effort. Perhaps it was better to have learnt the lesson privately rather to have ever formed an attachment with someone and then be rebuffed. I had no desires to marry soon, but now my lack of fortune might take the decision of marrying ever out of my hands entirely.

Amelia

Lydia climbed into the lumpy bed next to me, her feet cold. From the room next door came the explosion of male laughter. Normally I'd want to know what the Webster brothers were laughing about, maybe even have tried to join in, but now I just wished that they'd shut up, and said as much to Lydia.

'I know,' she sighed. 'But it is their house. Mrs Webster said this room belonged to the sons now at sea, but I fancy some of the others must've been sleeping in here and we have turned them out.'

'So we must bow and scrape and put up with their nonsense, grateful for their charity?'

'I did not say I was happy about it but that is how they may see it.'

'Do you suppose this is how our life will be like now?'

'I am afraid so, unless we do something about it.'

'What can we do?'

'I do not know. I can work more hours at Syrett's, Mother could get work, you could make money from dress making. That way we could at least support ourselves.'

It seemed like a life of drudgery.

'What if one of us was to make a good marriage?'

'You have been reading too many of your romances,' Lydia said patronisingly, as if she was twenty years older than me rather than two. 'Not even men of our previous station will want to marry us now, unless they are fools who don't plan for the future.'

'That is very bleak,' I said.

'As is the world. We will bring no money whatsoever to our marriages.'

'But Mama has trained us with good household skills. That is something, isn't it?'

'I fear it is a very secondary consideration. We shall have to make our own way.'

She blew out the rush light, and as she did it illuminated her high cheek-bones and striking face. Surely, I could not be only person to think her beautiful? Then I remembered Mr Syrett always had a smile for her. He could provide her with a comfortable life, and by extension Mama and I.

'What of Mr Syrett? Why do you not pursue him? I fancy he has a romantic nature after the poetry he reads, and is already established in business so has no need for you to bring money to the match.'

'Amelia! How could you?' she sounded outraged. 'I work for him! Besides, he is in his fifties at least.'

'All the more reason. He will not live so long, and then he may leave you his shop in his will.'

'Stop it! I will have no more of these jests-'

'It was not a jest,' I said.

'No more of it, please,' Lydia said. 'I think I would prefer to make my own way than to try and entice or depend on a man. Looking at what depending on a man got Mother.'

'Do not start criticising Papa again!'

She sighed. 'Very well.'

The thought that I would again wake up in morning in a world without Papa bought tears to my eyes and I started to shake with crying.

'Come here,' Lydia said, holding me to her. As I calmed down, I felt sleep mercifully washing over me, until another roar of Webster laughter and a round of raucous singing caused me to start awake. Lydia was right, we'd have to learn to support ourselves to escape this dependency, but the idea of sewing pretty dresses that I could never wear for ungrateful girls like Abigail Hughes filled me with despair. If Lydia would put no effort into securing a husband of means, then it was up to me.

*

The next couple of weeks passed slowly. Mama visited most evenings for dinner and we saw her at church on Sunday. Lydia returned to work at Mr Syrett's. When we were together, Mama and Lydia spoke furtively about ways in which we could support ourselves. Mama was to set up a pie making business and Lydia would continue at Mr Syrett's. They told me I must apply myself to dress making, not taking a moment to consider my feelings on the subject.

I was good at it and enjoyed making my own things, but the thought of slaving away for other people and catering to their whims became increasingly abhorrent to me. However, I was not asked about this.

Loneliness crept up on me. I had not thought quite how alike Mama and Lydia were in all things. They could both be described as intelligent, practical women, which I knew I was not considered to be. Papa had appreciated me as I was, but maybe that was because we were more alike. Both with a love of music, both considered more fun I didn't doubt.

Now, I was alone in my family with those traits. It made me think no wonder Papa had been driven to gambling, he needed his own enjoyment if Mama had treated him so; setting him up as her accountant – something which he had no great passion for - while she fulfilled her ambitions with the hotel, no thought for what he might want. I did not even know what he truly wanted for his life. He had sometimes taken me to see musical concerts, maybe that was what he had wanted for himself before Mama harangued him.

It made me determined that I would not have my skills exploited for her schemes. I wanted wealth of my own, and I wanted to pursue my interests in music and sewing without having to suck all the life out of them by making a living out of them. Papa had always said I would marry well, that I would make a rich man a good wife. Why should that change? It would be harder now, but I was sure I could still do it.

Often in the day, with Mama still at The Fitzwilliam and Lydia at Syrett's, I sat in the parlour with Mrs Webster, reading to her as she sewed or set about other chores. We were sometimes joined by her two daughters-in-law, who Mrs Webster indulged greatly as she'd lost her eldest daughter-in-law, John's wife, to a particularly gruesome sounding miscarriage which was only ever discussed in hushed tones. The surviving daughters-in-law were married to her second and third sons, the much-feted navy officers, Philip and Richard.

Mrs Philip Webster fretted constantly over her husband's safety at sea and the child she carried, so she was trying company. I had thought the child was to be the first Webster grandchild, but Lydia reported Papa said it was the first *legitimate* grandchild and Mama told him to hold his tongue.

Mrs Richard Webster, or Betsey, was jolly company. I remembered the brief scandal around her marriage to Richard two years before. We hadn't been told directly, but Lydia found out the truth by listening at doors and relayed the story to me. We had been shocked, but I had thought it was romantic as well. Betsey was the youngest daughter of plantation owners from Clifton, and her parents had been against the match thinking the Websters beneath them. Richard and Betsey were undeterred and eloped to Gretna Green. The Websters had been delighted at the match, and to hide the scandal Betsey's parents at least pretended it was what they had wanted.

Betsey seemed to like me, and often sat next to me on visits. She said when I was out of mourning, maybe I should like to come and stay with her a while, and I said I should like that. Since the Websters were our family's oldest friends in Bristol I was sure it would be permitted.

Chapter 8

Jessica

Two weeks after the funeral, in the last few days of the final guests' stay, I received a completely unexpected visitor.

There was a knock on the kitchen door and I opened it to find Captain Parnell standing in the rain, dressed in his sharp civilian attire.

'Hello sir, what brings you here?'

'I wondered if I could speak with you on a matter of business.'

Perplexed, I stepped back and he entered.

'Tea? I just brewed some,' I said pouring a fresh cup. I was rather determined to use all the leaves in the kitchen before I left. 'Please sit.'

He did so, after shaking off his hat and over and hanging them up.

'So, what is the business?'

'Do you…this is, perhaps indelicate, do you remember that I bought a house with the intention to rent out while I was at sea?'

I blinked at him, jolted by the memory of our merry conversation on *that* morning.

'Of course, there is no reason why you should remember-'

I shook my head. 'No, it isn't that. I remember perfectly. You'd just come in from the rain then as well. It is only after that conversation that everything starts to blur.'

He nodded, regarded me, then seemed content that memories of that day were not about to reduce me to a sobbing wreck. 'While I am away, I would need someone to manage this house.'

My heart leapt, but I smothered it. That statement could mean any number of things.

'This person could live there as well, pay a much lower rent and oversee the other two lodgers. Maybe providing some meals, keeping the place clean and tidy. As Bristol is a port town and has the spa, I imagine the lodgers may be short term so the landlady would have free reign to choose respectable replacements.' He paused and I willed him to get to the point. 'I was wondering if you might consider acting as the landlady?'

This time I allowed the thrill of happiness in my chest to grow, but I did not to show it in my expression. I must ensure I was stepping into a secure position. 'So, I would be going into business with you?'

'Yes.'

'And why me?'

'In honesty, of all my acquaintances it is you who is the most qualified for this. It is you who will be doing me a service. I have stayed here. I know what a good landlady you are.'

I realised something. 'You must be aware I am about to be evicted, to offer this.'

He paused. 'Yes.'

'You came to the wake didn't you, is that how you know?'

He nodded. 'I saw your daughter at the church, where I had gone to pay my respects. She invited me.'

'Yes, she insisted on going-' I stopped. 'You recognised her?'

He smiled kindly, which caused me to relax a little. 'Not initially. I noticed she was alone. It is a hard thing to be young and alone at funeral, so I went to speak to her. I thought perhaps she was your nephew or cousin, the resemblance between you two is so strong, even when she was masquerading as a boy. It was only once we got back to The Fitzwilliam her manners changed, then when she vanished upstairs and came back down as herself my growing suspicion was confirmed.'

I raised my eyebrows at him, relieved he didn't seem to view Lydia's actions harshly. 'And you want to go into business with a woman who would let her daughter behave so?'

'A woman who lets her daughter behave so is exactly the sort of woman I want to go into business with.'

I gave a small laugh at his amusement, and I realised I hadn't laughed weeks. Then I realised Henry might hear and come down. Captain Parnell saw me glance upwards.

'Should you like to see the house, Mrs Fitzwilliam? It seems the rain has stopped for now.'

'Yes, I think that would be a good start. Which is not to say I've made up my mind yet.'

'Of course. I could never go into business with a rash woman.'

*

We walked to the Hotwells, near the spa. We chatted about the sights of Bristol, and when I asked, he told me how they compared to Liverpool. It seemed like Bristol, Liverpool had some very grand places as well as poor, and the docks heaved with ships from wondrous places all over the world.

'Here we are.'

We stopped outside a small but clean looking house. He opened the door.

It was sparsely furnished, but that was to be expected since he'd only recently completed purchasing the place. He gave the tour. There was a parlour, a pleasingly sized kitchen and three bedrooms upstairs.

'I was hoping you and your girls could share and we could rent out the other two rooms.'

I nodded, that seemed fair enough. We had stopped in the biggest bedroom, the only one with a bed, wardrobe and bookcase. It must be where he slept. For all the sparseness of the house the bookshelf was overflowing; there were books in what looked like Latin, as well as navy texts, history books, biographies and a good few novels.

'You ought to visit Syrett's, Lydia works there.'

He nodded. 'I have been meaning to go.'

I stepped into the hall and we went down to the kitchen, which I wanted to look over more thoroughly. There was a good oven and larder. Relief flooded me. I could make the pies my venture with Mr Webster and Mr Thomas. easily, and even take in baking for the rest of the neighbours at a price. In the rest of the kitchen, he had some quality utensils and an iron. Two shirts were hung up to dry along with collars and cuffs.

'You don't send them out to be washed?'

'My mother was a washer woman,' he said, which surprised me. 'It means I am quite fastidious with cleaning clothes, which helps when one must wear a uniform.'

'My own parents were servants. My father a gardener, my mother a cook. I was training to work with her before my marriage.'

'Gives you quite a work ethic, doesn't it?'

'Do you mean working in service or being poor?'

He barked a laugh. 'Both.'

'What did your father do?'

'He was a sailor, though not an officer.' He didn't disguise the pride in voice for his own rise, and why should he? 'My grandfather, on my mother's side, he was a cab driver. He wanted me to go into service. It was my father who made me a sailor.'

'The navy is a good place for men to make themselves. Better even than service.'

'Yes, it is.'

'So, I assume you didn't go to the naval college. You worked your way up?'

He nodded. 'I've been a sailor since I was eight, then joined the navy twenty years ago when I was fourteen.'

I nodded, glad I had never been parted from the girls when they were so young – or that I was not parted from own mother at that age.

'What do you say then?' he asked, breaking my thoughts. I imagined my life here. The big bedroom was large enough for me and the girls. The location was convenient, the house pleasant, if I had a say in the lodgers…this seemed all too good to be true. Fear of losing it swept over me.

'Will we sign contacts, Captain Parnell?'

He nodded. 'You can even name the lawyer.'

'And…what of your family? Do you have any?'

I hoped not to sound too abrupt, but I didn't want any family taking everything away should something happen to him, which given the nature of his profession wasn't unlikely.

'I have some cousins on my mother's side in Liverpool, but I am not close to them. Others scattered to Australia.' He paused and I wondered if that meant he was related to convicts. 'My mother's parents came from Italy and lost contact with the relations they left behind. My father was from Dublin. As for the rest, I am not married and have no children. My father died over ten years ago. My mother and grandfather died just before I joined the navy in an outbreak of sweating sickness.' He paused again, and I thought of what he'd said about being young and alone at a funeral. 'I have no nieces or nephews, my siblings all died much too young for that.'

I nodded. 'I'm sorry.'

He shrugged. 'It is not so uncommon where I am from. I understand why you asked. May I ask the same of you?'

'Just my two daughters. My parents married late and the two boys they had before me died as babies. My father was the last of his line; my mother had two sisters, one to London, the other to America. The one in London died, the one in America, she lost touch with. I suppose we are both alone.'

'Well, I am sorry for your losses as well.'

'It is the way of the world. Especially for those born poor.'

'Indeed.'

I looked around the kitchen and imagined a fire in the heath, pies in the oven, the girls sitting about the table with me. I looked to Captain Parnell. I did not know him that well, but I supposed we were friends. He knew of hard work as I did. If he was to go back to sea, we wouldn't see much of him and I would get Edward Webster to draw me up a good contract. I might not be as wealthy as before, but I could do well here.

'Have you ever been part of a similar venture?' I asked.

'Yes, I bought a house in Liverpool which my aunt ran. She had been a housekeeper. I sold it after she died a few years ago.'

I held out a hand. 'I would like to accept your offer and go into business with you.'

'Excellent.'

He shook my hand as if I was a man and we laughed nervously.

'Should you like to stay for dinner?' he asked. I was about to refuse, but then why? There were no dinner bookings tonight, Henry wouldn't miss me, the girls were dining with the Websters at their in-laws' grand house in Clifton, I had no husband awaiting me. I was a widow, and for the first time I realised what that meant. I was free.

'Yes, I would like that.'

'It's not a fancy fare, I'm afraid.'

'Well, I could-'

'Mrs Fitzwilliam, I did not invite you to my house so you would cook for me. I am not that hopeless. Maybe it might be pleasant for you not to cook.'

'I love to cook,' I said, but even as I spoke I felt weariness around my edges. 'But you are right.'

I sat down while he assembled dinner from the larder of bread, cheese, wine, cold pies and meats, all of which looked delicious.

'Aha, so you are not cooking after all, I see?'

He grinned as he set the table. 'You've caught me out.'

I raised a glass as he sat. 'To this house.'

'And our business.'

We toasted and started to eat. It struck me suddenly that I had never been quite so alone with a man. With Peter we had first lived with his family, then in the hotel with my mother – both buildings always full. Now, here I was with a man I barely knew all alone in a house and intending to stay that way for the course of the evening. How strange then, that I felt so at ease with him. A strange, daring thrill went through me and I smiled, which to my pleasure he returned.

'This is good food, and excellent wine,' I said, in part to cover for my smile but also because it was true.

'Thank you, though as you say I can hardly take credit for it. Have you cooked all your life?'

'Yes, my mother was a cook and her mother before me and so it went back. We'd worked for the Roberts, the family who owed the land next to the Fitzwilliams, for generations.'

'What was it like? The countryside? Glastonbury, isn't it?'

I looked at him, wondering at his interest.

'I was born in a city and spent my life at sea,' he said. 'I know little of the countryside.'

So I spoke of it and found I was glad to; no one had asked me for an age. I told him of the open skies and fresh air, stories about paddling in streams and the fun of markets days, the freeing feeling of being able to run through fields barefoot and the thrill of seeing the first spring blossoms.

'When I was there, I think I always wanted to be away, I didn't appreciate it. I liked the village when it was busy, and knew if I went to a city there would be more busyness to enjoy. It seemed the country was a bad place to be poor as well, if you lost your job there were less places to find a new one. Less places to thrive. My mother didn't stifle my way of thinking either, in fact she encouraged it She used to say she wished she had the courage to go, as her sisters had.'

'And there we were in the city thinking the country was all bliss- a cornucopia of food we imagined it,' he hesitated before continuing with a twinkle in his usually serious brown eyes. 'That was why we thought country folk so simple, they never had to work for anything.'

'Simple indeed!'

He chuckled. 'I see now I was much mistaken in that rude assumption.'

'I was warned city boys had no manners at all.' I shook my head and we laughed, more relaxed this time. My whole body was starting to feel less tense, as if warming up on a summer's day. It could of course be the wine, or it could simply be that I was enjoying myself. I wanted to continue in his company, in this house for as long as I could.

'And what of your youth?' I asked as he topped up our wine glasses.

'I think I am better at being an adult than I was at being a child,' he said, smiling at the memory. 'I went about the place with Our Luke and Our Kathy-' he stopped, having slipped into a Liverpool accent. I gave a half smile of amusement, which he returned and continued. 'They were my siblings. The others, sadly, died as babies. Us three were always trying to make some money with various schemes, and we helped our mother with her washing and the babies. The room we lived in-' he stopped again and looked at me, embarrassed. He had said 'room', revealing he had been much poorer than I, raised in a little cottage. I carried on eating, pretending I had not noticed and he pressed on. 'Always smelled of lavender, soap and babies, the sheets and clothes of the wealthy hanging up everywhere. My grandfather - Nonno, we called him which is Italian for grandfather - drove a cab and I loved to help him with that, encouraging customers outside the theatres and such, riding up top with him. At the time, it seemed a struggle, but looking back, there were happy times among it.'

He stopped, and looked down as if he had said too much. Maybe he thought he had, in too true an accent, but I liked it and I liked that I was gaining a fuller picture of him. I wanted to know about this man who I was to go into business with; who wanted to go into business with me.

'And you then you went to sea?'

He nodded. 'My first voyage was only a quick one, a couple weeks on a small passenger ship to the Isle of Man, then a few days after that I went to Spain on a merchant ship.'

'And you were eight?'

He grinned. 'Sailors start young. My father knew some of the able seamen so they kept an eye out for me. The next time I went on a voyage, to India, I took Our Luke with me and I was very proud to look after him.'

'So when did you learn to read?'

'One of the things I did to make money on land was help market traders set up for the day. There was a woman, who had fallen on hard times and she had a book stall. I used to like helping her set up, looking at her atlases first of all. She taught me letters, then the man who managed the stables where Nonno worked taught me a bit more when I helped out there, then a petty officer on a ship…scraps here and there. I tried to teach bits to Our Kathy and Our Luke as well. Kathy was quite good, poor Luke couldn't understand it. Later, Captain

Perkins took my education in hand so I could sit the officer's exam. How did you learn to read?'

'Cookbooks. My mother taught me from them, as she was taught and I taught the girls. I do not think I am so great a reader but I am very proud of how confident the girls are with letters.'

'They do both seem to be very prolific readers, so you must be better than you give yourself credit for.'

It was rather silly but that hadn't ever occurred to me before, and no one else had ever pointed it out. To divert attention from the compliment he had paid me, I asked him about how he had been promoted.

'I took a job on a navy ship, even though it was just before the relief laws so it was illegal-'

'Forgive my ignorance, it wasn't just illegal for Catholics to be officers in the military before the relief laws, you could not serve in any way at all?'

'Yes, but of course people often did because the navy wants young, healthy troops above all things. So, there I was. I found ways to assist the petty officers, and then the captain's servant got sick so one of the petty officers, Cogan, recommended me to Perkins as a replacement. For that voyage I was the Captain's servant. I worked hard and I enjoyed it. At the end of the voyage the captain said if I considered converting, I ought write to him and he would recommend me to become an officer.'

'But then the relief laws came in and you didn't have to?'

He shook his head. 'Not exactly. The first relief act in seventy-eight allowed Catholics to join the military but not to become officers. It was relief act of ninety-one which allowed Catholics to become officers.'

Inwardly I ran through quick calculations. If he was about my age, in 1791 he would have been in the middle of his twenties. Even with my limited knowledge of the navy I knew that was rather old to be a midshipman, the starting rank for navy officers.

'So you converted to the Church of England?'

He nodded and looked away. 'It always made me feel ill at ease, but I could see no other option. It was my only chance to rise. In ninety-one, I quietly reverted back to Rome and since most people had always seen fit to assume I was foreign and Catholic anyway, it made little difference to my life outside the navy. You shall think me quite without a backbone I am afraid.'

'Not at all,' I said quietly as a realisation dawned on me. Around the same time he had chosen between religious conviction and poverty, I had married. Both of us had made difficult choices, at a young age in hopes of a better life. His had worked out rather better than mine.

'May I ask, what I happened to Kathy and Luke?' I spoke gently, knowing they must have died but hoping they had lived well before then.

'Well…' he took a sip of wine. 'It was the smallpox outbreak. Our Kathy, Our Luke and I – we all got it.'

I went to ask if he was scarred but stopped myself; that was unfeeling. He caught my eye then tugged down his collar to reveal some pock marks on his neck. 'It is a strange, peculiar luck to have, to not only survive smallpox, but to have most of the scars on my back.'

'That is something, at least,' I said fearing what was coming.

He hesitated. 'It would be, if it had not blinded Luke and it killed Kathy. I was the eldest and… It did not seem just.'

Such sympathy welled up in me that I had reached out and pressed his rough hand before I thought on it. It was improper, but it seemed wrong to do nothing.

'My mother went into a melancholy which never left her,' he sighed and I felt a wrench of pity in maternal sisterhood. To have already buried some of her children and then to lose another would be unbearable. I did not know how women survived such things. 'A few months later the sweating sickness claimed my mother and Nonno. By then I had already met with Captain Perkins. I thought about not taking him up on his offer so I could look after Luke but he was a good lad, he wanted to contribute as well. Luke met up with our cousins who were…well, to be frank, they were always up to some mischief or other. They promised him some sort of dubious work, and it led to him getting into a fight with some other boys. Luke dashed his head open on the cobbles.'

I gasped.

He looked away. 'This next part I am not proud of, but I was so angry. I sought out the perpetrators and fought them, then I fought my cousins. I did not come off particularly well but I cared not. I was lucky that my father sought me out and braved my young man's fury,' he gave a hollow laugh 'He convinced me to go to take Captain Perkins' up on his offer. He said after the luck we'd had, what good had being Catholics done us anyway? My father never wanted that for himself, but he was happy for me. The navy was the best thing that ever happened to me. I made Midshipman by the time I was sixteen. My father even lived to see me become a lieutenant when I was twenty-two.'

He took a deep drink of his wine. 'My apologies, that is not something I speak of often but now you know what sought of a person you are to go into business with.'

I did now indeed now him a deal better, and felt reassured. He was hard working and ambitious, qualities I respected. What I found myself respecting more was how fiercely he had loved his family, and I was very sorry for him that he had lost them. 'I appreciate your honesty,' I said. It made me see he had come from even poorer circumstances than myself, so hopefully not treat this house and business lightly.

'So, what of your time at sea? You must've been to some very interesting places.'

'You want to hear about that?'

'Of course. I always see people coming and going but I've never left the West Country. Where was the first place you visited?'

'Well,' he said, seeing the bottle empty and looking at me with a cocked eyebrow. I smiled, nodded. He went to fetch another from the larder, while I heaped more cheese onto my plate. 'It cannot simply be me, telling you my stories all night. It must be like for like. I'd like to hear how a country girl came to run one of the best hotels in England.'

'In England? Please!' But I saw he was waiting for me to go on, so I did. 'Well as I told you it was my mother's idea. When I married, we were promised some money from Peter's family but he was the youngest of four sons so we would have to go into trade in some way. His family were gentlemen farmers, but he had no inclination for farming or land management and had never trained to be a lawyer or a clergyman so had no way to earn a living' I gave a laugh, feeling very foolish. Now I thought on it, what real qualities had he had to recommend him? How dare his family think he was so superior to me simply for the station he had been born into. If not for me, he would have squandered everything much sooner. The Fitzwilliams must have been delighted to relieve themselves of the responsibility of looking after him, and foist him off onto my mother and I. Taking a sip of my wine in a hope it would soften my rush of anger, I carried on, knowing it would not do to speak so ill of Peter whatever I thought. 'My husband was very pleased with the idea of owning an inn. He liked to be around people, he must've guessed my mother and I would do much of the work. My mother was very pleased, it had been a dream she had long harboured without the means.'

'And you?'

'At that time, I wanted what my mother wanted. I wanted her to be happy. And I liked owning an inn, but the older I get the more I see we like it for different reasons.'

I leant slightly closer, conspiratorially, I had never spoken so frankly about my mother and Peter, but was emboldened by the exaggerated clarity which comes with drink. 'My mother wanted to own a fine establishment, she wanted to have the lords and ladies, the very wealthy as guests. She was always pleased to work for the Roberts for they were the richest family in Glastonbury you see, and loved the idea of having the great and good staying at her hotel, so she may become acquainted with them and have their praise. It was the reason she wanted the hotel in Bath.'

'Why did you not end up there then?'

'It was me,' I said. 'I think the only time I went against her. We visited. I liked it, it was very pretty and beautiful – but it was stifling. The thought of working for those people, of the grovelling and pretence every day was too oppressive. I thought we would get guests for the spa and the society but Bristol is a port, so we could get even more guests that were travellers, merchants and people bound for adventures. I rather thought I would prefer a hotel that could both be luxurious but also comfortable, make people from different backgrounds feel welcome, and as if they were having a treat but not so there was too much ceremony. I always felt out of my depth in those days, with Peter's family making me feel very much the poor relation that I was. I just wanted a place where anyone could relax. And I wanted the food to be good; large good portions of proper West Country fare to be available – not the grim things you get in some places, or anything too over fussed and fashionable so guest are left hungry and confused. I said, let us look to Bristol and Peter had visited there and liked it, and so it was settled. I love the energetic feel of Bristol and I love the idea of travel, though I have not done it much. My mother ended up happy as we still got some wealthy guests but I just liked to accommodate everyone.'

He made no judgment, as I always had feared, that I was ungrateful for my lot.

'Well you succeeded, I have never felt more at ease in a hotel than I did in yours.'

We talked for hours, him telling of exotic places, me talking about cooking and The Fitzwilliam, and the girls, then just talking about our cities. By the time we'd got through the second bottle of wine the rain had turned into a storm. We stood at the window watching it a while. I could feel the heat from his body, but I did not reach out to touch him.

'You can stay the night, if you wish,' he said. 'I can sleep in the parlour. You can have my bed.'

And, free as a widow, I agreed.

Chapter 9

Amelia

Mr and Mrs Webster took us and their sons to dine at the Browns' house in Clifton. They were Betsey's parents, so she was there. The dinner party was a large one, with several other families of the Browns' acquaintances present.

I must confess I had hoped for a somewhat fancier house, given they were plantation owners and having seen all the fine fashions worn by their daughter. The decor was very dated and the food was not especially nice. Even the rest of the company was rather dull; lawyers, merchants and a clergy-man, with equally dull wives. Aside from the Websters, there were no young men whatsoever.

Lydia was quiet, and Betsey was engaged in conversation with everyone else. After we had eaten, we sat in the parlour and Lydia was called to play cards with some of the dull wives. I smiled; she would beat them all. When she left, Betsey at last came to sit with me.

'Enjoyable evening?' she smirked, rolling her eyes.

I grinned back at her. 'Oh, delightful,' I whispered.

She chuckled. 'When I first married, I was so pleased to get away from these dry occasions, yet they insist on inviting me back. Which reminds me, I have had an invitation which may be of interest to you.' She snapped her fan open. 'My Aunt Tindal, a childless widow, has invited me to go visit her in Bath. She has said I may bring a friend. I was rather hoping you would be that friend.'

My eyes widened. 'Do you mean it?'

'Of course.'

I grinned, heart soaring. 'Thank you!'

'Now, brace yourself for here is the tedious part. My aunt is very poorly, so we may have to do our fair share of looking after her and keeping her company. But don't worry, we shan't play nurse-maid the whole time. In the evenings I will take you to parties and as I am a married lady, I shall be chaperone. I know plenty of people there we can have a merry time with. So, you will come with me?'

I nodded. 'I would love to, but do you suppose it is proper?'

'With the mourning? I would think a change of scene will do you good.'

'I will have to get Mama to agree.' I hesitated, she did not know Betsey very well. I supposed saying we were staying with the aunt would count in our favour and Mrs Webster could vouch for it all. Betsey pressed my hand. 'Should you like to hear what the parties will be like?'

I nodded.

Jessica

Blinking, I sat up in an unknown bed with an aching head. The bed smelled of a man, of the Captain, of soap and starch and the sea. I momentarily panicked, before my mind went over my steps last night. I had come up to bed alone. Of course the bed smelled of him, it was his bed but for last night at least, he had remained downstairs.

My dress was hung up, and I was still wearing my stays and petticoat. The memories of yesterday's strange events flooded back to me; ought I have stayed the night? Should I have drank so much? Yet I was hardly a young maiden, I was a widow of five and thirty. Henry would not notice that I had gone, and even if he did who would he tell? He did not know I'd been alone in a house with a man; I could say I stayed at the Websters. I ran my hands through my hair, but nothing untoward had happened, and it seemed I'd come out of the day much richer than I started so it could not be all bad. I just hoped when I got downstairs, Captain Parnell hadn't had a change of heart.

*

The smell of porridge drifted from the kitchen. Hoping I had nothing to be embarrassed about I took a deep breath and stepped inside.

Captain Parnell looked up from doling the porridge into two bowls.

'Good morning,' he said. 'There is tea in the pot.'

I poured it and we sat down together.

'My apologies,' he said. 'I ought have tried to get you a cab last night.'

I shook my head. 'In that storm? You would have had a job finding one. And it probably would have drawn more attention had I arrived home in the middle of the night during a storm. This way, I doubt anyone has noticed apart from us.'

'Yes, apart from us.' He laughed then turned to the window. 'The storm has quite cleared now. It looks as if it will be a good day.'

The sky was blue, and the sun was shining; there was even the hint of a rainbow. Everything was new. 'Yes, it does, doesn't it? So,' I said, bracing myself for rejection. 'Shall I set up an appointment with a lawyer?'

He nodded with a smile. 'Yes. When would you like to move in?'

I returned his smile. With his question he cemented the reality of my new situation. 'My last guests at the hotel should be leaving tomorrow. Does that suit you?'

'Yes. I will be here for another few weeks. I can move my things into one of the smaller rooms, and you and the girls can have the bigger one.'

'Thank you.'

'Do you have a lawyer in mind?'

'As a matter of fact, I do. Edward Webster, the son of my friend. Maybe we could call at his offices after breakfast.'

'Excellent.'

I took a drink of tea and it did something to ease my headache.

'May I ask how your head fares this morning?' I asked. 'Mine is a little tender.'

He chuckled. 'Mine also, but hopefully this porridge will set us in good stead. I must have my wits about me if I am to deal with your lawyer.'

I went to protest, but saw he was teasing.

'Indeed you must,' I smiled.

Lydia

The bell rang and I looked up from my book. Mr George Thomas entered the shop.

'Miss Fitzwilliam, I did not expect to see you here so soon.'

I straightened up and shrugged. 'I must earn my living, now even more so than before.'

He nodded, looking abashed. 'Of course. And how do you fare?'

It was a question to which no words could answer. There was a constant pressing on my chest and tension in my muscles, an anger not just at the thought of the debt which whirled in my mind but also at the suddenness of it all, the violence that had killed my father. The fact that he'd had no time to put anything right, that I had spied on him yet not been brave enough to confront him, that I had avoided playing cards with him in the last few days of his life, which left a great hollowness in my core.

'I am as you see, sir.'

'Yes…I came to see if you had any more books, but it is no matter-'

I reached behind the desk and pulled out a stack of four; three from his list and one which I had thought might be useful anyway. As I explained this, he stepped closer with a small smile.

'What excellent condition they are in.'

'Yes, they belonged to a doctor who was quite fastidious.'

'Oh, these are marvellous,' he said as he examined them. After he paid, he slapped a hand to his forehead. 'I quite forgot, my father said to remind you of his offer for you and your family to dine with us. He asked if the twenty-fourth would be convenient?'

'I think so. I will check with my mother and send confirmation.'

'Excellent. We shall look forward to it.'

With a tip of his hat, he strode from the shop.

*

When I arrived back at the Websters', Mrs Webster smiled to see me.

'Your mother is in the parlour. She has good news that she wishes to share with you and Amelia before anyone else.'

I hastened to the parlour, where mother sat waiting with Amelia.

'Just tell me-' Amelia said as I burst in.

'What is this good news?' I asked, thinking some clause in the will had been discovered or that Uncle Henry had decided to show charity; the first seeming far more likely.

Mother smiled. 'I have found us somewhere to live, and a way to make a modest living.'

Amelia's eyebrows shot up. 'What is it?'

'I think we shall need to keep our other forms of incomes as we discussed-' a look of annoyance crossed Amelia's face. 'I have been asked to manage a lodging house.'

'That's excellent news!' I smiled. It should not be so different from before, and hopefully this time Mother would be able to keep more of the money, as a widow. Mother returned my smile, though Amelia's looked forced.

'How has this come about?' I asked.

'Do you recall Captain Parnell who stayed at The Fitzwilliam?'

I nodded. He had spoken with me at the funeral.

'Was he Lt. Driscoll's foreign looking friend?' Amelia asked.

'Yes,' Mother said. 'Only don't say it in that tone Amelia, you sound disparaging. He is half Italian.'

'That's still foreign.'

'Amelia-'

'His lineage is hardly the point,' I snapped. 'What's he got to do with this?'

'He bought a house with the intention of renting it out while he was at sea. He knew of our predicament and given my experience at The Fitzwilliam has offered the position of running the place to me. There is a large bedroom which us three will share then we shall rent the other two out. We shall pay a rent to Captain Parnell but it shall be much lower than what will be charged to the other lodgers, and our places there will be guaranteed for six months should anything happen to him.'

'But you won't be paid to run this house?' Amelia asked.

'I will be paid and there will be a discount to our rent. We are only paying a fifth what the tenants will pay; it is very generous.'

'Where is it?' Amelia asked.

'Hotwells.'

Amelia sighed. 'That is near the spa I suppose, I had hoped you might say Clifton.'

'Come now Amelia,' Mother chided. 'This is much more than we had right to hope for.'

Amelia shrugged. 'At least it means we don't have to live with the Websters anymore.'

'Yes,' Mother nodded. 'And we will have full rein over which tenants to take. Though we won't be as near to town as we are used to, it is not so bad a walk. We will be closer to the country as well, so we might take trips and such like.'

Amelia nodded, looking slightly more cheerful. I took Mother's hand. 'This is a stroke of luck,' I enthused, hoping to make up for Amelia's attitude.

'When can we move in?'

'Tomorrow,' Mother beamed.

Chapter 10
Jessica

After Lydia asked Mr Syrett if she could take the day off to help with the move, he kindly agreed and offered to drive us and our belongings in his trap. He first picked up the girls, their luggage and the cats from the Websters, then he came over to The Fitzwilliam.

The last of the guests finished their breakfasts and I bid them farewell as they left. I told Henry last night that I was leaving. He did not ask where I was going, or what was to become of his nieces.

When Mr Syrett's trap arrived, Lydia came in to help me move the bags and the boxes of our remaining books, a basket of food, bed linens and a few ornaments, pictures and small pieces of furniture which I hoped Henry would not question. He retired to Peter's study and did not stir. I hesitated by the glasses in the cupboard which had belonged to Peter's mother. I had decided not to take them since Henry would surely know they'd been his mother's but suddenly, out of annoyance I decided that I would. Henry had made no comment on them during his stay and his mother had given them to me. I would take them for myself and the girls. Lydia came to help me wrap them without question and we hastened away.

I turned around as we rode down King Street; my home, my life, my work became obscured by busy people hurrying by and grew smaller behind me. I had never thought how much my life could change, how the place I had adored and worked for could be so easily taken from me. I swallowed the tears that rose and Lydia pressed my hand. I must concentrate on our new start.

When we pulled up outside the house, our new home, Captain Parnell came out to greet us.

'Hello,' he said, shaking hands with Mr Syrett, then patting the horse. 'What a fine stead he is.'

'Yes,' Mr Syrett said proudly.

Captain Parnell offered a hand to help me down, then the girls, before taking off a crate.

'Lead on, Mrs Fitzwilliam.'

The door was open so I led the girls in, noticing the unimpressed look on Amelia's face as she released the cats from their basket. What had she expected would happen to us? Young though she was, couldn't she see this was the best we could hope for?

As Captain Parnell set the crate of Lydia's books down. One fell off and she lunged for it, but he got there first. The book was her much thumbed copy of *Vindication of the Rights of Woman*. For a moment I panicked then remembered how he hadn't disapproved of her dressing as a boy.

'Is this yours, Miss Fitzwilliam?' he asked.

'It is,' she said, extending her hand for it.

He gave it to her. 'Is it any good? I have read her *Vindication of the Rights of Men* which I found slightly naïve, but the sentiments were laudable.'

Lydia held the book close to her chest. 'Yes, I like it very much. It is more passionate than well-argued, but nonetheless valid and important.'

She spoke quickly and colour rose in her cheeks. I saw she was waiting to be mocked or dismissed, but the Captain smiled warmly. 'Well, it sounds fascinating. I should like to read it sometime.'

Lydia held the book back out to him. 'Here,' she said. 'You may borrow mine. Perhaps we could discuss it before you set sail.'

'Thank you,' he said, taking the book. 'I shall look forward to our discussion.'

'Are these your books?' Amelia asked. The full bookshelf which had previously been in the largest bedroom was now in the parlour.

'Yes. I thought instead of hoarding them I would leave them available for yourselves and the guests to read while I am away.'

Mr Syrett grinned at the shelf. 'A very eclectic mix here. Ah, you have Cook's *A Voyage to The Pacific Ocean*. I love that book.'

'As do I. I must admit I am still disappointed not to have made it to Australia or New Zealand yet.'

Lydia picked it up.

'You ought read it,' Captain Parnell said to her. 'A like for like, then we can discuss that before I sail as well.'

Lydia nodded. 'Very well,' she smiled.

'Oh, you have some novels which I have not read,' Amelia, at last, graced us with a genuine smile.

'Help yourself, Miss Amelia. Mr Syrett, shall we unload the rest of your trap?'

Mr Syrett nodded as Lydia piped up that she would help.

As they unloaded everything, Amelia and I made sandwiches and poured small beer. Once all was unloaded we all sat around the kitchen table, and started to eat. As Amelia asked Captain Parnell his opinion on various plays and poems while Mr Syrett and Lydia chimed in with their own views, a calmness and tranquillity descended over me. I was home.

Amelia

The house was not so bad as I had expected, and Lydia was right. At least we were no longer with the Webster boys. The room I was to share with Lydia and Mama was a large one. Lydia and I had a double bed and Mama had a single.

Captain Parnell did not seem so bad, nor keen to interfere with our lives which was a relief. He mentioned that he would be often out of the house attending to matters aboard the ship he captained, HMS Aries.

Lydia asked if she could see it, to which he said she would not be allowed aboard, but we could talk a walk to see it. It was arranged we would take a trip see the ship, then picnic on the Downs if the weather was fine before an expedition to buy some furniture. While Lydia was excited and Mama was intrigued, I could think of nothing duller. Hopefully there would at least be some handsome officers around.

As we settled into bed, tired from all our unpacking, I decided to broach the topic of visiting Bath with Betsey Webster, since Mama was in a good mood.

'Mama, I have been invited to Bath.'

She looked up from shaking out her bedding and Lydia raised her eyebrows at me.

'By who?'

'Mrs Betsey Webster,' I said.

Mama started to unpin her hair. 'Richard's wife? The one from Clifton?'

'Yes.'

Betsey being from a wealthy Clifton family would count in my favour.

'Just you and Betsey Webster?' Lydia asked, and I detected jealousy in her voice.

'Yes. She is in her twenties and a married woman so can chaperone. We will be staying with her elderly aunt, Mrs Tindal, so I am sure it will be most respectable.'

'Well... Maybe a trip would do you good, but I must talk to Mrs Webster, the *senior* Mrs Webster, before I make my mind up to get a clearer picture of Betsey's character.'

'Mama-'

'I barely know Betsey and it will be your first trip away from Bristol alone, darling.'

I went to argue more but realised I was in a good position from the look of annoyance on Lydia's face.

'Very well Mama, thank you kindly.'

The next morning, I was last to awake. It took me a few moments to realise where I was, then it all came crushing down. I was not in my bed, nor in the Websters' house, but in this new place. The grey morning light, which leaked in through the window, showed the room as shabby and bare. From somewhere I could smell damp and there were faint cracks in the ceiling.

'Amelia!' Mama called up the stairs, her voice too bright and cheerful. I heaved myself out of bed and descended the cold stairs to find Mama and Lydia already eating breakfast. My stomach jolted to see them sitting at a kitchen table without Papa or even a place set for him, even if this wasn't his house or our old kitchen he should still be here, yet Mama was excitedly talking about the paints she had asked Captain Parnell to fetch so she could decorate the house.

'What do you think of pale blue for the guest bedrooms?' Mama asked. 'Or sage green?'

'Sage green looks warmer, but blue looks cleaner,' Lydia said. Since when did she care a fig for such matters?

'I think green for the bedrooms,' Mama mused, passing me a plate of toast. 'I shall paint the stairwell blue. I fancy Captain Parnell might be persuaded to get some new curtains for the parlour.'

Of course he would be persuaded. It was in his interest to leave all this dull nonsense up to her. 'What of our bedroom?'

'That will have to be done last I'm afraid,' Mama said. 'When we have made a little profit, which is not to say we cannot decorate it with our things if you wish.'

'As long as Lydia doesn't put up her gruesome carcass sketches.'

It suddenly seemed bitterly unfair that Lydia could still draw as many carcasses as she liked but I was not to have my piano. No one had even the mentioned the loss of it; though doubtless how Papa had come to acquire it overshadowed it in their eyes.

'Will I ever have a piano again?'

Mama paused in pouring the tea. 'Maybe someday, if you marry a rich man or if we save up enough, but I don't think one would comfortably fit in this parlour. Maybe we could see what smaller instruments you could play.'

As if to play another instrument would be as easy as that, and a smaller one? Would she have me play a pipe or fiddle like some Irish tinker?

'Perhaps you could busy yourself in the garden.'

She gestured to the yard through the window.

'We'll be growing some of our own food,' Lydia enthused.

Lord, had it come to this? Were we to scratch about like country folk?

'You could grow flowers,' Mama carried on.

'We don't know the first thing about growing plants-'

'I do. Do not forget your grandfather was a gardener.'

And the other was a gentleman farmer, emphasis on *gentleman*, who got others to doing the dirty farming work for him. Father would not see me work on my hands and knees in the mud, this was not his intention. He didn't come from so near the gentry to have me reduced to this!

The thought of busying myself in the garden as a replacement for my music was insulting. Was that to be my leisure time after slaving over dresses, to be kneeling in the mud, bending my back over turnips and potatoes with the odd flower for compensation? I expect if I did grow flowers, they'd want me to sell them as well.

I stood up.

'I'm not hungry.'

'You must eat.'

I stormed from the room, wanting to be gone.

'Amelia, you must take care coming down here in your night dress. Suppose Captain Parnell was here.'

'He's a sailor, isn't he?' I snapped, thinking of the conversations the Webster boys hadn't bothered to keep quiet. 'I'm sure he's seen plenty of girls in less than their night dresses!'

'Amelia!' Mama followed me to the parlour and now stood aghast. For half a moment I feared she would do what she had never done and strike me. She wouldn't have even thought of such a thing if Papa was alive.

Instead she ran her hands through her hair. 'Enough. Please, we must try to make the best of things. It could be much worse.'

There she was showing her true self - a servant, not a lady despite her fine dresses and manners, always ready to scrape and serve, first the guests at the hotel now Captain bloody Parnell. Papa would never have approved of her working for a Catholic.

'Amelia, I know you feel your father's loss. We all do, but I know you feel you were closest to him-'

'Because I was, and I can see he only made a mistake, I don't blame him-'

'Yes,' her lips thinned. 'He made a mistake, he didn't intend for us to be poor but here we are. We have nowhere else to go. We all wish he hadn't died, and it hadn't come to this. Maybe it will do you good to go to Bath, but you must behave like a young lady not a churlish girl. Can you do that?'

I nodded begrudgingly.

'Good. I know it is hard to give up our nice things but hopefully it will only be for a time. Now, we have a pleasant day ahead with decorating and seeing the ship, do we not? Depending on your behaviour I will talk to Mrs Webster tomorrow.'

So, blackmail was it? Well, I would simper and serve if it got me to Bath, for once I was there, I wouldn't have to put up with this anymore.

'I do understand. My father died when I was younger than you remember.'

She didn't understand at all. She told me herself she had always been closer to her mother. Just as she was now to Lydia.

The door sounded and I realised Captain Parnell would be coming back, so I ran upstairs to get dressed.

Before dressing I took a few deep breaths, sitting on the bed. The two cats came to sit on my lap, nuzzling at my hands. They helped to calm me, and though I still believed myself in the right I saw I had conducted myself in a very rash, unladylike manner. I ought not to lose my temper, and even though she might show it differently I supposed Mama was trying to do what she thought was best. My stomach rumbled. She was right about eating breakfast. I dressed quickly hoping there would still be some left when I went back downstairs.

Jessica
We set off with Captain Parnell after breakfast, and Amelia's spirits improved once she'd eaten. With Peter gone, I realised how much he indulged her and I had let him, since it seemed better than him wishing for a son. It was no wonder that she missed him, but whilst I didn't want to be too hard on her I also didn't want her to become unruly.

I lost my own father in my sixth year, so only had fleeting memories of him; a quiet, old man. I was more used to not having a father than having one, so I could pretend to understand what the girls were going through, but I couldn't really. Losing my mother had been painful. The girls had been small and she had been living with us. It made me realise how much I'd depended on her, and I was grieved that she would miss the girls, and the hotel, growing.

It is perhaps the years at the end of childhood, as one becomes an adult that people need their parents to guide them, and though it was always obvious in our small family that Lydia was more like me and Amelia like Peter, I thought they both still had a mix of both our traits; but now with Peter gone, his likeness to Amelia was more striking. She looked so much like him; she frowned like him and had the same expressions of boredom or annoyance if a subject was uninteresting to her, the same happy, enchanted focus when something took her eye - which little had done of late save this trip to Bath.

We walked through the bustling docks, watching merchant ships being unloaded with silks and spices, sailors hanging from ropes cleaning navy ships, families boarding passenger ships. The familiar yearning rose up in me, the longing to follow the ships. When we arrived at the HMS Aries both girls brightened up; Lydia at the sight of the ship and Amelia the sight of the officers - I was not so blind.

It was a huge great vessel, that seemed to overlook all the other ships. The head was a very finely sculpted model of the God of War wearing a gleaming chest plate and a crown made of oak leaves. The sails billowed proudly in the breeze. Some men were busy at work, cleaning, mending and polishing on the deck. When they saw us they gave cheerful salutes and returned to their work.

'Are we truly not allowed on?' Lydia asked.

'I'm afraid not. An admiral's wife would be allowed with her husband, but no other respectable woman is really supposed to set foot upon a navy ship I'm afraid.'

I noted his use of the word 'respectable' and realised what other sort of women might be allowed aboard. There were a few of them were laughing loudly with a group of sailors not far behind us.

'Well,' I said briskly. 'Thank you for showing us. She really is a lovely ship. Shall we go to our picnic?'

The Captain flagged us a cab and we set off up Park Street towards the Downs. When we arrived, he asked as to where was best to situate ourselves and I felt embarrassed not to really know. I had rarely visited the Downs, rarely left the hotel, the city centre and the society of our friends. The girls were happy to take the lead and soon we were sitting in a pleasant spot, overlooking the Avon gorge.

'Is it true you must be a mathematician to be a sailor?' Lydia asked, looking down at a boats sailing in the River Avon.

Captain Parnell nodded. 'For those who go to the college it is taught there.'

'And you?'

'I picked it up from my father, badgered everyone else and, you shall be pleased to hear, combed second-hand bookshops in every port we landed in. I do not think I have a mind naturally disposed to mathematics, but with practise I got there.'

'I think Lydia has a mind disposed to it,' I said proudly.

'But what good is that to anyone?' Amelia said. 'It's hardly as if she can join the navy.'

'It is always helpful to have a logical mind,' Captain Parnell said.

Amelia shrugged. 'I'm to pick some flowers.' She left us.

'My apologies for my daughter's behaviour,' I said.

Captain Parnell shrugged. 'She is young.'

Lydia looked up from watching the river. 'You oughtn't let her go to Bath if she behaves so.'

I shot Lydia a look but she stared back at me unperturbed.

'Bath might do her good, a change of scene,' I sighed. Peter's death had not caused such a change in Lydia, but she was hiding her grief. I could not think of Peter without a confusing mix of sadness and anger at the state he left us in, but knew to talk to the girls about my anger at Peter was not a good thing. Again, I remembered I did not know what it was like to lose a parent at their age. But Captain Parnell did.

I turned back to him

'You lost your mother when you were a similar age. Do you think a change of scene would be good?'

Captain Parnell paused, as if surprised to be asked. 'My change of scene was joining the navy, which did do me good. However, I am not sure if idling in Bath would have the same effect.'

'She needn't be idle,' I said.

'I didn't mean she was, but Bath does have that effect on people doesn't it?'

'Well, I gather she will be a companion to the aunt of a family friend, Mrs Tindal,' I said.

'You should insist she visit some of the Roman ruins and other cultural sights to keep her mind occupied,' Lydia interjected.

'That could be beneficial, if I may say so,' Captain Parnell said. 'As would tending to this Mrs Tindal. To keep her busy could be welcome, that is what I found at least.'

*

I sat with Mrs Webster in her parlour.

'How trustworthy is Betsey?' I asked.

Mrs Webster looked offended. 'She is my daughter-in-law—'

'I am considering entrusting my daughter to her care. She seems rather young.'

'She is three and twenty. We were both mothers by that age, were we not?'

'I suppose, but she seems younger.'

'That's what being raised rich does to you,' Mrs Webster spoke with an odd pride. 'But it also means while she seems young in some ways, she is well versed in other matters, such as how to act and who to know in society.'

I hesitated, recalling there had been some scandal when Richard married her.

'Did they not go to Gretna Green to wed?'

'Well yes,' Mrs Webster admitted. 'But that was the fault of her family, it is all forgotten now and there was nothing inappropriate I assure you.'

'Why did they go there then?'

Mrs Webster thinned her lips. 'Her father refused Richard. He had not quite realised what a well-respected officer he was. It was a misunderstanding. Mr Webster and I certainly had no objection. The young people were just in love and eager to be wed and it has all worked out for the best.'

I nodded, not entirely convinced but Mrs Webster's tone suggested the matter was at an end. No child had been born implausibly quickly after the wedding, so I supposed that could be further evidence that nothing untoward had happened.

'I am not-'

Mrs Webster cleared her throat and gave me a look which reminded me she was my senior by twenty-five years. 'You ought not hold it against my son for marrying up, just as you yourself did, Mrs Fitzwilliam. Surely Betsey's actions merely show a lack of snobbery and prejudice. She has a romantic nature.'

Mrs Webster's words caused me discomfort. Was it never to be forgotten that I came from more reduced circumstances than my late husband, even though it was now known to the world he was gambler and a bankrupt? Perhaps it was best to change my line of questioning.

'Is Mrs Tindal quite infirm? Will they spend much of their time tending to her?'

'Oh yes, she is an old invalid. She will have them reading Fordyce to her all morning and writing her correspondence all afternoon. She will probably insist that poor Amelia sees all the Roman ruins as well. I expect there won't be time for the young women to be distracted, even if they wished it.' She reached over and pressed my hand. 'You've all been through such an ordeal, let Amelia have a bit of an escape in Bath, eh?'

My friend's words rang true, and the presence of this serious Mrs Tindal was reassuring. It would be good for Amelia to get away, and it was an opportunity I would never be able to provide her with. As a final precaution I decided to write to Mrs Tindal introducing myself and Amelia. Her prompt reply came within days. Its tone was firm but friendly, saying she was greatly looking forward to receiving her niece Elizabeth, and was keen to make the acquaintance of my daughter. She echoed what Mrs Webster said about Amelia being kept busy as a companion, whilst still being able to enjoy the culture of Bath. She even hinted that if Amelia pleased her, she might consider taking her on fully as a companion or recommending her to one of her friends, which would be an excellent position. I did not tell Amelia this, knowing it might cause her to sulk about how I always wanted to make money, but if it came to it, I suspected she would prefer such a path to dress making.

On the morning of Amelia's departure, after she had been sunshine all week since I confirmed she could go, I bid her farewell as she climbed into the stagecoach with Betsey.

'Please take care and be good.'

'When aren't I good?'

'Come now darling, you know what I mean. I am hoping you will gain a lot from this experience so please help Mrs Tindal in every way you can.'

Amelia nodded. 'Very well, but you make it sound as if I am to be her servant.'

'No dear, but you will be a guest in her house and she is an old lady in want of company and assistance, is she not?'

She kissed me on the cheek and was helped up into the stagecoach by a young man who regarded her with keen eyes, causing my stomach to twist. Mrs Webster assured me Betsey was more sensible than she appeared, and Mrs Tindal's footman would meet them at the other end. Betsey herself had even assured me she would take the best care of Amelia. All would be well, why would it not be? Young people go to Bath every day, but as the stage coach pulled away tears formed in my eyes.

Amelia had slept away at the Websters, the Hughes and other friends during her life but this would be the first time she would be in a different city from me. They expected to be gone for six weeks. I swallowed, selfishly wondering whether she would miss me as I headed back to the house.

Chapter 11

Lydia

The invitation to dine at the Thomas' had also been extended to Captain Parnell. Together we took a cab up to Cotham.

The door was opened by a young, negress maid and we were shown to the warm parlour, which teamed with floral prints, framed pressed plants and live flowers. Mr Thomas rose to meet us, his rosy cheeked wife on his arm and George just behind him. We were introduced to the other Thomas children, from the sixteen-year-old Miss Ruby Thomas, who would be joining us for dinner and had taken more of her father's darkness than the others, to the younger Hyacinth, Matthew and Flora who would shortly be going to bed.

Mrs Thomas took Mama's arm, ready to introduce her to the rest of the company. Mr Thomas poured Captain Parnell a brandy and George came closer to me.

'You shall be sitting next to Ruby at dinner, Miss Fitzwilliam,' George said. 'I asked it of my mother, for I think you two shall get on famously.'

'Indeed?' I smiled. That was the sort of thing people said to Amelia. No one before ever assumed I would get on 'famously' with other people.

'As luck would have it none of our parents' friends have daughters close to her age, and if we go out into society it is hard for her to make new acquaintances with young girls.' He paused and I realised her darkness was probably why. She was standing with the younger children by the fireplace, fixing her sister's bow, but she glanced over at us. 'I think your personalities are well matched. Should you like to meet her properly?'

I nodded. Beaming, he beckoned her over, and she came, head bowed, hands clasped.

'You see Ruby has a head for books as well, don't you gal? She and mother are quite the botanists.'

He looked encouragingly at his sister.

'You may have guessed about the botany from the decor in this room and our sisters' names.' She spoke quietly but there was a hint of a grin as she chanced a look up.

'It does make sense, now you mention it.'

George was called over by his father for a brandy.

'My brother has told me a great deal about you,' she said. 'He said you are quite the biologist. How did you come to be interested in the topic?'

She spoke in a rush, as if she had prepared beforehand.

'I think it comes from being in the kitchen at my family's hotel. I took an interest in the butchery of the animals. My mother encouraged it, but my sister and father thought it quite gruesome.'

'I am sorry to hear about your father,' she said, concern softening her eyes.

'Thank you,' I said, the ever-present knot in the pit of my stomach tightening, and decided to change the subject. 'Will you tell me how you and your mother came to be interested in botany?'

'Her father, my grandfather, was a gardener.'

'As was mine.'

She smiled at that, a layer of tension visibly leaving her.

'He worked in Clifton, for one of the slave trading families, the Knights. It was how my parents met. My father was a household slave and my mother lived on the grounds with her family.'

Her eyes flashed with anger as she spoke, and she looked at me challengingly. I realised the family's blackness was something the fair skinned George always avoided or spoke around. Ruby had come out and mentioned slavery in our first conversation despite her obvious shyness. I liked her for it.

'I had not realised your father was a slave,' I admitted. 'Foolishly perhaps, I never gave it much thought, perhaps easing my conscience in assuming he was born a free man.'

'My great-grandfather on our father's side was a slaver himself, a Knight cousin, though my father did not know him. Doubtless you have heard of such things?'

I nodded. 'My employer, Mr Syrett, has abolitionist pamphlets in the shop.'

'Father is trying to get everyone to sign the latest abolitionist petition. You will sign it, I trust?'

'I will, but I am only seventeen…'

'We must get your mother and her friend to sign it then.'

'Of course. May I ask if your father was born in the West Indies, or here?'

'The West Indies,' she said. 'He came over to work for the lady of the Knight house when he was about eight.'

I nodded; young Negro boys were quite the fashion accessory.

'Since my mother and father were a similar age, they became friends and my maternal grandparents felt pity for my father. My grandfather and my father used to talk about plants, for since he spent his early years on a planation my father knew something of them even for one so young. When my father was fourteen the Knights planned to send him back to the plantation to toil in the fields. My grandfather sold all he could and bought my father, then adopted him and my father took my mother's family name of Thomas. They left the Knights' employ and set up the grocer business.'

I admired the passion with which Ruby had related the history, though the facts turned my stomach, especially the complicated and cruel family tree of the Knights. They must be aware that some of their slaves came from unions, probably forced, between the male members of their family and their female slaves but clearly turned a blind eye. Mr Thomas was a cousin to those who had owned him yet because his grandmother was a slave, he and his parents were little more than animals to them.

Mr Thomas was laughing with George, Captain Parnell and some of the other men. To think of the harrowing start to his life was quite a jolt to the normally merry man I was used to. Slavery was something which even with Mr Syrett's pamphlets and the boats in the dock had always seemed at a distance, but now it was much closer and the urgency for it to end was suddenly glaring.

'I fear I have made you ill at ease,' Ruby said, nervous once more. 'My brother will be cross. He said I ought hold my tongue on such matters until closer acquaintance.'

'You ought not, Miss Thomas,' I said. 'The abolition of slavery is a pressing concern. We ought to feel the extent of the grief it causes. I am the same when it comes to the question of emancipation of women.'

'You are? As I am.' Her face lit up. 'Have you read Wollstonecraft?' she asked in an excited whisper.

'Indeed I have.'

'Oh Miss Fitzwilliam! We have so much discuss! Loath though I am to admit it, it seems my brother was right!'

As we sat down to eat Ruby told me who the rest of the guests were; there was a young, friendly, blond Methodist minister, Mr Bradley, an older more serious, ruddy faced Methodist minster, Mr Taylor, and an elderly Negro gentleman with an African accent called Mr Ashanti.

The conversation turned to the abolition. Mr Ashanti told us horror stories of the middle passage; the months long journey many Africans endured from their native land to the West Indies and Americas. Mr Thomas did not speak of his own experiences on the plantation or the Knights household, but facilitated the conversation and spoke about petitions, then asked Mother if she would use sugar produced by free men in the pies for their venture (which she said she would).

The question of what would become of the slaves after freedom was raised. The Methodist ministers argued that the scheme to start a colony of freed slaves and their families in Sierra Leona was as a good idea, it just needed more care in the management which so far it had sorely lacked, Mr and Mrs Thomas were not keen on the idea, since as Mr Thomas said he had never been to Africa in the whole course of his life, so why should one such as himself up sticks now? George looked positively repulsed by moving to Africa. They agreed when

Mr Bradley said when slavery was repealed, the navy should be sent out to be set to chasing down slavers from other countries.

'An excellent notion,' Captain Parnell said. 'But sadly I feel the Empire would rather look for some other way to make more money, rather than to lose it.'

'Indeed. There would only be a moral victory in chasing down foreign slavers,' Mr Thomas said. 'No profit whatsoever, so they shall not bother.'

I sat enraptured with Ruby, listening eagerly to such spirited conversation. All the men spoke eloquently while Mother and Mrs Thomas listened attentively. The only person who looked uncomfortable was George. The young minister, Mr Bradley, started to speak about how abolition could signal a new age of freedom and love for all.

'Come now,' Captain Parnell said as the main course was bought out and more claret poured. 'You surely don't believe there will ever be freedom for all, do you?'

'I certainly don't,' Mr Ashanti said. 'Even without Europeans in Africa, slaves were traded - though without the wretchedness of the middle passage across the ocean to these plantations in foreign lands. Your Empire would crumble without oppression.'

Mr Taylor spluttered on his wine. 'The British Empire civilises, it doesn't oppress-'

'Our whole conversation leading to this point has been about how it actively profits from oppression,' Mr Thomas said. 'I am sure that when we abolish the enslavement of Africans, some other sort of slavery or indenture will have to take its place. It all comes back to making a profit to feed the Empire. Look at how well we live, and if you forgive me my friends, we are not exactly the *Beau Monde*, are we?' He was rewarded with chuckles and Mrs Thomas jokingly telling him to speak for himself. 'Not a baronet amongst us, yet we are profitable because the Empire is profitable, and the Empire is profitable because it can produce sugar and cotton for free and sell it for however much it chooses.'

'And there was slavery before, with the Ottomans, Romans and Vikings,' Captain Parnell said. 'I cannot think of a great empire which has functioned without it. It is the human condition to oppress others.'

'I rather think it is not the Ottomans, Roman and Vikings you think of when you say it is the human condition to oppress others, but emancipation for Catholics?' Mr Taylor said wryly.

'I never claimed to be unselfish,' Captain Parnell said. 'Then there is the treatment of the working class in general.'

'Hear, hear,' said Mr Thomas.

'But look where egalitarianism got the French!' protested Mr Taylor

'Not everyone gets it right first time.'

Mr Thomas chuckled. 'Their intentions were noble, were they not? I should very much like to see where they stand in another ten years. Look at the Americas, what at exciting time to live in such a place, if you are white at any rate, to see the birth of a nation ungoverned by monarchy. What a brave notion.'

Mr Bradley looked at Ruby, who was listening rapt, then at the other men. 'Once the Negro is liberated, assumedly a freed slave would just join the working class? If we do not send them to Canada or Serra Leone, we must provide better for them and the rest of the poor. And why can we not have more tolerance for religion? I should not care how a man worships, as long as no one is harmed, if he is kind to his neighbour and works hard.'

'And his first loyalty is to the crown,' Mr Taylor said pointedly, alluding to the foolish fears which many people had that every Catholic was embroiled in a plot akin to that of Guy Fawkes. I cleared my throat.

'If I may say,' I said and earned a smile of encouragement from Ruby. 'People that are drawn into the sort of assassination plots which Mr Taylor alludes to would doubtless find some other way to cause the realm mischief if not for faith. I rather think it is a certain kind of mind drawn to such actions, rather than a religion.'

Mr Taylor flushed and went to speak but Mrs Thomas cut him off, with a twinkle in her eye. 'And what do we think of the emancipation of women?'

'I think if a woman has a husband, she need not worry about such matters,' Mr Taylor said.

'And if she does not have a husband, a father, a son or a brother?' Mother said, her voice gaining strength as she spoke. 'And if perhaps when widowed, she found she had been deceived in the living her husband had promised her and in his character?'

'Well, surely that is a rare example–'

'I doubt it,' Mrs Thomas said.

'I think,' Mother continued. 'On the issue of the emancipation of women, a man and wife should have joint control over their assets, especially if like Mrs Thomas and I, they work for it with their husband or if she brings it from her own family. A widow should at least be left with what she entered the marriage with, no matter how large or small the amount. That is not so much to ask.'

Colour rose in her cheeks as she spoke, but she regarded the men with steely eyes, and I noticed Captain Parnell returned Mother's look with something that could have passed for admiration.

Amelia

My first week in Bath was mostly spent in Mrs Tindal's parlour, reading aloud from *Fordyce's Sermons to Young Women* while she and Betsey embroidered a very dull tapestry of a lake. We went out once, on Sunday morning to church. It was painful. All that could be happening beyond these walls - the society, the sights, the parties but Mrs Tindal made no mention of it. We may as well have been in the middle of nowhere.

She was very small, old and frail, half deaf and blind so that her stitching was awfully slow. Betsey was no great needle woman either and I did not volunteer my services, since I could think of nothing so dull as stitching that big blue lake. Mrs Tindal insisted that I read Fordyce, since she was shocked when I said my Mama had never read them to me.

'But she sounded so proper in her letter.'

By evening, there were visitors but my hopes of anyone exciting were quickly dashed. They were just other elderly ladies with their equally elderly husbands, or middle-aged daughters and companions. The conversation ventured to nothing amusing or even political - lord I would have taken politics for some diversion at least, that could have ended in some disagreements, but no, it was all about the weather, or the passage of time, or the various aliments suffered by their acquaintances. Even Betsey was dull and simpering their company. Only by night did she seem to be my friend again and chatted happily in the room we shared, telling me how she had written to various people of her acquaintance whom she knew in Bath and once they replied, and we had settled in to Mrs Tindal's liking, we could call upon them.

'It won't be like this for the whole trip I promise,' she said. 'Once we have settled, Mrs Tindal will allow us diversion.'

Every day my hope faded that we would ever get to see more of Bath than Mrs Tindal's house. I might as well have stayed at home for all the good this trip was, but then on the eighth day Mrs Tindal did not come down to breakfast. Betsey went to speak with Mrs Haywood, the housekeeper, then met me in our bedroom.

'Mrs Tindal will not leave her bed today. She is greatly fatigued by the exciting first week of our visit,' Betsey rolled her eyes. 'However, she has said we may use her carriages to make social calls and see the sights, and of course since I am a married woman you are entrusted to my care.'

She pressed my hand and I beamed. Free at last!

She hastened over to her wardrobe and pulled out a pretty floral dress, made of Indian muslin. 'Here,' she said. 'Borrow this!'

'But I am in mourning.'

She held the beautiful gown against me. 'Yes, but no one here needs to know that, do they?'

I returned her smile. She was right, though as I changed into the dress I couldn't shake the feeling I was betraying Papa.

Betsey insisted we take a tour of the city in the carriage so I could see the fine houses, crescents and parks. It was not as big as Bristol but was so much more elegant that I felt instantly at home. Once the tour was done, we called on Betsey's friends, the Davisons, who were 'the good sort' of navy people, by which she meant Lt Davison had come up though the navy college. They had taken rooms in one of the large crescent houses. Once we were shown to the parlour, the fashionably dressed Mrs Davison, who was of an age with Betsey, greeted us warmly.

'My darling! I began to wonder if we would see you at all and my heart was quite broken to be deprived of your company. This must be your little friend, Miss Fitzsimons was it?'

'Fitzwilliam, Ma'am, Amelia Fitzwilliam.'

'Ma'am! You make me sound like my mother, I'll have no ma'ams from you, sweet thing. You *are* pretty, just as Bee said you would be. Come, you must meet the boys.'

We followed her into the next room where three men stood talking. One was very familiar.

'Lt. Driscoll!' I exclaimed.

'Miss Amelia,' he smiled warmly and stepped forwards.

'You two are acquainted?'

I nodded. 'We met a few weeks ago.' I nearly said at my parents' inn but that seemed vulgar, but I felt bad for thinking it.

Lt Driscoll looked to Betsey and Mrs Davison introduced them.

'I met some of your Webster brothers-in-laws at the same Bristolian ball where I danced with Miss Amelia, and they asked me if I knew the Davisons, which I did. Lt Davison and I were in the same class at the college. It was always my intention to visit them after Bristol.'

'What a happy coincidence.'

'Allow me to introduce my brother-'

'Half-brother-' A man who looked like an older, plumper Lt Driscoll interrupted him with a smirk and an English accent. He was expensively dressed in a rather Romantic style, with dark velvets and jewel coloured silks.

'-Mr Charles Snowden.'

He took my hand and kissed it, 'Enchanted.'

'You have the same mother then?' I asked, wondering at the difference in surname.

'Same father,' Mr Snowden said. 'Difference is, my mother married our father. Poor Miss Driscoll did not.'

Colour rose in Lt Driscoll's cheeks and the full weight of Mr Snowden's words sunk in. Lt Driscoll was *illegitimate*. Well, he'd certainly kept that quiet and little wonder.

Mrs Davison looked to the other man in the room, who was tall with thick red hair.

'May I introduce my husband, Lt Davison.'

'Miss Fitzwilliam, pleased to make your acquaintance,' he said with a Welsh accent. I nodded and smiled, then chanced another look at the two half-brothers. Lt Driscoll was fiddling with his cuffs, while Mr Snowden sipped tea with a smug expression before letting his eyes drift over to me. I did not shrink from his gaze, which amused him.

Driscoll was the handsomer one, though they both had brown hair, big eyes and clear, pale skin. Snowden's rotundness gave him a softer look, which was at odds with the sharpness in his eyes. Driscoll had a stronger chin and cheekbones, a prettier mouth (which made me wonder if it came from his assumedly temptress of a mother) and his eyes were all bright eagerness. While Driscoll was a dandy, his clothes were more fashionable and less eccentric than Snowden's, who carried off his more artistic taste very well.

'I must be off,' Mr Snowden announced. 'Remember the ball and do bring Miss Fitzwilliam.'

My heart leapt at the thought of a ball!

After he had gone, Lt Davison shook his head. 'I don't know why you put up with him.'

'Come now,' Mrs Davison interrupted. 'He is rather amusing and has such good connections.'

'I'd rather he didn't insult my guests in my home, brothers or not.'

Lt Driscoll adjusted his cravat. 'That's just how it is.'

'Yes, but you don't have to see him. You told me your father good as abandoned -'

Lt Driscoll gave him a sharp look. 'I'd rather not talk about it any longer.' He then turned to me with a smile. 'Now Miss Amelia, you must tell me all about your stay in Bath.'

Chapter 12

Jessica

The morning after the dinner party, a lengthy letter from Amelia arrived, detailing Mrs Tindal's house, the habits of their day, and how she hoped to soon be permitted to explore the city. I was satisfied that she was being kept busy enough by tending to Mrs Tindal, and I hoped she may be allowed to see more of the town or she might start to resent her host and reject the opportunity of becoming her companion should it arise.

My head buzzing with Amelia's letter and the controversial conversations from the Thomas' dinner, I put the finishing touches to breakfast. I had baked a loaf of crusty bread, which the butter melted into as I spread it.

Alone in the kitchen I licked the remnants of the salty, creamy butter from the knife before retrieving the baked eggs from the oven. They were near perfect, just a sprinkle of seasoning was needed. The whites were speckled with thick ham and the yolks looked still to be wet. My mouth watered at the thought of spooning them out onto the bread. What a blessed relief it was that my new home had a good oven.

'Smells delicious,' Captain Parnell ducked into the kitchen, wearing a darned shirt and some faded breeches. It was the first time I'd seen him not looking sharply attired, but I thought it suited him just the same. I handed him a plate and gestured to the coffee pot.

'A good breakfast will set us up well for today. There is much to do, I see you have come dressed for it.'

He smiled; he was to paint the parlour today. We had decided it was prudent to carry out repairs and renovations ourselves since he was to be in town a few weeks and we were both able bodied enough. It would save us a deal of money.

After breakfast he got to work painting the parlour the pale green I had chosen, whilst Lydia and I set up in the yard, under warm spring sunshine, to sew the curtains.

We lunched on salmagundi, which I made enough of so we could have it for dinner as well. One can never have enough in my view; the lovely fresh lettuce leaves with the bitter, sour anchovies and pickles, both balanced out with the chicken. Come evening it would taste different, sharper again, having had longer time to sit together.

Satisfied after lunch, I went upstairs to fetch more of the curtain fabric for the bedrooms. As I retrieved it my gaze fell on the last unopened trunk and my stomach clenched. It was full of Peter's clothes.

On the morning we left The Fitzwilliam, I hastily packed all my clothes and when only Peter's were left hanging in our wardrobe a rage burst up in me. Would Henry even get his clothes as well? They were of good quality, I made sure of that. I hadn't done so for Henry to wear or sell them.

Quickly forcing Peter's clothes in the trunk hadn't been emotional, it had been exhilarating, as if I was taking Peter with me, rescuing him from the clutches of Henry. But now I had a trunk of his clothes in my new house, clothes that he would never wear, that myself and the girls obviously could not wear.

Drawn to the trunk, I knelt down and opened it. Peter's smell of wood, cinnamon, pipe tobacco and ink drifted up. How I had missed that smell without even knowing it! Pain rose in my chest.

My husband of twenty years was gone. He had been taken so senselessly. His smell, his clothes were confined to this trunk. Never again would I hear him snore, hear his pen scratching, see him pat his belly and laugh about his indulgences, look fondly at our daughters, smile as he played the piano.

I skimmed over the top layer; a jacket of blue wool. The only one left; his brown one he'd been killed in and the black one he'd been buried in. He used to wear this jacket when he went out of an evening. He called it his lucky jacket and I'd thought nothing of it. Bitter tears stung my eyes.

Even now I could not think of him with forgiveness. I wanted to mourn him properly as a true wife for all the happy years I'd thought he given me, for his kindness, for his loving ways, his compliments and his indulging of me, but he'd indulged himself more and it had cost me. Maybe one day I would be able to forgive, forget and mourn properly but his lie now marred all the other good parts of him; as if our happy memories and stable life had never existed.

These clothes were a reminder of his presence. As angry as I was, I did not wish him dead. Maybe in time he would have tried to right his wrongs. He had been making large repayments. Maybe he would have told me…maybe, maybe, maybe. I couldn't deal in maybes, I had to deal with the here and now.

Lydia's footsteps sounded on the stairs and I swallowed a burning knot of anger and sadness.

'I was wondering where you had got to.'

'I was just looking at your father's things. Can you…can you fetch Captain Parnell for me?' I said, deciding as I spoke. 'I'll need help moving this trunk into the attic.'

Amelia

Mrs Tindal's health did not improve, but it meant she slept a great deal. I read to her for an hour at breakfast, and an hour before dinner but otherwise we were free to explore Bath and she made no objection to us attending Mr Snowden's ball.

I had only brought my mourning clothes with me but on our outings, I borrowed dresses from Betsey. Mrs Tindal asked if we had anything suitable to wear to the ball, and Betsey said I would need something so Mrs Tindal let us have some fabric she had stored in a trunk. I hadn't held out much hope for whatever the old lady had, but it turned out to be beautiful blue silk from India. She said just this once she was sure it would be well if I relaxed my mourning clothes as it was my first ball in Bath.

It meant I spent a few days making the dress, but I enjoyed working for myself once again – no petty demands from Abigail Hughes, but the dread loomed over me that I would have to make a start on her hateful dress whenever I returned to Bristol. Pushing that thought to the back of my mind I continued to work on my dress. Maybe if it was pretty enough I would not have to return to work on Abigail's dress at all, for it may help me to catch a husband of my own. A pleasing thought indeed.

Betsey read to me when she was not making calls, not from the prescribed Fordyce's but from scandalous novels, such as *The Monk*, in low tones, still managing to do all the voices.

Mrs Davison called a few times and gossiped gaily, mostly about people I didn't know but her stories were very amusing. We also met her a few times when strolling about the assembly rooms and once she was accompanied by her husband and Lt Driscoll.

'Would you take a turn about with me, Miss Fitzwilliam?' Lt Driscoll asked.

'Of course.' I took his arm.

'I must apologise for my brother's behaviour the other day.'

'Oh,' I said, realising he meant the references to his illegitimacy and that I did not mind about it. I still liked his company, although it did make me cautious in wishes for anything deeper than a acquaintanceship. 'Do not think on it. We are friends as ever we were. Now, let us discuss this ball. I am rather excited at the prospect.'

He chuckled. 'I suppose this will be your fifth ball?'

'How do you know?'

'You told me when we danced together last. Which reminds me, may I request the first dance from you again?'

'You may, though I hope you won't be late this time.'

'I will do my best.'

'Will you be staying with your brother while you are in town?'

'No, I stay with the Davisons. Charles stays in our father's house.'

I nodded, trying to be tactful. 'So, am I to assume that Mrs Snowden is still alive?'

'Indeed she is. She will not be there, but the servants might tell her and our father can't be bothered with the hassle of it.'

'Oh dear,' I said, thinking Mr Snowden senior sounded a very cold sort of a person.

'May I ask about your mother?' I said, letting curiosity get the better of me.

He raised his eyebrows.

'Forgive me,' I said embarrassed. 'I have been improper.'

'No, not at all. It is just no one ever asks about my mother.' Lt Driscoll took a deep breath. 'She is a very good woman, my mother. I suppose everyone says that about their mothers, but she is. Very devout, very kind and gentle, but she is so fragile.'

I nodded, feeling ashamed. It was not the sort of picture I had in my mind. I had thought her a seducer. 'Mr father is an English merchant. He was the youngest son of a mill owner, and so not imagining he'd inherit, he set up in business.'

'What business?'

'Cotton. He lived on his plantation in the West Indies some years before returning home. During his absence both his older brothers died, so he inherited the mill as well. He married Charles' mother, who is of Anglo-Irish stock-' he crinkled his nose at this, '-an old landowning family, with some distant noble connection. It is thanks to that union that he came to be in my mother's part of the world. Charles' mother inherited some ramshackle piece of land after a distant relation died. My father came over to Ireland to wrangle out the details, and met the lawyer dealing with the case, who was my uncle. My uncle was my mother's guardian, since their parents were dead. She was thirteen, my father was forty-five.'

He hesitated and I expected a tale of a long courtship and a forbidden love, but when he next spoke his voice was devoid of its usual joviality.

'When my father departed Ireland two months later, my mother was with child.'

I thought of the older men who stared at me for longer than they ought at the inn and how Papa would glare at them. No one had done that for Miss Driscoll, and the poor Lieutenant had to live everyday with that awful knowledge. A chill passed through me as the unspoken horror of what had happened came over me. I couldn't help but to give his arm a squeeze and he gave a small smile of recognition. 'She was lucky my uncle has a soft heart and didn't pack her off to the nuns. He wrote to my father who gave her a cottage, and she feigned widowhood. We did not hear from him until I was fifteen when it turned out my uncle had contacted him and demanded he make provisions for my future. My mother wanted me to go and work for my uncle at his solicitor's office, but while my uncle was kind to us, he would never been seen with us in public. My uncle and father paid for me to go to naval college. When my father arranged this his wife and legitimate children discovered my existence and Charles, who is his youngest legitimate son, was intrigued by the scandal more than anything else and wrote to me. I see him a few times a year, which is more times than I've ever seen my father.'

I could barely keep from gasping so stunned I was by his frankness, no bravado as I had seen in Bristol.

'So you put up with Mr Snowden as he is your only link to your father's family and fortune?'

'Yes, though one day I shall make my own fortune. I work hard and Captain Parnell says I show much promise and have a head for the mathematics involved in sailing.'

That surprised me, as I'd never heard Captain Parnell say much of him at all, but then I hadn't asked.

'Thank you for your honesty.'

'I am sure Charles would have regaled you with my history if I had not.'

I thought of Mr Charles Snowden, preening in the Davisons' parlour, smugly trying to embarrass Lt Driscoll. His saying 'poor Miss Driscoll' had been very nasty indeed and the thought of it now made my skin crawl. 'He is not very gentlemanly, is he?' I said.

'No, he most certainly is not.'

'Perhaps then,' I said trying to think of the right thing to do but rather wishing there was another alternative. 'We ought not go to the ball?'

'Ah Miss Amelia, that is very sweet of you but I will not deprive you of your fifth ball.' He flashed me one of his charming grins, banishing all seriousness from his face and I was relieved. 'The first rule of Bath is to attend every ball you are invited to, especially if the hosts are not to your liking, for it is at their expense!'

Chapter 13

Amelia

On the evening of the ball, I watched many grand, beautiful people disembarking from their carriages as our own pulled up.

'Come along,' smiled Betsey while I carried on gawking as a footman held out his hand to help me down. We walked up the steps to the house and awaiting us in the hall were two statues of kneeling Negroes wearing only loincloths, holding aloft trays of fruit. What a spectacle!

I plucked off some strawberries with a giggling Betsey as we moved down the corridor with the other guests. As requested, everyone wore masks and no women wore white or cream, but a whole variety of colours, which matched the men's brightly coloured jackets. Betsey procured me a mask with peacock feathers, whilst her mask was black and catlike, in a pleasing contrast to her red dress.

I suppressed a gasp as I entered the ballroom. Such wonderful flowers were positioned everywhere, and the band was the largest I'd ever seen. A man wearing a draped cape, antlers and a full white mask turned his gaze on me and he made his way over while Betsey conversed with the purple attired Mrs Davison. He bowed and presented his hand.

'Why Lt. Driscoll!' I exclaimed and Betsey laughed. I took his hand and he led me to the floor. Through my glove his hand felt a deal plumper than I remembered but maybe it had swollen in heat of the ballroom. The music started up and aside from Lt Driscoll I was in a set of strangers.

'How do you like Bath then?' an English accent asked from behind the white mask. I gasped in horror. It was not Lt. Driscoll but Mr Snowden. How could I have been so foolish? That was why his hands were different and his draped cape hid his plumper figure! Otherwise he was the same height as Lt Driscoll, had the same hair, had obviously been trying to mimic his movements. Had Betsey laughed because she had known? My cheeks burned with embarrassment. The dance had started and I had to carry on, but dread clenched my insides. What would Lt Driscoll think if he saw? I would not want him to think I had been in on the joke. I glanced over my shoulder to see a man with a pretty mouth, green coat and leopard skin mask watching us as he approached Betsey. It was too late, I realised with a heavy heart.

'I am not speaking to you,' I snapped.

'But I am the host,' Mr Snowden said. 'You must.'

'But I was promised to your brother.'

'Half-brother. But as the host I really ought to get what I want.' He laughed and I responded with a stony silence, only fulfilling the bare minimum about of dance steps.

'No one will think ill of you, they all know it is my party and that I am quite spoilt so I must always be seen with the prettiest girl!'

Out of the corner of my eye I saw Lt Driscoll join the dance with some girl I'd never met. No one objected to them tagging onto our set. Was this to be the longest dance in Christendom?

'I see you are enjoying yourself,' Lt Driscoll said in an accusatory fashion when it came his turn to spin me around.

'I did not realise, I thought he was you!'

'He is very clearly wearing stays.'

A woman next to us looked shocked at the mention of such an item and I was swept back by a smiling Mr Snowden. 'I think I have made poor Dara and all the other men here quite jealous by hogging you, m'dear.'

He clapped loudly. The music stopped and the doors were thrown open to the garden.

'Friends!' he called as everyone quieted to look at him and I tried to edge away. 'Let us continue our revelry under the stars!'

A cheer went up and taking me by the arm, Mr Snowden led the way to the garden. If Driscoll was so vexed by it, I wished he would have taken my arm. Where was Betsey? Could I just pull away or would everyone think me stupid and childish? Everyone was watching us, so there could be nothing untoward in Mr Snowden's actions but I would much rather not have his sweaty hand clutching at my elbow.

The crowd followed, with servants bringing trays of drinks and the band setting up outside. From the trees emerged gypsy-like people who started to preform feats of acrobatics, juggling and fire breathing, which I might have enjoyed at any other time. When I clapped Mr Snowden smiled indulgently at me, which made me instantly regret doing so. He gave me a glass of champagne, telling me it was the finest that money could buy.

'If you'll just excuse me there is a matter of business to which I must attend.'

He stepped away and I watched the acrobats clambering on to each other and flipping over, trying to take deep breaths and gather myself. Surely it would be very silly to find Betsey and ask to go home? She would only laugh.

'Miss Amelia, everyone is talking of you and my brother.' Lt Driscoll was at my side. 'Maybe I could ask Mrs Webster to take you home.'

'I do not know where she is,' I said. 'And people would think me foolish.'

'People may already think that after you let yourself be paraded on his arm like that.'

'Why didn't you offer your arm to me?'

'I can hardly afford to upset him in our father's house, can I? It would draw to much attention to my presence.'

'And that leopard skin mask doesn't?' I snapped too quickly. I wanted to be mad at his brother not him, but his inability to act then blame me was infuriating.

He sighed. 'My apologies, I was only thinking of your best interests-'

'What are my interests to you?'

'I…'he straightened up. 'I must return to sea in the next few days. I was hoping you would allow me to write to you.'

I hesitated, it was a compliment and a romantic notion to have a such a handsome man wishing to write to me but at that moment I was so annoyed at him and at his whole family.

'I thank you but I cannot think about that now. I need to find Betsey.'

'She's there.'

He pointed towards the rose garden where she was giggling, surrounded by a company of rowdy looking young men. I swallowed and headed back towards the house, sipping the champagne to steady my nerves.

'Miss Amelia, where are you going?'

I waved a hand, I just wanted to be away from this suffocating place. I would take our carriage and then send it back for Betsey.

Chapter 14

Jessica

As Lydia left the kitchen carrying a tray with Mrs Pemberton's breakfast, Captain Parnell stepped in, dressed in his crisp navy uniform. It was a jolt to see him wearing it again, the past few weeks I had only seen him in civilian clothes, but today his ship was to set sail once more.

I stopped myself from complimenting his attire and busied myself by seasoning the baked eggs.

'All ready?' I asked.

'Yes,' he said, pouring three cups of coffee. 'I left a trunk of my belongings in the loft.'

Lydia came back in, and together we carried the baked eggs over to the table as Captain Parnell brought the coffee.

'When will you set sail, sir?' Lydia asked.

'Depends on the winds, but hopefully before midday.'

'And you will be back at Christmas?' Lydia asked.

He nodded. 'And how is our lodger this morning?'

'She was well enough.'

I nodded. Mrs Pemberton was our first lodger and she arrived yesterday, a matter of hours after we had put a sign in the window. She was in Bristol to take the waters at Hotwells and was an elderly widow from Derbyshire with her maid Mary, who was to sleep in her room on a truckle bed. It made us realise that it might serve to change the attic into a room for the servants of our guests, although the project would need some thought as we would also wish to make the loft not just habitable but comfortable as well. Mrs Pemberton didn't mind that her maid was to sleep in with her, but she was initially puzzled by Captain Parnell and my relationship.

'You are not married?'

'No, but this is purely a business arrangement,' Captain Parnell said. 'I am in the navy so I will be rarely here. I own the house, Mrs Fitzwilliam, who is a widow, manages it.'

Mrs Pemberton nodded sceptically so I took care when giving her a tour to emphases the sleeping arrangements. Whatever she made of us, she decided to stay and paid her first month's rent in advance.

Captain Parnell rose to leave, and I followed him into the parlour.

'Well,' I said as he picked up the small bag he'd first brought to The Fitzwilliam. 'Take care of yourself.'

He smiled. 'And you.'

'If you get the chance you ought to write to us to let us know how you fair.'

He nodded. 'I will, I have left you the best admiralty address for you want to write to me – especially if there are any problems.'

'Yes.'

There was a pause and Lydia came in. 'Goodbye, Captain,' she smiled and gave a mock salute which he returned. 'I shall try and save some seafaring books for you at Mr Syrett's.'

'That would be greatly appreciated. I shall seek out any medical books for you at port book shops.'

Lydia smiled appreciatively, and Captain Parnell looked between us. 'Right,' he said. 'I shall see you in December.'

'Yes.'

'Yes.'

With that he was gone, leaving me wishing that I had been able to think of something more meaningful to say, but I wasn't sure what. I returned to the kitchen to tidy away the breakfast things and Lydia hurried out to Mr Syrett's leaving me with a kiss on the cheek.

I sat down to write Amelia a letter and package gifts for her birthday. My youngest daughter would be sixteen next week and I hoped my letter and the small presents would reach her in time. I managed to get her a selection of ribbons, as well as some sheet music for she said Mrs Tindal had a piano and finally a book of poems from Mr Syrett's by Joanna Baillie which Lydia said she had not read yet.

Had Peter been alive and our finances been as healthy as I'd trusted they were, I expect we would have been able to buy her some fine fabric to make a gown from but maybe I would be able to get her more next year. By then hopefully we would have a steady stream of customers. As I finished writing the letter there was a knock at the door and I answered it to find a thin woman a little younger than myself enquiring about the spare room in an American accent.

Lydia

It took longer to reach Mr Syrett's from Hotwells but I enjoyed the walk, seeing the city wake up and watch it go about its business. As ever, Mr Syrett had a cup of tea waiting for me and, as he had since Father's death, asked me how I was with concern in his eyes. I answered honestly; I was well enough.

Night-time was the worst, I could not sleep as well as I used to, especially since we unpacked and I realised that we left Father's cards and cribbage set behind. It made sense that Mother left them since the cards were the cause of our downfall and were kept in his study which Henry had claimed, but still…a skill for cards was one of our common grounds. To think of the set we played on gathering dust in what was now Henry's study – or indeed who ever had bought The Fitzwilliam - was troubling indeed.

It got me to worrying how I might have handled everything differently. Had I confronted father about the irregularities in his accounts when he was alive he might have had a chance to change the will before his accident…ifs, buts, and maybes. These thoughts which kept me awake, that and the dull ache in my stomach which had not desisted from when I had seen his body.

'Time is a great healer,' Mr Syrett said quietly. I asked what we were doing today, not wishing to dwell. He was sorting through books from the latest estate sale and gave me a box of scientific books to go through whilst I manned the counter. He stayed in the back to sort the others. As I got to work the bell rang with our first customer of the day and I looked up, pleased to see the smiling face of Miss Ruby Thomas.

She invited Mother and me to dinner on Thursday, which I gladly accepted. She helped me shift through the science books, as we chatted about them. I offered to loan her the titles on botany, but she insisted on paying for them, taking three in total. She stayed for most of the morning, chatting pleasantly to Mr Syrett and me.

She said her brother had tickets to a dissection and that I ought to come along. She even stopped to ask me how I fared with my new house, and all the changes in my life. I gave her the same answer I had given Mr Syrett, then paused. Our conversation was so easy I found myself tentatively confiding my fears about the cribbage set. I had not even told Mother for fear that she would blame herself for not packing it. Ruby nodded thoughtfully as I spoke and pressed my hand.

Thursday came around and after my shift, Mother met me at Mr Syrett's and we caught a cab up to Cotham to the Thomas'. Now that we had two lodgers, Mrs Pemberton and Miss Atwell, Mother was more relaxed. We had two guaranteed sources of income, and though Mrs Pemberton was crotchety, she paid in advance and kept herself to herself.

Miss Atwell dined with us in the kitchen regularly and conversed with Mother in a friendly manner, confirming all the forwardness and relaxed manners one expects in Americans. She had come to track down a long-lost relation who a lawyer had written to her about. Mother liked to hear her tales of her journey across America and the ocean. In our room at night Mother commented on how brave Miss Atwell was, and how admirable it was she had travelled so far alone.

'It's strange, isn't it?' she said. 'All the people we saw at The Fitzwilliam, and probably all the people we will see here, going on their journeys and I have never been further than the distance between here and Glastonbury, which I think is not more than thirty miles.'

'Maybe when Captain Parnell is back to watch the house we might take a holiday, maybe to Lyme Regis, London or Brighton.'

She hesitated then smiled. 'I had not thought of that, but then he would be here without us…although I suppose it is his house after all.'

In the coach, she wondered what topics would be raised at the Thomas' that evening.

'I ought to have read up on the slavery movement again or some other pressing issue of the day,' she said. 'I haven't even seen a newspaper.'

When we arrived the party only consisted of the Thomases and the younger Methodist preacher from our last visit, Mr Bradley. He spoke with Mr Thomas and George, while Mother was engaged by Mrs Thomas. Ruby made her way over to me, though I did not miss the disappointment on Mr Bradley's face as she left his side, nor the glances he kept throwing her way.

'Come with me,' she smiled. 'I have something for you.'

She led the way from the parlour, upstairs to her bedroom. Her two younger sisters were both in bed and peered at us excitedly as she entered the room. She raised a finger to her lips, picked a large parcel off the desk and quickly exited.

'Here,' she handed me the parcel wrapped in linen.

'What is it?'

'Open it and see.'

I did so and gasped. It was the cribbage set. 'How on earth?'

'I only just managed it a few hours ago,' she said. 'I called on The Fitzwilliam after we spoke earlier in the week, and it was empty, but a sign said that they were having an auction today. I did not tell you before for fear it would be too painful, but I went with George and this was one of the first things to come up. We bid on it, I will admit a very lowly amount, and we were accepted!'

Relief washed over me at holding the item in my hands again. 'Thank you,' I said, tears welling up in me. 'How can I ever repay you? I can get you the money, but it's worth so much more–'

'You don't owe me anything,' she said. 'That's what friends are for.'

Amelia

The next morning I had been prepared to tell Betsey I had hurt my ankle and been obliged to go home but she did not ask. Instead she was keen to tell me that at the party she had made the acquaintance of a third son of Viscount, The Honourable Mr Marmaduke Fontaine. She described his handsomeness and the attention that he paid her as if she were not a married woman.

Regrettably, he called in the afternoon and brought with him his friend, Mr Snowden.

They called every day in the week leading up to my birthday. Mrs Tindal kept to her bed, but Mrs Haywood the housekeeper, made sure to let her disapproval be known with sly looks and tuts, though it only amused Betsey as opposed to putting her off. I wondered privately if Mrs Haywood had a point, but I wasn't sure how to tell Betsey, I did not want her to think me a prude. Perhaps she was just friends with Mr Fontaine, and I could embarrass myself by trying to question about it. They were all so easy going about it, I doubted myself for feeling uncomfortable in their presence. Perhaps this simply was how things were in Bath. A small part of me wanted to speak to Mama, but that seemed childish so I suppressed the urge to ask her advice in my letters.

The Honourable Mr Fontaine took Betsey on promenades in the parks, carriage rides through the streets, walks in the assemblies rooms and to concerts, plays and a ball his friend was throwing, to all of which I trailed along after her with Mr Snowden at my side.

We went shopping and Mr Snowden asked my opinions on hats, cravat pins and handkerchiefs, saying I had a good eye. He also insisted on buying me 'trifles', which included an ivory bracelet, a ruby pendent, jewelled necklaces, a diamond broach shaped like a rose, a bonnet and towards the end of the week he said he would commission a dress made for my birthday present. I ought to have refused, but when else would I get the chance for such indulgence and it seemed he had the money to spare. After traipsing around after Betsey, I might as well get something out of it.

He spoke of his love for poetry, his intention to write more and the plays he he'd seen, the books he intended to read. If I questioned his opinion on books as sometimes they wouldn't make sense or he would go back to talking about something that was of interest to him, such as his club in London or his friends' exploits.

Betsey said if I wanted him for a beau – and who would not want such a rich beau – then I must indulge and flatter him. In truth, she said, what was of interest to me would not be of interest to a man of the world. If I wanted to be his wife, then I would have to put up with a life time of his prattle so best I learnt to put up with it now. I stared at her.

'But I do not want him for a beau, much less a husband.'

She laughed at me. 'Dearest, how many other chances are you likely to get – especially with a man like him – in your current circumstances? You need to take this opportunity.'

I nodded. She was right of course, my marriage prospects were slim and I wanted a rich husband but I shuddered at thought of Charles Snowden. He was a self-satisfied toad. For all of Betsey's talk of marriage, he had said nothing on the subject. I was not so naïve as to be unaware that men want other things from girls with no prospects. He may be just like his father in that regard.

If was to marry him I must put up with a lifetime of his talk. It wasn't unpleasant talk, but it seemed better that I listened passively rather than question him. When I had questioned his views on *Romance of the Forest*, since it sounded as though he was speaking of another book, he looked put out and said, 'I thought we were just having a pleasant conversation, not a quarrel.'

'I wasn't quarrelling I was only saying-' but he'd looked so disappointed I apologised. I did not want to upset the company by picking fault with all he said as though I were Lydia.

Chapter 15

Amelia

When I came down to breakfast a small parcel was awaiting me, and I recognised Mama's handwriting on the label. I smiled, unexpected homesickness welling up, though it was not the homesickness for the place Mama now lived but the home that was lost – The Fitzwilliam, with both Mama and Papa, the bedroom where Lydia and I had read and laughed together, the piano, the kitchen…I was glad I was alone in the breakfast room and quickly dabbed my eyes on the napkin before opening the parcel.

There were three fine ribbons in velvet and silk; blue, pale red and yellow, a battered collection of poems by Joanna Baillie, doubtless from Mr Syrett's shop, a long letter and - my heart leapt - a fruit cake! I had not eaten a fruit cake in months and Mama had remembered it was my favourite…but then that was it.

I flushed with guilt, thinking how my mother's birthday gifts paled in comparison to the 'trifles' Charles Snowden had bought me. I shook my head. I ought not compare them. If he did want to marry me then through the match I could help Mama out of her current poverty. I cut myself a piece of cake as Betsey swept in.

'What's that?'

'It's from my mother. Would you like some?'

'Yes please.'

As we tucked into our cake, the footman came in and poured us tea, then fetched the plumb pudding. Not long after the door opened again, and a negro I recognised as Mr Snowden's valet came in carrying a box.

'A gift from Mr Snowden,' he bowed as he set the box on the table. 'I am to await your reply.'

Betsey grinned at me and I leant over to open the box. I gasped, then aware of Mr Snowden's servant's eyes on me, forced a smile.

'How divine!' said Betsey.

'Yes,' I said quickly, uncertainty inching up me. The dress was a much darker red than I would have chosen, with far more gold trim and a lower neckline. I swallowed, touching it and feigning happiness. How expensive had it been? How could I turn it away? The simple answer was that I could not. Hidden in the folds of the dress was an envelope. I plucked it out and read aloud to Betsey.

'For the enjoyment of Miss Amelia Fitzwilliam, a party is to be laid on at the residence of Mr Charles Snowden. Please arrived by seven thirty to enjoy the feast of pleasures that await.'

'You will be there then, ma'am?' the valet asked.

I nodded. 'Of course, please tell Mr Snowden that I am most gratified.'

'I will, good day to you.'

He left us and Betsey snatched the gown out of the box.

'It isn't what I would wear,' I said in a small voice, my throat pressing. It wasn't out of childish disappointment but more of confusion. Had he gone against my wishes on purpose? And what was meant by that low neckline? A blush spread over my skin at the thought of it and I felt stupidly naive.

'It's better than what you wear,' Betsey chided, twirling around with the dress held against herself. 'This is a woman's dress, the ones you like are still was a tad childish don't think? You should be flattered that Mr Snowden sees you as a woman, Amelia. What else did you expect?'

'I do not know,' I said quietly.

As she twirled the dress, she knocked the ribbons from Mama onto the floor, so I bent to pick them up, fighting the urge to cry.

Lydia

Mother was keen to accompany me to the dissection.

'No need to look so surprised, dear. I am open to learning new things. And I was butchering longer than you, so I doubt I will be squeamish.'

We met with the Thomases outside and Mr Thomas greeted us by saying, 'I am not sure about all of this, I must admit. I doubt I shall be much of a gallant chaperone, ladies. I fear I much prefer seeing artichoke hearts than human ones!'

Mrs Thomas chuckled, but George and Ruby rolled their eyes. It gave me a momentary stab, a memory of father calling me his savoury and Amelia his sweet and us wearing the same expression of the Thomas siblings now; one of annoyance and embarrassment. I ought have appreciated my father's jokes while they lasted.

We went inside, Mrs Thomas asking after mother's day and mother telling her of our lodgers.

'How peculiar!' said Mrs Thomas on hearing of Miss Atwell's quest.

'Is she to be left a great deal of money?' George asked with a grin.

'Don't be so crude,' sighed Mrs Thomas before raising an enquiring eyebrow. 'But is she?'

Mother shrugged. 'I think she is reluctant to say one way or the other, but she has lived such a life. Born in the American revolution, her mother followed her father about the camps-'

'Which side were they?' asked Mr Thomas.

'For American independence, I think. She has worked as a governess in Canada and Mexico! Mexico sounded marvellous. I could hardly imagine such travel, so silly when we see all the boats.'

We were shown to our seats in an auditorium, In the centre was a shrouded figure and a serious looking man with two nervous looking young men readying themselves nearby. Ruby and I exchanged grins of anticipation.

I asked George how his reading was going and Ruby said she was reading the books as well. We fell into a discussion which was cut short when silence was called for and we focused our attention back to the stage.

The serious looking man stepped forwards and introduced himself, before naming the other two as his assistants.

'I notice some ladies in the audience tonight,' his gaze fell on our party, which contained the most females. 'I trust you will not become too squeamish and if you are distressed will alert the men accompanying you to escort you outside instead of making a scene.'

I bit my lip with anger and Ruby rolled her eyes.

'The cheek!' hissed Mrs Thomas. 'I did not birth five children to be called squeamish.'

Though she had not spoken loudly her voice carried to the few rows in front of us and with satisfaction I heard a few titters. The doctor scowled.

'As to the subject,' he said, 'This young man '

He whipped off the shroud to revel a naked, male corpse. It gave me a small start, not because he was dead but because he was naked. Of course he was going to be naked! I had seen sketches of the male anatomy in medical books, as well as in historic books about Romans and Greeks but the first naked man I saw in real life was a dead one!

The thought was so absurd it almost made burst out laughing, but I mastered myself. This was exactly what the doctor had spoken of, worse in fact for not a drop of blood had been drawn yet. I focused as the doctor pointed out the bruising on the man's neck, a result of the noose; his punishment for house breaking. He raised a scalpel and made his first incision.

A few days later, Ruby walked with me on my way home from Mr Syrett's as she was to join us for dinner. She said George tried to draw what he'd seen when they returned home, and Mrs Thomas and she spent the next day dissecting plants and vegetables trying to examine them in a similar way to the pompous doctor. Her father joked they were all crazed for the sight of blood.

As we neared Hotwells we turned down a road, not far from the spa. Two well-to-do looking boys were playing behind the houses. One of them clambered up a wall, while the other screamed encouragement, waving flags fashioned from sticks and handkerchiefs.

The one yelling turned at us as we passed, staring rudely at Ruby. I'd spent enough time with her to know the difference; around the centre of Bristol hardly anyone stared at all, same as when we were close to her house, but in other areas people did stare – sometimes just curious, sometimes with malice. Around Hotwells it wasn't usually so bad, unless people came from some rural place to visit the spa. I guessed that was the case with these boys.

Just as we passed them there came a cry and a sickening thud. We spun around to see the climber sprawled on the cobbles, staring in horror at his leg, the foot twisted the wrong way. The other boy, assumedly his brother, gawped. After a few moments of stunned silence both boys began to wail and Ruby and I hastened over to them.

We knelt at the injured boy's side. 'What is your name?' asked Ruby, but he carried on crying.

'What's his name?' I asked his brother, who gulped and replied, 'Geoffrey. I am Arthur.'

'Where are your parents, Arthur?' asked Ruby.

He blinked a few times.

'You aren't in trouble,' she said. 'We want to help.'

'They are at the spa. We were supposed to wait for them. We only meant to be a few moments.'

'Can you run and fetch them?' Ruby asked. 'We shall stay with your brother and you shall be quite the hero.'

He nodded and, dropping his flags, ran off.

Geoffrey continued sobbing.

'There now,' I said uselessly. 'Maybe we should have told him to fetch a doctor as well?'

Ruby bit her lip. 'No need,' she said, looking at the boy's leg. 'You can set that.'

'Me? I do not think so-'

'Why ever not? You have read all the books, cut up the animals-'

'Animals are hardly the same. This boy needs a doctor.'

'You don't need to be a doctor to set a break, labourers do it all the time! At least look at it, 'tis a clean dislocation I think, but you'd know much more about that.'

It couldn't hurt to look could it? She was right, it did appear to be a simple dislocation. To snap such a thing back into place was always described as an easy and straight-forward thing, and as she said people who were not even doctors could do such things, so why not I?

As if to help stiffen my resolve the boy asked, 'Do you think I'll ever be able to walk again?'

'Not if someone doesn't do something quickly,' Ruby gave me a pointed look.

'Very well,' I said. 'Geoffrey, you must be brave. I am going to try and reset your ankle. You must be still. Miss Thomas will hold you tightly.'

Ruby as good as pounced on him and his sobs muted into breathy weeps. Bracing myself I removed his shoe, then took his leg and foot in my hands.

'Don't look,' I said. 'One, two-'

I twisted as I had read about and practiced on butchered animals. There was a crack, he yelped but I felt his bones slide and lock back into place. Ruby sat back and he peered at his foot, relief flooding his face.

Ruby clapped. 'Well done!'

'We're not clear yet,' I said, dabbing my brow. 'Geoffrey, could you please try and move your ankle?'

He rotated it, slowly and with a flinch. 'It hurts,' he said. 'But it works.'

'Excellent. Miss Thomas, could you please pass me those flags? I will fashion a splint.'

As we finished tying the splints, Arthur rounded the corner followed by a man with the boys' red hair and a woman with their blue eyes.

'Geoffrey!' exclaimed the woman as the man hurried to pick him up.

'How are you?'

'Better,' he said. 'Look, this lady fixed it.'

The couple looked from their son's leg to Ruby and I.

'Arthur said your ankle was all twisted around,' the man said.

'It was,' Geoffrey said. 'Like I told you-' He pointed at me. 'She fixed it and-' he pointed at Ruby. 'She helped.'

'And you can move it?'

'Yes.'

I stepped forward. 'Probably best to take him to a doctor,' I said. 'Just to be sure, but it seems fine.'

The mother nodded. 'My thanks to you Miss, and your girl I'm sure-'

I realised with a crawling of my skin she assumed Ruby was my servant, or worse, my slave.

'Miss Thomas is my friend,' I said.

'Oh, I see,' the woman swallowed. 'Well thanks to both of you so much, we are very grateful. Thank the kind ladies, Geoffrey.'

'Thank you,' he said sincerely.

'It seems you have done us a great service,' father said. 'My thanks.'

With a touch of his hat, which the boys copied, and a cheerful wave from the mother, the family set off. Ruby looked at me, grinning. As soon as the family were out of earshot we set each other off giggling with the surprise and victory of it all.

Chapter 16

Amelia

Betsey assured me that the dress suited me well, but had the maid lace my stays extra tight and I felt as though I was going to burst out of it. When we arrived at Mr Snowden's the other guests were awaiting us and they applauded as he made his way to me.

'How ravishing you look!'

He beamed but I did not think that was much of a compliment, especially given his father's history, it made my skin crawl but still I thanked him for what else could I do? From his coat pocket he produced an old fashioned, clunky pearl necklace with a hideous coat of arms in the place of a pendent. 'Here,' said affixing around my neck without asking. 'Let us see how you suit real pearls.'

It was cold and heavy, but Betsey made a fuss of it.

'See, I have invited all your friends,' Mr Snowden said, gesturing to the assembled company. They were all his friends who I'd only met in passing, aside from the Davisons who I didn't know very well either. I had a pang for The Fitzwilliam and longed to see Mama and Lydia, though I did not think they would approve of my dress. I wished for my fruit cake in our old parlour with the Hughes sisters, snobs though they were, and the Webster boys gathered around. If I was to have a birthday party, it would be they I would rather have here. And maybe even Lt Driscoll, at least he would try to make me laugh. Where was he now? Back at sea? I ought have let him take me to my carriage when I left Snowden's ball, I ought have let him write to me.

Mr Snowden led me about on his arm. We talked to his friends about topics I knew nothing about, and he was quick to take credit for every compliment I received, telling everyone how he commissioned the dress and paid for my jewels. I grew increasing light headed as I hadn't eaten much all day so not to spoil my appetite, but it seemed the food was mostly snacks passed about on trays and Mr Snowden kept giving me champagne.

I looked about for Betsey but she was chatting to her The Honourable Mr Fontaine who was openly ogling her décolletage.

'Now time for games! Let us start with nonsense!'

Everybody cheered and we sat down. I was relieved for I told Mr Snowden nonsense was my favourite game. He started off, but soon all of his friends were using their own private jokes - crude sounding ones at that, and I could not help feel as though I was being mocked, and it was the same when we moved onto Bridge of Sighs. Then Mr Snowden said it was such a lovely night we may as well take things into the garden, and though there was no fireworks or music like last time I was glad of the fresh air.

'Let us play hide and seek!' Mr Snowden declared. 'I shall seek!'

The partygoers tripped off into the garden, mostly in pairs, Betsey on the arm of the viscount's son. Feeling stupid, I stood alone, then decided I had better get on with it and hide. I crouched behind a rose bush feeling a fool, everything starting to spin.

'Aha!' Mr Snowden stood above me. 'That didn't take long, almost as if you wanted to be found.'

I forced a smile as he bent to help me up, but he lunged in for a kiss. I stumbled back.

'Sir!'

'Come now, don't be alarmed. Everyone is surely entertaining themselves so we could use this time to get better acquainted.'

He leant into kiss me again, but I linked arms with him instead and moved so he only kissed my cheek.

'We can walk and talk,' I said. 'Now, let us seek your friends!'

Lydia

I lay awake, thinking of the satisfaction of clicking the boy's ankle into place.

Mother was delighted for me. She even made a cake to celebrate. Would I ever get to behave so again? Should I lurk about awaiting accidents so I could leap into action? A foolish notion but I had another thought which was even more foolhardy.

I still had those boy's clothes I'd worn to Father's funeral. What if I used those? Not to pose as a fully qualified doctor exactly but some sort of saw bones...or surgeon. Could I serve out an apprenticeship? The thought crossed my mind to apply to St Bart's as George had, but the risk of being caught out seemed too high, but surely if I was careful? That aside, we could not afford the fees! I sighed. If I could stay here but fulfil an apprenticeship that seemed less risky...

Should I broach it with Mother? Was it lunacy? I sat up, 'Mother?' I hissed.

'Yes?' she said sleepily. I lit my rush light and crossed over to her bed, perching on it. 'I have been thinking about what happened today...'

She sat up. 'What about it?'

'I was just thinking...I should like to do it again. It made me feel like it was what I was supposed to do. Does that make sense?'

She blinked. 'It does. I feel like that when I am cooking, but cooking is rather different to doctoring.'

'I know.'

She regarded me in the dim light a few moments. 'Back in Glastonbury it was old Mother Faulkner whom people would call on when they were sick, with all her remedies and draughts. That sort of thing is harder in a city though...'

'I was thinking,' I paused. What was I thinking? 'Maybe I could use my boy's clothes and...'

Mother frowned. 'And?'

'And I am not sure. We cannot afford for me to go and but...maybe I could become an apprentice, so I could become a surgeon?'

'Dressed as a boy?' mother repeated slowly, as if she had not heard me correctly.

'Yes.'

She took a deep breath. 'Your father's funeral was one thing but...'

'But?'

'But...come now Lydia, you know why. It's not respectable, but then I believe you are smart and hard working enough to be good at it. If you were a boy it is a path I would be heartily encouraging. But what of a future husband?'

'I think that unlikely.'

'Come now Lydia, you are very pretty and a clever man would want a clever wife whom he might converse with.'

'Mrs Webster told Edward I was no longer a good prospect for him and he did not argue with her.'

Mother looked taken aback, then tutted. 'There are better prospects than him in the world. We are on our way to being nearly what we were-'

'Mother, I do not want to wait around for some man who may or may not take me while we rebuild our fortunes. I would rather work hard to contribute to that. I could make more than I do at Mr Syrett's in the long run-'

'But Mr Syrett has been good to you, he's been good to us.'

'I know - but I can't work there forever, just like you couldn't work at the Roberts' forever.'

She ran her hands through her hair. 'How about if we had you apprentice as a midwife?'

'I do not think many people would want a midwife who had not had children herself.'

'You are right,' she gave a surprisingly bitter laugh. 'And yet we don't mind young doctors, do we?'

'Indeed.'

She paused. 'Very well. Tomorrow we will discuss it further, and together we will make some sort of a plan.'

I nodded, my heart unexpectedly soaring.

Amelia

I awoke with a sore head and memories of Mr Snowden's lips lunging for mine. My stomach turned. What had I gotten myself into? Luckily, he thought my refusal innocent and charming, but how long would that last if we kept up an acquaintance?

He was delighted as we found his guests together, and they all shrieked with delight. When the party resumed Betsey's hair was askew and I didn't want to know what she'd done with the viscount's son, though she dropped a few hints - forgetting perhaps that I'd known her husband, Dick Webster, longer than I'd known her.

I was glad when it was time to go home, for Mr Snowden continued to laugh and joke with his friends, who fawned about him. I sat at the side of the room, nursing champagne and wishing for more food; Mama's fruit cake or her mock turtle soup.

*

There was a knock at my door and Betsey wandered in, clutching a flannel to her head. 'The maid said you had a headache as well. Will you go down for breakfast?'

I nodded.

'We must go and see my viscount today, I promised I would.'

I didn't point out that he wasn't a viscount at all merely the younger son of one, nor how much it set me on edge that Betsey was apparently prepared to be free with her affections despite her marriage.

'There was talk of him and Mr Snowden organising a trip to Brighton.'

'Oh?' I said feeling relieved that he would be gone.

'Yes and he said they would pay for us to join them.'

'But Brighton's on the other side of the coast!'

'What's gotten into you? It'll be an adventure. It's even more fun than Bath and nearer to London!'

'What about Mrs Tindal?'

Betsey shrugged. 'I am your chaperone, remember? If The Honourable Mr Fontaine and Mr Snowden are paying it would be rude to refuse, wouldn't it?'

My stomach sunk.

Chapter 17

Jessica

When I had awoken, I hoped my conversation with Lydia had been a dream, but deep down I knew better. Over breakfast, Lydia had said she just wanted to enquire to see which local surgeons were looking for apprentices. I told her I would think on it. I could not call upon a surgeon I knew. I did not want to be harsh, but I was at a loss as to what to do otherwise. I was being too indulgent, yet at the same time a small part of me wanted to see how far she could go. It would just be easier if she wanted to be a midwife, but she was right – no one would trust a maid to be a midwife and no respectable maid would become a midwife. Of course they wouldn't become a surgeon either but…

She left for her shift at Mr Syrett's and I promised to think on the matter. There were plenty of doctors around the spa so maybe one of them would offer some sort a solution. Maybe they would want a housekeeper? I heard the tinkle of Mrs Pemberton's bell and the scurrying of Mary's feet. *She* saw a great selection of medical men. Maybe one of those would do. I would quiz Mary later and maybe pretend there was a family friend in want of an apprenticeship or some such.

Satisfied with this thought I put on my apron. There was much to attend to today. Mr Webster and Mr Thomas were coming around in a few days with their wives. They would be trying some pies and deciding which ones they thought would sell well, so today I was going to make some practise versions.

I had a pig's shoulder and a pigeon which Lydia had already skilfully butchered to go into pies as well as apples, rhubarbs and berries. These would feed Lydia and me, as well as Mrs Pemberton, Mary and Miss

Atwell for the next for days. I was looking forward to the gamey pigeon and tart berries. As well making them into individual pies I could make another and combine the two ingredients, the same with the apple and pork.

I was sorry Miss Atwell could not join us for the dinner with the Websters and Thomases, because her lively stories would make excellent conversation. Maybe she would even have some ideas for pie fillings, hitherto unknown to me. Her vivid descriptions of her travels had encouraged me to pick up the well-thumbed copy of Captain Cook's adventures, so beloved by Captain Parnell, Mr Syrett and now Lydia. I was quickly beginning to understand why they enjoyed it so; the places described seemed to be beyond imagination.

I made standing pastry for the pies, which would make them sturdier and easier to transport. Calm washed over me as I boiled the butter before adding it to the flour, salt and lard. The pastry would be hand risen and would need a few hours under a damp cloth after kneading before modelling but already the satisfaction of the work was filling me. I hummed as I kneaded, missing Amelia's playing on the piano, and was interrupted by a knock at the door. It was a delivery boy. I expected the letter to be from Amelia and was excited to read her missive, hoping she would be telling me she was coming home soon, or at least she had been offered a position as a companion, however the handwriting on the envelope was not her swirling, loping letters.

It was the neat handwriting of Captain Parnell. Unbidden, a thrill rose in me and I felt it was a strange betrayal of Amelia. While I would rather a letter from her, something from Captain Parnell was a pleasing, unexpected compensation.

As I covered my pastry with the damp cloth before settling down to read his letter, the memory of the delicious cheeses we had eaten came to me; the crumbly Cheshire, the creamy Cheddar, the salty Parmesan…I wondered if he had tried macaroni and cheese and thought myself foolish for neglecting to ask him. I had heard the basics of making macaroni was very similar to pastry. Peter dismissed macaroni as a foreign fad, but was happy to use the term as an insult for any fashionable young man who crossed his path. Maybe next time Captain Parnell was in town, I might attempt to make it.

The letter said that he was now stationed in Portsmouth due to the weather and that they would be setting off again soon. He hoped I did not mind that he wrote to me, and asked after my health and the girls before enquiring after the house. He said he was thinking of buying a house in Portsmouth, but he thought it might simply be easier to rent it out to one family as opposed to getting another person in to run it as a lodging house since he doubted he could find someone to match me in that capacity.

As I folded his letter and thought on how to reply, the smile did not leave my face.

*

As the day and the pies progressed, another post arrived. I was sure this time it would be from Amelia but no, it was for Mrs Pemberton. But then Amelia did not write every day, though it had been at least four now since her last letter. Amelia could simply be busy or her letter could have gotten lost in the post. Maybe there was not much to report, and she was being prudent with her money – though Amelia was never prudent with money. I thought she would write to at least thank me for her birthday gifts, however small, and tell me if she marked the day in any special way. Maybe if I heard nothing in a few days I would write to Mrs Tindal.

When Mrs Pemberton returned, she greeted me in her stiff way then retired to her room, leaving Mary to get her a cup of tea.

'Mary, I was wondering if you could help me.'

Mary looked startled.

'A son of a friend of mine is looking for an apprenticeship as a surgeon. I wondered if through your work with Mrs Pemberton you had encountered any surgeons in want of apprentices?'

She looked at me intently, brow furrowed, as the kettle boiled. 'There are a lot of surgeons and quacks around the spa. Most of them have apprentices, but there is one who doesn't.'

'Yes?'

'Well, he is rather gruff ma'am, but he is good. He specialises in broken bones. Mrs Pemberton-' Mary lowered her voice '-she sees him because one of her ills is that she broke her wrist years ago and it never set right so gives her pains. He thinks she should let him break it again and reset it but she wouldn't have that, so he just prescribes things to soothe the pain,' Mary shrugged. 'Anyhow, his name is Mr Campbell and I have his address written down so I shall bring it to you later.'

'Thank you, Mary.'

A gruff doctor wasn't quite what I had in mind, I had pictured some sort of medical version of Mr Syrett, however the only true way to determine his character was to meet him for myself.

That evening, I told Lydia the news. She beamed.

'I am sure I shan't mind how gruff he is,' she said. 'As long as he teaches me well.'

'We can add him to our list,' I said. 'If his manner is so rude he ought not be our first choice.'

Amelia

The Brighton trip was arranged alarmingly quickly. It only took a few days from Betsey's words until we were speeding along in a carriage. I knew I ought to write to Mama, I knew I ought to refuse to go but there was the small lingering doubt – if not now, when would I ever get the chance to go to Brighton? Especially at no expense. It was foolish, but I was hoping to find some way of avoiding Betsey and the men while I was there. Betsey said she would notify Mrs Webster Senior of our move only after we arrived in Brighton.

'But why not before?'

'I suppose there isn't much difference, but there might be a fuss if we do it before and once we're there it can't be undone can it?'

'But what of Mrs Tindal?'

'She has gotten so ill she probably doesn't want visitors.'

The housekeeper, who had seemed put out by our presence was even more put out at our hasty departure. 'But my mistress enjoys your company.'

'Are we not a strain on her when she is so ill?' Betsey said. 'Always coming and going and she is unable to receive us. It is best we leave her in peace.'

Mrs Haywood shook her head and left us. When I went to say farewell to Mrs Tindal, the housekeeper was keeping vigil over her bed with the doctor.

Mrs Haywood gave me a cross look, but the doctor stood to give me his seat.

'Mrs Tindal, Betsey and I are to leave for Brighton with our friends.' Saying friends did not feel right. 'We have been invited, you see.' I half wished the old lady would grab my hand and pled with me to stay but she did not so much as stir. 'Well,' I sighed after a long pause. 'Thank you for letting us stay with you. I have had the most marvellous time, you have been terribly generous.'

When I left, I found Betsey ordering the maids about, packing my things.

'Where are my papers? I am going to write to Mama–'

'I told you to save that until we are there.'

I don't know why I didn't argue. Part of me wanted to go to Brighton and I knew Betsey was right, Mama and Mrs Webster might make a fuss. Another part of me didn't want to go to Brighton like this.

The next morning the carriage arrived for us. Betsey gaily boarded with The Honourable Marmaduke Fontaine or her Unhonourable Honourable as she had taken to calling him. Mr Snowden stepped out to help me in. I glanced backwards but I was not called to the house. The viscount's son popped a bottle of champagne and Betsey laughed shrilly.

'Is all this champagne not rather unpatriotic?'

Mr Snowden chuckled. 'Would you rather ale? No indeed you wouldn't, come along, up we get.'

I could have walked back into the house myself and found a way to go home, but I feared Mrs Haywood might not let me in or that I was just being a fool. After all, this was what I should want, wasn't it? Where had behaving properly gotten anyone? Mama slaved away all her life and had never been to Brighton. I would not be like that.

Tentatively, I peered into the carriage. It had velvet seats and gold trim, the horses were white, even the footmen's livery was expensive. I braced myself, then let Mr Snowden help me up into the carriage.

Lydia

Mama made an admirable list of surgeons whom were unknown to our family but were based in the area. I set about writing letters, inquiring if they were in want of an apprentice and signing the name Hugh Sommers. Mama and I agreed I would use her maiden name as well as the name she would have given me had I been a boy. I rather liked the sound of it.

I awaited the post everyday, my nerves a mixture of anticipation and dread. I received a few prompt replies from my letters and excitedly opened them, only to find them informing me that the doctors in question already had apprentices. A few of them said that while they did not have apprentices, given my lack of schooling or recommendation they would not consider taking me anyway.

It was hard not to feel defeated, but Mother said that all I needed was to have one person say yes.

'When your father and I looked for an inn to make The Fitzwilliam, it took months,' she said. 'But we got there eventually.'

I supposed that was true, and The Fitzwilliam had been a fine hotel, had it not? It was not much longer that I got a reply from a Mr Ashley saying he would be interested to meet me. That caused more nerves than all the disappointments put together.

With Mother's help I dressed, ponytailed my hair and headed to meet him. When I reached his house, the housekeeper showed me to his study. He looked up at me, then raised his eyebrows as we were left alone.

'Hugh Sommers?' he said.

'Yes sir,' I said, taking care to keep my voice low.

He looked at me searchingly, causing a flutter of worry in my chest, and stood up.

'Have always had a failure to thrive, Master Sommers?'

'I beg your pardon?'

'You say here you are seventeen, yet you look very young.' He came closer to me. 'Short, thin, no sign of even the faintest of hairs on your upper lip or chin.'

'My father was late bloomer,' I lied quickly.

He shook his head and looked at me very severely. 'I think I must submit you to a medical examination.'

'What? Why?' My heart started to pound.

His nostrils flared. 'Something to hide?'

'No-'

'So then why not-'

'I didn't say no-'

'Well let us get started-' he advanced.

'No!'

He folded his arms. 'I thought so, *Miss* Sommers, it is my business to know the human body – do not forget! Leave this place at once before I have you arrested for indecency and fraud. Put this foolishness to bed. I shall be letting all my friends know not to pay any heed to letters from Hugh Sommers, do you understand?'

I nodded, too alarmed to talk, and hurried from his house.

Jessica

The evening of the pie tasting arrived and there was a knock at the door at seven sharp. Lydia hastened to answer it whilst I added the finishing touches to the pies; a scattering of herbs for the savouries and a dusting of sugar for the sweets, then stepped back and viewed them with satisfaction.

'Lydia, how well you look!' came Mr Webster's voice. I stepped into the parlour and greeted our guests, offered them drinks and, after small pleasantries, I asked Mrs Webster if she heard from Betsey.

'Oh yes and what a fine time of it they are having, eh? To be young again and to be in Brighton!'

'Brighton?' I asked with a smile, assuming she had misspoken, but she nodded. 'Yes their lodgings sound quite divine.'

'Amelia and Betsey are in Brighton?' I asked. 'I thought they would be home soon.'

'Change of plans. I got the letter from Betsey yesterday. One of her old school friends met them in Bath and invited them to Brighton for a few weeks. They even covered the costs!'

'But what of Mrs Tindal?'

'I daresay she can amuse herself!'

'Oh,' I said, a sense of disappointment and dread settled on me. Why would Betsey's school friends have covered the costs? They must be very rich, but such rash spending sounded irresponsible. 'And you got this letter yesterday? I have not heard from Amelia for several days.'

Concern flickered across my friend's face but she relaxed it into a smile. 'I daresay her letter just got lost or with all the excitement she hasn't had a moment to send it.'

The latter seemed thoughtless, too thoughtless. The letter must have gotten lost, unless she wished to conceal her journey from me, but why would she do that?

'And Betsey took Amelia with her?'

'Yes indeed, she was quite explicit about that.'

'Could you give me the address?' I asked. 'I shall write to Amelia and say her letter got lost.'

'Of course, I don't have it to hand but I'll bring it over tomorrow.'

'Thank you.'

Before I had time to dwell another knock at the door heralded the Thomases. Unable to do anything else about Amelia now, and trying to convince myself it was just some lost letter or misunderstanding, I concentrated on serving the pies.

Chapter 18

Amelia

From my window I could see the sun setting over the sea. Such a pretty scene, I would have to save it for my letter to Mama. I would tell her that Betsey's school friends, were the Snowdens and they had covered our costs as that was what Betsey had suggested. Parents and a sister had been invented for Mr Snowden to make us seem respectable, though so far we had done nothing unrespectable, Betsey's insistence on fabricating this lie made me wonder how long she wanted that to remain the case.

The lie made my insides twist with guilt, but I didn't know how else to explain the situation without causing a fuss. Mr Snowden and the viscount's son rented their own rooms in the same building as us and sometimes would drunkenly sing outside our front door much to Betsey's amusement, my embarrassment and the annoyance of our neighbours in the building.

I would not tell Mama about the sapphire necklace which I now wore, nor the matching blue dress which Mr Snowden had ordered to be to made so tight it dug into my skin and was cut so low Betsey called it 'delightfully French'. Soon I would have to go to the party at the assembly hall and see all of them again…There would fun involved to be sure; the games, the glamour, the clothes, but mostly I found Mr Snowden's friends bores who were desperate to shock.

I could take these sapphires to a pawn shop and have enough money to get a stagecoach to Bristol with plenty to spare. But what waited for me there? Working back at Mama's new lodging house?

Waiting to marry some tradesman? Going blind as I strained to make dresses?

I left my bedroom, after downing a glass of madeira and waited in the parlour for Betsey. Our maid, Ines, came and poured me another glass of madeira. There came giggles from Betsey's room as she joked with her French émigré hairdresser, whose bill the viscount's son was paying. I sat back and continued to drink my wine. If I joined Betsey in her bedroom I would have to hear more anecdotes about the viscount's son, and I'd had my fill of those, especially as I was present when most of these 'amusing' incidents had taken place.

'More wine, ma'am?' Ines asked and I nodded, surprised I had emptied the glass already. As she finished pouring there was a knock at the door. Ines scurried off to answer it and I tensed as the loud voices of Mr Snowden and the viscount's son drifted into the parlour.

'-cheeky scoundrel! I told him where to go!'

'Quite right, old chap!'

'Miss Amelia!' Mr Snowden exclaimed. 'We thought we could all get a carriage together.'

'Where's Betsey?' asked the viscount's son.

'Getting ready.'

'Marmaduke?' she called. 'Are you here?'

'Yes m'dear!' he said with a wink. 'What's taking you so long?'

'I'm nearly ready, you mustn't come in!'

He laughed roguishly and started to rattle her door, causing more laughter. Must they all be so childish? They were older than me!

'I do not think I will attend tonight-' I started to say, when Betsey burst out of her room and my words were lost. She worn a dazzling diamond necklace, ostrich feathers in her hair and a dress of white silk. The viscount's son put his hand on his heart and pretended to swoon, before he and Betsey left for the carriage arm in arm. Mr Snowden rolled his eyes and looked at me.

'I think I will stay here.'

'But you look so pretty.'

'Thank you-'

'Come on,' he took my arm and started to walk, bringing me along with him. 'Jealousy does not become you. I want to show you off.'

'Jealousy?' I asked.

He raised his eyes brows in a way he must have thought was knowing.

'You are far more beautiful than her, she is all practised airs and overdone gaudiness.'

He thought I was jealous of Betsey, rather than annoyed by her. I knew he would not listen if I tried to explain this, rather he'd just assume I was protesting too much. We reached the carriage and once again I let him help me in against my better judgement, hoping I might make some new friends of my own at the party or at least have a few moments away from Mr Snowden's.

Lydia

I had not told Mother the truth about my encounter with Mr Ashley, I simply said he'd chosen another apprentice. He must have been true to his word for the only other response I received from my enquires was one telling me not to write again; the rest of my letters went unanswered.

That only left Dr Campbell, the supposedly gruff doctor Mary had spoken of. Mother said we'd go and see him together. She did not want me working for someone who'd been described as so uncouth without making her own mind up first. I was glad of her company, feeling if Mr Campbell felt as Mr Ashley did he may not act so aggressively if Mother was there. I had replayed the scene in my head so many times, each time wishing I had acted differently but I hadn't known what else to do. If Mr Campbell acted the same, I was worried I would have to give up this foolish hope once and for all.

I waited until Mrs Pemberton left for the day before I emerged in my boyish ensemble. Mother eyed me up and down with a smile before I put my hat on, as she left breakfast out for Miss Atwell.

'Let us hope he is not too gruff,' she said as we set off.

Mr Campbell's abode was in a shabby part of Hotwells and when we knocked, it took a few moments for him to answer, though there was a great deal of clattering and swearing, causing Mother to raise her eyebrows.

When the door opened it was by a tall but crooked man with rough, smallpox scarred skin stretched over big bones. He must have been ten years older than mother at least and his black hair was streaked with grey.

'Yes?' he barked as he fastened his cravat.

'I heard you were in want of an apprentice?' Mother said.

He looked from her to me. 'See my advert, did you?'

'Actually,' I said, thinking it would show initiative, 'we made a few enquires.'

'And in those enquiries,' he fixed me with a harsh stare. 'Did you discover I have high standards for my apprentices? Most of 'em can't hack it.'

'I suppose we did hear you had high standards, but that wasn't how it was phrased.'

His eyebrows shot up and Mother went to speak but he burst out laughing. 'No, I bet it wasn't! Dear me, 'wasn't how it was phrased'! Diplomatic little tyke, aren't you? So,' he drew breath. 'What do you call yourself?'

'Hugh Sommers.'

'And this is your mother?'

'I am sir,' Mother said.

'Well unless Hugh is a milksop, I am not sure why you are here.'

'My son is no milksop,' Mother said. 'And I have a right to see where he may work.'

He looked her up and down, then turned his gaze back to me.

'Any experience?'

I started to list the books I had read but he waved an impatient hand. 'Any experience?'

'He's an excellent butcher,' Mother said causing Mr Campbell to raise his bushy

eyebrows. 'I'm a cook,' she added. 'So I should know.'

I took advantage of his be-wilderness to explain about the boy with the ankle.

'And you learned this from books and butchery?'

'Yes.'

He frowned. 'Well, you best come in.'

It was settled that I would start the next week. I had not imagined it would all move so quickly! He stated from the off he had no intention of a live-in apprentice, which was what mother and I had hoped for anyway. His home was the cramped first floor of an old house; with plants, books and tinctures as well as jars of what looked like bones and animal remains clogging up every surface.

He advised me to continue to dress in a sober fashion – I realised he was referring to the dark colours I had chosen for father's funeral. He seemed pleased that I had not attended any school – 'a corrupting influence!' Mother added I'd done some shop work to make me seem as though I had experience of the world. I did not know what we would have done if he asked for a reference, but he blustered on, seeming to take this at face value.

'Used to handling money then?'

'Yes.'

'Good, because you know this ain't for free. It's my living, and if you intend to make it yours, you'd best get used to charging for it.'

'Yes sir.'

I was to attend him at seven every morning, six days a week (though people would get ill on Sundays as well so I'd best believe he'd send for me if needs be) and not finish until the work was done. As I walked home with Mother I was elated.

'I start training to be a surgeon next week!' I beamed.

'You must take care not to let him ruffle you,' Mother said. 'Or to be put off by his rough ways.'

'I won't be. It is better than I could have expected. Do you think he suspected anything?'

She shook her head. 'No, he's the sort that would have said – even in jest – if he thought you a little girlish. I suppose you might have to act a bit rough to keep the pretence up.' Mother pressed my arm. 'I am proud of you. You conducted yourself well and this could be the start of a very bright future, so long as we are careful. Oh, but we must tell Mr Syrett.'

'Yes, I hope he shan't be too offended, but whatever shall we tell him? That you need more help with the housekeeping maybe?'

'No,' Mother pursed her lips. 'I believe we should be as honest as possible with Mr Syrett; he is a friend and has been good to us. Tell him that through Mrs Pemberton you have made the acquaintance of a surgeon who has invited you to become his assistant, or housekeeper of a sort. It is unorthodox yes, but does not sound so shocking. Mr Syrett knows you and your enthusiasm for medical and scientific knowledge so he wouldn't find it too surprising, then we could even suggest a replacement.'

'A replacement? You mean Amelia?'

'No, I think she would tire of it quickly. I was thinking of Miss Thomas. Mrs Thomas was saying how admirable it was that you worked in the shop, but how difficult it must be to find a respectable employer, without going the whole hog and packing Ruby off to be a governess. She hinted it was hard for Ruby because finding a husband might be difficult and some people might not want to employ her–'

Mother paused. 'But I think Mr Syrett would, for he is an abolitionist and Ruby has visited you in the shop, so she knows about it.'

'That is an excellent idea, I shan't feel so bad if I can offer him a replacement. I will go and call on Ruby before I go to work!'

'Mind you get changed first, dear!' Mother laughed as she put the key in the door. When we stepped into the parlour, Mary was singing from the kitchen. Mother and I exchanged alarmed glances. I would have to be more careful in my comings and goings. Mother took a long coat off the hook and I wrapped it around myself before hurrying up the stairs to change.

When I came downstairs, Mother was sitting on the sofa reading a letter.

'Amelia's letter?'

Mother looked up and nodded with a smile.

'Did it get lost then?'

She paused. 'No, I can tell by the date, but she makes no apology for writing late.'

'I suppose it is all the excitement.' I wasn't sure why I was making excuses for Amelia. Hadn't it occurred to her Mother might be worried?

'Does she say why she is in Brighton?'

'Same as what Mrs Webster said Betsey wrote, they met Betsey's old school friends. She says lots about how comfortable the rooms are and how lovely the sea is.'

I nodded, noticing Mother's smile was waning.

'Does she say when she is coming home?'

Mother shook her head. What on earth did Amelia think she was doing? And more to the point, what kind of a chaperone had Betsey Webster turned out to be?

Chapter 19

Jessica
Miss Atwell came downstairs holding her bags and a letter.
'What time is your stagecoach?' I asked.
'Ten.'
'Manchester, was it?'
She nodded. 'I must meet my cousin's lawyer and then, well…' she smiled. 'We shall see if I am to become rich or not. Either way I shall pass through here again if you will have me.'
'Certainly. Will that be upon your return to America?'
'I wish to see the rest of Europe before I go back. If I am to be rich, I will travel in style and if not, I will find away.'
'How determined you are!'
'Well, it is so close, how can I resist?'
'I hope you shall find Italy and Spain as exciting as Mexico.'
'Everywhere has its own charm,' she smiled. 'As you will find when you travel.'
'Oh, I don't know about that-'
She looked astounded. 'Why ever not?'
'Well I couldn't possibly-'
'Why?' she asked again as though the notion of not going was more absurd than actually going.
'My daughters-'
'Are both almost grown.'
'The lodging house-

'Will always be here.'

'To speak bluntly, the money-

'You are a resourceful woman Mrs Fitzwilliam, and have a whole host of talents, which can keep you in funds in a respectable fashion.'

'I suppose you are correct,' I said, seeing how easily she had vanquished what seemed like rational reasons and made them into mere excuses.

'You must promise me you will travel.'

I laughed.

'I am serious.'

'Very well,' I said. 'I promise I will travel.'

'Good,' she pressed my hand. 'When I return a rich woman, you can take me shopping for you are the most stylish woman I know-'

I laughed.

''Tis true, then I shall give you some tips on traveling, eh?'

I nodded. 'Well, I am looking forward to my return already!'

After she left, I was alone in the house. Lydia was completing her final shift at Mr Syrett's while Mrs Pemberton and Mary were out seeing one of the many doctors. I was making my first batch of apple pies for Mr Thomas when a knock at the door heralded a letter. Once again, I expected it to be from Amelia, and once again it was from Captain Parnell.

He was still in Portsmouth. It was a pleasing to think of having an on-going correspondence with someone. I only ever had such a thing with Peter's Mother, once we moved to Bristol and Peter could never be induced to write often to her, so I had - nervous at first at my uneducated penmanship but soon finding her letters and my expected replies could be very formulaic.

Captain Parnell asked my opinion on many matters - either serious or fleeting and wrote of things that might interest me, he also told me about the food he had eaten and asked if I had made certain recipes. I realised this was something I would have to replicate in my own letters but was happy to do so - I wanted to know more about various things he knew - especially as concerned to travel and since I would sometimes wonder on his opinion on various matters, and it was gratifying that he seemed to wonder about mine as well.

That afternoon, after more baking and a thorough scrubbing of the kitchen there came another letter, and this time it was from Amelia.

After my nervous wait last time, having one follow so quickly was a pleasant relief and she had written pages, crossed as well!

She wrote in detail about the fashions in Brighton as well as new dances she had learned and plays she had seen, though despite all that I couldn't help feeling her letter told me nothing at all. She did not say when she intended to come home, much to my annoyance. There was no mention of her opinions or if she was actually enjoying herself. I tried to shake the thought away – of course she was enjoying herself, she was going to balls and the theatre, but I could not help the lingering doubt. Amelia was never good at checking her emotions - and happy or sad, she would often declare it.

I sighed, I missed her presence in the house – her singing, her happy laugh, her way with stews and savoury pastry, but most of all I just missed her. If she and Betsey had kept to the original plan, instead of going to Brighton, she would be home by now. Her absence was always there in the back of my mind and the longer she was away the worse it became. I would write and urge to come home. If she wasn't enjoying herself hopefully my letter would give her cause to come home, I would even offer to pay for her fare.

Lydia

'But how will this help?' I snapped.

Mr Campbell raised his eyebrows. 'Who is the teacher here?' he paused, the silence demanding an answer.

'You.'

'And so you do as I tell you.'

'But surely as the apprentice it is exactly my place to ask questions-'

'You didn't go to some fancy school, did you? No. You came here, so no questions. Now, this time in alphabetical order of ailments.'

He left the room, slamming the door behind him. I waited a few moments before the front door shut as well before releasing a string of curses which would not have been becoming for Miss Lydia Fitzwilliam.

Fool that I was, I arrived filled with such hope. I'd known it wouldn't be easy but at least thought I would be working alongside Mr Campbell, seeing patients, but no. He left me in his house everyday to reorganise and catalogue his collection of specimens.

From the confusing way they were strewn about the house I could tell various people had tried to catalogue them at various times and failed miserably. There was no clue as to what some pieces were, so I looked them up in his books which were equally badly catalogued. After my third twelve-hour day I finally finished cataloguing as he wanted, in order of species, only to have him tell me to do it again in order of age and now he was asking me to do it again. Surely this would not last forever, would it? How long should I keep at it? It had been a week now...but then who else would take me on? I sighed and started again. At least now I knew what they were I could be quicker each time.

I left for the day when Mr Campbell told me to make myself scarce. I dreaded to think how the specimens would have to be rearranged tomorrow.

'Mr Sommers!' In the evening street I was startled to hear my own pseudonym and turned to see Ruby. Aside from Mama, she was the only other person who knew the truth about my apprenticeship. We had not even written to Amelia in case Betsey read her letter and was scandalised. I told Ruby after I offered her the job at Mr Syrett's, when we were alone in her parlour. The worlds came tumbling out, as all my secrets seemed to when around her and she whooped with pleasure and embraced me.

'I thought to see you at home,' I smiled, the sight of her easing the tension I was feeling. She was dressed beautifully as ever, her gown made of a fabric with a bold botanical print.

'I thought I would surprise you and I wanted to see you in your boyish garb. Now isn't it proper to offer a lady your arm?'

I chuckled and did so, and she giggled at our charade.

'So, how is the shop?' I said, missing Mr Syrett's kindly ways.

'I declare it is a dream,' she smiled. 'I think I have proved a bit of a curiosity but-' she shrugged. 'No one has been rude or caused offense and he has such a nice lot of regular customers.'

A pull of longing for my old job with all its comfortable pleasures tugged at my insides.

'And how is Mr Campbell? And the apprenticeship?'

'Oh, you know marvellous, but busy,' I started with the lie I peddled mother so not to disappoint her, but I could not go on with it. 'No, I must tell someone, it is terrible.' I gave her the true account of my week and she listened intently.

'Apprenticeships often start off hard though don't they, to test your mettle?'

'I suppose.'

She pressed my arm. 'Do not get downcast, I am sure he won't keep you at that, forever will he? He must want someone to help eventually with his trade or he wouldn't have taken you, would he?'

'I suppose.'

'This must be some sort of initiation. I think men do this sort of thing all the time, lord knows why. He probably wants to see if you are serious.'

'But I am.'

'So, prove it, hold your tongue and don't argue. He doesn't realise you are a girl and have never had it easy, does he? He thinks you are a boy, and must learn the hard way since boys are rarely denied anything.'

Amelia

'Good Morning ma'am,' Ines entered my bedroom with the breakfast tray as the clock struck ten. I sat up.

'Is Mrs Webster awake yet?'

'No ma'am, and she asked not to be disturbed before midday.'

I nodded. 'Ines, could you prepare me a small picnic hamper. I intend to go out today.'

'With Mrs Webster and the gentlemen?'

'No, just by myself. I will leave after breakfast.'

'Very well, ma'am.' Ines opened the curtains and left me.

A few nights ago at a card party a young man had spoken to me very animatedly about the beautiful beaches and countryside around Brighton. I suggested to Betsey and 'the gentlemen' that we should take a trip, at least to the beach if nothing else, and while they greeted the idea with enthusiasm, everyday there was some excuse as to why they could not go, so I resolved to go myself.

I rehearsed what I would say to Ines and was prepared for every possible refusal or problem but none came. Even the weather was on my side, all was sunny and clear. I dressed in one of my simple mourning dresses, and packed some papers and pencils to draw with as well as Castle Rackrent by Maria Edgeworth.

I stole from our rooms, and hurried from the building, hoping not to disturb Betsey or that today wasn't the day when Mr Snowden and the viscount's son decided to stir before lunch and call on us. Luckily, the only people I met on the stairs were our middle-aged neighbours.

Once outside in the fresh air, I hastened for the beach in the bracing wind. Standing upon the pebbles I looked out at the sea. I had not expected to find the sight so overwhelming; in Bristol the sea was forced into harbours, here it was open and free. The smell of salt was strong and the waves, although small, crashed with majesty on the shore. It bought a smile to my face and taking a deep breath, I set off on my walk excited at what else I might see.

Chapter 20

Lydia

During the fourth week, I finished Dr Campbell's cataloguing task a good half an hour before he returned home, so I made tea after washing his scummy pot.

'What's all this?' he asked when I presented him with a cup upon his return.

'I finished in good time.'

'Did you indeed?' he slurped his tea. 'So, where is the malformed hoof of the goat?'

'Next to the malformed hoof of the sheep.'

'Show me.'

This was the first time he actually made any enquiry as to how I had completed my task. 'And the monkey's fingers?'

'Next to the monkey skull.'

'Which monkey skull?'

'The chimp, which is next to the gorilla skull.'

'Show me. Ah yes. And you are quite satisfied that is a gorilla skull? I never told you it was so.'

'You never told me what any of them were, but I referenced it in your books.'

'Tell me what makes this gorilla's skull? And how is not to be confused with my human skulls?'

I reeled off the differences, which he neither contradicted nor confirmed.

'Now, how can you tell the difference in my human skulls in age and gender and condition in life?'

I lead the way to the largest part of his collection, the human remains, which I had stacked in their jars and boxes in the back room which may well have been a dining room had someone other than Mr Campbell lived here but he had made it a mausoleum.

'They are arranged in order of age, as requested,' I said. 'This skull is that of a baby, only three months old by my reckoning and born with syphilis given the condition of the nose-'

It was only with the chiming of nine from his clock (which actually meant it was quarter past the hour) that he grunted. 'Very good.' He went back into the hall and returned with his black doctor's case. 'I think you have catalogued all to my satisfaction.'

He dropped his case with a clang and opened it. A smell of wet leather, metal and rot drifted up. 'Tomorrow you can start cleaning all of my instruments.'

He patted me on the shoulder and as I headed for the door I realised the cataloguing had been a test which I passed. It taught me a great deal about the anatomy regardless of the strange method of it. Well, as grim as his cleaning his equipment sounded, I was another step up the ladder.

Jessica

We took in an elderly woman named Mrs Nutall to replace Miss Atwell, and she soon became fast friends with Mrs Pemberton who extended her stay. My pies of apple and pork, and pigeon and berries sold well at the Webster's butchers' shops, and Mr Thomas asked for more of my pear and apple pies, and blackberry pies to sell. We discussed what different ingredients we could use at the seasons changed. I visited Mrs Thomas' greenhouses in her garden and she explained with much enthusiasm the harvests they would bring.

Mr Thomas said the big houses in Clifton and even a manor house out in Somerset, where many of the fine folk lived, (he gave a chuckle and a wink at this, acknowledging my awareness of his egalitarian views) thought my pies excellent and he was sure we could charge more for them.

Lydia worked hard at Mr Campbell's, and though she told me how well it all was going I saw how tired she was and how she didn't go into detail about what she was doing. He mostly had her cataloguing and cleaning. I knew most apprenticeships started off with drudgery but I hoped it would not wear her down.

When her eighteenth birthday came, we went with the Thomases and Mr Syrett to a dissection. She was greatly relaxed to be with our friends, even though after we came home and indulged in cake and wine she could not stay awake long.

Miss Thomas visited often for diner in the evenings after her work at Syrett's, much to Mrs Pemberton's and Mrs Nutall's bemusement, and would be collected by her younger brother Matthew or Mr Thomas on their grocer's trap. She often brought medical and cookery books for Lydia and me, and as tired as Lydia was it lifted her spirits to have so good a friend.

As summer passed to autumn, Mr Campbell did at last start taking her out on visits. She said most of his patients were very poor and desperate but she was glad to be working. Over the late summer and autumn months Amelia's letters continued, but more and more they described her countryside ramblings, and included numerous sketches, which improved week on week. Whilst I was pleased she seemed happier, I continued to be anxious for her; my youngest child in a place unknown to me, with no fixed date on when she might return. I missed her terribly and wanted her here or at least settled. Had I known the trip would last this long I might not have let her go.

I also heard from Mrs Hughes demanding when Amelia would return to make her daughter's wedding dress, so I told her I was terribly sorry but that did not seem likely Amelia would be coming back to make it. Mrs Hughes wrote back to say the whole thing had been handled very ill.

I had not heard from Captain Parnell for a while since his ship had left Portsmouth again. There had been a happy flurry of letters between us whilst he had been there, and he detailed his purchase of a cottage which was rented by an old sailor and his wife. Now he had returned to sea there were no more letters from him, and I missed them more than I felt I had right to.

Chapter 21

Amelia

Betsey and her Unhonourable Honourable carried on their intimacy, so I took more walks and feigned a few illnesses to escape some of the parties. I enjoyed planning my routes and discovering new things, and avoiding the constant society of Betsey, the viscount's son and Mr Snowden made me feel liberated. At the parties I did attend, it seemed Mr Snowden had found himself a Miss Butchart and while this troubled Betsey, I was glad of it.

As for his other tiresome friends, I found them more tolerable the more champagne I drunk. None of them were married or respectable, they were all rich boys with their 'favourites', who I soon came to realise were their mistresses. They gambled away fortunes, probably more than Papa could ever have imagined. I tried my hand at cards a few times but I found the gall of losing more bitter than the thrill of winning, so I started to hoard the money Betsey or Mr Snowden gave me to spend at the tables.

Despite all the glamour, my favourite part of Brighton was not Brighton at all, and required no money. It was my walks; admiring the sea, cliffs and beaches. How I would have scorned these even a few months ago, but now they were a blessed relief.

Walking alone I did not have to listen to anyone or laugh or make merry, as I always did with Mr Snowden and Betsey, so much so that my face ached. Sometimes when I reached a secluded spot I would just sit and cry for Papa and for the deep sadness that followed me around for his loss.

Lydia

The smell of blood and rotten meat was strong; just like a butcher's shop.

'Hold him down!'

I did as I Mr Campbell commanded, and clamped my hands over Thorton's arms.

''Ere,' his friend said, emptying a bottle into his open mouth then planting the wooden bit between his teeth.

'Ready?' Mr Campbell flexed his fingers, an unmistakable gleam of pleasure in his eyes as they studied the broken bone protruding from the skin.

Thorton started to say the Our Father and I watched as Mr Campbell checked Thorton's leg was tightly tied down then picked up his saw and got to work. Thorton's stifled cries caused his friend to grimace, but we both held his thrashing body down as he struggled to free himself then went limp from loss of blood.

'Will he live?' his friend asked. Mr Campbell was still too engrossed in his work to answer.

'We will have to see,' I said. 'I can still feel him breathing. You did your friend a service by summoning us. Better this than have it rot, that is a ghastly way to go.'

His friend swallowed and nodded. 'Yes, thank you sirs.'

Thorton survived the operation, but we would have to be back in the morning to change his dressing. We left Thorton in his lodging and Mr Campbell went onto a tavern. I took his case back to his house, and thoroughly cleaned his instruments then double checked the appointments for tomorrow, writing them out on the slate at his bedside so he would remember in the morning. As well as Thorton we had another sailor whose finger had been amputated, an elderly man with consumption and a child with a persistent cold, then the afternoon saw us gravitating towards the spa where we had appointments with an invalid and a wealthy widower.

Mr Campbell had only recently allowed me to come on the spa visits with him, having first had me accompany him on the more desperate visits to the sailors' taverns where many of the barmen knew him and passed on his details to sickly customers, for discounted rates on their own treatments which often seemed to stem from promiscuous behaviour, whilst the sailors' injuries stemmed from the dangerous nature of their work. Showing me the seedier side of his clientele first was evidently meant to shock me, but I tried to remain strong in the face of it and in truth, it was fascinating.

It took a good few months for me to be permitted along on the much more sedate spa visits and whilst they were still very interesting, I missed the cut and thrust of the dockside patients.

Luckily for me, Mrs Pemberton had no more appointments with Mr Campbell so our paths had not crossed. I managed to avoid her, Mary and Mrs Nutall when going to and from the house often wearing a long coat I had purchased from a reach down shop. It looked more suspicious in the summer months but through autumn and winter no one would have cause to question it. What was starting to look odd was my long hair. I noticed more young men forsaking ponytails and wearing their hair short.

When I reached home and made it to my bedroom I shook my hair out. Mother was downstairs in the kitchen, getting our dinner ready. Taking the scissors, I drew a deep breath, faced myself in the mirror and started to cut. Mother's footsteps sounded on the stairs, but I carried on. She would know the truth soon enough.

She gasped as she entered the room.

'Shut the door!' I hissed.

'Is your ponytail not sufficient?'

'It gets in the way and it is going out of fashion for young men, it would draw attention for me to look different.'

She swallowed.

'It's only hair Mother, and it isn't as pretty as yours.'

'Of course it is,' she sighed and kissed my forehead.

'We can sell it as well,' I said.

'Things aren't that desperate.'

'Yes, but we might as well as not.'

Frowning, she observed the uneven hacks I had made so far, shook her head and taking the scissors started to cut it for me, doing a much better job.

*

As we dined at the Thomases, Mrs Thomas spoke of her niece's recent engagement after a brief courtship to the wealthy son of a wool merchant.

'How brief was the courtship?' I asked Ruby.

'A month!'

'Do you think there is love after so brief a courtship?' I asked, thinking it was the sort of thing Amelia would wish to know.

Ruby shrugged. 'Some might say if a rich man sets his cap at you as long as he is not a brute, what else is there to do?'

'Would you do that? Marry for money?'

'It's not likely a rich man would want me -'

'I-'

'Come now, it's the truth. But if I liked him and he was rich, it would make me independent of my parents. I could run my own salons and have as many green houses as I chose.' She laughed.

I nodded, unsure if she was joking or not, and caught sight of Mr Bradley, the young Methodist minister. He glanced over at us, or more to the point, glanced over at Ruby.

'I think there is one here who likes you.' I swallowed. 'But I don't know how rich he is.'

'Who?'

'Mr Bradley.'

'Truly?' she blushed. 'Mama said the same, but I cannot see it.'

'I can hardly miss it.'

His looks at her continued all evening and I regretted my words; she fidgeted every time he looked over. It did not stop him.

'I don't think I meant what I said earlier,' she said as we parted. 'I was only thinking how nice it was to be rich was all, and what really worries me is being a spinster.'

I raised my eyebrows. 'Why should that worry you?'

'Oh Lydia, I would always be dependent on George or Matthew for charity, would I not? And as kind as they are, who knows who they will marry or where their careers will take for them, for they could pass as part Spanish, or maybe even full blooded English if someone wasn't too observant, and what would I be, hanging around reminding everyone we are mulattos? It is alright for you, apparently you are set to be a surgeon, but we cannot all be men.'

'I am sorry for unsettling you.'

She sighed and spoke in a hushed rush, her eyes widening. 'I was foolish to never think of Mr Bradley before, but now you have said it, I think if anything does come of it I will have to have him for no one else would have me. It makes me so panicked, even though he is perfectly nice.'

'I am sorry.' The thought of her being Mrs Bradley twisted my insides. She pressed my hands and Mother called me to the cab. I left feeling as though we'd quarrelled and a great heaviness settled upon me. When I got home I stayed up later than Mother, worrying about Ruby, Mr Bradley and myself. Lord, life would have been so much easier had I really been a boy. How much longer would my charade continue for? I unpinned the wig mama had insisted we had made from my shorn hair for social occasions. I wanted to push forward in my career, but I was not sure I could pretend to be a man forever, despite the freedom it gave for it was so strange living a double life.

Chapter 22

Jessica

For the week leading to Christmas we were to have no lodgers, though Mrs Pemberton said she would return in the spring then ominously added, pressing her chest, 'God Willing' to which Mary rolled her eyes. We had a booking for the new year, for a married couple and their invalid daughter so I was not worried for my finances which was a welcome feeling.

It was strange to think of having a restful period. The hotel had always been open for Christmas and the girls and Peter had always been merry, but Amelia was still in Brighton though writing regularly, and Lydia was working all the hours God sent. Mr Campbell rightly predicted that as midwinter approached more of 'weak' would fall ill. She was rushed off her feet with falls in the bad weather, colds and fevers of all sorts.

I gave the house a good and thorough clean. Though I was satisfied with my labour I found it hard to sleep, my mind beset with worry about both Lydia and Amelia. Lydia came in as the clock struck ten, and I hastened downstairs to meet her and give the food I had saved. She ate quickly and wordlessly, clearly exhausted before heading up to bed.

As I cleaned away her plate there was a rattle at the front door. I froze. My first panicked thought was that it was burglars, but I tried to shake it off. It could be Amelia come home unexpectedly. My heart soared at this thought. The door creaked open and, though I hoped it was Amelia, I still grabbed a knife as I stepped into the parlour, then gasped with relief.

'You gave me quite a fright!' I chuckled, raising my rush light to illuminate the face of Captain Parnell.

'My apologies,' he said. 'I sent a letter saying I should be home this week.'

'I did not receive it, but it must have gotten lost. Never mind that, welcome back.'

As we paused for a brief awkward moment it occurred to me that I had never thought on how tall he was before, but that was probably because he was well proportioned with it – not lanky. I had not noticed either that while his Roman nose might be called long by some, it was not bulbous and was in perfect proportion to the rest of his face; large eyes, long eyelashes, high cheek bones, and his skin tone looked a very healthy olive – not swarthy or sallow. How odd that I had once thought him only *almost* handsome…

Colour crept up my cheeks at these thoughts and the realisation that my hair was down, and I only wore a shawl and night gown. He was very well turned out in his naval uniform – buttons and boots gleaming in the rush light.

'Should you like food?' I asked, pulling my shawl tightly around myself. 'Let me make you something-'

'I can manage-'

'I insist,' I said. 'Let me go and quickly put on something warmer then I will put together a meal, I cannot sleep anyway.'

'Oh well, if you cannot sleep anyway.'

We both laughed, the awkwardness melting away. 'Go wait in the kitchen, I will be down presently. I want to hear all your adventures.'

'Very well,' he smiled. 'Though that is sure to help you sleep.'

I hurried upstairs and, careful not to wake Lydia, I pulled on a neat black dress and pinned my hair back a little, then donned my cap. I hesitated at the door, Peter's cribbage set on Lydia's bedside under a pile of books catching my eye. What was I doing? Why did I feel so nervous, so flighty…so happy?

I swallowed. That was silly, foolish, I was not a girl but an old widow. I took a breath, well maybe not so very old, but still a widow. I had been startled and this was all just relief that he was not been an intruder. Taking a deep breath, I headed down the stairs.

He was waiting in the kitchen, rush light lit and uncorking a bottle of wine. He was *so* much taller than I remembered and he smiled at me in a way I didn't remember either, so open, so happy, so pleased. I looked away, headed towards the pantry and started to busy myself.

'What do you want?'

'Nothing too heavy.' I heard the wine being poured. 'Here, come and try this. I should like to know what you think.'

I came out of the pantry with some bread, cheeses, cold meats and the leftovers from some of the pies.

'Are these your famous pies?' he handed me a glass and we clinked.

'Yes, they are the winter varies; beef and mushrooms, pigeon and chestnuts.'

'I have been looking forward to trying some, but come, tell me what you think of the wine.'

'Why should you care about that?'

'You must have a much more refined palate than an old sea dog like me.'

'Not so very old,' I allowed myself to say before sipping the madeira. 'It's very good, nice and fruity and light. It would go very well with a salmagundi or maybe a fruit pie. I am sure we can put it to good use here. So, what do you think of my pies?'

I stopped, wondering if I was babbling.

He generously praised the texture of the pastry and the richness of the meat, as well as the surprise of the mushrooms and nuts and how much better it made everything taste.

'And how goes the house?' he asked.

'Well,' I said. 'We have a new family of lodgers taking both rooms for two months in the New Year and Mrs Pemberton and Miss Atwell said they would both like to return.'

'Cheers to that,' he said and we drank again.

'How is the other house in Portsmouth?'

'Not as nice as this one, but good enough and the family are tidy and punctual with their rent.'

'What more could you ask for?'

'Pies?' he said and I smiled.

'How is everything else?'

'Amelia is still in Brighton.'

'Driscoll mentioned he saw her in Bath.'

'Did he hope for an attachment?'

'I think he did. At first I thought it was just a flirtation, but I think he became very fond of her.'

'Oh,' I said. I had almost forgotten about his interest in Amelia when he'd stayed at the hotel since so much had happened since then. I took another drink of wine. 'You must think me a very terrible mother but she is chaperoned, I have written asking for her return months ago-'

'I shall not be on shore very long or I would have taken you to Brighton myself, however if she does not return shortly perhaps you should go. You could even not pay rent for that month-'

'Who could manage the place?'

'Could Miss Fitzwilliam?'

'Well, no, you see she is busy.'

'At the shop?'

'Not quite, but she is in employment.'

He raised his eyebrows.

'It is a respectable line of work ...' I trailed off. He once said he had no problem with Lydia dressing as a boy for her father's funeral but masquerading as one for a career could sound absurd, lewd and dangerous.

'She is assisting a doctor, but I won't say more without her.'

'I am sure between us we can muster some friends to cover for your absence should you decide to travel to Amelia in the new year.'

We picked at the food and ate in silence for a while until I saw a small parcel on the table I had missed. He saw me look at it and I blushed, embarrassed for my nosiness but he pushed it towards me.

'I found it in a shop in Portsmouth, have a look.'

I opened the canvas wrapping and saw a small book written in a language I couldn't read. I looked at him quizzically.

'This is for you, but it is not an unselfish gift. It's an Italian cookbook. In your letter you wanted to know about macaroni and cheese, the recipe is in there. I can help you translate it.'

'You speak Italian?'

'Very poorly, mostly slang if I'm honest-' we chuckled. 'But I have been trying to teach myself to read it so I have dictionary and a phrase book.'

He told me in his letters he tried macaroni and cheese in a restaurant in London and had it a few times in his childhood, his grandmother cooked it on particularly good Easters – good, I guessed, because cheese and eggs could be afforded. His letters described the rich melted cheese and the silky pasta as clear as if it happened yesterday.

'A lot of pressure for me to get it right.'

He laughed. 'I could count the amount of times I've eaten it on one hand, and honestly the last one poor Nonna made she burnt it.'

'So as long as I don't burn it.'
'Even if you do, you can always blame the translator.'

Amelia

Betsey looked up from her letter as we lunched together.

'Mrs Davison is coming to Brighton,' she groaned. 'We shall have to meet with her I'm afraid.'

'What is wrong with that?' I asked. 'She is your friend.'

She smiled smugly. 'We move in rather different circles now. Mrs Davison's father was a school master.'

Her husband was a butcher's son who did well for himself in the navy, and from what I could tell for all the talk of Betsey's parents being rich, they were rather poor as far as plantation owners went and she was their youngest child. I did not say any of this however, I actually found myself pleased at the thought of seeing Mrs Davison.

'Well, I could entertain her if you have plans with your honourable.'

Betsey laughed. 'Oh you are sweet.' She planted a kiss on my cheek and swept from the room. 'Don't forget the ball tonight. Mr Snowden is losing interest in you, I fear! You ought make an effort, he deserves something for all the gifts he's given you.'

Gifts in his taste which I had not asked for and which had mostly dried up. I knew there was no point answering Betsey but I did not mind, I was happy in my solitude for now.

I headed off for my walk. The weather was a lot colder now but I filched Betsey's furs, and tried to make myself believe it was bracing rather than bitter. I wondered what Mama and Lydia were up to and hoped the next post would bring word of them.

When I arrived home a few hours later Mrs Davison was sitting in the parlour, with a flustered Betsey and a bored viscount's son.

'Amelia!' Betsey leapt up when I entered. 'Mrs Davison's letter got waylaid on route, so you see she is here already only The Honourable Mr Fontaine and I are expected elsewhere, but now you are here the problem is solved.'

'Good day to you, Mrs Davison, I hope your journey was comfortable.'

'As much as can be expected,' she said distractedly looking at Betsey, who was already being helped into her pelisse by Ines, as the viscount's son put on his hat.

'Well, I am sure you have much to acquaint each other with, I shall see you both soon.'

With that Betsey and the viscount's son hurried from the room, the door slamming carelessly behind then. Mrs Davison frowned, and moved to the window where she tweaked back the curtain to watch them drive away. I asked Ines for some tea, even if Mrs Davison didn't want any I needed warming up.

Mrs Davison sat back down, with a look of dejection. 'So, the rumours are true?'

'Rumours?' I asked.

'That our dearest Bee has formed an attachment to that rake,' Mrs Davison hesitated, looking at me imploringly despite what she had just witnessed.

I nodded. 'Nothing is confirmed yet, or at least I do not think it is, but as you can see there is an attachment worthy of gossip.'

Mrs Davison sat forward and whispered. 'This might be indelicate – especially given your youth-' I stopped my eyes rolling at her patronising comment. 'Do you suppose she is his mistress?'

'I …' I shrugged. 'I do not think it is long before she will be.'

Mrs Davison sat back. 'She always did have this foolish romantic streak. She married Captain Webster against her parents' wishes you know. She thought she was ever so in love with him at the time, and that she was so daring for marrying socially beneath herself, but I rather think in material terms her husband is not a poor man.'

'No. He did well on prize money, or so his mother said.'

'If she doesn't stop now she will be quite undone,' Mrs Davison sighed. 'And the folly of it, she is supposed to be chaperoning you! Oh dear.'

Mrs Davison stood up and started to pace. 'I must be frank Miss Amelia, though our acquaintance is only a short one, rumours are starting to circulate about Mr Snowden and a young woman from trade. Is that yourself?'

I swallowed, blushing with embarrassment. 'Betsey would like it to be and for a time I think he liked it to be as well but now I think his affections lay elsewhere.'

'And you have done nothing untoward?'

'No.'

Mrs Davison looked around the room.

'Are you often alone these days?'

I nodded.

'Come to me tomorrow afternoon, I shall arrange to have you sent home. We can both try and persuade Betsey to join you but if not I promise I will get you home at least.'

Relief flooded over me in waves, bringing tears to my eyes. I had not realised quite how badly I longed for home. 'Mrs Davison, you are so kind!'

*

That afternoon I set to packing. I had Ines take the dresses Betsey lent me back to her wardrobe, and I sold the two ball gowns Mr Snowden bought me to a reach down shop for a good price, before taking some of the jewellery to a pawn shop to have it valued.

The dealer eyed me in my morning garb and offered condolences. I realised he assumed I was freshly bereaved, selling off the family jewels.

'Dear me,' he said as he examined the jewelled necklaces under a magnifying glass. 'These two are paste you know.'

I felt sick, I thought them diamonds and sapphires, Mr Snowden told me so. 'Would they be worth anything?'

'A little,' he said. 'This ivory bracelet, ruby pendent and broach are quite valuable on the other hand and this one-' he held up the large pearl necklace with the coat of arms Mr Snowden had draped on my neck at the ball he threw for my birthday. 'Is real and quite old I think.'

I nodded as he told me his price. It was not as much as I'd foolishly allowed myself to believe, but it was a good amount. I decided jewels would be easier to transport than money, so sold him the paste ones as well as the ivory bracelet and left. Once back at the apartment, I sewed the pendent, broach and pearl necklace into the hems and lining of my clothes before packing.

As I manoeuvred my case into the parlour there was a knock at the door. Ines hurried past to answer it.

'Has Mrs Webster not been home all day?' I asked her, glancing at the clock which showed it quarter past six.

'No Miss,' she said as she opened the door to reveal Mr Snowden, red faced and worse for wear.

'There you are!' he exclaimed, barging past Ines.

'Sir-'

'Do not worry Ines,' I said straightening up, uneasiness creeping up my spine. 'But pray, would you please stoke the fire and perhaps dust the mantelpiece?'

'But miss ' she looked from me to Mr Snowden as he stumbled across the parlour. 'Of course.'

'You know what everyone is saying, don't you?' he asked.

'What is that?'

He sat on the sofa and patted the place next to him. 'Talking about your Mrs Webster and my friend Marmaduke.'

'Yes, I heard something.'

'How nice and free and easy it must be for them.'

'Depends on your view of nice.'

'When did you become such a prude?'

I shrugged.

'Come,' he said, still patting the space next to him. 'Sit next to me.'

'No thank you, I think you ought to be going-'

Quicker than I would have thought he grabbed my wrist and yanked me to sit down next to him. The ornaments Ines was dusting clattered.

'Let go of me-'

'Why?'

I swallowed, my mouth dry with fear. 'Please let go of me.'

'Why? I bought and paid for you.'

'What on earth do you mean?'

'What were all those gifts for do you think? Before you turned into a cold fish?'

'I am sorry if I have not behaved to your liking, but I never asked for anything-'

'But you took my gifts! Now let me-'

He went to push me back onto the sofa. 'Sir please! What about Miss Butchart?'

'Oh her, just like you. Another damn cold fish. Hang the lot of you, teasing me, leading me on-'

'I didn't mean to, I didn't realise-' I yanked myself free, ripping the sleeve of my dress. One of the ornaments smashed as Ines hurried to my side.

'If Marmaduke may have Betsey, then I will have you-'

He sprung up, but I leapt back and at last his drunkenness started to inhibit him as he staggered. Arms linked with Ines, I ran into the corridor, slamming the door behind me. Lord, that would hardly hold! Would he be put off by making a scene for the neighbours? With Betsey's behaviour maybe they would just ignore it, thinking I was his woman anyway. Ines produced the key from her apron as his footsteps and curses rumbled towards the door. She quickly locked it.

'It won't hold him for ever,' she said as we hurried away.

As I walked through the streets towards Mrs Davison's address it started to sleet and I only wore my dress, slippers and a borrowed shawl. I saw Ines to a townhouse where her cousin was a lady's maid so she could seek refuge for the night. The cousin lent me a shawl before closing the door, clearly doubting my story and inferring with every raise of her eyebrows that I was Mr Snowden's mistress.

'Remember to bring that shawl back!' were her parting words.

The cold was piercing, chilling me through to my bones, my slippers were leaking water that was sharp with cold. I found that I was weeping, and I couldn't stop no matter how much I scolded myself. Nothing too bad had happened, I had gotten away. Of course he wasn't following me…was he? What a naïve fool I had been in Bath to accept gifts from him, I should have known it would all end horribly. He spent money on me, maybe it wasn't so wrong that he expected something, maybe I was just a silly, selfish, fool…there was no maybe about it. I shivered. I must stay alert, lest he was following me, or in case of any other braggart – a few undesirables shouted lewd comments at me from a tavern.

'Oi!' yelled a woman of the night near the theatre, where I paused among the crowds going in to catch my breath. 'This is my spot!'

Horrified, I hurried on. What must I look like in this tattered shawl, wandering alone in the evening? The bitter chill was moving up my shins, causing my legs to feel heavy and numb, my fingers and face as well. I was nearly there, I knew the street name from my walks. It was not as well-to-do as where I had been living, but it was respectable. In fact, when I stopped outside, a warmth rose in my chest. It looked so much like *home*, not The Fitzwilliam, but the lodging house.

I hammered on the door and a scowling woman answered.

'We don't do handouts–'

'I'm looking for Mrs Davison,' I managed through chattering teeth.

'Mrs Davison?'

'Yes.'

'And who are you to the master's sister-in-law?'

'I am her friend, Miss Amelia Fitzwilliam. I was supposed to call tomorrow, but something has happened, something very alarming. Please may I see her?'

'How alarming?'

'Please may I see Mrs Davison?'

'Hmm, wait here.'

She shut the door in my face. The joy dissipated into more tears. What if she did not fetch Mrs Davison? What if Mrs Davison changed her mind? The door opened again, with Mrs Davison peering behind the old woman's shoulder.

'Oh goodness! You poor dear, come in. We shall put you to bed straight away and Mrs Smith here will send you up some dinner-'

Gratefully I stumbled through the door.

The next morning, after a deep sleep I awoke with a slight fever so Mrs Davison told me to stay in bed; she would arrange for my luggage to be fetched and the tatty shawl returned to Ines' prickly cousin. I was too tired to argue, so slept again for the rest of the morning. Mrs Smith, the housekeeper bought me my lunch at midday, followed by Mrs Davison who handed me a letter once we were alone. There was no address, simply my name in Betsey's elegant hand.

'What is this?'

'I do not know,' Mrs Davison replied. 'But your rooms were empty this morning, even Betsey's belongings were gone.'

'How queer, what does the letter say?'

Mrs Davison shrugged. 'I have not opened it.'

I smiled at the thought of what Lydia would have done and opened it myself. The smile vanished as I read the letter.

'She has run off to London with Mr Fontaine!' I gasped.

'To live as his mistress?' whispered Mrs Davison.

I nodded.

'Heavens, has she told Captain Webster?'

'She doesn't say, she just talks of her love for Fontaine and how they want to be together no matter what. '

'Foolish!' Mrs Davison sat back and shook her head. 'Shocking! She has ruined herself, and nearly you. Do you feel well enough to leave tonight?'

I nodded.

'It is best you pretend you came over here yesterday afternoon and stayed. Do not tell anyone about what happened with Mr Snowden or they shall think you are as bad as her.'

I nodded, a weight settling on me. Ines' cousin had treated me as such contempt, it was not hard to believe others would do the same.

Chapter 23

Lydia

'Good Morning Lydia dear,' said Mama.

I sat up. 'I think I fell to sleep before you followed me up,' I said, so tired that I felt as if I had not slept at all.

'Captain Parnell arrived last night.'

'He is here, now?'

'Yes. He will stay until the next lot of guests arrive.' She perched on the edge of my bed. 'I told him that you were no longer working at Syrett's but did not tell him what you were actually doing. I thought it should be up to you if we tell him the truth or not.'

'He has seen me as a boy before, has he not?'

She nodded. 'And he guessed.'

'Did he?' I asked, surprised.

'Oh,' she smiled. 'Yes, I didn't tell you? He said it was the resemblance to me. At a glance he assumed you might be my nephew or cousin but then he worked it out.'

A spurt of annoyance rouse in me. 'Did that mean everyone else guessed?'

'I doubt it, I expect Henry would have had some words to say on the matter. And I fancy your father's other brothers are not very observant.'

I gave a snort of laughter. 'Or there could be another reason,' I said. 'Captain Parnell noticed me because I look like you, he said it himself.'

A blush rose in her cheeks. 'Oh Lydia, you must not talk so!'

I grinned and she swatted at me, but I found that I did not despise the thought of Captain Parnell liking her, not half as much as I hated the thought of Mr Bradley and Ruby.

When I descended the stairs, I did so in my boyish attire without a coat. Mama was already in the kitchen with the Captain, she pouring coffee whilst they both looked over a battered tome. I'd told her I would tell him the truth but I don't think she realised I would present myself as Hugh Sommers for breakfast. As I stepped into the kitchen they both looked up.

After a pause, Captain Parnell asked. 'And so how exactly is it you make your living?'

My mouth was dry, his surprise was apparent and so was his amusement, but I could not tell if that meant approval or not. It was with a sudden terror that I realised how badly I could have endangered the business – if a guest found out what I did there could be quite a scandal.

I licked my dry lips. 'I am an apprentice surgeon under Mr Campbell.'

'Does he know-?'

I shook my head.

'What does he call you?'

'Hugh Sommers.'

'Mr Campbell seems very pleased with her so far,' Mother interjected. 'She is capable and able, so why ought she not pursue it?'

'You intend to live as a man for the rest of your days?'

I shrugged honestly, that did seem such a large undertaking. 'I do not know, but I want to how far I can go. I think I should at least be allowed to qualify and then see where that takes me.'

'Mrs Fitzwilliam, I see you are not only the sort of woman who allows her daughter to dress as a boy but to train as a surgeon.'

'Indeed I am, Captain. Does that make me the sort of woman you want to continue in business with?'

After a pause, where the Captain raised an eyebrow and shook his head they both laughed, and it strengthened my belief that there was something between them.

'So,' I ventured, 'I am not to be scolded for bringing disgrace upon the lodging house?'

The Captain gave me an apprising look. 'It is very irregular I dare say, and I cannot offer wholehearted approval but it is hardly my place to scold you when I spent thirteen years pretending to be a protestant.'

I raised my eyebrows but Mother was not surprised by this revelation. They must have had grown closer than I realised. I sat down and Mother poured me coffee.

'I think not enough people are allowed to see how far their ambition can take them,' the Captain said. 'But then, how many changes does one make before one loses oneself?'

'But when you cannot succeed as yourself what choice is there? Despite all the limitations you have faced because of your religion Captain, you are still a man. There are still more options available to you than me.'

'Indeed. It is perhaps society then that should change though, as opposed to the individual.'

I nodded. 'But I doubt that will happen soon. Look how they have lampooned Wollstonecraft instead of heeding her words.'

'This is turning into a Thomas dinner party,' Mother sat down with the plumb cake.

'What patients will you see today?'

'We have some appointments with some of the elderly and the young ones suffering in the winter and we have an open surgery in the afternoon for sailors-'

There came a scraping and the front door opened.

'Who-?'

'Mama?' came Amelia's voice. Mother and I hastened to the parlour and there stood Amelia, looking exhausted, with a coachman setting down her bag. Mother embraced her.

'I am sorry I did not write but I knew I would beat the letter-'

'Do not worry about that, my darling!'

The coachman looked to me for a tip and I realised it was because of my boyish attire so I hasty gave him coin. When he left Amelia stepped back from Mother, looked at me and laughed. 'Goodness Dia, what on earth are you about?'

'I am training to be a surgeon.'

Amelia laughed harder, but not mockingly, only joyfully.

'Why of course you are!' she said, drawing me into an embrace

Amelia

The journey had been over four days, but I had made it; tired and aching back to Bristol. Mama sat me down for a large and welcome breakfast of plumb cake and coffee, with bread, cheese and meat gathered from the larder. Lydia readied herself for her work.

'Why did you not tell me of this in your letters?'

'I was afraid of committing it to paper.'

'And what will you do when you qualify? I am to always have a brother now? Or a cousin from the country? What will we say has happened to my dear sister?'

'I...I do not know.'

With another kiss on the cheek she hurried off to see Mr Campbell.

'Is he at least eligible?' I asked.

'Oh Heavens no,' Mama said. 'He is unmarried, but is quite a gnarled old creature.'

I giggled at her surprising show of meanness and she shrugged.

'He may have taken Lydia on but I think he works her too hard and is very ungentlemanly.'

Speaking of gentlemen, Captain Parnell bid me welcome and left us, although not before I carried out Mrs Davison's request. When I asked how I could repay her kindness, she said that I must remember her and her husband to Captain Parnell. I said I would, realising her motivations for helping me were not entirely selfless. She wanted to help her husband's career by getting in the good graces of a senior officer.

'Mrs Davison, Lt Davison's wife, helped me secure the ride and paid for the cost as Mrs Webster has gone on to London.'

Captain Parnell raised an eyebrow. 'How charitable. I shall see she is reimbursed.'

'No, I can-' Mama started but Captain Parnell raised a hand. 'That is why she did it, Mrs Fitzwilliam, to get my attention. I'll deal with it.'

'It was a good thing, what she did,' I said.

He nodded. 'I shall treat it so. Good day to you, ladies.' With that he left us.

Mama sat opposite me as I gorged myself on the breakfast which was more welcome to me than all the pastries and cakes in Brighton; indeed I had forgotten how good her food was.

'My darling,' she said. 'Have you lost weight?'

'A little,' I said. '

'How are you?'

'Good,' I said. 'Glad to be home.'

She reached over and pressed my hand. 'Did anything particular cause your trip to end so abruptly?'

The truth hovered at my lips as I looked at her eyes, and I had a childish urge to tell her but what would that achieve? It would only worry her and she could do nothing about it now. She might blame me for accepting his presents and not coming home sooner. Or worse she may even blame herself. I swallowed and looked back at my food, I still had not answered her question and a straight out no would not do. I sat back and weighed my words.

'Betsey Webster eloped with the youngest son of a viscount.'

'I beg your pardon?'

'Your ears did not deceive you, Mother.'

Mama raised a hand to her mouth. 'Do the Websters know of this yet?'

'I doubt it. I left as soon as I could, trying to lessen any scandal attached to myself.'

'Though doubtless there will be some.'

'Not as much as if I stayed in Brighton.'

'I thought she seemed increasingly careless, but she has been an even worse chaperon than I feared. Did you suspect anything?'

I hesitated and almost lied, but admitted the truth. 'I knew as soon as we left for Brighton that there was a flirtation between her and the viscount's son, but I never expected this would happen.'

'And you went to Brighton anyway? That was why you did not write to me wasn't it?'

I nodded, shame filling me. 'I do not know what I was thinking, only very foolishly that I wanted to see Brighton. I realise now how silly I was, how silly the whole trip was really. I…'

Her arms were folded, and she looked crosser than I'd seen her since we argued the morning we went to see the HMS Aries.

'That was so irresponsible of you, I do not care if she was supposed to be the chaperon, you must have known then she was doing a bad job. Could you not have stayed with Mrs Tindal or just come home? We could have raised the money.'

My shame was causing the colour to rise in my cheeks. 'I…' I wrung my hands, searching for a way to explain my folly and the actions which now seemed like those of an entirely different person. 'I do not know why I behaved so, only that I felt a mixture of being half asleep but also in a rush to experience as much as I could.'

'And was it all as dazzling as you expected it to be?'

'No,' I said. 'Not at all. Different maybe, not all bad, but it didn't make me feel any better.'

'Better?' her expression softened. 'Better,' she repeated, not only understanding what I meant but also making me understand. All the follies in Brighton and Bath had not cured the ache of Father's death, nothing ever would. It would always be with me and I would not be the girl I was before, nor this girl I had been trying to be. I must become someone else.

Tears burnt my throat but I swallowed. 'I think I am going to lie down now.' I kissed her cheek and stood. 'I am glad to be home.'

'And I am glad to have you home.'

Lydia

When I finished work that evening, it was late after another busy day, but Mother and Amelia had waited up for me. I dined on stew whilst they chatted about their day. Amelia told me of the scandal of Betsey Webster and Mother said she did not think the Websters knew about it yet but she was unsure if it was her place to tell them.

'Amelia could have come home on her own accord,' I said.

'Yes but it feels rather dishonest and they have been good to us.'

'Some of the boys saw father gambling,' I remembered. 'Mrs Webster said that. And they never told us.'

'Yes, but she said she wished they had,' Mother said.

I shrugged.

'When they know Amelia is home, they will know we know and I feel no desire to shield Betsey from them.'

I nodded. 'Then I suppose you must tell them.'

Her conscience assumedly cleared, Mother fell asleep quickly. Next to me, Amelia tossed and turned.

'Not tired?'

'I slept a lot today,' she whispered. 'I only woke up in the late afternoon.'

'Very nice.'

'Yes, but not so nice now,' she paused. 'When I came downstairs, Mama and Captain Parnell were chatting, thick as thieves.'

'Hmm, they do that,' I said keeping my voice low. 'They wrote to each other while he was away with such frequency. I think it cannot all have been business.'

Amelia propped herself up on her elbow. 'Truly?'

'Yes.'

'So you think there is an attachment brewing between them?'

'Maybe,' I said. 'I do not think either of them has been inappropriate at all, nor has there been any suggestion of anything like that, always 'Mrs Fitzwilliam' and 'Captain Parnell.''

Amelia stifled a giggle and Mother stirred. 'C'mon,' I hissed, taking her arm and we snuck into the hall.

'Is he here?' I asked, looking towards his room as I light a rush light.

Amelia shook her head. 'No, he went to a naval dinner or some such. He did not invite her as his guest.'

'Maybe he does not want to presume to much.'

'She is still in mourning, he should not presume anything at all,' Amelia said, her rag tied hair bobbing up and down as she spoke. 'He is not much like Papa, is he?'

'No,' I said. 'Not at all. Not in looks, or background or mannerisms and his politics couldn't be more different.'

'Is that so?'

'I expect had he been born a gentleman he would have been a dissenter, but as it is he must work for a living.'

'I expect that makes you like him then.'

'Of course.'

'If he had been born a gentleman, he might play at being a dissenter but no true gentleman can be a dissenter, they are all too lazy and vacuous.'

'Oh!' I gave a low chuckle. 'Spoken from experience.'

'Yes,' she said sharply. 'So, what do we really now of him? Even if there is no affection, I think we ought know a little about the man whose house we are living in.'

I nodded, pleased she was now here to be the lookout.

'If he comes back, cough. And we can say since the other spare room was empty we were in there gossiping so not to disturb Mother.'

Amelia grinned, nodded then went to stand at the top of the stairs. I lit my own rush light and crept along the corridor. Carefully I pushed his bedroom door open. It gave a louder creak than I would have liked, but I slipped inside.

All was neat and minimal. There was a leather satchel on the desk with a pile of books, shaving things by the wash basin, a trunk and that seemed to be it. Investigation of the trunk proved fruitless, it had already been unpacked. I opened the wardrobe and saw clean uniforms and a couple of civilian suits, with a pair of boots. I patted down the clothes and found they concealed nothing.

In the satchel, tied in string were letters from my mother. I skimmed over a few of them – very happy in tone, praising how I helped her which I felt guilty about now I was prying, speaking of Amelia's gossip, small paragraphs on the business and then anything else that seemed to occur to her, food, gossip, fashions, news items, books – they were not love letters but they were extremely friendly and as they went on their tone became increasingly warm and familiar…and he, who seemed to have so few other possessions – no trinkets, no ornaments, no letters from anyone else, had kept them. Next to them were pamphlets about life in Australia and the Americas. I tensed. Was he thinking of going? Where would that leave us and the lodging house? Finally, there was a slim book. I opened it. Accounts!

He had owned a house in Liverpool, run by a Mrs Marks, which was now sold, and a house in Portsmouth from which he seemed to make tidy profit. It seemed as though he had very few outgoings, no debts or creditors, and my eyes rounded quite a bit at the amount he had made prize money from 'heads and guns', ships won in previous battles. What did he intend for the rest of his substantial fortune? Then my finger stopped, there was page for outgoings after all, only these outgoings, fairly modest though they were, all went to one person in quarterly payments. Mrs Parnell. I swallowed. He had definitely not said he was married, and he said his mother was dead…so what did that mean? That he had lied?

'Lydia!'

I looked up to see Mother, ashen faced and framed in the doorway. Amelia coughed and scurried over from the top of the stairs, her jaw dropping at the sight of Mother, whose expression turned to fury. I shoved the book back in bag, then the three of us hurried back to our bedroom. We waited it silence as his quiet footsteps sounded on the staircase and the door of his bedroom opened and closed. Amelia was wide-eyed, looking halfway to laughing but Mother's cold expression put a stop to that.

'Well?' Amelia asked.

'I-'

'No,' Mother said. 'I don't want to hear it.'

Then she blew out the rush light and in darkness we got into bed.

Jessica

I did not sleep well that night. By Amelia's breathing I could tell that she fell asleep quickly and Lydia was not far behind. Perhaps I should have let them tell me before sleep what had been uncovered, it was my own fault that they thought they could pry.

But I thought he had been honest and upfront, yet judging by Lydia's face and her keenness to tell me, there was somethings that he neglected to tell me. I swallowed as I heard his feet on the stairs; they were quiet, the kind of footsteps which leant themselves to sneaking about; dishonesty and crime. He may well be an officer in the navy now but he'd come a long way from where he'd started. Social climbing would be a lot easier if one was dishonest... I tossed and turned, listening as he moved quietly around his room, the creaking floorboards giving him away for otherwise he did not make a sound – not crashing into things and cursing as Peter had done after a night out.

When sleep came it was fractured and I dreamt I was alone in the house, with no news as to where the girls or Captain Parnell was so I set out in a panicked search for them. As I looked, I grew older and my clothes became more ragged. When I did find the HMS Aries it took a while for me to persuade the sailors to let me on. Below deck, it was no longer a navy ship but a gambling den – or at least how I imaged one to be; dark, smoky, reeking of spirits and sweat, with loose women hanging off men. In the midst of it all my daughters, my husband and Captain Parnell played at cards – all ignoring my presence, even when I pleaded with the girls to come with me. When I left the ship, I tried to get home but found no trace of the house or The Fitzwilliam anywhere.

I awoke with a start to find Amelia still sleeping but Lydia dressing. Lydia looked at me with her eyebrows raised.

'Sorry I looked through his room last night-'

I held up my hand. 'I understand why you did it, but you caught me by surprise. So,' I sat up and drew a deep breath. 'What did you uncover?'

She sat next to me. 'I am not sure. A few things, all which could mean something or nothing.'

'Yes?'

This, it seemed, was enough to wake Amelia up who rolled over and propped herself up.

'Pamphlets about life in the Americas and Australia.'

'There is nothing wrong in that. He is a sailor, there could be hundred reasons why he has such things.' I spoke with confidence but the news jolted me. Why had he not told me that? If he left the country what would that mean for the house …and our friendship? I ought not be surprised, those who go to settle in such places are either down on their luck dreamers, or ambitious hard workers who find the barriers of class and religion prevent them from truly succeeding in Britain. He was very much the latter. But yet, why had he not confided these ideas in me if that was the case?

'When I looked in his account book…'

My stomach knotted.

'He owned a house in Liverpool run by a Mrs Marks-'

'She was his aunt,' I said quickly, relieved I could explain that away.

'He sends quarterly payments to a Mrs Parnell.'

'Scoundrel!' said Amelia.

My mouth went dry and for a moment I felt as if I'd been hit. I breathed through my nose trying to centre myself.

'He said his mother was dead? And his father's family, did he not?' Lydia said.

'Yes.'

'So he must have a secret wife-' Amelia whispered.

I wet my lips. 'There could be another explanation.'

'What?'

'I do not know…' I reply, feeling dizzy. He had no provision for her when he had drawn up the legal papers for this place yet…yet…if he was married, why ought I care? But as his friend at least he should have told me, even if he'd married her in youth and folly I deserved to know.

I stood up, feeling the worry and panic whirling inside of me.

'You have put me in an impossible position for how am I to challenge him about this without saying you have been going through his things?'

The girls looked blankly at me.

'I must make breakfast,' I said and started to dress, dreading the thought of seeing his face.

As I toasted yesterday's bread and made the porridge I wondered how I could broach the topic. We had never discussed our romantic histories. I was obviously a widow who had married young, but he was a bachelor and a sailor. Anything could have happened. A vision of foreign beauties suddenly washed over me; fashionable French ladies, exotic bibis, Irish girls with bright red hair, Spaniards clad is black lace…there was a pain in my chest, like a clawed hand squeezing, which was not the sort of feeling one was supposed to have if one's friend or business partner turned out to be married.

On our first night in this kitchen I was sure he'd said he was not married, but then how had he phrased it? Maybe he was just an outright liar so had not told me about his wife for his own reasons though I wasn't sure what they could be. Maybe she was sickly or mad…

'Good morning,' he said as he entered the kitchen.

I forced a smile. 'How was your dinner?'

'Very good. There were some officers I had not seen in a good few years.'

I nodded. 'They were all in good health? Any marriages or children in the intervening years?'

'A few,' he said.

I nodded. 'Did they find you much changed?'

'No, they said not. They all said they would ask their wives to find me a wife, despite me not asking for it.'

'You do not wish to be married?'

He hesitated. Did he not wish to be married because he was?

'It is not that, maybe one day, but I have no wish to be set up with someone. I want to reach a certain standard before I marry.'

'A certain standard?'

'I would like to be able to support my wife in comfort.'

'You have always thought this way?'

'For the most part. And I fancy my friend's wives would set me up with girls. I have no wish to marry a girl, I should like a woman closer to my own age. Marriage should be a partnership, which does not seem attainable with a young girl.'

'So you want to be able to support a wife, but from what you say she would have a hand in your affairs?'

'I suppose that is true,' he said. 'I would not want her to work because we have to, because of a fear of poverty, rather I would want to have enough money so she did not have to worry, but that if she wanted a hand in my affairs she could so without the stress of everything coming apart. Does that make sense?'

I nodded. 'It does,' I said, thinking it did better than just making sense, it sounded wonderful. And yet, was this another lie? If this was what he believed, and he was apparently well known as a confirmed bachelor among his fellows, who on earth was Mrs Parnell?

Chapter 24

Amelia

The next few days proved to be busy ones. Lydia worked dawn 'til dusk, and the upkeep of the house required cleaning of the kitchen and parlour as well as cooking which I helped Mama with. Captain Parnell had ship matters to attend to. I tried to watch him closely but discreetly. There seemed no hint that he had a secret wife; all letters which arrived for him looked official and he opened them at the breakfast table. There was nothing but unwavering friendship and warmth towards Mama - which while was not inappropriate, might have been if either were married.

Mama received word that not only had her previous lodger and friend Miss Atwell inherited a substantial amount from the will she had been chasing down, but she hoped to stay with us for a few days over Christmas before she set off on a tour of Europe, so I helped Mama prepare Miss Atwell's room. Every time the post came I was nervous that it would be a letter from Mr Snowden even though I had left him no forwarding address, but if he wanted one all he had to do was ask Betsey Webster. That woman was a pressing problem which to be dealt with. On my third day back, Mama and I could avoid it no more and she said we must pay Mrs Webster a visit and break the news, if it was not already known.

As we walked across town, I tried to come up with various ways to tell Mrs Webster.

'Maybe I could say I did not realise when I left-'

'No-'

'Maybe I could say I did not know who she went off with-'

'No-'

'Maybe I could say I did not know for most of the time what she was up to with the viscount's son-'

'Is that true?'

'No.'

'Well then, do not say it. I think we must be honest. The Websters are forthright people, and lord knows must have been on the other side of this kind of nonsense with their sons.'

'Mama!' I gasped.

'Well, 'tis true,' she sighed.

'I had not heard you own to it before.'

'I am not so blind Amelia, I just choose not to dwell on unpleasantness or at least, I used to have that luxury.'

When we arrived, Bertha let us inside.

'I shall just fetch Mrs Webster for you,' she said as she opened the parlour door. 'You will be pleased to see Captain Richard Webster is back with us.' She lowered her voice and smiled. 'I did think you might bring news of his wife …' she waited for me to respond but when I said nothing she merely raised her eyebrows and stepped back, allowing us entrance to the parlour.

As her footsteps faded away, Richard stood to greet us. In looks, he was one of the more middling Webster brothers, though his uniform and a scar under his eye from his naval adventures gave him a rather dashing edge. As the second eldest he had more maturity and gravity than some of the younger, flightier ones. I bit my lip. Betsey had picked a good Webster to simply cast aside.

'Mrs Fitzwilliam, how long has it been? Three years at least! I was sorry for your loss, but you look well.'

'Thank you-'

'And Miss Amelia, dear Millie I think we called you as a girl - but you are all grown up now. My wife sings your praises, you are quite her bosom friend, I hear. Where is she? The last letter I had was dated two weeks since and she said she was still in Brighton.'

'When did you return sir?'

'Only a few days ago. I think I will go to Brighton to seek her out. I wrote this morning to tell her so. I am keen to meet these school friends she speaks so well of.'

'Richard,' Mama said gently. 'Captain Webster, perhaps you ought to sit down.'

He looked between us, confused.

'Had something befallen my wife?'

'Not exactly,' I said and Mama shot me a look. We sat and heard his mother upon the stairs. I thought such a man might be mortified to have such a tale related to him before his mother, it seemed to degrade him even more.

'Dickie,' I said using his childhood nickname and speaking quickly so to get it out before Mrs Webster barged in. 'Betsey has – Betsey met someone. A man, a third son of a viscount-'

Richard paled.

'I am sorry, but she has gone to London with him, that is why I have come home.'

Captain Webster's face tensed.

'Good Morning ladies-' Mrs Webster smiled as her son stood up and stormed over to the window. 'What on earth has happened?' she asked, her voice high pitched. 'Is it Betsey?'

'Yes,' Captain Webster said and slammed his hand against the window frame making me jump. 'Yes, it damn well is Betsey.'

'Is she-'

'She has run off with another man, according to Millie at least.'

Mrs Webster looked at me.

'Is this true?'

'Yes Madam.'

'Well, what did you do to prevent it?'

I blinked. 'Nothing – well, I made it obvious I did not think much of Mr Fontaine-'

Mama stood. 'If you could remember Betsey was supposed to be my daughter's chaperone, not the other way round. She left Amelia to make her way back to Bristol alone.'

Mrs Webster blinked rapidly then hastened to her son, tried to lay her hands on his shoulders but he shrugged her off and rounded on me.

'The braggart she has gone off with is a Mr Fontaine?'

'Yes. The Honourable-'

Captain Webster gave a bitter bark of laughter.

'-Mr Marmaduke Fontaine, son of The Viscount of Avon.'

'You know where she went?'

'London.'

'London is a big place. Can you think of where?'

I wet my dry lips, my heart pounding. 'Bloomsbury,' I said quietly.

Captain Webster yelled for Bertha to fetch pen and paper and then stood over me whilst I wrote the viscount's son's name as well as a list of places in London which he had boasted to frequent, as well as houses his family owned.

'I think that is quite enough,' Mama said. 'I shall take Amelia home now.'

Mrs Webster nodded. 'Yes, and thank you,' she pressed Mama's hand. 'For coming to us with this. Please do not tell anyone else – not the Thomases', certainly not the Hughes or…your navy man. It would not do for the other officers to know of this.'

'Captain Parnell is not my navy man.'

Mrs Webster raised her eyebrow. 'I will see you soon, I think things will get unpleasant here.'

Captain Webster was calling for his coat. 'I will go to the butchers',' he said. 'Then my brothers and I shall ride to London and seek them out. I think I could even get some *trusted* friends from the navy-'

'We do not want word of this to spread-'

'Mother, I will have her back, do you hear me? I will have her back if only to give her a hiding! She will be punished for this! And I will call him out, damn him!'

Mama took my arm and we hastened from the house.

'I did not think the Webster boys would march on London for her,' I said.

Mama sighed. 'What did you expect?'

'Why did we tell them then if they will beat her?'

'They deserved to know. I would rather someone had told me about your father, even if I could not beat him. Married couples ought not lie to each other, they ought not betray each other. Come on. It is up to them now.'

I hurried behind her, mulling over her words. 'You ought not compare Papa to Betsey-'

Mama spun around. 'Why? Because he did not run off with a viscount's daughter? He still betrayed me, Amelia. Richard Webster may have been cuckolded, his honour may have taken a blow but he still has his own money, he can still work, he will not be cast from his lodgings. Because of what your father did I lost a lot more than my honour, I lost everything, twenty years of my life's work, so do not tell me that Papa was better than that silly girl. He was different, but he was thoughtless and selfish just the same and I have suffered more than Richard Webster will.'

With that she marched off, and I hastened to keep up, stunned into silence and for the first time feeling a fool for not viewing father's actions in that way.

Jessica

Back at home, Amelia was quiet but set to helping me with the housework and readying Miss Atwell's room. Captain Parnell came home for a lunch of mock turtle soup and told us he would be dining out in the evening.

'Any one we know?' Amelia asked.

'You might Miss Amelia, do you know the Donnells? They are friends of the Davisons?'

'I do not know the Donnells, though I think I may have heard them spoken of.'

'Perhaps another time I could introduce you all.'

'But not tonight?'

'No, it is to be a small party tonight,' he said. 'Captain Donnell has contrived to introduce me to his cousin Miss Donnell.'

I tensed. 'One of the young ladies they are trying to match you with?'

'I think so.'

'And what does she have to recommend her?' Amelia asked.

'Amelia!'

'I do not mind. She has been described as very pretty by several people, a good reader and is called pious-'

Amelia laughed and the captain raised his eyebrows mockingly. 'Of all the words to choose,' he mused with a smile. 'Pious does not strike me as particularly complimentary.'

'You would not want a devout wife?'

'Pious and devout seem two different things.'

'Indeed,' Amelia paused. 'But then do they mean she is Catholic? Surely they would not sell you a pious protestant?'

'Lord I hope not,' he laughed along with Amelia.

'I fear,' she said 'A pious Catholic lady would be more glamorous than a pious protestant. At least a Catholic would come wrapped in black lace. A pious protestant is a very austere creature.'

'Does this idea come from your gothic novels?'

'Indeed, what other way could I possibly have to inform me of the world?'

'Very good, Miss Amelia. You are not to be patronised I see, accept my apologies-'

Of course Miss Donnell was Catholic. I suddenly felt very stupid that I had not even considered the real difficulty a difference in our religions would cause. I gripped my spoon. A greater worry was still the mysterious Mrs Parnell. And…why should I care anyway? But it was a folly to even argue with myself this way, when it was obvious I did care, at least a little.

'- She is only one and twenty, which to many seems welcome but I think it rather a hindrance.'

'Surely you are not so much older,' Amelia smiled and I felt a flush of anger wondering when my youngest daughter had become so confident with men.

'Come now Miss Amelia, I am fifteen years older than her.'

'Age gaps are not unusual. Papa was twenty years older than Mama.'

Did she mean to give him licence to like a younger woman, or remind everyone I was a widow or both? Either way I lost my appetite.

Lydia

Mr Campbell eyed the elderly patient, then looked to the man's grown son.

'You think this damp place is a suitable space for an invalid?'

'Well, no sir but it is all we have-'

'You would do well to keep him warm as best you can-' As Mr Campbell spoke the man's chest rattled with another cough, prompting him to produce a glass bottle from his case.

'Give him two doses in the morning and evening, but it will cost extra-'

'Will it help?'

'Undoubtedly. He needs all the help he can get stuck in this wretched place.'

The son quickly handed over enough coin for two bottles and we headed off.

'What was that medicine?' I asked. There was no label and I had not seen it before.

'Boiled water, a fist full of herbs and a dash of gin.'

That was not a concoction I had heard of. 'What does it do?'

Dr Campbell shrugged. 'It might take the edge off but I doubt there is even enough gin in there for that.'

I stopped in my tracks, despite the cold, wet street. 'So you sold him a lie?'

He looked at me eyebrows raised. 'You don't have to put it like that,' he said. 'Sometimes a bit of hope does the trick, you know. And besides, it won't hurt. The family think we've done their best.'

'But you haven't, we could have researched some new methods-'

'Found the elixir of life, have you?' he gave a snort. 'He's old and sickly. He's going to die, a little bit of hope doesn't harm anyone and the extra money helps me out when times are tough.'

'Some of your other medicines…' I said slowly. 'I thought they were genuine but are they watered down?'

He shrugged. 'Some. Most I should say. They don't work anyway.'

'That's not true-'

'It's luck more than anything if those potions work. What good we really do is setting bones and operating, but only then on the strong. The rest will sort itself out.'

I had grown used to his brisk ways but to see him speak so callously still came as a surprise. I turned to go. 'I have a mind to go back and tell those people that you have tricked them!'

He grabbed my arm and pushed me against the wall. 'You do that and I swear to God you'll feel the back of my hand.' He spat in my face as he spoke and his hot breath stunk of spirits and tobacco. 'And that won't be all. I will find out what it is you are hiding, Hugh Sommers.'

He looked at me triumphantly.

'What do you mean?'

'Clever boy like you didn't go to school? Not even on a scholarship or to some two bit house run by a broken down vicar, seems awfully odd. I'd guess that you weren't always poor enough to be uneducated. Did you go and couldn't take the bullying, or are you sick? Your family go bankrupt in some scandal?' He pushed a finger against my skull. 'Sick in the mind? Go do-lally? Or maybe you're a molly, is that it? Though you can't be *that* because I have seen how you sniff around that pretty mulatto-ess of yours…is it something to do with her? Or your pretty little Mama? You aren't someone's bastard are you, Hugh? There has to be a reason you've stuck with me, most people do because they've got no other choice.'

'No!' I exclaimed, my insides tense with dread. 'I don't know what you are talking about!'

'Let's leave it that way, shall we? Don't tell my secrets and I won't try and find out yours.'

He released me and I stumbled away.

'I will see you tomorrow, young man,' he said. 'That is, unless you want me to start digging.'

I hurried off, too shocked to argue or defend myself, afraid any denial would make him realise what my secret really was.

Amelia

Once again Mama and I were left in the house, as one real man and one pretend one went off to work. I found, much to my surprise, I rather liked this rhythm we'd fallen into. I even started on the pile of dress repairs, and asked what had happened about Abigail Hughes' wedding dress. Mama looked up from her mixing bowl, annoyance tensing her brow.

'I would rather you handled that better.'

'I never said I would do it,' I snapped. 'You did and everyone just assumed.'

Mama pursed her lips. 'They found someone else, though Mrs Hughes does not call anymore. I have only seen her at social gatherings and even then she is only just civil.'

'Because of the dress?'

Mama hesitated. 'It was before that I think, as soon as it was revealed we were penniless. I was too caught up to pay it much heed at the time.'

'*I* noticed,' I said. 'So, how was the wedding?'

'Mrs Webster said it was a very showy affair, and Abigail and the groom fawned over each other awfully.' Mama shrugged. 'But I suppose it made them happy.'

'You are too good, Mama.'

'And I fear you might become too wicked.'

She smiled as she spoke and I tried to smile back, squirming inwardly. If only she knew... Just then there was a knock at the door.

'Ah,' Mama said glancing at the clock. 'That will be Miss Atwell I should think.'

She hastened to answer it.

'Hello there Mrs Fitzwilliam!' came a jovial American accent and I stepped into the parlour to see Mama being embraced by a freckled woman a little younger than herself, dressed in a brown riding habit and top hat. She grinned when she saw me.

'You must be Miss Amelia,' she strode towards me beaming.

'I am yes, Miss Atwell I assume.'

She nodded and looked between Mama and I. 'Well, she's even prettier than I imagined! And what a strong resemblance!'

I smiled. 'Everyone says it is Lydia who resembles Mama, not I.'

'Well, Lydia does look like the spit of your mother, but you two do look alike; the hair, even the way you stand and move! You two are so elegant.'

'You are too kind, Miss Atwell,' Mama smiled – and not just the smile she reserved for ordinary guests, but the really warm one that reached her eyes. Still, it was not as glowing as the expression she saved for Captain Parnell.

'We want to hear all of your adventures in the North,' Mama carried on. 'Please sit, I shall fetch us some tea.'

'Do not worry Mama, I shall do that and I'll take Miss Atwell's trunk upstairs. You have much to discuss.'

'Thank you, Amelia.' The two women sat down, happy as little girls. 'So, where did you end up? Was it Manchester?'

'It was and such machines and factories they have up their you would not believe – smoke billowing up into the sky and the noise! I tell you, I took a tour around one-'

'Can you do that?'

'I asked. My, all that whirring and great movement I could not believe, though the conditions they have the workers '

When I came back with the tea, they were deep in conversation about Miss Atwell's second cousin's (for that was who left her the money) lawyer.

'Great big front teeth and pointed whiskers so he looked like a mouse, but an angry mouse. He asked so many questions, all about me and my family history, but at last he was satisfied.'

'And so you inherited?'

She smiled. 'I am so pleased. I thank dear Cousin Alfred in my prayers every night. It was one of those mills he had owned and sold, that was why he was so rich you see, but he never married. I think it's rather nice that the fortune of a bachelor can pass to a spinster, don't you?'

'Indeed,' Mama smiled. 'But you oughtn't call yourself a spinster just yet-'

'Why not? I am proud of it. I am as in charge of my own destiny as a woman can be, and I am not fancy enough to disgrace any relations.'

'An excellent way to view it.'

'Yes,' I said. 'Yes, it is a very interesting way to view it.'

'I fear you are too pretty Miss Amelia, to enjoy spinsterhood.'

I shrugged. 'We are poor though.'

'And so are plenty of folk. Like myself, you never know if you might be in for a windfall.'

Jessica

The next morning Miss Atwell expressed a desire to buy some sheet music for her fiddle so I asked Amelia to take her. Amelia happily agreed, her previous feelings of animosity towards the instrument assumedly forgotten.

'Are you off to the ship today?' I asked Captain Parnell.

'No, I am at my leisure.'

'I wonder if you could give me some assistance with this macaroni then?'

Captain Parnell grinned. 'Of course, though I am not sure how useful I will be. I will fetch the dictionary and join you.'

In the pantry I gathered what I guessed to be the ingredients: to be eggs, flour, cheese and excitement built in me at the thought of cooking a dish so unfamiliar to me. I opened the book and looked over the strange words, trying to form them in my mind.

'Here we are,' he set the battered dictionary down.

'So how much Italian do you actually know?'

'Honestly? Mostly curses,' he gave a chuckle. 'And familial terms; nonno, nonna, zia and such like. My grandmother never spoke English, but apparently she wasn't even speaking Italian but Neapolitan so that is no use, unless we were to find ourselves in Naples.'

'So, you are telling me unless I want swear at a relation, you aren't much good to me?'

'But I do have the dictionary.'

'And you do know what this is supposed to taste like.'

'I will take my duty as taster with utmost seriousness.'

'How does it taste?' I asked. 'Like soft pastry?'

'No, not at all–'

'Surely not like an unrisen loaf?'

'No. It's very hard to compare to any English food. Maybe barley? But even that's not right.'

I smiled, a thrill going through me at the new flavours I would soon try. 'So, how do we begin?'

He read, then flicked through the dictionary. 'Separate the flour?'

'Sieve I imagine.'

'Then add salt.'

'So far so good,' I said as I reached for the sieve.

'Then you need to make a ...'

'Yes?'

'Something to put the eggs in, it says *well* but that can't be right.'

'That is right, see like this.'

'Ah...'

'Let me see,' I asked curiously and dared to read aloud the next sentence in a poor accent, then considered what I'd said. 'Agiatare? Is that to stir or mix?'

'It is, how did you guess?'

'It sounds like to agitate, doesn't it?'

'Any praise I give for your quick mind will seem patronising when I'm relying on this dictionary.'

'I was not seeking the praise of a confessed foul-mouthed rogue.'

'A wise woman.'

After mixing it needed to be left in the larder to cool, so I got to work making the cheese sauce.

'Have you ever been to Italy?'

'No, but I would like to go.'

'Which part would you visit? Naples?'

'Yes, but I would like to see all of it. Florence is supposed to be especially beautiful.'

'Do you think you will?'

'I plan to before I am forty.'

I hesitated at the memory that Lydia had found travel pamphlets in his bag. 'Would you travel anywhere else?'

He fixed his gaze on me. 'Yes. I think I should like to go to Australia or the Americas.'

'To settle?'

He nodded. 'I think there are so many more opportunities there.'

'What of this house?'

'I will not leave you destitute, Mrs Fitzwilliam,' he said gravely. 'Do not worry.'

'But what of the navy?'

'I have gone as far as I can go in the navy. They will not promote me higher. I could maybe take a commission in the navy stationed in Australia or Canada, or I could become a half pay captain The navy was good for me, but it was a means to an end, the only way for me to progress in the world.'

I nodded. 'I see…and what of Miss Donnelly?'

'I do not think she is cut out for making a life in a new world, she seems too delicate.'

My insides were tense as he went back to flicking through the dictionary. Was I cut out for a life in new world? What did it matter? I wasn't sure how I felt about him. He was handsome, he made me laugh, I was always pleased to be around him and looked forward to his letters – when I stopped to think his presence did fluster me but mostly I felt remarkably at my ease with him, able to make jokes and speak my mind, when he wasn't here I was always thinking of things to say to him…but he was a Catholic, I wasn't even sure if we would be allowed to marry without one of us converting. Would he convert again? He wanted to move away and I still had not solved the riddle as to who Mrs Parnell was. I knew him well enough to guess that he did not talk wistfully about things. If he wanted to do something then he would. But then, I grew increasingly restless, I wanted to travel – as Miss Atwell had, as he had – all responsibilities aside, it made me sad to think I should die and never see more of the world than Glastonbury and Bristol.

'I feel foolish for saying this,' I ventured. 'But I am still yet to see London or the fine beaches that are so relatively close to Bristol.'

'The weather could prove for a precarious journey this time of year, but next time I am here we shall take a pony and trap down to Clevedon, that is not so far.'

'Just the two of us?'

He smiled. 'The girls could come if they wished,' he said. 'Or it could be the two of us, after all a widow does not need a chaperone, does she?'

'No,' I said. 'Very well, let us do it when the weather is fine.' And then because she was still worrying around the edges of my thoughts, I said 'But if you are courting Miss Donnell it may not do for you to take me to the seaside.'

'Maybe she could accompany us and you could chaperone her,' for a moment I surprised myself with the quickness of the lead weight that formed in my stomach, the horror that he saw me as a fussy old chaperone but then he chuckled and I laughed, relieved. 'I do not think there is anything between Miss Donnelly and I.'

I saw a chance to enquire about Mrs Parnell, in a roundabout way.

'You must've have courted much to know after so short an acquaintance. What was it, one dinner?'

'I have courted enough.'

'Indeed, but never married?'

He hesitated and my breath caught. 'No, never married. Nearly, once, but the engagement was broken off.'

That was not the answer I had expected or dreaded at all. 'Nearly?' I softened my tone. 'May I ask what happened?'

He shrugged, though I sensed he was trying to look more nonchalant than he felt.

'She decided she would prefer a husband who was not away so much and engaged herself to a legal clerk instead.'

'Oh, I am sorry to hear that,' I lied, trying to conceal how pleased the confession made me.

'I had not intended to become engaged young, but she was the daughter of my Captain and I did love her a great deal. She *liked* me a great deal, but she did love that legal clerk. When I landed in Southampton I headed to her house and saw them together in the street, there was nothing untoward in their behaviour, but I had never seen her so happy and there you are. It was for the best, I think. She would doubtless have grown resentful, and the thought of marrying young and with little money made me anxious.'

'You seem very at peace about it.'

'It has been ten years since,' he laughed.

'I only ever courted Peter,' I said. 'And that was barely a courtship. He noticed me, decided he liked me and that was that. I think it was always my mother's plan for me to marry up and I was happy to oblige. I liked Peter well enough but I suppose loving him came later.'

Captain Parnell nodded. 'So, he was your first love?'

'No,' I realised. 'My first love was Lydia, then Amelia and I loved them both so much, there was so much love in me then that I loved their father.' The further truth that I was afraid to speak aloud was that I could not remember loving Peter, much less liking him, yet I knew that I had, I knew there had been happiness and peace with him, but I could not find it, as though it had slipped out of my hands when I discovered his betrayal. Now all I could remember was his faults, and the times when I had felt bored, alone and listless yet been afraid to acknowledge it.

I looked up at Captain Parnell and he looked down at me with such warmth that I took a step towards him. He set down the dictionary. He reached for my hands; his skin was rough and chapped. Peter's never were; it always amused him that he had softer hands than mine. Captain Parnell held my gnarled cook's hands like they were made of gold.

We moved closer still and I felt the heat from his body, craned my head up to look into his deep brown eyes. A clatter shattered the silence as the front door opened and Amelia and Miss Atwell's loud conversation filled the house. We both knew the few seconds it would take them to cross the parlour to the kitchen; especially if they were removing coats and bonnets so instead of parting, we savoured the last few moments of our near embrace.

'Mama, we are home and what a lark we have had!'

'Indeed, I had that man searching all over his shop-'

We broke apart as they entered the kitchen and I reached for a pan, trying to busy myself.

'Let me make you sandwiches!' I burst.

'What are you cooking?' asked Amelia.

'Macaroni and cheese,' said Captain Parnell.

'Oh, delicious!'

'It will be a while yet, I have yet to make the sauce.'

'We can make our own sandwiches then,' Amelia said. 'You carry on with what you were doing.'

I nodded, stifling a laugh at Amelia's words while the Captain raised an eyebrow at me.

'Very well,' he said and opened the dictionary. I dared to look at him again and he gave me a dashing half smile, unobserved by the others who were raiding the larder. I smiled back.

'So,' he said loudly. 'You need to make a base-'

Chapter 25

Lydia
I often felt like a thief escaping the scene of a crime as I slipped out to work in the morning, a large coat over myself lest the neighbours see my attire.

There were often beggars around, huddled and sleeping. The ladies of the night could sometimes be seen wandering back to their lodgings, along with sailors and rakes all in a dazed manner. Occasionally it would thrill me to see a man dressed sombrely leaving a house with a medical case under his arm – a doctor! I would tip my hat and be delighted when they returned the courtesy as if we were brothers-in-arms.

Aside from them, there were the knocker-uppers and night men, and some eager housewives and servants, cleaning the steps and windows of their homes or shops. Mr Campbell's house was treated to no such washing.

He did not keep a servant, probably for the same reason he did not have much luck with apprentices, and I was always pointing out to him the line between apprentice and servant, which he found heartily amusing.

Today he was not to be amused. Since the medicine argument he barely spoke to me. He jerked his head at the sight of me, stepped out of the street to join me instead of inviting me in and set off at a near march. When I asked where we were going, he made no reply. We reached the dwelling of an elderly woman, racked with coughs, and whilst he conversed with the woman's relations he made no effort to talk with me, only issued commands followed by a muttering of 'wretched boy', which some of the patient's relations caught and raised their eyebrows at. Once we finished with the lady and he sold his placebo medicine with a vicious glare at me, we headed off.

'Where next?' I asked.

'You are going back to my house,' he said. 'There is a deal of washing to do.'

'I am not your valet–'

'No but you are my apprentice, you smart mouthed braggart. The washing is old bandages and disused jars from patients' samples.'

He left me and with a heavy heart I returned to his house. There was a pile of dirty rags, bandages, jars and tools in the kitchen all with a look of not having been washed in years. I swallowed, feeling defeated by the task before I had begun. I just made a big step back in my progress, but I rallied and set off with a bucket for the pump.

The day was long. The boiling of water and scrubbing had me working up quite a sweat so in the end, worried though I was that Mr Campbell would return, I stripped off my jacket, and waistcoat. When he did come back, I'd hear the door so could quickly dress again, covering my girlish form. He did not return until very late in the evening, once I finished my task. I helped myself to a few pieces of bread and sat reading one of his medical books. When at last he returned, the key rattling in the door and cursing at its stiffness he scowled when I came to greet him.

'Still here?' he said. 'Be off with you!'

I gratefully obliged, and saw him eyeing me with suspicion as I donned my cloak but was glad to get away.

The streets held a strange mirror to those of the morning; the ladies of the night were still about though were much more exuberant than in the morning, brazenly touting their trade – some offering themselves to me. Sailors and rakes drunkenly roamed about, cheering and laughing, calling after the women while link boys lit the way for the staggering rakes. The December night was too cold for anyone else to be lingering on the streets, but some people were salting in front of their houses in case of frost, men who looked like clerks were hastening home and once more I saw doctors making house calls. Carriages rattled passed, the horses going quickly as if they, like everyone else, wished to be out of the piercing cold.

When I reached home a surprisingly merry scene awaited me, and I felt a flare of jealousy for having missed it. The cats were curled up before the warm fire, Amelia and Miss Atwell were cheerfully reading aloud from *A Midsummer's Night Dream* and Mama and Captain Parnell were sat listening. At the sight of me Amelia jumped up and came over.

'You must join us, we are having such fun!' She went to take my coat, but I stopped her, throwing a look at Miss Atwell. Amelia rolled her eyes at me, as Miss Atwell continued to read.

'I don't think she would care a jot,' Amelia whispered.

'Too many people know already and I think Mr Campbell is suspicious of something. I will go upstairs and change.'

'Very well but make haste. Oh, there is a letter on the bed for you.'

I did as I was bid, and found the letter in Ruby's hand. Lord how I missed her! I had not seen her in week, I wished to tell her all about Mr Campbell's behaviour but dared not commit it to the page. Her letter invited us to the party they were having on Christmas Day and my heart soared, surely Mr Campbell could not begrudge that? Ruby said her mother would write to mine so all could be arranged but she hoped we could all come, including Captain Parnell and any lodgers.

The roar of laughter from downstairs acted like a beacon, and dressed like a girl I headed downstairs where Mama made a space for me between her and Captain Parnell. She gave me a bowl of what looked like macaroni and cheese.

'How exotic!' I smiled.

'Taste it, it's divine!' Amelia enthused, just as Miss Atwell declared it would 'warm you right up!' and Captain Parnell poured me a glass of madeira after Mother nodded her consent. Soon I was laughing along with everyone else.

Jessica

On the morning of my first Christmas without Peter, without The Fitzwilliam, I awoke early, my breath fogging the air. The girls were still asleep, cuddled up like babes. I was thankful that Mr Campbell had received an invitation from his sister to spend Christmas with her family out in Shirehampton so Lydia had a few days off work.

If Peter was here he would still be sleeping, if I was at the hotel I would be preparing breakfast for the guests. As it was, I dressed quickly in the cold then crept downstairs tend to the ham that would do us for lunch, along with the leftover Christmas pies of goose which Mr Thomas and Mr Webster said sold very well. The thought of the salty pork caused my tongue to tingle, before stirring memories of Peter. Ham was one of his favourites, Christmas being a time for all his 'one indulgences'.

Suddenly, I was strangely untethered, disorientated, expecting to open a door and end up in The Fitzwilliam – I tried to shake the feeling by cutting the breakfast plum cake but I had to stop to take a breath. After a few moments I moved to the parlour. I must focus on the Christmas to come not Christmases gone; how many wonderful gifts and feasts on those days had been funded by Peter's gambling which I had happily accepted?

I started up the fire in the grate and hung stockings for the girls, as we'd used to in our parlour, although this year Lydia had protested, but I had done it just the same. They contained an orange each from the greenhouses of Clifton (thanks to the Thomases) as well as a book each.

As I arranged breakfast on the table Captain Parnell came in.

Seeing him now, so soon after my thoughts of Peter, made me think I ought to feel some sort of guilt – but I refused to. I had done nothing wrong. I poured him coffee and he thanked me, our hands brushing, eyes meeting as he took the cup. We stood close again, and his hand rested on my waist whilst mine was on his chest.

'Happy Christmas, Jessica,' he said and it warmed me to hear him say my name.

'And to you, James.'

Then Miss Atwell's footsteps thudded down the stairs. 'Goodness, ain't it cold!'

Captain Parnell, James, jokingly rolled his eyes and stepped back from me. 'I'll stoke the fires, shall I?'

'Splendid.' She sat down, complimenting me on a fine spread and tucking in. She was not long followed by Amelia who had the Christmas stockings in one hand and a very tired looking Lydia linked to her other arm. They both still wore mourning, Amelia's dress with frills and Lydia's with a high neck, and suddenly it struck me how much they looked like women instead of girls, but then Amelia flashed a grin of unbridled pleasure as she wished me the best of the day and asked if she may open her presents.

Later, Captain Parnell went to the Catholic church while Miss Atwell accompanied the girls and me to our local church. I attended every Sunday and exchanged well wishes with the other parishioners who had grown familiar to me over the past months. Strange though it was, I was glad to be known only as a widow among them not as Peter's wife. It was not the same church we had worshipped at with Peter and I was glad, I think that would have been too painful for Amelia, who wept at the service and said we must all pray for Papa, which I did.

After church we passed a merry afternoon of eating, reading and parlour games then in the evening donned our finery for the Thomases' party.

Mrs Thomas greeted us warmly on our arrival and said the parlour had been rearranged so that there might be dancing for the young or, she chuckled, the not so young. Hyacinth was playing a soft tune upon the piano. George and Ruby came over to Lydia's side, all smiles, leaving Mr Bradley, whom they had been conversing with to talk with Mr Taylor. I watched Mr Bradley's eyes follow Ruby but she did not seem conscious of it, her own gaze fixed upon Lydia.

Lydia smiled happily to see her friend and introduced her and George to Amelia, whilst Captain Parnell was beckoned over by Mr Thomas for claret with Mr Syrett and old Mr Ashanti. I made the relevant introductions of Mrs Thomas to Miss Atwell, and as I had thought they chatted as merrily as old acquaintances. There were other people to be introduced to; three married couples; all part of the abolitionist movement with a few younger children between them and two older sons who were friendly with George and openly made eyes at Amelia.

The maid, Janey, ushered in a few more guests; an elderly woman and another middle-aged couple I did not know, and a small group of bachelor abolitionists, who looked to be in their twenties. The Websters had been invited, but did not seem to be in attendance. Whether this was because of Richard's troubles or their views on the Thomases I did not know.

'Well,' Mr Thomas clapped to quiet the company. 'What a busy party we have become. Let me assure those not wishing to dance the dining room is available for cards and conversation. Let us raise a toast to the season then the dancing may begin!'

'Happy Christmas!' exclaimed Mrs Thomas, and we all toasted and wished each other likewise.

Mr Bradley practically fell over his own feet asking Ruby to dance, and I saw Lydia send a wistful look after them as they moved to the centre of the room. George was quick on the up take and offered her his arm, as one of the young men who'd been watching Amelia darted towards her. Mr and Mrs Thomas said they would start off the first dance and Hyacinth would play, but people must not expect them to dance all night. To my astonishment and pleasure Miss Atwell headed to the floor with one of the bachelor abolitionists.

I watched happily as the music started up and the dancing began. Some of the others around the side started to file out, including Mr Syrett but Captain Parnell stayed and I did not feel quite old enough yet to shuffle off and play cards.

George chatted gaily to Lydia, but her eyes kept flicking over to Ruby, who Mr Bradley was engaging in conversation - but she kept meeting Lydia's gaze. It must be a nervous time for Ruby to have a man interested in her and I could understand her concern, but she was lucky to have the attention of such a handsome, respectable fellow.

Amelia and Miss Atwell were in the same set and laughed with their young men. Amelia, as ever, made me worry that she was bordering on flirting, but then why must a girl enjoying herself be a flirt? There was no provocation in her moves, just fun. As the song finished Captain Parnell came to sit with me

'You enjoy the dancing?' he asked.

'Oh yes, I used to love to dance, but then once I was married Peter never liked to,' I hesitated not wanting to sound resentful of Peter but also realising I had barely danced in twenty years. I tried to change the subject. 'I like to see the girls enjoying themselves.'

Amelia joined Hyacinth on the piano and another young man asked Lydia to dance, Ruby stayed with Mr Bradley and George took up with Miss Atwell, as the Thomas' retired.

'Would you like to dance?' Captain Parnell asked me quietly. Our eyes met, and I felt as silly as a girl in one of Amelia's gothic novels, but there was such a pleasure in being asked, in seeing the admiration in his handsome expression.

'I am still wearing mourning,' I sighed. 'These are my friends, but I also do business with them. Mr Thomas knew Peter, despite Peter not holding a high opinion of him. Then there is the girls' reputations-'

'It would be enough to know that you would like to.'

I looked into his serious, dark eyes and remembered the feel of his hands on mine. Inside my gloves I flexed my fingers.

'Follow me in a few moments,' I whispered, a sudden thrilling thought occurring to me. 'I fancy cards.'

I left the room, feeling sure all were watching me and when I was in the hall asked Janey to fetch me my cloak and his coat.

'Are you leaving, ma'am?'

'I just need some air and Captain Parnell will see I am well.'

She fetched them for me. Nervously, I waited for him, thinking he might not follow but he did. He looked at me inquisitively but said nothing until we were in the garden.

'I have visited the Thomas' enough to know that if we stand in this part of the garden-

He cocked his head. 'We can hear music from the parlour and not be seen?'

I nodded.

It was dark, but the light from the house and moon illuminated us in the coldness, our breath fogging the air.

'You are not cold?' he asked.

'I am, but a dance will warm me up.'

'Just the one?'

'We shall have to return before we are missed,' I said. 'And before we freeze.'

'Very well,' he smiled, before bowing as I curtsied, and offered me his hand.

Chapter 26

Amelia

I stepped out into the yard, the ground frosty, my breath fogging the air. I did not think I had ever been the first in the house to awake, but after last night's festivities everyone was sleeping soundly, as well they might. It was only Miss Atwell and I who had no employment in this house, and the worse for me since Miss Atwell was a guest. Perhaps today I could start breakfast and get the fires going, once I cleared my head.

It was strange last night to see how my mother and sister had moved on in Papa's absence. They were very much ingratiated with the social circle of dissenters and liberals. Lydia had a bosom friend in Miss Thomas, and even Mr George Thomas seemed as if he rather liked her, though Lydia has never been adept at noticing such things concerning herself.

Mama and Captain Parnell spent a lot of time together, talking like old friends. I wondered if they would only be friendly inside this house for want of what others would say, but apparently not. Mrs Thomas gave them interested looks; Mama still in black. I supposed Mrs Thomas was not friendly with Papa, even if Mr Thomas had business with him, so perhaps to all at that party it was as if he never existed at all. I wiped away a tear. Life went on, of course. And Mama was right, after how Papa had left his affairs I supposed she had no cause to sit about, mourning forever.

Should I have liked to marry someone twenty years my senior if she bid me do so, as her mother had done to her? Definitely not. Would I not prefer someone closer to my own age, who was coming up in the world? But Papa always looked at her with such affection and she returned those looks; we had all been so happy. Now, Captain Parnell looked at her affectionately, and spoke to her, always so interested in anything she said or did as she was with him, and they were always laughing and darting amused looks at one another.

It could all come to nothing. It could all be a lot worse; loathe as I was to admit it, I did like the Captain. If she was my friend rather than my mother, I would likely encourage the match though what they intended to do about their differences in religion was anyone's guess.

I went back inside, deciding to busy myself. I gathered breakfast food from the pantry and decided to bake some eggs, though not before starting the fire, a frown crossing my face at the thought. The task messed my hands and as I fumbled with the flint Miss Atwell came into the parlour.

'Good morning,' she said, looking at me quizzically. 'That is a queer way to light the fire.'

'I was never much good at it.'

She laughed. 'Evidently, here let me tend to it.' She squatted next to me and dexterously set to work. 'My father insisted I learnt to light fires when I was very little. We often moved about as well so I can light a campfire as well as any Indian.'

'My father never really insisted I do anything practical.'

'As is often the way. But yesterday you played the piano with great skill. Who taught you that? Ma or Pa?'

'That was my father,' I said sitting back on my haunches as the heat spread through the room. 'He could play very well himself and had a good singing voice. Sometimes we would duet…'

Miss Atwell pressed my shoulder before we got to our feet.

'Come,' I said. 'I was making breakfast. Would you like baked eggs?'

'That would be delightful. Your mother praises your cooking skills, you know.'

I smiled. 'Yes, I am the savoury and Lydia is the sweet.'

'And you are an excellent needle woman.'

'Mama taught me that,' I said as I stoked the oven after she lit it.

'May I ask how you found Brighton and Bath?'

I cracked the eggs, wondering at her reasons for this line of questioning. 'They were both beautiful places, but I did not have as a good a time as I hoped, perhaps it was the people.'

Or more, how I behaved around the people. 'What is your interest? Do you intend to go before the continent?'

'Perhaps, but it is more likely I will go at some other time. I ask as I am trying to sketch your character. I think we have gotten on rather well these past few days, would you agree?'

'Yes.'

'Your mother is a good woman, and you were excellent company at the party last night.' She drummed her fingers. 'What I mean to say in my round-about way, was that I was thinking of asking you to be my companion for my European excursion. What do you reckon?'

My heart leapt. 'Truly? Oh Miss Atwell I am honoured, but will it do for two ladies to travel unaccompanied on such a long journey?'

'I am a wealthy spinster, I may do as I please. If it comes to it I can pretend to be a widow or invent a husband, that is a rather fun trick I have tried before.'

'I never thought to see Europe! I should love to come!'

Miss Atwell smiled. 'Good. I fancy I could do with a companion. I have travelled alone along time, and I think it would do me good to have a friend. Your skills with the needle and with cooking set you in good stead; both things I can do but without any flair.'

I thanked her again, but a nervousness rose in me. Was I not unworthy, given all that had passed in Brighton and Bath? Was I not glad to be home? Yes and yes, but then when was I likely to get this opportunity again? A second chance, more than that…a chance to see Europe. Mama would approve, she would like me to be a companion I knew, and it was a step above being a seamstress and even helping with the lodging house, better than being a governess, than working in Mr Syrett's…so what troubled me? That I could not be trusted, that people we met could not be trusted? All of it, yet Miss Atwell was not Betsey – whilst she was fun she was sensible and had her own means. She had no need to fortune hunt viscounts. It seemed she had no real need to show men any consideration at all. Maybe with that in mind, being her companion would set me in very good stead indeed.

Lydia

Much to Mother's delight Amelia actually made breakfast and started the fires. The baked eggs were *very* good, but Amelia was not boastful of them. She was quiet as Mother discussed the Thomas' party with Miss Atwell and Captain Parnell read his book on the life of Benjamin Franklin, although he did exchange a few happy glances with Mother which caused me to look at Amelia, to see if she noticed. Her expression reflected my own thoughts on the matter. It was all well and good, but we still did not know who Mrs Parnell was.

Last night at the party, Mr Syrett gave me some medical journals he had gotten from a house sale. They were a few years old, but detailed the discovery of Mr Jenner, and his belief that curing smallpox could come from exposure to cow pox, and that administering the virus to the young could help stop it. He learnt this from milk maids, who were daily exposed to the virus and it seemed were immune to smallpox. I looked up again at Mama. There was a pause in her conversation as porters were sipped.

'Mother, you sometimes milked the Roberts' cows, did you not?'

She looked at me. 'Yes, quite often if my mother was in need of milk for her cooking. Why do you ask?'

'You've never had smallpox, have you?' I asked, even though I knew the answer.

'No,' she looked between Miss Atwell and Captain Parnell, bemused.

I reached over and took her hand, touched the scar on the back of it, that had come from cowpox. 'That's the cowpox scar is it not?'

'You know it is.'

Everyone was looking at me as though I had gone quite mad.

I pointed to the pages before me. 'I am just reading of Mr Jenner, and his ideas that having had cowpox makes you immune to smallpox. He is suggested infecting children with cowpox to halt smallpox.'

'Do you suppose it would work?'

I nodded. 'His reasoning and tests seem sound. Perhaps you are proof, Mother.'

'There is sense in it,' Captain Parnell said. 'Once you have had smallpox, you cannot get it again.'

'It is the same with many other serious illnesses I believe,' Miss Atwell said. 'I have read of people inoculating themselves with the smallpox scabs, so they only get a milder form.'

'Yes,' Mother said. 'I have heard of that, it sounded dangerous to me.'

There was silence as everyone considered this.

'May I see that?' Captain Parnell asked. I handed it to him, and Mother almost reached out to him, but stopped herself – seeing that I noticed. He noticed as well and gave her smile. 'I am fine, Mrs Fitzwilliam.' He then looked at me. 'My family was caught by an outbreak of smallpox when I was child. My sister died, my brother went blind and I survived.'

'I am sorry to hear that,' Miss Atwell said.

'You are lucky sir, your face was not afflicted,' Amelia said.

He looked at her.

'No, forgive me,' Amelia said, touching her own face. 'It is awful, just awful I was only trying to bring cheer but it was badly considered-'

'Do not fret Miss Amelia, it is what everyone says and I must acknowledge it to be true.'

'Do you suppose such a thing will be commonly available?' Miss Atwell asked.

'There is a fortune to be made here,' Captain Parnell. 'So I imagine they will charge for it.'

'But would it not be in the interests of all to see it eradicated?' I asked. 'To stop it spreading?'

'Indeed.'

'Well, 'tis the season for miracles is it not?' Mother said with a small smile.

Jessica

After breakfast, as Amelia helped me tidy away, Miss Atwell asked if she could speak with me.

'Of course.'

'I was speaking with Miss Amelia this morning,' she said and at this acknowledgement Amelia smiled nervously. 'And I was thinking for my travels on the continent I should like to take her on as my companion.'

Selfishly my first thought was that Amelia had only just returned to me, but I forced a smile. This would be good for Amelia, to have such an opportunity to travel and it was what I wanted for her; to be a companion was a very agreeable position and it would suit her better that it be to a younger, cheerful woman like Miss Atwell as opposed to an elderly woman like Mrs Tindal.

I sat down at the table, nodding trying to find some words. 'That is very good of you to think of Amelia, Miss Atwell. We are most flattered. And this-' I looked at Amelia. 'This is what you would like?'

She nodded. 'Yes Mama, I would dearly love to go.' Of course she would.

'Very well,' I said, already feeling worry starting to rise. 'I grant my permission, but may I ask do you have a proper itinerary?'

'I am finalising it now, and I shall give you a copy before we set off so you may rest assured. I will look after Miss Amelia as if she was my own daughter.'

'That is good of you to say. Where you will be going?'

'To London first then, then onto Belgium, Holland, Sweden, Italy and Spain. I should like to go to France but fear it may be too dangerous at present.'

I nodded and looked at Amelia, who was beaming with excitement.

'This all sounds very exciting,' I said. 'You will be sure to steer clear of any fighting?'

'Certainly,' Miss Atwell said. 'Plenty of people are still travelling managing to avoid the conflict. I will plot the route especially to ensure we are safe.'

If Miss Atwell was pleased with Amelia as her companion, when their travels in Europe were over supposing she decided to take her back to America. I swallowed, I would never see Amelia again in all likelihood should that happen. That would have to be met with if it occurred, I told myself. 'Well,' I said. 'This all sounds very exciting. May I please have a moment alone with Amelia?'

Miss Atwell nodded and left the kitchen, leaving Amelia eyeing me anxiously.

'I promise I will behave and I will work hard as a companion. I will write more frequently than I did in Bath-'

I embraced her and she stopped talking, holding me back tightly.

'You will be greatly missed,' I said. 'You must take care this time.'.

'I swear it, and I think Miss Atwell is a good deal more sensible than Betsey Webster.'

'Of course she is, but how strange it will be two women travelling such a distance alone.'

'You think it improper?'

'No, but others might, it will not stop me from letting you see the world. It is too good an opportunity to forego.'

'Thank you, Mama,' Amelia said planting a kiss on my cheek.

Together we stepped back into the parlour where Miss Atwell was eagerly awaiting us.

'I am happy to entrust Amelia to your care,' I said.

Miss Atwell nodded. 'I was about to suggest the three of us go shopping. I have long wanted you to advise me Mrs Fitzwilliam, what say you?'

'An excellent idea,' I said.

Chapter 27

Lydia

I was asked if I wanted to join the shopping expedition but declined. In a few days I would be back at work and wanted a more restful day today. Since Captain Parnell had also gone out, I was left alone in the house, so sat in the parlour reading until I fell into a doze and awoke with a start. It was dark outside and still no one had returned home, although the clock said it was only four o'clock.

How lucky for Amelia to be able to go to Europe. If I had not been working with Mr Campbell would I have gotten to know Miss Atwell better and been chosen to go instead? Was it a wasted chance? Would I be like Mother and never travel? But surely, I would have a trade and so could travel then, but would that involve travelling as man? It would certainly be easier to travel as a man; easier to live as a man in many ways.

If I had dressed as a man last night I could have asked Ruby to dance, I could have stopped Mr Bradley monopolizing all of her time. He did not stop looking at her all evening, but I knew she did not want to spend all her time with him for she kept sending me glances. I had not been the only one to notice his interest in Ruby for I heard her mother and sisters discussing it in hushed tones. Theirs was not the only attachment that was discussed; so was my mother's and Captain Parnell's.

They were inseparable all night; whether they had been watching the dancing or going off to play cards, in groups or just the two of them and yet we still did know not the identity of Mrs Parnell. Mother seemed content to live in ignorance, but she had done that with Father and look where that had gotten us. Quickly I made a decision. Since they were all still out I would find some answers of my own.

I hastened up the stairs and knocked on his bedroom door lest he returned while I slumbered but he had not, so I stepped inside. I searched the wardrobe and luggage again and found nothing, then carefully started to read through the account book. Her name was still there, this Mrs Parnell, and the amounts that went out to her quarterly. It seemed that he had been doing it for some time. This book dated back three years ago – and the stipends were in place since then.

The door sounded downstairs and I froze but it was only the voices of Mother, Amelia and Miss Atwell and their footsteps headed towards the kitchen. I went back to the account book as the clatter of dinner preparations arose with the sound of laughter. Then there was a creak and I looked up. Captain Parnell stood in the hallway looking at me through the open door with an expression of puzzlement which was quickly turning to rage.

'What are you doing?' he demanded.

I swallowed, with no idea how to explain my way out of it.

'What are you doing?' he repeated with a threatening edge to his voice. I could not even stutter, I was so mortified. What must I look like? I was still sitting at his desk, account book open before me, there was no explaining it away. He would have us out on the streets, or me at least. How had I let myself get caught?

'Lydia-' Amelia sang up the stairs then stopped dead when she saw the scene. 'Mama!'

I stood up and started to stutter apologies as Mother came up the stairs.

'She has always been full of curiosity,' Mother said. 'It is my fault for not checking her-'

'She still has not answered my question. What were you doing?'

I stepped from the room.

'With everything that passed after Mr Fitzwilliam's death,' Mother was saying. 'It is only natural that she should worry, I will speak to her.'

But here was an opportunity to have a question answered directly even if it would bring more ugliness. I could have just agreed with Mother and pleaded for forgiveness, instead I said, 'I wanted to find out who Mrs Parnell is.'

'I beg your pardon?'

'I wanted to find out who Mrs Parnell is.'

He looked from the account book to me. 'Mrs Aofie Parnell is my father's widow.'

'Your step-mother?' Amelia said.

'Yes.'

Mama put her hand to her mouth. 'But you did not mention her before...'

The Captain looked between all of us. 'I was introduced to her in Dublin by my father when I was three and twenty. The second and only other time I met her was after my father died and I went to tell her the news. Maybe I ought have mentioned her, but she figures very little in my life, I do not think of her as my relation in truth, cold as that may sound. It was not as if she was a step-mother who raised me. Since she has no claim on my properties, she would never have been a threat to the stability of this house. You know already this place would pass to some of my cousins in the event of my death, with the stipulation you must be allowed to stay as a tenant at your current rate for six months.'

'I'm sorry -' Mother started.

His frown deepened. 'This is not the first time Miss Fitzwilliam has pried into my accounts, is it?' He hesitated and none of us could respond. 'Had you asked to see them, I would have shown you.'

'Both times I acted without Mother's knowledge! I only told her afterwards.'

'It is my fault,' Mother said. 'I should have ensured she didn't do it again, explained to you. I should not been so indulgent towards her.'

'I appreciate the way you raise your girls, but there has to be a limit. Have I ever shown you signs that I was untrustworthy?'

'No, but neither did my husband. Lydia was only trying to protect us.'

'I am sorry,' I said again, seeing the hurt on Mother's face, on his face, that they were both trying to mask.

'I do not break my word, Mrs Fitzwilliam. I said you would be secure here. I know what it is to be poor so I would not put you in that position, I told you this.'

'I know, you did...I...'

'I am going to go out,' he said. 'I only hope you don't do this to all the guests.'

'I do not do it to all the guests,' I said weakly. Although Amelia raised her eyebrows, it was the truth, I didn't have the time to do it any more like I had at the hotel.

'I do not know then if it is better or worse that I have been singled out,' he said.

'You don't have to go out,' Mother started.

'I think I do, if only to clear the air. Good night.' With that he left.

Amelia's eyes were like saucers. 'Will he evict us?'

'He can't, we have a contract,' Mother said faintly, before slowly turning to look at me a look of such disappointment written across her features I had never seen. 'Oh Lydia, why could you just not have left it alone?'

'I am sorry -'

She raised her hands as I went to her. 'I must go and make dinner,' she said and stormed down the stairs.

Jessica

Stupid, foolish woman! I should have known something like this would happen, letting Lydia be unchecked for so long…it was my fault entirely. Of course, she had a right to be worried after all that passed with Peter but I ought have been firmer and insisted I would find out about Mrs Parnell. Now what a mess we were in.

He would not evict us, but he could give me notice. What must we look like? Snooping around, prying and spying. Had he children who had done the same to me I would be mortified and he was so proud, and careful and forth right. I chopped the vegetables to smithereens.

'Mrs Fitzwilliam, is all well?' Miss Atwell entered from the parlour. I could not tell the truth lest she think Lydia had been spying on her.

'Yes yes,' I said. 'Just a small misunderstanding, all resolved now.'

I did not look at her, but carried on peeling the turnips so hard my hands started to hurt. Her footsteps went upstairs as Amelia's hurried down.

'Lord!' she exclaimed. 'I never thought anyone would ever catch Lydia!'

'Don't.'

'Mama- ' she drew nearer after a pause. 'Please sit down, let me make dinner.'

I looked at her in surprise. 'Am I really so bad?'

She shrugged. 'It has just been unpleasant, has it not?'

I let her take over and sat down, embarrassed that it had all shaken me so badly. I wished he had stayed so we could smooth things over, I wished I found the courage to somehow ask him earlier…the last few days I had truly been at peace after such a tumultuous year and it all had been dashed away again.

Amelia

After Mama and Lydia went to sleep I stayed awake, having too much nerves to sleep; my mind flitting between Lydia's being caught and the chance of travelling to Europe. It was a chance that I would not squander. I would be useful to Miss Atwell, I would be well behaved and try to learn and take in culture and arts and such like. There would be much to learn from Miss Atwell about how one might survive as a single woman as well as the possibility that we may cross paths with eligible young men - men who I was relieved to think Miss Atwell would scrutinize more closely before forming an acquaintance with than Betsey had.

The thought of meeting yet more men seemed suddenly both dull and terrifying - if Mr Snowden was anything to go by their conversation could be boorish and self-centred, yet if they felt they were owed something - if one even showed them you were even slightly interested they could turn dangerous. I shuddered at the thought of Mr Snowden lunging for me, his eyes wide with drink, spit spraying when he spoke and the loud rip as he tore my dress. It was unpleasant enough to hope we did not cross paths with any young men.

The next morning Lydia was retaining her position of silence that she had adopted since her discovery, whilst I helped Mama with the breakfast. She crashed about haphazardly - her mind obviously occupied. Captain Parnell entered the parlour and without a word she swept out to him, closing the kitchen door behind her. I tried to meet Lydia's gaze but she was staring determinedly at her porridge.

'You needn't be such a martyr,' I said.

'I'm not a martyr, but a fool,' she sighed.

I did not argue - for her not to have left the Captain's room as soon as the front door opened seemed very foolish. Admittedly we were making so much noise it was hard to distinguish who was in the party, and he had not said anything as we entered the house but even if Miss Atwell had seen her instead of Captain Parnell it would hardly have been better. What was she thinking to go snooping without a lookout - I would not have let her be discovered!

Mama entered the kitchen again as I heard the front door open and close.

'Well?' I said.

'He was perfectly civil.'

Oh dear, civil was hardly good.

'He said I needn't apologise more it was done, but he received new orders yesterday. His ship is sailing this morning, so he has to go.'

She sighed and a swell of pity and annoyance rose up in me that we must part on awkward terms when all had been so merry.

'So he will not evict us?'

'No,' she said. 'No. But I just worry we may not have as much of a cordial friendship as we had before.'

Cordial indeed!

Mama took a deep breath and ran her hands through her hair, as if pushing away all that had passed. Her jaw clenched and her eyes flashed.

'Enough on the subject,' she said briskly. 'We have much to think of with your upcoming journey, Amelia. We must start packing. Lydia, Mr Campbell will be at his sister's until after new year's, is that so?'

Lydia blinked, waking from her stupor. 'Yes, unless she sends him away in exasperation.'

'Well then you can help us in our efforts to ready Amelia.'

The trunk which I had so recently unpacked was retrieved and we spent the day repacking it. Miss Atwell had some errands to run so it was just the three of us, a combination I was glad of.

We bought some pretty fabric yesterday in pale blues and floral prints – I would be out of mourning, and Miss Atwell insisted that I have a new wardrobe for the trip. She asked Mama and I to help her chose fabrics for new gowns for herself as well and we knew her colouring would suit greens and russets. I was to make most of the dresses, but I did not mind, and these modern dresses were so simple that it would not take me long.

'No more mourning for us,' Lydia said. 'How odd.'

'Yes,' I nodded, though we had been allowed to forsake mourning for the last couple of months I had not to make up for my forsaking it in Bath and I think Lydia did not for she rather liked sombre colours. Poor Mama had to wait until April before she could wear colours again.

'White is hardly practical for a day dress though,' Lydia said.

'That is hardly the point,' I said. 'Anyway Lydia you like these styles, you said last year you find them less restrictive.'

'It is true, but they are still not breeches are they?'

I hesitated in my dress sketching and Mama, who was watching over my shoulder, looked at Lydia.

'What are we to do?' she said. 'It is hardly as if you can wear breeches for ever.'

'Where did you think it would lead?' Lydia demanded.

Mama shrugged. 'I scarcely know. These past eight months have been such a fog I hardly know what I thought about so many things.'

They lapsed into silence.

'Well,' I said. 'You have started it now have you not? You may as well finish it.'

'What books will you bring to Europe?' Lydia asked, standing up after a pause. 'We could go and see Mr Syrett and get some before you go. He might even have a guidebook, and he goes up to London once every few years so he may have some recommendations for the first leg of your trip.'

'As nice as he is, I do not know how useful his London recommendations will be to me.'

'Oh, tsh Amelia,' Mama said. 'He will know the attractions – just because he is elderly! He would know the parks at least. You really must take care before you turn into the most frightful snob.'

I blushed. 'I am trying-'

'You certainly can be trying,' Lydia said with a grin, but I could not help but feel wrong footed, as though we were slipping back to the old ways of them uniting against me. Mama put her arm around me.

'Come now,' she said shooting Lydia a look. 'I have noticed that you are trying and not in the way that Lydia means – even if she jests. I did not mean to speak so harshly. Now, Captain Parnell said there was a book about London on the bookshelf you could take with you if you wished.'

'He said that?' I said.

Mama went to fetch it while Lydia's eyes rounded. 'Why do you suppose he said that?'

'I do not know why, perhaps he meant it to forgive us,' Mama said as I thought that it was hardly 'us' that needed to be forgiven, it was more Lydia. 'He said it rather like it was out of duty than any personal favour-' Mama hesitated for a moment then pulled the book out. 'But whatever his intentions you may as well have a look.'

Jessica

I took the long way to the Websters', despite the bitter cold, my mind going over the events of yesterday morning. He had not been uncivil. Half of me wanted to be angry - it was only a slight infraction, Lydia did not mean any harm, she was just curious - but those were excuses that one would give for a child, not a young woman. He had been very formal and had the papers with his orders in his hands as if to prove he was not inventing an excuse to rid himself of my company.

'I am sorry- ' I said again.

'You do not need to apologise again, ' he said but he did not say I had been forgiven. His bag was already packed and I knew when I went up to the room there would be no trace of him; it would all be ready for the guests.

'I wished you could have stayed longer-' I said. Did it sound whining, desperate?

I could not read his expression and he said, 'I must obey my orders.' Words that left me none the wiser as to if he would prefer to stay or not.

'Well I wish you a safe travel then,' I said, trying to look reserved, to cover any sign of weakness.

He nodded, and gestured to the bookshelf saying Amelia could borrow the London book before he hastily left. It was not how I imagined our parting to be at all.

I pushed on, though it had started to rain, and pulled my cloak tighter around myself. I would not hail a cab, it was an expense I could do without. I offered to pay some of Amelia's way in Europe, more as a courtesy than anything else, for in truth I could not have afforded it but Miss Atwell refused saying that was not the point of a companion and that she would even provide Amelia with an allowance but still, I was determined to send Amelia off with some money, no matter how small in case something went awry. Not that Miss Atwell was untrustworthy, far from it, but she may fall ill or succumb to an accident or her boldness may lead them to some other kind of trouble. Amelia must have some money of her own. I had to trust that she would not spend it on trifles.

Last Christmas she was a child, after Peter died I feared she may grow unmanageable, whatever the full extent of her exploits with Betsey were it seemed to have checked her little. She would always be flighty and prone to vanity, but she did have a helpful streak – a willingness to please - more so than Lydia .When she was very little she used to love to help, just so she could be around me whereas Lydia was always happiest in her own company, entertaining herself.

How odd to think now she would be across an ocean from me, that she would see so much more than me - already she was so well travelled, but it was the right thing to do. Here she would grow bored and Miss Atwell would be a good influence.

I stopped outside the Websters, not sure how I would be received. I hoped they would not think I had come to pry. I was quickly ushered to the parlour by Bertha, and sat waiting alone, the house remarkably quiet. Mrs Webster emerged from the hall, bags under her eyes, with a weary step.

'My dear-' I stood to greet her but she sat down, gesturing for me to do the same. 'What has occurred? I am here out of concern and I have bought some pies -'

'Thank you, yes,' she said, her voice reedy, reminding me that she was over twenty years my senior, something she rarely seemed but now it appeared glaringly obvious.

'There was a duel,' she sighed.

'Over Betsey?'

'Indeed. I was just as incredulous as you, m'dear, what a waste over such a wanton bit of baggage, but it is all about honour you see…how fortune you are to have daughters. Had mine lived they would have been a great comfort to me at this time.'

'Was Richard injured?'

'Indeed he was, shot in the arm though he shot that viscount's son in the shoulder.'

I gasped.

'I know,' she wrung her hands. 'Richard is laid up in some London infirmary now, the wound festers-' her voice broke. 'I am to travel up this evening….'

'Oh my goodness, I am so sorry. Who is with him?'

'Tom and William, though they scarcely know what is to be done. Mr Webster often says Edward took more than his share of the brains so there was none left for Tom and William. I always thought those words harsh, but they let Dickie's wound rot and encouraged this fight and the letter only reached me yesterday for they did not think to write for days.' She dissolved into tears, and I pressed her shoulder, profoundly glad for the first time since Peter's death that I did not have any sons.

Chapter 28

Amelia

Miss Atwell bought a carriage and hired a driver, Albert Goss. He was a stout man of few words which exactly he had been hired - he hadn't asked if any gentleman relations would be joining us. Mama stood next to me wringing her hands and checking that I had everything, whilst Miss Atwell boarded the carriage. Lydia embraced me.

'We must write more this time,' she said. 'Tell each other everything, properly. You will see so much. I want proper documentation about all you learn.'

'Like Mary Wollstonecraft's travels around Scandinavia?' I asked, teasingly.

'Exactly so,' she replied with seriousness. I vowed I would, her letters would keep me grounded and we had already agreed to code so she could tell me of her doctoring adventurers. We were to refer to her as being Mr Campbell's housekeeper.

As she stepped away to talk with Miss Atwell Mama embraced me, crushing me. Tears came to my eyes. I vowed to be well-behaved and write often, meaning it this time, before she handed me a basket of food and helped me up into the carriage.

Miss Atwell thanked Mama again for sparing me and reached over to embrace her, before sitting back down. Lydia took Mama's arm as Albert shut the door and climbed up into the drivers' seat. The reins cracked and we were away. I turned and watched the house and my family grow smaller, waving in the same place until we turned the corner. I sat down and Miss Atwell smiled at me. I smiled back, trying to remember that London awaited.

Lydia

The house was quiet with everyone gone. Mother made jugged hare and spoke about Amelia's possible adventures in London and beyond. Her chatter was nervous, and as much as I tried to contribute the weight of humiliation from being caught prying like a nosey child rested on me, and what it might have cost her. She seemed to have forgiven me, but I still went out of my way to help her tidy up the rooms for the next set of guests. The Winthorpe family had requested two bedrooms; one for Mr and Mrs Winthorpe, and one for Miss Miranda Winthorpe and her maid, Lizzie.

We set to tidying Miss Atwell's room first. She left a small case of belongings which she had asked we put in the attic for her, and another pile which she said we could have to wear or sell as we pleased. There would have been a time when that might have been insulting, and from anyone else, put so bluntly maybe it would have been, but Miss Atwell meant it in kindness and we were in no position to turn it down.

I had lost weight since I started working for Mr Campbell, which mother commented on whilst she held the couple of thick gowns up against me. They were in browns and blues, and since more than six months had passed I was no longer in mourning, although I had rather liked the easiness of wearing black.

'But where would I wear them?'

'It is better to have them than not,' she paused. 'And how do you think this will all end?'

'What do you mean?'

'This,' she gestured at the breeches I was wearing. 'Do you really intend to live as a man forever?'

'I …I do not know.'

'We had best think about it, this charade is getting increasingly dangerous. When I agreed to it…' she folded her arms. 'I did not think it through. I think both of us were still blinded by grief and panic.'

'But I am capable!'

'I know you are, more than capable. I just…we ought to have planned it better. Maybe it would be better to move away where no one knew us and you could be my son, but then where would that leave Amelia? And we would have to start from scratch again and…we still have no money. An apprenticeship is seven years-'

'Do you want me to quit?' I asked my stomach tightening. 'I don't think I could, I-'

'No,' she shook her head. 'No I am not saying that, I am proud of what you have done. I just think we ought to consider how long we can keep this up and if you want to keep it up forever then, we must be even more careful than we have been.'

'I will give it some thought,' I said. She nodded and took Miss Atwell's old dresses to hang up in our wardrobe.

When we came to tidy Captain Parnell's room it was entirely empty of his meagre belongings and it made me feel worse to think he had so little and I had still rifled through it. I said this to Mother, who was on her knees giving the floor a good scrubbing.

'You must not dwell on it,' she sighed.

The next day I went to Mr Campbell's. I let myself in, to find him shovelling a breakfast of cold meats and cheeses into his mouth, washed down with beer. I had never seen him eat so much, and though I did not say he must have read my expression for he said. 'It's from my sister. Don't you dare think of pinching any, I know what's here. I need you to tidy and unpack for me today.'

'Sir!'

'Don't you bloody sir me,' he was already ambling towards the door, dusting crumbs from his jacket and reaching for his wig.

'When am I to go out on rounds with you again?'

He grunted.

'At least let me make good use of my time and mix you up remedies that might work. I have read widely on the subject and have a friend who is a botanist.'

His eyes swivelled back to me. 'Do you?'

'Yes.'

'Well, maybe write me some proposals for these remedies and we'll see but only after you unpack my trunk!'

Jessica

The Winthorpes arrived in the freezing cold. Mr Winthorpe carried his sickly daughter from the carriage and lay her on the sofa, Mrs Winthorpe was supported by the robust looking maid.

'Do we have our own parlour?' Mr Winthorpe asked.

'No sir,' I said. 'Though you will only have to share this with my daughter and I.'

'Indeed? And there is no dining room?'

'We eat in the kitchen, or a table can be set up here.'

He looked at his wife. 'You knew this?'

She looked down.

'I described the living conditions very carefully in the letter to your wife, and she said you had met Mrs Pemberton through friends. She knows the arrangements very well.'

The maid suppressed a giggle and the wife continue to stare at her feet. I surprised myself with how brazen I was being but given his abruptness I wasn't sure I wanted him to stay under my roof, money or not.

'Well,' Mr Winthorpe said. 'We shall have to see about this. I might have to find us more suitable accommodation.'

'Would you like to see your rooms first?'

'You best look at least, Papa,' Miss Winthorpe said weakly, and Mr Winthorpe nodded at me.

On seeing the rooms, he declared them satisfactory, although he might seek out others tomorrow, and ordered his women folk up the stairs. The maid Lizzie threw me a look as Mr Winthorpe closed his bedroom door behind his wife. 'He'll stay,' she said in a thick Yorkshire brogue. 'It is only that he is rather fond of being displeased.'

Luckily for me they spent most of the time out of the house at the spa and consulting various doctors. Miss Winthorpe had a small wheeled chair which Lizzie pushed, whispering and chuckling, whilst Mrs Winthorpe shuffled after Mr Winthorpe as he bustled about. They treated the parlour as their own, spreading out on the chairs, leaving books and hats everywhere as well as asking for a table to be set up so they could dine there - 'as a family' Mr Winthorpe said, meaning he did not expect to dine with me. I did not miss his company but did not appreciate being treated like a servant in my own house. He demanded to know where my daughter was so I told him the lie we had concocted, that she was a housekeeper nearby. They never rose early enough or went to sleep late enough to see much of her.

Lydia

Whatever occurred over Christmas with Mr Campbell's sister's family had made him more agreeable. He sometimes took coffee with me in the morning before he scuttled off, leaving me to clean his equipment or write up and organise his notes. He said that if my botanist friend and I could concoct some feasible and cheap cures and tonics then he would happily sell them, it would save him the trouble of making up his own and if they worked, which he highly doubted they would, all the better. One evening he even invited me to stay for port when he returned from his rounds.

I thanked him and drank what he poured, whilst he moaned about his patients and the other medical men of Bristol, who either undercut him and were crooks or looked down on him.

'Do you have much cause to socialise with them?'

'Heavens no. Occasionally I might pass a few words with navy surgeons in port but I have no desire to talk endlessly with pompous fools.'

'Do you read many medical reports and journals?'

'I used to…' he said. 'But many of the editors of medicals journals only tend to publish their own friends so what is the point of that?'

'You tried to get published?'

He poured himself another drink. 'Oh yes many times, chiefly about my specimens…' he trailed off, his gaze drifting to the row of jarred animal feet on the mantle piece.

'Have you read of the smallpox cure?'

He glared at me. 'Oh I have bloody well read of it, my damn nephew is training to be a doctor no less, at Guys of all places, and he likes to regale us all with that dangerous nonsense.'

'You think there is no truth in it?'

'Miserable as smallpox is it is a fact of life, it must be endured and we are just here to ease it along. It is another way to separate the weak from the strong.'

I blinked at it. 'You do not think it can be cured?'

'They aren't curing it,' he said. 'They are preventing it from ever happening in the first place. I do not believe in that at all, and if they are right, and they can stop ills before they happen we will soon be out of a job!' he laughed.

'That will take a long time to eradicate all diseases,' I said. 'And people will still break their bones, birth children and grow old.'

He sat back and gave me a hard stare. 'I suppose they will.'

'May I ask sir,' I said, bolder with the port, 'why you became a surgeon?'

'It all seems so long ago now,' he shrugged. 'My father was a surgeon, an army surgeon. So that seemed the thing to do. I always liked my specimens, collected them on my travels.'

'With the army?'

'No. I was a surgeon with the East India Company,' he said 'A fine adventure for any young man, especially a curious one like yourself.' He chuckled, a far away look in his eyes. 'Those were the days; balmy nights, pretty savage girls – that sounds like it would appeal to you a great deal, judging by your little mulatto-ess, eh?'

I blushed, not liking his tone but liking that he referred to Ruby as mine. If I was Hugh Sommers, she would be. There was no doubt in my mind. Well, for tonight maybe she be Hugh Sommers'.

'She is very pretty, is she not?' I said quietly, trying it out. He slapped his thigh. 'She is indeed. Here young Hugh, let us have some more port. Now tell me, are you courting her then or is she your mistress? Do not tell me that you are just great friends.'

I sunk into Hugh Sommers' imagined life as happily as sinking into a warm bath. 'She is not my mistress, sir. Do not suggest such a slur upon her character. We are courting.'

He raised his eyebrows and I sipped more of the port. The next words I spoke I did not mind if he heard or not but I knew they were true and that I had to say them to someone. 'I love her.'

He snorted, but I did not mind for I had not spoken for him and a great peace and calmness came over me at having reached that realisation.

'You will marry her?'

'I would like to.'

'Well,' he sighed. 'Maybe you ought. It does happen, from time to time, marriages between the races. In India a few sahibs married their bibis…perhaps I ought to have married mine.'

A sadness fell over his face and I sat forward, waiting for more but he waved an impatient hand.

'Let us talk no more of love!' he roared, pouring yet more port. 'Have you ever been to the bear baiting?'

*

When I reached home there was still no letter from Ruby. I had written to her days ago with plans for making the cures for Mr Campbell but had had no reply and had not seen her since Christmas. The weather was bitter so it was little wonder she had not been to see me and I had been working very late but I gave the letter to Mr Thomas when he collected the pies and he'd been several mornings since for more and bought no reply. To pass letters through her family's rounds was normal for us and meant that we often wrote to each other a few times a week, more when we did not see one another but still there was nothing and my proposition was so exciting! What could be taking her so long?

Amelia

Travelling to London in our own private carriage was far more agreeable than by stagecoach, and we stopped at several pleasant inns along the way, with many of the rural inn keepers charmed and intrigued by Miss Atwell's American accent. She was a merry travelling partner - employer I supposed - though she did not make me feel inferior as Betsey Webster had done. She was very excited to see the English countryside, pointing out similarities and differences with other places she travelled and telling me whether or not it was how she had imagined it. Despite her easy manner and openness, I made sure to always be useful, I ordered tea and discussed arrangements with the inn keepers and Goss. I found I liked to do it. I knew what should be expected in a good inn, and found pleasure it charting our progress in my mind through my brief conversations with Goss. Miss Atwell was always quick to thank me and call me her dear girl.

On the morning we were due to ride into London I was terribly excited. We stayed in small town that was mere hours away but it had already been decided we would rest there, and I wasn't childish enough to beg we press on no matter how much I wanted to; the horses were fatigued and we could be beset by highway men in the night, after all. As we rode in, passing through the countryside and watching as it gradually built up into a city I gawped in wonder, feeling no shame for Miss Atwell did the same. 'Well, gosh, what a metropolis! I ain't never seen the like!'

The streets heaved with people, some jostled to beg from our carriage, others gave a few rude gestures, most passed by as though we were invisible as they hurried about their own busy lives. The people seemed to range from the most beautiful to the most ugly and desperate, with everything in between.

There seemed to be building works everywhere – not dissimilar to Bristol and Bath – but on a much larger scale, the atmosphere of the place permeated our carriage, a frantic desperate manic energy, everything was possible yet everything could be lost. What a place! What I bumpkin I did feel, and I was glad Miss Atwell pressed my arm and said, 'How pleased I am to have such a fashionable companion as yourself, I suspect with your loveliness at my side going about in society shall be much pleasanter, otherwise I would quite stick out as a pretender.'

'Oh no Miss Atwell, you could never be so, you are so learned and witty and-' I paused suddenly wondering where Betsey was in this throng of faces. 'I suspect most people are pretenders here. I think that is rather the point.'

She laughed. 'How right you are.'

Miss Atwell had booked us a large room in a grand London inn, which she had arranged by correspondence. She advised me, as I was noticing she was often want to do despite her predictions of me being too pretty to be a spinster, about how a single lady must conduct herself in such a situation.

'For a single lady travelling alone, organisation is the most important thing for it is more dangerous for a woman to be without a place to stay than a man. I ended at your Mama's lodging house after the place I had organised turned out to be owned by a letch, another dangerous pothole for a single lady, but I did not resign from that lodging until I found someone else more secure. I shall never forget my relief when your pretty Mama opened her front door.'

The inn keeper of our London residence was neither pretty nor friendly, but the room was large and clean and she sent us up tea and sandwiches without being asked. I stared out of the window, we were not far from Regent's Street and all was busy and bustling. Bristol was busier than both Bath and Brighton but I was still unprepared for this volume of people - so many forcing there way along, old young, rich, poor, and such fashions; all the ladies looked like fashion plates in their Grecian style chemise gowns - and as for the gentlemen! So many uniforms, so much style, frothy cravats, polished boots and smart jackets, all like the illustrations of Beau Brummel.

Miss Atwell joined me at the window before saying she would go for a lie down, and then once refreshed, we could take a walk. She had high hopes of seeing the British Museum this afternoon. I smiled at her eagerness, and felt a pang for Lydia for doubtless she would dearly love to go to such a place. I would have to pay extra attention to compose an excellent letter for her.

I also went to lie down but was so filled with joyous anticipation that I could not sleep. Looking around our room my eyes fell on our trunks. I resolved to unpack them, Miss Atwell would be pleased I had done so when she awoke and I enjoyed handling our new pretty clothes. Once that labour was done I was sure to be able to sleep for a few hours.

Chapter 29

Lydia

Ruby visited me, just after I had breakfast. Luckily the vile Winthorpes were not awake yet, for doubtless Mr Winthorpe would have made his disapproval of her race clear, and the women would have gawked. He had already commented that Bristol was crawling with Negroes and savages, and that he had often been obliged to take a different route to avoid such unsavoury types, which I thought was somewhat of an exaggeration.

Ruby's visit was announced with a knock at the door. Her younger brother Matthew jumped down from the cart to present me with a crate of vegetables for Mother, smiling and wishing me a good morning. He made no comment as to the reason why I answered the door in a long coat or that my hair was cropped so short.

'Matthew will be back in a little while. He had to make a delivery down the road, so he will pick me up when that is done and take me to Syrett's.'

I nodded, as Matthew touched his hat and climbed back up to the carriage. I ought to invite Ruby in without hesitation but a panic overtook me. Suppose Mr Winthorpe came downstairs early? He would be furious if he saw her. I had already done much to endanger our place here. I swallowed. No, I would not talk to Ruby on the doorstep. I stood back and invited her inside. She sat on the sofa, as such a close friend should, but I felt worried again and guiltily wished we had gone into the kitchen.

'Well,' I said, overly cheerful to hide my unease. 'What a pleasant surprise this is.'

Ruby smiled. 'I got your letters, I am sorry I did not reply earlier. I have been occupied a great deal recently.'

'Occupied how?'

She looked away. 'Mr Bradley has been courting me.'

'Oh yes of course,' I said spitefully, his very name setting me on edge. 'Mr Bradley.'

'Yes,' she turned to face me again, her eyes sharp. 'And what is wrong with Mr Bradley?'

'How do you know I think there is anything wrong with him?'

'Your expression, your tone of voice.'

'Well, I …I think he does not know you-'

'That is the point of a courtship, so he may get to know me.'

'He is so dull, so bland-'

'He is not-'

'He's not as interesting as you, as pretty as you, as-' I stopped before saying as lovely and started to pace.

'He is interesting,' Ruby said. 'He is an abolitionist, and very liberal in many of his views. He has an interest in travel and geology. He reads widely and he is kind…'

She trailed off.

'So,' I said, tersely. 'You would have him if he proposed?'

'Yes I would,' she did not even hesitate.

'Do you love him?'

'No,' she said in a small voice. 'Of course not yet, but we do not all have that luxury.'

'What about his family? Will they approve?'

It was her turn to look wounded. 'His young brother lives in India, his sister is married to a Scotch man and lives in Aberdeen and his parents are dead. I am under no illusion that this has helped him feel comfortable in courting me. There are no immediate relations to disapprove. He inherited the family home in Redland and that is where we shall live, though we may travel to find more liberal circles. He does not have a great income but at least he has the house.'

'So it has all been decided?'

She nodded, tears suddenly welling in her eyes. 'It would seem so, all he has to do is ask. Mama, Papa, they are delighted. They never thought I would be married. Fleur thinks it paves the way for her to marry, and George is beyond relieved – a white, blonde gentleman wants to marry me! My children could be pale enough not to shame him! I cannot refuse, Lydia. This is my only chance.'

Her tears came more freely now, and she wiped her eyes on a handkerchief embroidered with roses.

'I knew you would be angry with me, but you are the only one I can talk to.'

I sighed. We were friends, I ought be happy for her. Happy that she was attaching herself to some mediocre man? But then she was right, there were worse men than Mr Bradley and not everyone would see her as they should. I sat next to her.

'I think I should like to be mistress of my own house, and he has a very lovely garden that he says can be mine. That should make me every happy. I could never marry a man without a garden.'

'I know.'

She gave a brave little laugh. 'I wish…' she paused. 'Last night I wished that Hugh Sommers could be real, and that he would like me, and we could have our own garden and perhaps we might run an apothecary together. How merry we would be.'

Her words wrenched my heart, she had just put into voiced all that I wanted.

'But Hugh Sommers is a fiction,' she sighed. 'And so I must be grateful for gentle Mr Bradley.'

I reached over and pressed her hand. 'If only we could be wealthy heiresses and not have to marry at all.'

She gave a hollow laugh, before straightening up. 'And now for the other reason of my visitation. Your proposal for selling Mr Campbell some tinctures.'

'Yes,' I said trying to gather myself, despite the dread which was inching up my body.

'I think I should like it to be part of the venture - only Matthew must be my face, if Mr Campbell requests a meeting.'

'Matthew?' I said.

'I am assuming you have not told Mr Campbell my gender?'

'No-'

'And I cannot dress as a boy, Lydia-'

'You-'

She held up her hand. 'It is a lot to take on and I do not think Mr Bradley would approve-'

I gave a snort of indignation and she frowned at me.

'Besides, even if I was a boy I would still be clearly mulatto which Mr Campbell may not take kindly to. He's scowled at me the few times I have seen him as it is-'

'He scowls at everybody.'

'He might recognise me. I think he would be far more likely to accept Matthew as the maker of the tinctures. Matthew could pass as white, or maybe quadroon at worse and he is of the desirable gender. He is no good at botany – in fact, bless him he doesn't have much a head for book learning at all. But what he is good at is business. He will probably take over the family business, not George. George will be too busy living in Glasgow as a doctor and pretending to be white.' She drew a breath. 'Apologies, what I mean is Matthew might do well with Mr Campbell for he would likely negotiate a good deal. I will give him a portion of my share. Maybe if all goes well with Mr Campbell, we could even sell some tinctures through our business as well, so it would be good to have Matthew involved earlier.'

I nodded, it was a sensible plan but I was annoyed to have to share her again. 'It is a good idea,' I said, then couldn't help spitefully adding. 'But will Mr Bradley approve?'

'I do not see why not.'

'Very well then.'

A knock at the door told us Matthew had arrived to collect her. Ruby admitted to hinting to him that there may be an enterprise she would need his help with and that had he expressed an interest. She told me I may as well stay in my boyish garb whilst we broke the news to him, and I realised this meant staying in the parlour a while longer. If the Winthorpes did emerge, Hugh Sommers and two mulattos discussing a duplicitous business venture would definitely cause them much aggravation, so I suggested we go to the kitchen as truthfully the guests could come down and overhear us as they expected free reign over our parlour.

We sat in the kitchen, Matthew looking between us, waiting to be told. Despite Ruby's claim that he could pass as white, I was not inclined to agree. Whilst he was not as dark as her, he was not as light as George. Mr Campbell was sure to notice, wasn't he? Maybe he wouldn't mind, but Mr Campbell liked to mind about things, although this was going to make him money which was something he was rather fond of.

Ruby was outlining the idea of the tinctures. Matthew asked questions, his Bristolian accent the thickest in his family, something I was sure was an affectation to emphasize his English heritage. He sat back and folded his arms, his expression one of a serious old man. 'It's a good idea, I wonder we haven't done it before. Sound money maker I reckon. So, who are you intending to sell it to, Rue?'

Ruby looked at me.

'Mr Campbell,' I said. 'He is a local surgeon.' I hesitated, thinking how worrisome it was that more and more people were coming into my secret. What would Matthew make of it? Passing as something you were not was well known to his family, but I was aware my dressing as a boy could easily be considered more shocking, distasteful even. I could live a simple life as a woman if I choose, he could not live a simple life as a black man.

'I am his apprentice.'

'Apprentice? In what?'

'To become a surgeon. He thinks my name Hugh Sommers.'

'Hugh? Why on earth would he think you are called Hugh? A queer name for a girl…oh.'

'I told you he was not the brightest,' Ruby said and he swatted her, but then crossed his arms again, furrowed his brow. 'So you dress as a boy,' he eyed me and I unbuttoned my coat. He glanced at my hair again, eyes rounding as if just realising it was cropped.

'It is a strange sight,' he said. 'You look a milksop, but a boy nonetheless. I cannot see that you would ever look like a mature man though.'

'Yes,' I said. 'That might pose a problem, but for now Mr Campbell is interested in the tinctures.'

Matthew nodded. 'Is it against the law?' he gestured at me.

'I do not know,' Ruby admitted.

'I do not think it is exactly against the law,' I said.

'Well, it would be fraud at least, would it not? Possibly indecency. Lewd behaviour.'

'Why is Lydia lewd and incident?' Ruby snapped. 'She is clever and determined-'

Colour rose in my cheeks as Ruby spoke so well of me but Matthew held up his hands. 'But she is wearing breeches,' he said. 'It isn't done. I do not think this will end well.'

'Lydia is careful She will not be discovered. And there is money to be made.'

'Mr Campbell's main focus as a surgeon is not the welfare of his patients but the welfare of his pockets.'

Matthew's eyes brightened. 'Is that so? He will pay handsomely then?'

'I think so and he will sell it even more handsomely to his spa patients I expect.'

The thought of money decided it to for Matthew. He stood up. 'Very well, I will do it. Rue, you ought coach me on the botany in case he quizzes me.'

'Of course.'

He nodded, satisfied. 'And I must get used to calling you Sommers then?'

'Yes.'

'So be it. When do we meet this Campbell fellow then?'

Amelia

Miss Atwell was excited to attend the theatre and I organised tickets to the Royal Opera House. We did not know many people in London, but at least this would get us seen and maybe lead to introductions. I made us dresses in Bristol for the occasion, as attending the theatre had been high among Miss Atwell's desires and if Brighton and Bath had been anything to go by, I learnt that attending the theatre must be done in the best of style or there was little point.

Miss Atwell's gown was cream, in Indian silk with an edging of teal. My own was the palest pink and simmered in the candlelight. I secured a pink rose in my hair to finish the look, whilst advising Miss Atwell wildflowers and greenery looked very well with her reddish hair. While not quite as old as Mama, she was nearing thirty and looked very youthful, so could easily wear pretty fashions, even if she was more used to clomping about the place in riding habits. It was a pleasure to have the chance to make her look pretty – I rather wished Lydia would let me do the same to her but she would never stand for such a thing, which was a shame for she could be a great beauty with a few minor alterations to her dress, hair and toilette.

As we entered the theatre Miss Atwell was still clomping despite her finery, so I took her arm hoping she would calm her step to keep pace with me. There was already a crowd milling about and I was pleased to notice ladies glancing at our outfits – a few smiling without malice behind their fans. The gentlemen also smiled at us, a rake bowed his head in our direction, with mockery, so I ignored him. I was not about to titter at nonsense, Miss Atwell completely ignored it, engaged as she was at observing the architecture of the place and drawing my attention to various pretty details in the plaster work. We passed a group of cavalry officers – not nearly as dashing as one might hope, but their plain looks were boosted by their scarlet jackets and the least dull of their number brazenly stepped into our path.

'Ladies, may I introduce myself?' he said, laughter in his eyes.

'Perhaps later,' Miss Atwell said guiding me past him. I had to supress a laugh, which his fellows did not. Miss Atwell was perhaps not as unobservant and naïve as I had been thinking.

'He seemed the most tiresome bore,' she whispered.

'He barely said anything–'

'Oh, verbally yes, but he was the centre of his group, and in introducing himself to us he was trying to be the centre of our evening as well as the centre of the room. I suspect most of these folk guess we are new to this metropolis, they were watching to see what we will do.'

'You would certainly have confounded them then.'

'Good. Now we can get to the important business of the opera.'

As the gold leafing on an arch caught her attention, something else caught mine. A navy officer with thick, wavy dark brown hair, well-polished boots, frilled cuffs appearing from beneath his jacket. My heart leapt, unsettling me. Could it be Lt Dara Driscoll? Did I want it to be him? I drew myself up, smiled, expecting his cheery face as the man turned but it was not to be. A handsome man nonetheless, but not Driscoll. I quickly glanced away, not wanting to draw the attention of the stranger.

What would I have said to Driscoll anyway, had it been him? I had been very rude to him on our last encounter, and he had been presumptuous enough to want to write to me…if only our last meeting could have somehow been different and if only I had heeded his warning about his half-brother.

Chapter 30

Jessica

The duration of the Winthorpes' stay passed slowly, there was always some new grievance to address; the bed linen was too thin then too thick, the food too rich or had too much seasoning (how dare they! It seemed they wanted the plainest, driest food in existence), the fires were not stoked well enough or were too warm. Never in all my years of inn keeping had I met with such a querulous family.

Peter would never deal with the complaints; it was always left to me. If they were delivered to Peter he would always relay them to me with a disapproving air, saying that this hotel had been my idea I really ought work better at it. When it came to take the praise, which I dare say there was much more of, it was always 'our' hotel, or even 'his'.

When the Winthorpes were not complaining about their lodgings it was Bristol in general they found fault with, and all they met here. I was not sure if they wanted me to answer for it or just to agree with them. At first I thought it was the husband who was the chief complainer and the wife was down at heel, but perhaps that was why they fell in love for she complained to him then he complained to me. Their maid was the only one with any cheer, but most of the time she liked to complain about them which also grew wearisome. I was half tempted to write to hurry Mrs Pemberton's return.

Amelia's letters were a welcome escape from them, and thankfully she wrote more frequently than she had in Bath and Brighton. She wrote of her trips to the theatre, to church services at St Paul's Cathedral and Westminster Abbey, public balls, parks and the British Museum with much more enthusiasm than her previous letters had contained describing all they met, the fashions and sights, always giving her lively opinions in great detail. Miss Atwell wrote as well, often to assure me that Amelia was doing well and was quite indispensable to her – something which made me proud.

My other longed-for correspondence did not re-emerge. I heard nothing from Captain Parnell. I had started to think of him as James and now any intimacy had vanished. Sometimes I blamed myself for allowing the girls too much freedom, but other times I was angry at him for being churlish, and holding a grudge. Girls were wont to pry – maybe he ought to take it as a compliment that Lydia thought he was growing close enough to our family to warrant investigation! But then he was proud, he had few enough belongings to have them searched, he was honest and upstanding…but why had he not written? It was not beyond the realms of possibility that he was engaged with navy business. The newspapers and every gossip about seemed paralysed by fear that Britain should expect to be invaded at any moment by Napoleon. The navy was our best defence. Suppose he had come to harm? But then the newspapers would report it if the HMS Aries sunk and as his tenant someone would have to notify me, but the thought of his demise twisted my stomach and caused panic to well in my chest. Since everyday my mind whirled with these thoughts – and I was caught between this and the Winthorpes in the grim late winter months - I resolved to write to him myself.

I made no reference to Lydia's actions nor did I offer another apology, neither did I refer to the dance we shared - nor anything else which had made Christmas so pleasant. Instead I wrote of the present; news of the girls, the Winthorpes and our friends, as well as articles in the news and new recipes for the pies I was making. I sent it, filled with girlish hopes for a response but as winter turned to spring and the Winthorpes' stay came to an end, I had no reply. It did not stop me from writing once more however.

I consoled myself with the thought that he might not have replied as he would not have received my letter if he hadn't docked. The rumblings of invasions from the French in the newspapers only grew worse so my worries in that area were not assuaged but I found at least I could be easy in the thought that I was doing all I could to bring back the intimacy which had been becoming so dear to me.

Amelia

We made Mr Syrett's brother-in-law's acquaintance, and his married daughter was of an age with Miss Atwell so made a point of introducing her to her circle. They were all pleasant enough and introduced us at a few private balls as well as the theatre. All of them were involved in commerce and trade in someway and we did not make it obvious quite how rich Miss Atwell had become.

I do not think Miss Atwell would have been comfortable with that, nor would she have been comfortable socially with those who were now her financial equals, which would mostly likely be the wives of very successful industrialists, plantation owners and some lesser nobility. One of our group was a bluestocking, who took us to a few meetings where there were some more wealthy women but wealth and society introductions were not discussed, more politics, the abolition of the slave trade, literature and other pressing concerns. I found these meetings not as dry as I would have thought. Some of the women were earnest but a few of them had wicked senses of humour and an interesting way of looking at things which made me grow in sympathy with their causes.

Lydia

Mr Campbell eyed Matthew with the same contempt he eyed everyone.

'You look very young.'

'I am one and twenty sir,' Matthew lied, surprising me. I fought the urge to look at him. We had not agreed on the lie and, though I approved of it, I rather wished he had told me he was going to do it.

Mr Campbell grunted. 'And where are you from?'

'Bristol sir,' Matthew replied, his accent growing thicker.

Mr Campbell rolled his eyes and gestured at Matthew's face and hair. 'You know what
I mean.'

'My father is Spanish sir,' this lie came smoothly as well.

'The very south of Spain is it?'

Matthew looked stumped but nodded.

'Which town?'

'Barcelona...?' Matthew blushed as he spoke. Mr Campbell laughed.

'There a lesser known Barcelona in the south, is there?'

'I...'

'You do know Spaniards are basically all half blackamoors? You look rather like living evidence of that.'

'Sir-'

Mr Campbell turned to me. 'Think you can lie to me and get away with it?'

I knew I could but that was not the point. 'I did not lie to you, sir.'

'No but you left out certain truths, didn't you?'

'I just thought you might prefer-'

'I would have paid a white man full price if that's what you mean. Young Mr Thomas here can have three quarters and be grateful for it. If word gets out people will think I'm dealing with a witch doctor.' He turned back to Matthew. 'Am I?'

'No! Certainly not! My mother is a botanist-'

'Better and better, that would be tantamount to a witch a hundred years ago.' He snorted. 'I suppose you are the brother of Sommers' pretty little mulatto?'

Matthew went to bluster then nodded.

"There you are see,' he said with a wicked glint in his eye directed at me. 'Everything is much better when we are honest, is it not?'

Amelia

From London we went to Belgium, Antwerp to be precise. I had never travelled by boat before and Miss Atwell made it sound like an adventure, so I had rather been looking forward to it. How wrong I was not to be cautious.

Not long after departure a wretched nausea overtook me, which forced me to bed and kept me there for most of the voyage. Miss Atwell said sea sickness was quite common, but I did not think it would be this bad! I was quite debilitated, by the time we docked in Antwerp the dry land was a blessed relief. Luckily our hotel was very comfortable so I was able to rest and recuperate in peace.

Chapter 31

Jessica

The Winthorpes were gone and Mrs Pemberton would not arrive until next week, with an old widower called Mr Stichcombe taking the other room a few days afterwards, so I had some time to myself. It would give me time to try some new pie recipes and give the house a thorough clean.

I rose with Lydia and made her breakfast whilst in my house coat, before she went off for the day. Yesterday it had been one year since Peter died. It was a strange, unsettling thought that I could now come out of mourning. We had gone to church and prayed for him. We had yet to visit his grave and I wondered if we ever would. Henry would certainly not pay for us to go; he didn't even know where we lived now. I supposed I could save up, but then who would watch the lodging house whilst we were away? Would Mr Campbell allow Lydia a leave of absence to work?

A cold thought struck me that no one would have tended Peter's grave. I had seen the family patch, it was not a mausoleum or anything so grand but there were two large stones next to each other dating from Peter's grandparents, which also included their deceased children as well as Peter's father and mother, their deceased children and Henry's late wife.

I did not suppose the girls or I would be buried there. Had Peter died with funds he would have been buried in Bristol and we could have had our own small plot. The Fitzwilliam grave was doubtless clean, but who would leave flowers for Peter? What inscription did Henry give him? How unsettling to think of Peter in the ground with his ancestors and Henry's wife but never me or the girls. I shivered.

Though I would never openly own to it, the prospect of donning my old clothes again filled me with much excitement. To always be marked as a widow was a dreary thing, and I never really favoured dark colours. I liked my clothes, and almost felt that my widows' weeds were like wearing the clothes of someone one else. I missed being able to walk about without sideways glances of pity from strangers', without glancing down at myself to remember my husband was dead.

After Lydia left, I knelt at the chest with my old clothes in and opened it. The colours - greens, blues and teals - seemed to shine up at me and soft fabrics cried out to be touched but suddenly I felt sick and recoiled.

Peter loved the teal dress and on the morning of his death I wore the green, like a flash of lightning I remembered him grabbing my arm as a wore the blue...oh my God. My husband was dead, gone, and never coming back. He had loved me and like a surge I remembered how much I had loved him, always liked him as a girl and fell in love with him after Lydia was born, and loved him steadily until...until...until did it fade away? Or did it just suddenly stop when he died and all was revealed? How could such a feeling, such a regard that was there for so long, just have stopped?

A pain swelled as if in the centre of my head, filling out to a piercing headache. I stood up, backed away from the case of memories, a thousand more coming forth, laughing with Peter on a walk home from church wearing the green dress, seeing the love in his eyes as he looked at me in the blue, the feel of his hand on my arm through the sleeve of the teal...and my feelings towards him. I returned his sentiments, love rose in my chest and choked in my throat.

For a few moments my anger at him dissolved as I grasped all that happiness and contentment that he bought me but then the anger at his betrayal came back, strong and heavy like a black cloud. Had I betrayed him as well? My feelings for Captain Parnell...whatever they were, Peter had known the Captain, albeit briefly.

Would anything have happened if Peter had lived? Heavens no! James would have been just another guest. He would have had no reason to install me in the lodging house, so I owed what had been flourishing into one of the dearest friendships of my life to my husband's death had Peter not died would he carried on secretly paying off Henry, leaving me none the wiser? Still content, thinking him a good husband. Had he lived and paid off the debt I would never have known, and all could have continued as before. Overcome by my pounding head and racing thoughts I sunk back into bed.

I was surprised that I awoke with Lydia entering the room. She held a rush light aloft in darkness. I had slept all day, yet still felt fatigued.

'Are you well?' she asked sitting on my bed. 'The Evans' oldest boy just knocked on the door. He said when they tried to bring their bread for the oven earlier at the usual time you did not answer, so I took it in for them.'

'Thank you, I have a great pain in my head and feel tired, I think it is some sort of nerves bought on by your father's anniversary.'

Lydia touched my forehead and nodded. 'You look very weak but have no fever. I will make us some dinner then you can go back to sleep.'

I was too tired to argue.

Lydia

It seemed Mother had taken to her bed for another day. She rose only to bake the bread of the Evans' and some of our other neighbours, then come down to put together a dinner for me. She toasted stale bread and got cheese and cold meets ready, hardly up to her usual fare. She looked exhausted and the impression of her pillow was still on her cheek. I had never known her behave so.

'Mother,' I said checking her temperature but she was not feverish. 'You are ill. What are your symptoms?'

'I am just exhausted, my head aches and I am so weary ...' she drifted off, picking at the cold met on her plate. Melancholy, I thought. It occurred to me she had not had such melancholy last year. We had been so busy trying to make sure we had somewhere to live, then trying to make the lodging house ran smoothly. She swallowed, her skin grey, her hair limp.

'What brought on this headache?' I asked.

'I was going to unpack my old clothes,' she said quietly. 'I was looking forward to it, but now it seems rather wicked.'

'Why? Your mourning is done.'

She looked at me sharply, then softened. 'That is true, but I feel as if I have not mourned him properly, despite the black.'

'You had to survive, *we* had to survive.'

She nodded and I supposed she was thinking of Captain Parnell.

'You cannot help who you befriend now he has gone,' I said quietly. A weight started to press on my own chest. I had been busy, very busy for the past few days, so much so I had not said a prayer for him. I swallowed. But maybe that was what I intended. I had been without a father for a year and it seemed much longer. I did not dwell on his memory, but I found suddenly I could not quite remember his face, it blurred. Upstairs was a likeness Amelia drew. I thought that it was not a very accurate but I could not remember why. I reached over and squeezed mother's hand.

'We have not been to his grave,' she said.

'No, we have not.'

'Maybe we ought, say goodbye properly now life is calmer.'

I nodded, not sure I wanted to see it. Perhaps if he had been buried nearer and visiting his grave had been part of our daily routine, I would have grown used to it but the thought of journey to Glastonbury to see it did more than repulse me; it frightened me. What superstitious nonsense! I shifted in my seat. We ought to go; it was right and proper. 'Shall I organise a trip for us?'

She shook her head. 'No, you are busy. I will organise it. I think it would do me good to have some useful employment. I think if the weather remains fine, we should be able to go and come back before the next lot of guests arrive.'

'So soon? But what of my work?'

'Well, I can go alone-'

'No that will not do. I will go. I suppose I shall have tell Campbell a lie, he would want notice for such a trip otherwise. I will write a note and tell him I have a fever.'

'Wouldn't he want to come round to examine you?'

'I doubt it,' I said.

'Very well,' she said standing. 'Whilst you do that, I'll pack our things.'

We took a stagecoach the next morning, I dressed in a mourning gown and Mother was also in black. The coach was busy with farmers. We were the only women and I rather wished I stayed dressed as Hugh. The eldest farmer had an affected stately manner and made a show of treating us in an overly chivalrous way then looking at the other men, to impress upon them how great an example he was setting. I am not sure why when men are polite and considerate to women it is chivalrous and they expect all kinds of praise for it, whereas it would be shocking if a woman was not polite to a man.

For a large part of the journey he conversed with Mother - or rather spoke at her, telling her how he was also widowed and had several younger children at home who all needed a new Mama. I read my book, or pretended to then feigned passages Mother might be interested in that I had to point out to her. When it was lunch time his eyes grew wide at the food which came from our basket but when he was not offered any he turned out of the window and started sipping on his flask, which thankfully sent him to sleep. We arrived in Glastonbury in the evening, just in time for the old man to wake up and offer us a place to stay in his house which Mother declined.

'It might be good for you to stay with locals, you being a stranger in this town.'

'I am not a stranger in this town sir,' Mother said, her accent growing broader and his eyebrows raising. 'Which you would have known had you asked me.'

Mother made for an inn, which we had visited before when Amelia and I were children. We stayed with Henry's family on the two times we visited before but Mother always called at this particular inn for the cleaning woman had grown up with her. When we stepped into the place, a few of the locals turned to look, but Mother ignored them and saw who she wanted behind the bar.

'Mrs Peglar?'

A woman with course sandy hair and weather beaten skin straightened up. 'Jessie Sommers as I live and breathe!' She hastened round to embrace Mother. 'This must be one of your fine girls?'

'Yes Polly, it is Lydia, my eldest.'

'What a beauty she is! Don't you look just like your mother? Quite a fine lady!'

She pressed my arm. 'I heard about Mr Peter; I am sorry for your loss. How do you fare? None of the Fitzwilliam servants seemed to agree what your brother-in-law did about you and the girls.'

'He evicted us,' Mother said smoothly. 'But a friend of ours owned a lodging house and I have become the landlady of that place. We have been lucky.'

'Oh I am pleased. You'll be wanting a room then?'

'Yes please, for two nights. We have come to see Peter's grave.'

'Of course. I shall go and talk to Mr Coole. I am sure he has spare rooms. You ought come to visit my cottage tomorrow. My Samuel is of an age with Miss Fitzwilliam I fancy.' She chuckled with a wink and hurried off. 'Mr Coole! Mrs Peter Fitzwilliam, Jessie Sommers as was, needs a room!'

Jessica

The Fitzwilliam family grave was in the churchyard at St John The Baptist. I was surprised that after all these years how easy it was to find the family plot. As a child, with Polly, I wandered among the tombstones playing hide and seek when I was supposed to be running errands. The Fitzwilliam one was always the best place to hide.

Later, in the first few weeks of my marriage, when I lived with Peter in the Fitzwilliam family home, his mother would walk past the tombstone after church on a Sunday. Once she looked at me and smiled, saying in all earnestness, 'One day you shall be here as well, my dear.' The thought chilled me, and I avoided the grave until our move to Bristol.

The twice we visited, I stood back while Peter showed the girls and they traced the names of their family. I heard Henry mutter to Peter afterward that since they were girls they would be buried at their husbands' family graves not in his family grave. He hoped Peter explained this to them but Peter swatted him away and said it hardly mattered – though what he meant 'hardly mattered' I wasn't sure. Half of me wished he had got angry at Henry for his snide ways, but then what would that have achieved? It chilled me to think of myself alone in such a busy grave, my girls buried away from me, but now I doubted I would be buried there at all. It was a strange relief but also unsettling.

I stopped at the wall and tapped it as we entered the graveyard. Lydia gave me a strange look and I realised how quickly I had fallen back into old habits. Whenever I visited with my mother we had always tapped the wall. 'Hello Papa,' I would say.

One of my father's dying wishes was that we not waste money on a headstone no matter how modest for him, or any sort of burial finery. He was in an unmarked grave in the churchyard. He wanted to make sure not a single penny was taken away from the money that he saved for my future – pride rose in my chest for my mother had given me to Peter with a fifty pounds – rather less than what he might of expected from a girl of his own standing but a fortune from my own class. The pride was punctured painfully, searing in my throat. All that carefully saved money to secure a husband who would gamble it away.

'Mother?'

I blinked my tears away and told her the story of my father, omitting my own bitter thoughts. Arm in arm I led her over to the Fitzwilliam grave. For a few seconds I averted my eyes, my old fear pressing down on me, along with heavy memories of being here at Peter's side, his smell of tobacco and linen, his steady breathing. My eyes fell on the church, and my mind brought forth the image of Peter, so well turned out on our wedding day. He was the age I was now, so handsome, beaming eyes alight at the sight of me. He always looked so pleased to see me. Why, if that was the case, did he risk everything; our safety and security? His actions made a mockery of what he promised in that church, made a mockery of any feelings of affection he had for me.

'It is a deal smaller than I remember it,' Lydia said.

'Perhaps you are a deal bigger,' I said, thinking it just as imposing as ever.

'I suppose,' she said. 'I am going to take a turn around graveyard so you may be alone.'

'Very well.'

It was the good times I should meditate on here, all those happy years. The times when I felt safe, felt lucky, felt as though our union was meant to be, that he was the best thing that ever happened to me. I must not focus on how much of it might have been built on a lie and if he lied about his gambling - and was so reckless - had he ever felt the same? I cried, thinking of all that had been lost, of the bliss I had found in ignorance, in all that contented happiness that I would not have again.

'I loved you,' I said. 'And I thank you for our daughters and for the times we had in our hotel. I thank you for being of easy temperament ...' I trailed off, wandering if all his easiness had been because of his guilt at his gambling. I took a deep breath. Was it best to forgive him? Did I want to forgive him? There was a strange sort of power in not forgiving him, but that would only fester in me. I should try and forgive him and let go of all these questions, I could not change the past, I could not worry about what is over and done. I will not remember it now exactly as it was for all that has happened in between so I must let it lie and be grateful that I was not treated with cruelty, that I had living children and that I learnt how to manage my business and lived the life I wanted to.

Now, I found I did not want to go back to The Fitzwilliam. I liked the lodging house. It gave me more freedom. I liked making the pies. Did I want that forever? As to that I was not sure, but grief aside, I was happily situated.

'I loved you, Peter,' I said again, tears drying, resting my hand on his tombstone. 'And I forgive you.'

I went to find Lydia.

Lydia

Mother said she would meet me back at the inn and perhaps we could stroll up to the old pagan tor or some such. I agreed. Amelia would have loved to see such a thing. I eyed the grim Fitzwilliam tomb. Now, that I was here I wasn't sure what to do. I touched the stone bearing father's name - it said he was the 'second son of the above', making no mention that he was a husband and father in his own right.

I had not played cribbage in an age. Mother and Amelia were no good at it. Perhaps I could teach Ruby. I enjoyed the game or, perhaps more, I enjoyed the morning hour that I had Father to myself, when he was not praising Mother or Amelia for their beauty and femininity but sat engrossed in the game with me. He never played easy or let me win, in fact I never won. I see why now if he made a career as a gambler, an unpractised girl could hardly have been his rival. Had I been a boy would he have taken me to his gambling dens? Perhaps we would have made quite a team, or perhaps we would have lost even more money.

Sometimes in the evening he would teach me and Amelia other card games and watch us play. I could always beat Amelia so then I would play him and he would win. His chuckling face came back to me clearly, eyes crinkling at the sides. In life I had not quite realised how much Amelia looked like him. All I had was the colour of his hair. The ache in my chest twisted and I sighed.

I did miss his presence...I knew we were lucky to have a relaxed father. Even if he was not a radical, he was not a tyrant. What epitaph is that? Here lies Peter Fitzwilliam, not a tyrant, uncommonly good at cards until he wasn't, let his wife and daughters have some freedoms whilst he spent their money away.

I found I was crying; I had not wept in months. 'Hello Father,' I managed. 'And hello from Amelia.'

She would have got more out of this visit than I. Guilt rose in me at what she was always so quick to point out, that I am closer to Mother. The thought of Mother lying in that grave gave my stomach such a sharp turn that I felt sick, faint and physically pained all at the same time. Not that I prefer it this way, not that I am choosing it.

'You ought have let me help with accounts,' I said. 'I am a good book-keeper, I help Mother with it now.'

My mind whirled suddenly, recalling of the violent nature of his death, of all the dying I have seen this past year and I wondered if he lay dying on the cobbles before he was carried to us or if it was quick, a hard blow to the head. I hoped it was the latter, I hoped he did not suffer. I hoped he was thinking of ways to pay the debt off, not of how to gamble more. A chill went down my spine. I hope he did not walk out in front of that horse on purpose, the shame of the debt being too much for him. I swallowed, trying to banish the ugly thought. Please, I prayed, let that not be true, before I turned and hurried to find Mother.

Chapter 32

Jessica

Lydia was quiet after seeing the grave, and I too was pensive, it all seeming more final than ever before. There was a sadness and a relief, a beginning and an end. I made no secret of my stay in the inn, but did not directly call on or write to any of Peter's relatives, merely walked up to the tor with Lydia and visited Polly Peglar. Peter's relatives did not call at the inn nor did we see them about the village.

When the coach departed we were a much quieter party - a woman with her two young children, returning to Bristol after spending some months tending to her dying sister, a young lawyer going to take up a new position. He looked at Lydia discreetly, but she did not seem to notice.

We arrived at night and by morning Lydia was back out to work again. When I stood in the kitchen after she left, I started to cry - deep sobbing that shook me all over. It went on for a while, before I stopped. I took a deep breath, feeling as if I had been scrubbed clean. The likeness Amelia had drawn of Peter I would hang up in our bedroom, then I would sort through Peter's clothes, keeping the waistcoat Amelia embroidered, his favourite item, and sell the rest. After that I would take my dresses out of the chest and remodel them, giving something old a new beginning.

*

Mrs Pemberton arrived with a new maid called Molly to the hour that she had predicted. She commented with an arched eyebrow that I was out of black then asked as to Captain's Parnell's whereabouts.

'He is at sea.'

'Indeed?' said she, pausing on the stairs. 'That green looks well on you.'

She stayed for another six months and the other room was let to various other people; a few elderly widows and widowers, Mrs Nutall returned for a couple of months and we also had a couple of newlyweds.

Lydia worked harder than ever, and whilst there was a pause in Amelia's letters in the time she travelled from London to Europe, once she arrived she wrote often, detailing all the splendour both natural and man-made, as well as the fashion, food and music and people she met with. I hoped she might meet a nice young man, and whilst her letters carried hints of the odd encounter with potential beaus nothing ever came of it. She was happy however, taking her role seriously and enjoying Miss Atwell's company. They often sent gifts; lace gloves and collars, fans, scarves and the occasional book. We were quite spoilt.

When Lydia did have spare moments, I found she was enjoying learning about setting bones. Mr Campbell and she made a tidy profit selling the tinctures. Because of this we saw more of Matthew, who was generally a cheerful fellow and Ruby would still often visit even after she became engaged to Mr Bradley; something Lydia said very little about. I could not blame her, it can be hard to think of one's friend marrying before one's self but Ruby seemed determined to keep up the friendship.

Sometimes I would still miss Peter, like a lingering doubt, but I also missed Captain Parnell and his letters and regretted how we had parted. Over the months I wrote two more letters that went unanswered. He was at sea, he was busy and I was being selfish and childish expecting a letter, but it did not stop my heart from beating every time the post was delivered and being disappointed when nothing from him was forth coming. I tried not to dwell on the fact he could be injured or dead for if either of those were the case we would have at least heard of it, for legal reasons if nothing else.

On a crisp cold November morning as I baked pheasant pies and the area was thick with the spices I had cured the meat in, there was a knock at the door. It was a young sickly looking navy officer.

'Would you like a room? We have no vacancies at present-'

'No Ma'am. Are you Mrs Fitzwilliam?'

'Yes.' My heart contracted. This was the man who would tell me James was dead.

He produced a thick envelope from his coat. It was not edged in black. 'Captain Parnell asked that I deliver this to you.'

'Thank you.' I clutched it with both hands. 'Where is he?'

'He is still at sea. I have been released from duty.'

I nodded. 'Can I offer you refreshment?'

'No, I must return to my mother. I had to honour a promise to a friend, that is all. Good day to you.' He turned to go then paused. 'And can you tell me, are you a widow *Mrs* Fitzwilliam?'

'I am, sir.'

A small smile touched his lips. 'Good day to you.'

I stepped inside, closing the door on the cold air and opened the seal, half dreading news of an eviction, or worse, his marriage to another.

'The letter was dated almost a year ago - in January when I had written to him - and there were pages, thick as a pamphlet, all covered.

I sunk into the sofa to read.

'Dear Mrs Fitzwilliam,

I hope this missive finds you well, and that there is chance for me to send it soon. We did not part as I would have wished, and I hope you can accept my apologies for my conduct. I can understand Miss Fitzwilliam's actions, it is very likely I would have done the same in her situation. It was surprise that caused my wrath and having long been a bachelor I have grown used to solitude and privacy. As for my reasons for never mentioning my step-mother, I can only repeat to you that I have met her twice in my life and she has played no role in my up-bringing. Sending her a sum to live on is the only time I give Mrs Aoife Parnell thought.

I can now see why the name 'Mrs Parnell' caused more investigation on Miss Fitzwilliam's part, something which foolishly did not occur to me in the moment, since that name is associated primarily with my mother in my own mind and now Aoife. You may be assured that I am quite embarrassed by this oversight now, and whilst there have been two Mrs *Seamus* Parnells, there is yet to be a Mrs *James* Parnell.

My father married Aoife without my knowledge 'a few years' (he was never one for accuracy) before his death when we were serving on different ships. I now believe they may have been married, or at least have been well acquainted, for much longer than that. He surprised me with the news of his wife when I was docked in Dublin and he met me there, then took me to meet the woman. She was pleasant enough, but the meeting put me ill at ease, making me suspect my father of living a parallel life in Dublin to the one he had in Liverpool. He denied this, but also claimed as he often did that his only loyalty was to the sea. As you might imagine, when he spoke so I was greatly vexed since I had witnessed my mother's loyalty only to him and her suffering at burying five of his children while he was occupied proving his loyalty to the sea and now, possibly, Aofie. By this time though, my Father and I were well practised in arguing with each other so by the time we parted we were on good terms once more.

The next I heard was a few months later, a letter from his captain informing me he had died, succumbed to ill health which had been fading for a while. I had tried to encourage him to retire and let Aofie tend to him, which he said he would do 'someday'. It only occurred to me a few days after to write to the captain, asking him if Aofie had been informed. He told me there was no record of a second Mrs Parnell – in fact there had been no mention of a first Mrs Parnell either and since my father spoke of me and my late brother Luke so often with no mention of any wife they assumed any Mrs Parnell must have died at Luke's birth, or even worse, that my father was never married at all. This left me with mixed emotions at my father's conduct, which was not a foreign sensation in regards to our relationship as you may have already surmised from this narrative, however the guilt prompted by the news that he had proudly boasted to his ship mates of my rise drove me resolve to seek out the woman who called herself his wife.

I managed to get to Dublin within the next year where I sought out Aofie. She was deeply grieved at the news of my father's demise, and was quite ignorant of it. I had pondered if her marriage to my father was witnessed either by God or law, but she seemed a good, simple sort of woman and any corruption that had befallen her was the fault of my father. Since her union with my father had produced no children, she was quite alone, so I bought her a small cottage and settled on her a modest amount each year.

There, you see I could and ought to have explained that a deal better and should have done so on our first night in the house. It was done more as an oversight than by design, I assure you. Now enough about me, how did you fare? And the girls? How do you find the Winthorpes?'

I smiled as the tone of writing, could imagining his eye rolls and raised eyebrows. He had intended to mail the letter but had no time so it turned into a diary as he sailed towards France to blockade the French ports.

Sometimes the letter hinted at the darkness of war, sometimes it was very conversational, a few times he said Lt Driscoll had requested to convey his greetings to Miss Amelia. He had at first written every day, but seeing that he would have to conserve paper went to once a week. He spoke of the past, referencing family stories and I saw how much he'd loved riding the cabs with his grandfather. It did not surprise me when he said he dreamt of owning stables of his own, and I thought I would tell him I would like to own a fine hotel once more – for grateful as I was for the lodging house it was nice to have my ambitions rekindled.

He included, to my pleasure, recipes from all over the world. He endeavoured to interview the sailors on his ship, starting with the officers, about their favourite food they had eaten on their travels. They all become rather involved in the project seeking the most obscure and exciting dishes from their memories and trying to work out recipes, some were little more than descriptions, but many had thorough instructions.

Sometimes he referenced the irony at how he assumed he'd get the chance to send me this short letter which now had turned into something quite epic, but it was so warming, so gladdening to know I had been in his thoughts and he had been so constant. He concluded by saying his midshipman Mr Scallon had been given a leave of absence thanks to relatives high up in the admiralty, due to his persistent and worsening ill health. He hoped Scallon would convey the letter faithfully to me.

When I finished reading it the light had gone low, I had only risen all day to check the pies, light a rush and stoke the fire. I felt as if I had been in good company and now I was alone again. I sighed, before rising to write a reply. Like my other few letters, he would not get them for God knew how long, but they could wait at the admiralty for him and hopefully they would find him.

Amelia

Our first stop had been Antwerp, with its large buildings and Flemish sailors then onto Brussels, pretty little Ghent and old charming Bruges. We travelled onto Amsterdam, with its red-brick houses and canals for roads, through Hamburg to Copenhagen, then down to Berlin and through to Prague - a city that looked like a fairy tale but held grisly relics in its cathedral, then Vienna, before we travelled to Italy. When we journeyed over the Alps I filled my lungs with air so fresh. Every country held new wonders and marvels as well, as so many different cuisines and fashions that I was sure to try as many as I could and write to Mama and Lydia about them in great detail.

We went all the way down to the south of Italy so we could see it in the end of summer. I was glad we did for Ravello was a delight; the lemons were the size of my fist and the air smelled heavily of citrus. The whole town was built on a hill with crocked walkways. We managed to see Pompeii whilst the weather was still clement, before heading north again. We saw the elegant Milan, then Venice – another dream-like place with even more canals than Amsterdam and such charming buildings, it was everything one dreams Italy might be. Florence, or *Firenze* as the Italians have it, was so beautiful with its white domo, then Rome with all its ruins on such a bigger scale than even the baths in Bath, provoked such awe that could not be paralleled. I could not help my imagination running wild with thoughts of dashing gladiators.

We saw many an old fine church and paintings by 'the masters'. I persisted with drawing, mostly landscapes, but several self-portraits I was unhappy with and studies of Miss Atwell which pleased her.

We attended the theatre, the opera and musical recitals; some so marvellous I wept with pleasure, we danced at many public balls and even earned invitations to private ones. We made friends, there were the Camberwells, a young married couple who we met with in various cities and the Gemmels, two brothers on their grand tour with their tutor, Mr Smith, who was of an age with Miss Atwell. We saw them often in Belgium and Amsterdam.

The elder of the Gemmel brothers, Robert, painted my likeness and I had to admit it very good. He was very proud of it. During the sittings he valiantly attempted flirtation but whilst he was amusing he reminded me of a puppy and I could not help comparing him in my mind to Lt Driscoll to whom flirtation came so easily. That might be seen as a bad quality by some, but he did not flirt with everyone. I realised in all the social situations we had been in Bristol and Bath I had never seen him once direct all his easy charm and friendliness at another lady.

Whilst I pondered this, comparing the puppy-like Robert Gemmel from a wealthy landowning family to the person I began to think of with regret as *my* lieutenant, it took me a while to realise Miss Atwell was having a flirtation of her own with Mr Smith. They both drew each other's silhouettes, and discreet letters were exchanged daily. I said nothing until I saw Miss Atwell weeping one morning while she thought I slept.

'What is it?' I asked looking at the letter in her hand.

'Mr Smith has declared his love for me.'

'Of course he has.'

'I cannot have him,' she said resolutely.

'Why ever not?'

'I will lose everything, my fortune, my independence, I cannot give that up so easily.'

'But you shall share it with Mr Smith.'

'No,' she said. 'It will all be his. No matter how nice he may seem now I cannot risk that he be a fortune hunter and this all be a disguise, for he is not a rich man.'

I felt cold. 'So you shall always close yourself off to love?'

'I fear I will have to. The risk of losing it all is too much.'

Over the months, as we travelled, letters in his handwriting would still turn up for her and she would reply.

'Maybe there is another way to live,' I said in Venice when I handed her one of his letters. 'Not in traditional matrimony, but not in disgrace.'

'What do you mean?'

'I do not know, I was merely hoping there was some option for you and Mr Smith that had not been considered.'

'I think those are the two options; disgrace or marriage.'

'Did not Mary Wollstonecraft live with an American before she married Mr Godwin?'

Miss Atwell nodded. 'And it did not end well. He turned out to be a cad and she was disgraced.'

Aside from this private sadness, Miss Atwell was her usual merry self and was apt to make friends wherever we went, and wanted to see and do everything. It was infectious, and I found myself often reading about places we went before and making lists of things I also wanted to do, which she welcomed.

To travel so widely was a disconnecting experience – the whole thing feels like a dream, yet one truly is living and experiencing so much. In some ways one is aware what is happening is deeply important and altering, but the whole experience feels as though it is happening to someone else. Nothing felt at all real, even when I realised it was father's anniversary I spent the whole day in what felt like a trance, unable to take anything in or marry together the life and loving parent that I had lost a year ago, to the life I now had.

Lydia

A few months after Father's anniversary there came the anniversary of my first year of being Mr Campbell's apprentice. He did nothing to mark the occasion, of course. It seemed I had been forgiven for the most part for our quarrel over his swindling of the patients with his old tinctures, and he was doing a roaring trade with the new ones Ruby made.

His moods were often subject to change; and were directed at the patients as much as me, so if he was in a foul mood I would be confined to his house on some cleaning or organisational duty and if he was feeling in better spirits then I would be permitted to go with him on visits. I became quite good at helping him set bones, though he never owned it.

In the summer he started to invite me to come to the tavern with him, where he laughed at my splutters when I supped the spirits which he seemed to consume with ease and speed. I realised then the reason for the changes in his moods and felt a fool for not seeing before. He did not limit the drinking of alcohol to mealtimes and evenings; once I recognised the signs of him being inebriated in the tavern I realised that this often the case outside of the tavern. I tried to only drink ale if in the tavern for fear of getting too drunk and taking him into my confidence, for while drink made Campbell changeable it made me very affable and gave me the belief that all were my friends, which was a very dangerous illusion to be under.

Ruby's courtship with Mr Bradley continued and when he proposed to her, in her family's garden, she accepted him. She wrote to me straight away and I wrote back professing joy and wishing them the very best, though all I felt was a weight of sadness in my chest, which grew when she and Mr Bradley spoke of moving to London. Mr Bradley wanted to become more heavily involved in the abolitionist cause and it was felt that he and Ruby might be more accepted in such a big metropolis. I felt such a deep sorrow at this news that I could not face Ruby and made excuses to avoid meeting with her for two weeks. When I did see her, she was all happiness. Her ever curious nature was excited by all the culture she might see in London, and she had even made plans to have the guest quarters of the house they took furnished very comfortably in the hope that I may come and visit for an extended time.

'But my apprenticeship…'

Her face fell. 'But surely something could be arranged, I can just imagine us exploring London together!'

I smiled at her and the thought was thrilling indeed, though dampened somewhat by the idea of Mr Bradley lurking about at the edge of our happiness.

Chapter 33

Jessica

I wrote a few more letters. It was strange to think that they would languish in the admiralty, but I took comfort from the knowledge that somewhere on the channel letters were being written to me. The thought was both heartening but also worrying; the threat and danger of war was even more pressing than before – like an oppressive humour in the air and James was out there, part of the first line of defence.

The war even seemed to cause a delay in Amelia's letters; several arrived all at once, with a warning that she had heard future ones might be delayed in blockades across the channel and I wondered at the route the letters had taken and how many had been lost on the way.

Mrs Pemberton returned for Christmas, bringing her widowed daughter, Mrs Wharton and her son Jack. Mrs Wharton was quiet and spent most of her time fussing over her son, who was not half as fragile as she thought since he spent much of his time playing tricks on our cats.

When the Thomases extended the invitation for their Christmas party to our guests, Mrs Pemberton spoke for the whole family, telling me in no uncertain terms that they would not attend a party hosted by 'people like that'.

Our Christmas was quieter than last year; I missed Amelia, Captain Parnell and indeed Miss Atwell. For whatever reason, Mr Campbell was not invited to spend Christmas with his sister's family again so Lydia worked with him on Christmas Day, but thankfully she was able to join me in the evening. Mr Bradley was greeting guests with Ruby beaming on his arm, as if he were already a member of the Thomas family, which meant Lydia did not find much to enjoy in the party as she struggled to mask her disapproval of the poor man and seemed to take no pleasure in dancing both with George and Matthew Thomas.

I asked her to try and find pleasure in the evening, and while I pitied her, I did think she was taking Ruby's marriage rather too hard. They could still be friends upon her marriage and there was hope by keeping up the friendship Mr Bradley may have some bachelor friends who could be a good match for Lydia. When I tried to explain this Lydia scowled at me and said I did not understand. When I asked her to explain she merely waved a hand and apologised.

'Well,' I said. 'Just remember, if you had married first you would expect Ruby to be happy for you would you not?'

At these words Lydia looked as though she cry, which was so uncharacteristic that I feared I must have somehow spoken to harshly but I could not see how, before an unsettling thought came upon me that I had no wish to dwell on.

'Lydia you must at least feign happiness,' I said. 'Or people will talk.'

Lydia gave me a guarded frightened look before nodding. I swallowed a burning knot in my throat hoping my growing fear was wrong, and that Lydia was just confused for she never had many friends. It was the first time that I suddenly fervently wished Lydia married, that some handsome doctor could come and sweep her off her feet and banish all thoughts of Ruby. It was my fault for letting her dress as a boy and now she did not know what she ought be. But then, it was a waste for her not to be allowed to practise medicine, although if this was the result what ought I do? Lydia went to bed, and we did not speak of it again. I could not help but remember the happiness I had found this time last year and hope that next Christmas bought some more.

Spring came, and with it the second anniversary of Peter's death. Once again Lydia and I travelled to Glastonbury, and laid bunches of daffodils. It was strange I had been a year out of mourning, and the world had largely forgotten that there ever had been a Mr Fitzwilliam. Mr Webster was the only person who occasionally mentioned him, mostly how Peter would like my pies, and I found that I was glad of this remembrance. Peter *would* like my pies; especially the pork and apple one.

Sometimes I caught Lydia gazing at the drawing in the bedroom but she would busy herself and if I asked her about how she fared, she would say she was well. Amelia would mention him in his letters, mostly food that she thought he might like or piano recitals she attended that reminded her of him. She did that more than she used to; maybe she too was worried that he might slip away from memory and was trying to ensure that did not happen.

Lydia

I sat with Mr Campbell in The Hatchet, him deep in his cups. I had been supping the same pint of weak ale for an hour, much to his disgust.

'Hurry up with that! I did have a thought to take you to see the lady pugilists today but we can hardly do that while you are sober as a Quaker.'

'A ladies boxing match?' Despite myself, I was rather intrigued.

'Oh yes, they are more vicious than the men. Recently I set a few noses for them so they said they would give me free tickets,' he chuckled. 'Quite an interesting study of the human form, I can tell you.'

I drained my tankard and he yelled for a stronger beer and some gin, but it was not to be for a young boy stumbled into the tavern. The child looked about frantically, then fixed his gaze on Mr Campbell and hurried over.

'Mr Campbell, it is my sister sir, Mama begs that you come-'

'I told your mother it is nothing more than a childhood fever. It will pass.'

The boy blushed. 'Please-'

Mr Campbell frowned.

'I can go,' I said. 'You go to the boxing. A childhood fever won't take me long.'

Mr Campbell sighed, then nodded. 'Very well but make sure you charge them.'

I followed the boy from the tavern into the darkness of Frogmore Street and along to some ground floor rooms of a rundown house. Inside, the place was snug and cosily decorated. A woman sat at the bedside of a child, who could be no older than four. The child's skin shone a bright red. The little boy who had fetched me looked at me imploringly.

The woman stood up, wringing her hands. 'You are not Mr Campbell.'

'No,' I said, trying to deepen my voice. 'I am his apprentice. My name is Mr Sommers.'

'I am Mrs Leigh,' the woman said. 'Mr Campbell has already been once. I suppose he thinks I am being melodramatic, but this is not just some common cold.'

I headed over to the bed. The heat in the room was stifling, the heavy curtains were drawn and it seemed an entire forest burnt on the grate. It could simply be the heat which had made the child so red, for the mother was sweating as well.

The child was boiling to the touch. I opened her mouth and found a swollen tongue; peeling and going white. Her tonsils were also enlarged. On closer inspection, whilst her face was flushed the redness on her neck and chest was a bumpy, rough rash.

'What are her other symptoms?'

'Ann has had a sore throat and complained of aching joints, headaches…'

I nodded, the diagnoses forming in my mind. 'When Mr Campbell saw her, did she have this rash?'

Mrs Leigh shook her head. 'Well, she did have the beginnings of it but it was not so bad. He said it could be fleas.'

It did not look remotely like flea bites. It looked like scarlet fever. How could he diagnose it so wrongly? How could I possibly think that I knew better than him? But the symptoms were what I had read about, and both Amelia and I had it when we were babies. This all matched the story Mother had told us of.

'Your daughter has scarlet fever,' I said, making sure not to say 'I think'. Mr Campbell was also was definite; people looked to the medical profession for certainty.

Mrs Leigh nodded gravely. 'Just as I thought.'

'Has your son had it?'

She nodded. 'He had it as a baby, and I had it myself when I was a child.'

'Are there any other children here? Where is your husband?'

'We have no other children. Mr Leigh is a sailor, he is halfway between Africa and America on a triangular passage by now.'

'I see,' I said, realising that Mr Leigh worked on a slave ship. His wife and son continued to stare earnestly at me, and my principles about his work aside there was a job to be done. 'Well, we must bring her temperature down, so less coverings on this bed and let us reduce those flames. Also, we must fetch her something cool to drink. Has she been able to eat?'

'She has no appetite and her throat is so swollen, sir.'

'Have you tried preparing soft food? Mashing vegetables, for example?'

'No, I have not.'

'Well we had best get to it, ma'am.'

Mother and son sprang into action.

When I visited them the next day, Mr Campbell came with me, cursing all the way that I had made a mistake. When we arrived, Mrs Leigh greeted us warmly and thanked me for attending last night as well as Mr Campbell for sparing me. Mr Campbell grunted at her and went to the child's bedside. She was not a flushed as she had been yesterday and was sleeping soundly instead of tossing feverishly, but the rash was still visible on her neck. After telling Mrs Leigh to continue with the treatment I prescribed, we left.

As we walked down the street Mr Campbell told me Ann Leigh's continuing care was entirely up to me but I must fit it in around my existing duties and perhaps we could go to see the lady pugilists next week. I tried to suppress a smile, from him that was high praise indeed.

Amelia

We spent longer in Italy than we had intended, both of us falling in love with Florence. There were other British families in residence there, and several illustrious persons could claim a connection to the place including Lady Emma Hamilton. The surrounding countryside was also lovely and we ate a great deal of Italian food, something many of our British peers did not, but which Miss Atwell insisted upon. I was glad she did, for I could write in great detail about the food to Mama and I found their *pasta*, bread and fruit agreed with me a great deal.

We made plans to move onto Spain as spring approached, but had to postpone the trip as Miss Atwell came down with a fever. It was nothing too serious, but she kept to her bed. I sat with her, sewing, reading aloud and gossiping. On the third day, I decided to take a stroll unaccompanied around the market which Miss Atwell fully encouraged. I vowed to bring her back a gift.

As I set off I was glad to be in the fresh air; it was crisp as cool as a British spring. I wondered if I would see any new acquaintances at the market and what gift I could select to bring Miss Atwell the most joy.

'Miss Amelia!'

I stopped and looked about the busy street. A woman round with child was waving and making her way towards me. None of our

Florence circle were with child, so who could it be? And how did she know my name? She grinned broadly, and I realised although her belly was rounded the rest of her was very thin, too thin to be healthy. It was Betsey Webster.

'You are surprised to see me I think.'

I nodded, lost for words.

'Perhaps we should take tea. Let us go back to your lodgings.'

She had taken my arm with an iron grip, but I did not move with her.

'No,' I said.

'No?'

'Miss Atwell is ill,' I said. 'It will not do to bring strangers back to our rooms.'

'I am not a stranger,' her grin was still fixed upon her face but it did not reach her eyes.

'Not to me, but to Miss Atwell you are.'

'Could we not take tea somewhere nearby? It has been so long since we have seen each other.'

'It was you who chose to leave my company, not the other way around,' I replied.

She blinked. 'Yes, but there were circumstances, the viscount's son, you understand…' she swallowed. 'Please Miss Amelia, let us take tea together and become friends as we were.'

I wanted to wrench my arm from her grasp and leave her, but there was a desperation in her and I could hardly storm away from an expectant mother without drawing scorn from passers-by. The closer I looked at her, her cuffs were frayed, her bonnet faded, there was a slight tinge of gin on her breath and her coat was the one the viscount's son had bought for her in Bath; the elbows had been very nicely patched, but patched none the less.

'Very well,' I said.

She beamed, the first genuine smile I had seen since our interaction began.

Once we were seated, I asked how the viscount's son was.

She fiddled with her hair. 'He is very well, I believe. I think he is to be married next month to a Duke's daughter.'

'So, you parted ways?'

She nodded.

'And you did not want to go back to Captain Webster?'

She laughed too loudly and people on the next table turned to look. 'Come now Amelia, he would hardly have me back, would he? After Marmaduke injured his arm, it nearly had to be cut off, but that was surely an exaggeration for now he is back at sea with the navy, so all is well for him but he made it quite clear he never wanted to see me again.'

'So what happened to Marmaduke?'

'We…we stayed friends for a good few months, but then his father started insisting on this marriage business. We considered it a fine joke first of all, and Marmaduke thought his intended was going to be a hag. Only, it turned out she was not. Marmaduke liked her, you see.'

She hesitated and laughed again.

'Oh,' I said, not sure what else to say.

'But then,' she sipped her tea and I noticed her hands were shaking. 'Mr Snowden liked me…'She trailed off and stroked her stomach.

'Mr Snowden is the father of your child? Did he force himself on you?'

She shook her head. 'No, Lord where did you get such an idea! There was no force about it and Marmaduke found it all very amusing.'

I hoped to God no one could overhear our conversation and that it never made it back to any of our English friends that I had been seen with her.

'You are Mr Snowden's mistress now?'

She nodded. 'Marmaduke was very good about it, since no one is quite sure who this creature's father is.' She didn't even blush, she just laughed again, and I felt revulsion rise in me. 'Mr Snowden has taken me on this trip. There is an English couple who we will meet in Venice, it has all been arranged, distant cousins of Marmaduke. The wife is barren. They can return to England with this.'

'And you will return with Mr Snowden?'

She shrugged, gaiety gone. 'Marmaduke left him in charge of the money and he has all but spent it. He is repulsed by me these days, yet we still must get to Venice soon.'

I nodded. 'But you are further south than Venice.'

She blinked. 'Are we? Well yes, but I wanted to see you.'

'How did you know I was here?'

She hesitated. 'The Gemmels. We met with them in Switzerland. They are friends of Charles's family. Robert had those charming sketches of you and they told us all about your Miss Atwell. How we both pitied you!'

'Why did you pity me?'

'Why, having to work as a companion to some spinster, a bluestocking by all accounts and American, how uncouth. To be wasting all your beauty and youth away.'

'That isn't the case at all. You are quite wrong about Miss Atwell.'

'Lively, is she? On the prowl for a husband?'

'No, I can assure you she is not.'

'Come now,' Betsey smiled. 'Why else would a single woman with a fortune come to Italy? If not for a husband it must at least be for-'

'Betsey you must not speak so.'

'Maybe it is not male attention she is interested in at all. Goodness, I wonder if anyone else in Florence has started to wonder about the American spinster and her pretty companion.'

I stood up, horrified. Betsey reached out and grabbed my wrist with her claw like

hand. 'It was only a jest, please do not go.'

Anger was pulsing through me at Betsey's base assertions about Miss Atwell. 'Betsey, what are your intentions?'

She blushed. 'Sit down and I shall tell you.'

'You shall tell me as we are,' I yanked my arm from her grasp.

She nodded, the brief sneer that had settled on her features vanishing. 'Well, it could benefit you as well. Would Charles not make a suitable husband for Miss Atwell? He would be ever so grateful to me, he has assured me of that and to you as well if you wish it. He will see that we are both well cared for and he will treat Miss Atwell with kindness.'

Heavens above! How had I ever thought these people my friends? I placed the money for the tea on the table. 'Good day to you, Mrs Webster. I have errands to run, but please do not rush your tea on my account.'

I turned and hurried off, shaking with anger.

'Miss Amelia!'

I kept going, so as I reached the street I was almost at a run. I did not stop, afraid Mr Snowden might have been watching us and that he might spring from any alley. Once I was home, I slammed the door behind me, gasping for breath.

'Signoria Amelia?' Signora Ricci, our land lady, stepped into the corridor, her eyes round with concern. 'Is Problem?'

I caught my breath. 'I think we will be leaving soon,' I said. 'I must talk to my mistress.'

Chapter 34

Jessica

My Dear Jessica - if I may be so bold,
We have docked in Plymouth, where I had the incomparable pleasure of reading your letters which the admiralty saw fit to forward to me. It is my intention to set out for Bristol within the week, and I hope to be there by next Tuesday at the latest. If our lodging house is full, that is no matter, I shall stay at an inn, but expect me to visit often - if that is agreeable to you. I hope that we may even manage a trip to the sea, as we discussed now a year and a half since.
Yours affectionately,
Captain James Parnell

I must not get carried away, but this letter could not be misinterpreted as merely friendly at all. It was not a great romantic sonnet and held no declarations, but it had promise at least and news that my humble, doubtlessly badly penned letters held an 'incomparable pleasure'. Unfortunately neither of the guest rooms were free, Mrs Nutall was with us and an honeymooning couple by the name of Archer, so I set about making enquires at inns very nearby and reserved him a room in what seemed the most comfortable. I could not help the idle thought that if we had been husband and wife such a thing would be unnecessary - but then, where would Lydia sleep? Maybe I should have the loft converted into a bedroom after all.

On the morning of the Tuesday I burnt the toast and the eggs were a little over-done, so had to apologise to the guests but none seemed to have noticed, they were all chatting happily about their plans for the day. As they carried on, there came a clatter of hooves outside. Normally that was nothing of note but I was twitchy as a mouse, awaiting the sound of anything that could signal an arrival. I hastened to the door. In the street, James was dismounting from a cabriolet, and I stopped myself from exclaiming his name. He turned and smiled at me.

'Jessica,' he said warmly, advancing towards me. 'How well you look. This blue suits-'

'I say! What a fine cabriolet!' Mr Archer had pushed past me into the street, apparently taken with the smart black cabriolet and matching horse. 'Is it yours, sir?'

'It is a rental,' James threw me an exasperated look then turned his attention to Mr Archer.

'Mr Archer, this is Captain Parnell, the owner of this house,' I said.

'Jolly good to make your acquaintance, sir. What a fine job you chaps are doing thwarting the French and the Dutch and I know not who. I ought to have been in the army but I have weak ankles, you see.'

'Indeed.'

'Now this vehicle, where have you ridden it from? How is the suspension? Are those new wheels? And look at the hood, very fine-'

'The suspension is excellent,' James said, patting the horse's neck. 'It has lasted well for the trip from Plymouth-'

'Plymouth you say! Mrs Archer we ought rethink our plans for a barouche and get a cabriolet-'

He hurried back inside the house. I smiled at James, and came to stroke the horse next to him, remembering he had said how he liked them for his grandfather had been a cab driver. 'She's a pretty creature,' I said. 'The Roberts used to have black mare like this. It was their pride and joy. What was your grandfather's horse like?'

'He never owned one,' James said. 'He used to work for a man that ran a stable. There were two bays and a black. It was their great joke to call the horses after Prime Ministers, so one of the bays, Freddy North, was his favourite.'

I gave a laugh.

'The other bay, Grenville, had a foul temper – gave my uncle Giorgio a good kick once but that rather endeared me too her, since he used the whip a lot more than he ought. This one has a very good temperament, she is perhaps a little too soft but very hardworking.'

'The Roberts, the family my parents and I worked for, used to call their bulls and cows after kings and queens. There were a lot of Henrys, Edwards, Marys and Elizabeths. It was how I learnt history.'

Our fingers touched on the neck of the horse and we let them become entwined. For half a moment I let myself imagine that the horse was ours and he ran a stable and I fine a hotel, as we had spoken of in our letters. He glanced at me, gave me a half smile and I wondered if he was thinking the same.

'It is good to have you back, but I am afraid we are a full house. I have made a reservation for you just around the corner.'

'That is very good of you. Perhaps you ought show me the way.'

'Of course.'

'Here-' he helped me up with a grin. 'And lead on before Mr Archer returns.'

Lydia

'So,' Mr Campbell said, adding a generous splash of whiskey to his morning coffee. 'How is the patient?'

'She is doing very well,' I said. 'I daresay today will be my last visit.'

'Well it is a relief to know that you can be trusted with these trifling domestic patients. I think I shall pass more of them onto you, for they are very tedious to me and this way I can focus on the more interesting dockside patients.'

And the more lucrative spa ones.

'Yes sir,' I said, pleased that I was at last to have my own patients, but vexed that he would hog the broken bones and mysterious, tropical illnesses of sailors for himself.

I called on the Leighs and found little Ann sitting up, conversing merrily with her brother. Her rash was fading and her temperature was dropping, so after advising Mrs Leigh to burn the bedsheets and Ann's nightgown, I went on my way.

The rest of the patients Mr Campbell had given me were a range of old and young, middling and poor. Mostly they had simple fevers, but there was also one case of consumption and what felt like a tumour in a woman's stomach, as well as another case of scarlet fever in a little boy. I prescribed tinctures and bed rest where appropriate and for the second case of scarlet fever I prescribed the same treatment that I had for Ann. For the consumption and the tumour there was little to be done.

Some of the patients queried my age when I arrived, but when I assured them Mr Campbell thought me capable they all agreed to treatment.

'Well,' the woman with the tumour said. 'I ain't never known Mr Campbell to have any apprentice that lasted past a month, so you must be doing something right.'

When I returned to Mr Campbell's house he was not yet there but a young woman was waiting outside.

'Do you know when Mr Campbell will be here?'

'I cannot say for sure, but I am his apprentice. May I be of some help?'

'That's better than nothing I suppose, come with me.'

We hastened to her small house where a young man was laid up in bed with a serious fever. I examined him and found raised bumps all over his skin. An ice cold sweat trickled over me.

'Well?' demanded a middle-aged man, the father of the household, worry etched onto his face. He knew as well as I what those lumps meant.

I swallowed. 'I will have to confirm with Mr Campbell before making a serious diagnosis-'

'Spit it out, damn you!'

'I am sorry sir, but I believe your son has smallpox.'

Chapter 35

Jessica

Mrs Webster invited me to dine with her. When I asked if her invitation could be extended to include James she readily agreed. After leaving pies for our guests to eat, we made our way over. James offered me his arm, which I took with a smile. It was pleasing to think as we strolled along on the clement spring evening that to those passing us in the street we must look like husband and wife.

On reaching the Websters' we were welcomed inside. I wondered how they would be with James, since Mr Webster had been a friend to Peter, but he was all ease and friendliness. Of their sons, only John and Edward were present – the calmest two, even if John was a little too fond of claret it only served to make him more subdued. The conversation moved from the navy, with reference to Richard, Tom, Will and Philip Webster who were away at sea, to the threat of the French and Napoleon, to gossip about the Hughes and the news that Edward had recently become engaged.

There had been a time, when Peter had been alive and we were believed to have some money, when Edward had taken a fancy to Lydia, but that had long since faded and now he was engaged to his employer's daughter. Mrs Webster enthused as to what an advantageous match this was since Edward's employer had no sons of his own so would hopefully entrust more of the business to Edward, who smiled. Little mention had been made of the character of the young woman in question at all, but it was not my place to comment on the lack of romance employed by the Webster family.

John Webster drank steady and ate little. He was ten years younger than me and had become a widower a year before. He seemed no more at peace about it now than he had when it had happened, poor man. Mrs Webster had always said that he was the most romantic of her brood and that had loved his young wife. It seemed that she had been right.

After dinner, the men stayed in the dining room for whisky whilst Mrs Webster and I went to parlour for tea.

'You seem very friendly with your employer,' Mrs Webster said with a smile.

'I do not think of him as my employer,' I said, her choice of word unsettling me.

'What else is he then?'

'My friend,' I replied.

'Nothing more?'

'Perhaps,' I said.

She sipped her tea and her expression became grave. 'Have you thought this through, Mrs Fitzwilliam?'

'How do you mean?'

She set her teacup down and gave me a stern look. 'You and he, I will confess, do seem to have quite the bond. You get on famously; he has all the manners of an English gentleman and I will concede he is charming, handsome even, in a foreign sort of way-'

'He is not foreign-'

'Does he have any English blood? No, I thought not-'

'He was born in Liverpool, as was his mother.'

'And where were his mother's parents born? And his father? Ireland? His people are

Black Irish, I wager. There has been a lot of terrible trouble stirred up there of late-'

'That hardly has anything to do with him. He has been fighting the French, for Britain.'

'He is a Catholic, is he not? I do not mean to chastise you, but you must think about this. Put a halt to this attachment before it becomes anything to serious.'

I swallowed, anger rising in me. 'Your objection is his Catholicism?'

'Yes, of course.'

'And if he converted?'

'Has he said he would?'

'No but-'

'Even if he did, would he even be truly trusted?'

'Trusted? The navy *trusts* him to captain a warship.'

'They would not trust him to go any higher though, would they? Mrs Fitzwilliam, please heed me I mean no offence but your life, the lives of your girls, would be difficult if you were to marry him. There would be restrictions places upon you and any other children you might bear him. And what of the girl's marriage prospects?' She pressed my arm with a smile. 'As a friend you must allow me to say with your loss of fortune their prospects are bad enough without having a Catholic step-father to content with.'

She clearly thought she was being friendly. She was using her senior age to patronise me and I could tell from how she spoke she expected me to be grateful for her advice and to comply with it.

'I can see this was kindly meant-'

She nodded.

'You are right, I will have to give the matter of religion some serious thought however I am not dissuaded from *forming an attachment* as you say with Captain Parnell, far from it. I have long lived doing as I was told and what was right and proper, maybe for once I ought simply do what I want.'

Mrs Webster raised her eyebrows and it irked me to think her sons were so ill-behaved and I never preached to her about it, yet she thought she could bid me to be proper when I had done nothing so wild as *formed an attachment* to a respectable navy officer, who simply happened to a Catholic, who wasn't half as unsuitable or rough as her full blooded English protestant sons or indeed her harlot of a daughter-in-law.

'Tell me of the Edward's fiancée,' I said to change the subject. 'Is she pretty?'

*

As we walked home, my mind kept flitting back to Mrs Webster's words.

'Does something trouble you? You seem distracted.'

I sighed, looking for the right words and pressed James' arm. 'Mrs Webster thinks we should go no further with our attachment, since we are not of the same religion.'

'Ah. That explains Mr Webster's line of questioning.'

I cringed. 'What did he say?'

'I think he would have traced my lineage back to the ancients given half the chance,' he gave a short laugh. 'I told him I am about as foreign as the king.'

I laughed. 'You didn't!'

'I did, for it is true.'

'Whilst I do not agree with the Websters, Mrs Webster's words have given me cause to think. What are we doing? What will we do about religion?'

He moved so he took my hands in his and faced me.

'I suppose the word for what we are doing is courting,' he said with a smile and kissed my hand, sending a warm wave of pleasure through me. 'As for religion, we are hardly the first Catholic and Protestant to fall in love, however much it might scandalise the Websters, and I doubt we will be the last.' He sighed. 'We both know I have converted before. It is perhaps rather ridiculous to do it again but I would do it for you if you wished it.'

I shook my head, flattered though I was. 'Unless it is a legal impediment, I see no reason to over complicate everything.'

'It is not a legal impediment. A Catholic wedding is void unless it happens in a Protestant church anyway.'

'Is it?'

He nodded. 'Most Catholics get married in Catholic churches of course, then go and have the Protestant ceremony as a formality. The Protestant wedding is the legal one. Without having the Protestant ceremony, even if you have a Catholic ceremony it does not count under the law so any children would be illegitimate and other such rights granted to married couples would be forfeited.'

'Oh,' I said. 'My apologies, I have never given much thought to Catholic laws until recently.'

He gave a half smile. 'Until recently? That's interesting.'

I nudged him.

'There is Scotland,' he carried on. 'You can apparently just declare yourself married, or 'get married over an anvil', in fact the laws appear so lax I can barely make sense of them. Then there is Gretna Green, but I rather resent going there as though we have something to be ashamed of.'

I smiled as we continued to walk on, his use of the word 'we' in terms of marriage had acted like a magic spell, his arm was linked with mine just as it should be.

'You have been doing your research.'

'I have.'

'You mentioned children,' I hesitated. 'I am over five and thirty you know, it is still possible but I doubt there is a chance for a large family. I only have two daughters to show for twenty years of marriage.'

'I like your daughters,' he said, then with a grin he added. 'Better two like them than six Webster boys. I have no expectations or dreams of a tribe of children, Jessica. I want a partner, a friend, I want you above all things.' He paused and kissed the crown of my head. 'And whilst I think we would make a good family with your girls, I would not try and replace their father or stop any honouring of his memory.'

'So,' I said. 'We could marry in The Church of England. Would they not try and convert you?'

'I am sure they would try, but it is not illegal for them to marry us as we are.'

'And would you want a Catholic ceremony afterward?'

He sighed. 'They would also try and convert you, and we might face even more resistance to our marriage. So long as we are married legally, and you are protected as my wife under law I see no reason to complicate it further.'

I smiled, a warmth growing over me.

'But Jessica, there is a war on. I would not marry you to make you so soon a widow.'

'James-' I said, my hopes crashing down.

He stopped walking and looked at me. 'Please believe me when I say I want to marry you above all things, but I do not want to send you into widowhood so soon after you have left it-'

'I would still mourn you whether we were married or not.'

'I will make sure you are protected, but I will not inflict an Irish name on you if I am not there to protect you from those who would scorn you because of it. I will not have you in black, in mourning for so short a union. I like certainty, I like security. I want to marry you knowing there is a good chance that we will have our whole lives still ahead of us. There are dark times in this war looming ahead of us, Jessica – they could be the end of me, but more than that, such times are a chance for a man like me to prosper. I have done well on heads and guns in the past and I will do so again. There will be some battles soon and when they are done I will come home to you a rich man, so that we may go somewhere and make something of ourselves.'

Pushing aside my disappointment I saw sense in what he was saying. 'There are things I should like for myself as well. If I could I would like to travel more, to see more of the world. I think I should like to own a hotel again, a bigger one if I could, serving fine food and I think I should like to go and try something, somewhere different, as fond as I am of Bristol I find myself rather thinking it is time for an adventure. I think I would regret it if I did not.'

'I am pleased to hear that.'

He looked at me, his dark eyes burning earnestly. All that ambition was deeply compelling, attractive; all these plans for greatness and he wanted me to be part of it.

I stroked his face. 'Being poor again, it frightens you, doesn't it?'

'Yes.' He did not break my gaze, his fierce eyes locked onto mine. Good, I thought if poverty scared him I would be safe.

'Very well,' I said. 'I will trust you and your plan.'

We drew close and his arms were around me, and mine around him.

'I have waited my whole life to meet you Jessica, the only thing I could not plan for. Now let us be happy as we are, and spend as much time in each other's company until I must go back to sea again.'

'Yes,' I said and kissed him, briefly but firmly on the lips. I drew back with a smile. 'I must admit that I am rather enjoying being courted.'

He laughed. 'Well let it continue then.'

Lydia

Mr Campbell confirmed my thoughts when I brought him round to see the patient. It was smallpox. As we left he spoke to me quietly. 'There is another case, around the corner.'

Fear crept up my spine.

'Will either survive?'

I thought he might dismiss me, but he said, 'It is too early to say. I have seen patients in worse conditions survive and those in better health die. You have not had it, have you?'

'No.'

Mr Campbell had smallpox scars on his cheek; deep and old looking.

'I was about your age when I got it,' he said. 'I was quite handsome before.'

The sickness spread, within the week three more families in the surrounding street had been affected. Some people started to refuse to go out, or wore cloths over their faces like highwaymen. Many others came to us believing they had the disease and were beset by panic for the early stages before smallpox can easily be confused with a fever; before the pustules show themselves. Initially I was interested to watch the development of the condition but I was also afraid; more so than I had when treating any other illness.

I did not tell mother about the outbreak for fear she would stop me treating the patients, but she found out anyway for soon it was all anyone spoke of. I had been leaving earlier and getting back even later to avoid her in case she had heard, but she caught me one morning. One of the chamber maids in the hotel the Captain was staying in came down with it.

'Lydia, are you treating these smallpox patients?'

'Of course.'

'But you have not had it before. You ought ask to be excused.'

'To be excused? Mother, how can that be? I am training to be a surgeon, I cannot be excused nor do I wish to be.'

'Oh, but Lydia were will this lead?'

'I do not know, but it is my responsibility to see it through and to help the patients.'

'Can you not deal with Mr Campbell's paperwork as you used to?'

'No, Mother. We are very busy, I must be out helping people.'

'I have a good mind to forbid you-'

'Then how will that look? A boy would not be forbidden, then we would have to explain the whole mess to Mr Campbell.'

'Rather that than you die.'

'Do not be so dramatic.'

I hastened out the door.

'Lydia, come back!'

I did not, for I did not know how to placate her. She got her way anyhow for on the

fifth day Mr Campbell he said he did not want me tending to the patients anymore. 'But why? You need me '

'Have you been inoculated?'

'Yes,' I lied quickly.

'Are you sure?' He held up a letter in her hand between two fingers. 'Your Mother says differently.'

I scowled, betrayed.

'Now, you will stay here and clean my equipment, and sort the tinctures. It must be done. There are so many patients to treat I have fallen behind.'

He left and I sat down feeling fatigued, exasperated by being treated like a child.

Jessica

Though it grieved Lydia that Mr Campbell had confined her to his house I was delighted when she told me.

'You needn't be so happy,' she snapped, before heading off to work. I noticed she had not eaten her breakfast so chased her with it. She rolled her eyes and took it. 'Thank you. Enjoy your day at the seaside. I want to hear all about it.'

'You could ask Mr Campbell if you can join us.'

She smiled. 'Maybe another time. I rather think this trip is not for me.'

'But you haven't seen Captain Parnell since he has been back. I do not want any bad feeling between you because of how you parted.'

'Very well, since I am confined to Mr Campbell's house, I am sure to be home by the time you get home. I shall see him then, or I will make an effort to meet him for breakfast.'

I nodded and sent her off with another kiss and a wave.

Back in the kitchen I laid out the breakfast so it would be ready for the guests when they rose, they knew about my trip to Portishead today and thought it a fine thing. Mr Archer said I must tell him if it was worth the trip and how the cabriolet handled it. Nervous fluttering tingled my body at the thought of going to such a new place, of seeing the sea – not forced into harbour but open, endless and wide, with the beach and cliffs and such other wonders.

'Good morning,' James entered through the front door, and I crossed over to his arms. He looked down at me with a happy expression; as though I was better than I was, as though he could not believe his luck.

'Ready?'

I nodded, and fetched the basket. 'I have packed our luncheon.'

He helped me into the cabriolet and I adjusted my bonnet and cloak which he complimented. I thanked him, glad he noticed. The bonnet was new, well to me at least. I bought it from a reach down shop and remade it to my own liking. I complimented his clothes as well; he suited his navy uniform I told him, but today he was dressed in civilian attire and looked very smart and handsome in dark blue and grey. His cutaway coat, while not showy was the latest fashion.

'Stop now, Jessica, I will have to own to a fault. I am unforgivably vain and if you continue in this manner it will go to my head.'

'I would never have called you vain, you merely take care over your appearance. I do not think there is too much pride in that. Without offending your young friend, I would say Lt Driscoll is vain.'

James laughed. 'Oh he is, without a doubt.'

'Come now, if you expect his suit to succeed with my daughter you shall have to vouch better for him than that.'

'I shall by and by, I assure you. Lt Driscoll is quite a fine young man, but it is not his suit that concerns me at all today.'

He grinned at me rather dashingly and I allowed myself to laugh as the horse hurried through the morning streets.

'Now Jessica, there is a map under the seat, I believe we are to follow the river Avon-'

It would be a lie to say we did not get slightly lost, and indeed that getting lost could have veered into a squabble but it did not - quite- and we reached our destination in good time. I did not even mind that we nearly quarrelled over directions because it meant he had asked my opinion on directions in the first place - a novelty for me after twenty years of marriage.

As we neared the beach the smell of the sea was stronger than I had ever smelled - fresher - since by the harbour in Bristol it sometimes carried a rancid odour. We stopped at an inn where we stabled the horse and set off, me on his arm - an action that was becoming a most comfortable habit. He led the way along the coastal path and I hastened along until I could stand near the edge and feel the wind whipping at my face. It made me almost giddy at my height above the watery abyss. The sea stretched further than any field or forest it seemed to me, yet in the distance there was still some land.

'If we were to sail from this spot where would we end up?'

'Well, if we went straight we would reach Wales, for this is still the River Avon-'

'Oh. Forgive me but I thought this was the coast.'

'The River Avon feeds into the Bristol Channel which becomes the sea.' I nodded.

'To chase it any further would mean an

overnight stay somewhere.' 'So this is still the English coast, if not the British one?' 'Certainly. If we were to bear left we would leave the Avon and go into the Bristol Channel, then skim under Ireland and keep going until we reached Canada.'

I beamed full of childish joy at the thought.
'Would it be a hard voyage?'
'It would be a cold one, and if we hit storms it could be dangerous. Being on the open sea like that we would be very isolated.' I leaned in close to him and teasingly asked if he's ever seen any sea monsters. He laughed. 'Only French men and even they are not so frightening. One of my first voyages, on a merchant ship, we journeyed down past South Africa to India - tropical fish and birds in all colours you can imagine and a few sharks as well. That was my first time on a beach proper, when we had a bit of shore leave in South Africa. The sand felt so hot we thought it would scorch our feet.'

I looked up at the sky; what had started out as a lovely spring day now had clouds gathering. 'No such luck today then.' He smiled. 'The sea is at its best when it's gloomy.'

'You know,' I said smiled. 'Sometimes I forget you are a northerner, then you say things like that.'

He laughed, 'Come along then, my soft southerner, let me help you down to the beach.'
The sand beneath my shoes reminded me of thick, tightly packed snow – slippery and unstable. I gathered a few stones and shells of interesting shapes for Lydia and I saw a shell in a blush pink I would save for Amelia.

After we picnicked, we wandered along the beach further. James asked if I should like to go into the town but I did not, the costal paths and beaches were much more of an unexplored novelty. Without prying eyes in town, we could walk along together and it was as if the rest of the world did not exist. We saw the occasional fisherman or beachcomber but no one else and as much as I rather liked the notion of people mistaking us for man and wife it was better yet not to think of that, for those thoughts then led me to worry about the differences in our religions and Mrs Webster's words, whereas without those worries we could just enjoy ourselves.

I did not think I had ever laughed so much as when I was with him and I liked his sarcastic streak, which he used to poke fun at himself as well as everything else. At last as evening fell, we wandered back towards the cabriolet and I could not believe the day had gone so fast.

After we had been on the road a good while the horse jolted and we were flung forward, just as darkness was taking hold. James leapt down to look at the creature.

'Her shoe is come lose,' he said. 'Damn.'

'Well there looks to be a farmhouse over there.'

He looked in the distance sceptically, and I remembered him once saying he was a city boy who had spent his life at sea. 'They'll help I'm sure of it,' I said. 'They could be....untrustworthy.'

'Country savages, you mean?'

'That is exactly what I mean.'

I playfully slapped his arm. 'People aren't like that round here.'

'That is what they want you to think.'

'Come along, I'll show you.'

He helped me down with a mock grimace.

'I am sure you always honestly helped lost country folk in Liverpool, didn't you? Gave them the shortest and most cost effective routes on your grandfather's cab and such like?'

He raised an eyebrow. 'Country folk were our favourite type of customer.'

'Well,' I said with a jovial disapproval. 'I am sure you shall be repaid for all that kindness.'

We walked along the path to the farmhouse where music and singing could be heard. James knocked on the door. It was answered almost immediately by a strong looking older woman.

She looked us up and down and asked in a confused voice if we had come for the party.

'No,' James said 'Our horse has lost its shoe.'

'We were just hoping to re-shod it.'

'I thought I didn't recognise you, of course you can re-shod your horse. Do come in. I am Mrs Combes - we are celebrating the birth of our first grandson. I shall fetch my son to help you with your horse Mr-?'

'Captain Parnell.'

'Captain indeed? Army, navy?'

'Navy.'

'Oh my youngest son Bert is in the navy, he has just been promoted to midshipman. Do you know him? Bertie Combes.'

'No, I can't say that I do.'

'Well you must look out for him. David! David, come here. Now Captain, I will take good care of your wife and David here will help you with the horse.'

James threw me a dubious backward glance as he left the house with a young man who was the image of Mrs Combes. I rolled my eyes and smiled at him. Mrs Combes led me through the house, to the land outside where a bonfire was being stoked, a fiddle played and a group were carousing. She poured me a generous helping of cider and bid me sit with her daughters. 'Make room girls, Mrs Parnell's horse has thrown a shoe. Her husband is a captain in the navy so watch your manners please!'

They giggled and made room for me, then Mrs Combes asked if I had any children.

'Two daughters,' I said. 'From my first marriage.'

'He is your second then? Well, well you did do well I fancy.'

They cackled gleefully as they topped up the cider.

'No children with your new husband yet then?'

I blushed. 'No.'

'Well, I fancy there is still time, you are still young enough I think,' Mrs Combes said as though surveying a breeding cow.

'I suppose so,' I said, finding the thought of having James' child a very warming one. A whole future, a future these women assumed I already was living stretched out before me. A comfortable house with a larger garden so I could grow more produce to cook with, possibly somewhere in the new world where the weather was always like a fine spring day, some dark haired children - maybe even a boy, or maybe just more dear girls. James could leave the navy and we could laugh and explore together, have a thousand days just like this one.

He appeared with a tankard in his hand as my own was topped up.

'All settled?'

He nodded. 'Young David has been so blunt as to tell me what a lucky man I am to have such a pretty wife.'

'Well you are,' I smiled. 'Or you very soon will be.'

'I hope so,' he said, momentarily serious, before flashing a mirthful smile again. As he did so it started to rain and went from a drizzle to a down pour in moments. He took my hand and we dashed under a large tree, others ran into the house or barn. It seemed suddenly we were alone, though the sound of the Combes singing continued.

I was in his arms, pressed against his chest, craning my head up to look at him looking down at me. My lips found his and we kissed. We did not stop, we carried on, his mouth warm and inviting, his kisses urgent. The rain was only a shower and stopped far sooner than I would have wished it, the voices of our hosts grew louder as they emerged from their shelters to carry on their revelry and reluctantly we broke apart, stayed looking into each other's eyes for a few moments; before we headed out to re-join the party, hearing our names - or rather his name that I was trying out, being called.

Lydia

The day dragged; I was alone in Mr Campbell's, cleaning the equipment, making sure all his books were up to date. I sat down and dozed at one point, then awoke with a fierce headache doubtless from being confined to his stuffy house all day. He asked me to reorder his library and all the lugging of his ill kept tomes made my limbs ache.

When he returned he insisted we went for a drink, which being as fed up I was with being cooped up in doors all day I agreed to.

The tavern was hot and noisy, with many people loudly speculating about the spread of smallpox or exchanging takes of illness they had survived in the past. I found a seat and supped at the ale Mr Campbell bought; it doing nothing to either ease or make worse my aching limbs and head. After three pints I felt in danger of falling asleep again so I set off, leaving my mentor deep in his cups of gin.

Walking home was harder than usual because of my drunkenness, and because of the surprisingly warm spring night. When I reached home I saw a cabriolet and a horse waiting outside; presumably Captain Parnell's.

The parlour was in quiet darkness but light and quiet conversation came from the kitchen. I crept across the parlour, still wrapped in my cloak despite the heat, lest a guest emerge. When I entered the kitchen, Mother and the Captain both looked up, and were sat very close to each other. For half a moment I thought they had been holding hands, but I couldn't tell. I sunk into the chair opposite.

'Hello dear,' Mother said.

'How do you fare, Miss Fitzwilliam?' I was relieved there was only friendliness in the Captain's tone; our last encounter assumedly forgotten.

'Well enough generally, only very tired and dull today. Mr Campbell has confined me to his house on cleaning and tidying duties to limit my exposure to smallpox. If only I had been vaccinated. I think I will try to go and have it done soon if I am not too old.'

I concentrated on making sure my words were not slurring as I was starting to feel the effects of my three pints of ale. My eyes fell on a jug on the table.

'What is that?'

'Cider, from a farm we stopped at one the way home when the horse threw a shoe.'

'Is it good?'

'Yes but strong. You may try a little bit.'

I poured myself some and asked about their day as the cats leapt onto my lap. Mother became radiant as she spoke about it, and took the Captain's hand quite forgetting herself, but I did not draw attention to it. She was an affectionate person and to see her with someone so much closer to her own age made her appear so much younger and livelier than she ever had with Father – it was a sad thought, in a way, but it was true. Father was always happy with her, so perhaps it was not so sad after all.

The Captain said it was time for him to go, so Mother walked him to the front door. With them gone I poured myself a more liberal cup of the cider and drunk it down; it had a much more pleasing taste than the ale. The cats gave me an accusing stare. When Mother returned, so content she was she did not notice how much the cider had been reduced before saying it was time to go to bed.

I woke up early - hot, sweaty and nauseous. I stumbled from my bed, seized the chamber pot and managed to flee outside to vomit in the yard (lest anyone hear me). Damn drink. My head was throbbing but it was all my own fault. How did Mr Campbell live like this? Was he never sober enough to feel the ill effects of drink? Just the thought of another drink - alcoholic or not was enough to make my stomach swim. I had to hurry up and leave before Mother awoke in case she thought I was ill.

When I arrived at Mr Campbell's he was ambling out the door.

'There you are! What time do you call this? There is another case I must tend to. I have left you a pile of linens and bandages that need cleaning in the kitchen.'

With that he was gone. The stench of his house was overwhelmingly awful, stale sweat, alcohol, tobacco and just a general decay. Feeling I would be sick again I hastened to the kitchen, threw open the windows and gulped in the fresh air. Steadied by it, I turned my attention to the pile of blooded bandages. I heaved up the bucket, my muscles aching as I did so. I did not think pumping the water or boiling it would do much for my nausea but it would have to be done. Anticipating the heat I took off my jacket and loosened my cravat before setting to work.

Chapter 36

Jessica

Rabbit with cider would be a good filling for a spring pie. I fetched a fresh jug of water from the pump for the roses James bought me on our morning walk. He was out front, helping the Archers with their luggage and talking with Mr Archer about the much-envied cabriolet, which was stabled at the inn. Mr Archer's enthusiasm for the contraption had not waned and I rather fancied James was pleased to talk about it.

The situation gave me a pleasant daydream that I might once again own a hotel, this time with enough land for stables and James could talk with such enthusiastic riders as Mr Archer everyday about the horses he trained and bred.

I went through the larder and drew up another list of other possible pie fillings, if there were no rabbits from the Websters. Chicken also went with cider. I picked up the jug; it was lighter than I thought. Had we drunk more than I remembered? I felt a little sleepy this morning and suddenly I remembered holding James' hand in full view of Lydia. She had not commented on it so maybe it was not as obvious as I remembered. The front door closed and James entered the kitchen.

'The Archers have gone on their way,' he said.

'The room is free,' I replied. 'You might as well move back in.'

'It is the best room,' he said thoughtfully. 'Seems a waste for me to have it.'

'Seems a waste for you to pay for the hotel,' I replied, glancing at him and seeing he was watching me. He reached out, pulled me close and we kissed. All thoughts of cidery pies were banished as we carried on kissing, alone in our house – I had no thought for where it might lead, only that I wanted to stay in that moment. We drew apart, his arms still around my waist and mind around his shoulders, foreheads touching, smiling. Just as we came close for another kiss, we were disturbed by an urgent hammering at the door.

'What on earth?' we broke apart and I went to answer it, but he moved in front of me protectively, as the knocking become more insistent.

'Who is it?'

'Open up!'

'It sounds like Mr Campbell, I think.'

James opened the door.

Lydia cowered next to Mr Campbell, holding her jacket around herself, her waistcoat undone. She was not indecent but her girlish figure was clear. Heavens! when she looked up, I gasped with fear – it was far more terrible than I had realised. Her face was blotchy, spotted – no! Mr Campbell was yelling.

'What is this? I thought a milksop, a molly cove at first. Is it true as I have suspected – it is a hermaphrodite?'

Lydia swayed and fainted into my arms. Passers-by stopped and stared.

'Mr Campbell,' James snapped. 'I think the more pressing question is has she got smallpox?'

'Oh, undoubtedly but that was bound to happen. What I take issue with is the idea of letting a hermaphrodite loose, passing it off as a boy-'

'She isn't a hermaphrodite,' I snapped, holding Lydia's hot, shaking body. She did not seem to even know where she was. The red spots were growing before my eyes.

'She is a girl?' Mr Campbell asked, dumbfounded as James as good as dragged him into the house, away from the growing crowd.

'Will you treat her?' I asked.

'I have been lied to, hoodwinked!' he snapped. 'This is not to be borne. You are lucky I did bring her home, this is a disgrace to the profession.'

'It's a disgrace to the profession you didn't bloody notice sooner,' said James, suddenly sounding a lot more northern. 'Now, will you treat her?'

Mr Campbell frowned, thinned his lips then sighed. 'So Hugh is not a hermaphrodite at all? I was thinking for some time perhaps I could write a paper on it, wondered if he might donate-'

'Mr Campbell,' James injected, in a tone that sounded like he was issuing an order. It had the desired effect.

'Yes sir, yes I will treat her, get her to bed. I will be up presently to start blood-letting. Now, who are you?'

I guided Lydia up the stairs and hastily helped her into her nightgown. She was almost unconscious and she was hot to the touch. She lurched for the chamber pot but could only retch with no vomit. How had I not noticed she was so ill? I had been so self involved with my romantic entanglements? I should have insisted she stayed home, away from disease - never her let embark on this madness in the first place.

Mr Campbell knocked at the door and appeared with a bowl and knife. His gaze fell on Lydia, in her night gown, in bed. With a mild expression of surprise, he crouched at her bedside and made a deep insertion in her arm. I watched, tense with misery.

'How do you think she will fare?'

Mr Campbell shrugged. 'She is young and strong, remarkably so for a girl, but only time will tell.'

There was another knock on the door and James stepped in. I moved so I was next to him and he put an arm around me.

'What can we do?' he asked

'There isn't much -'

'Should we light a fire or open windows? Keep her hot or cold?'

Mr Campbell sighed. 'Feed her when you can to keep her strength up. She will vomit but she must be strong. As for the temperature, she is hot but don't cool her too much. I will be back later, you have my word on that. Watch her. There is little medicine can do now. Once smallpox has taken hold there is little left to do but hope.'

Mr Campbell left and I sunk down at Lydia's bedside, my thoughts thick as treacle. I reached out and took her hand, which was lumpy and hot.

'Lydia, dear?' I said. She grunted as if asleep, but her features were not relaxed. Tears blurred my eyes but I swallowed them back. 'We need to get her some food. I should cook.'

'No,' James said, his hand on my shoulder. 'You stay with her. There are pies in the larder, are there not? I will bring them up. I will see to everything, you just stay here with her.'

I nodded.

'With a fever,' he said, 'it can help to talk to a person, can't it? Or reading to them.'

He was right, it kept them in the land of the living. I reached for one of the medical journals by her bed, opened it and started to read aloud.

Amelia

Over the next few days Miss Atwell's fever faded and she was ready engage in society again, however she was not entirely ready to leave Florence.

'We shall leave in about a week, I think,' she said. 'Remember you have had more time to enjoy the city than I for you have not been in bed with fever.'

I thought to tell her the truth of my desire to quit the city but found my throat stopped. What would she say? She would never behave as I in Bath and Brighton, and to explain the full nature of Mr Snowden's and Betsey's behaviour and relationship I would have to give her a full picture of all that passed and then she might tell Mama, or simply send me back in disgrace. I could not describe to her that I had been friends with someone, a married woman, who had become a mistress to one man then another in such quick succession that she did not know the father of her child. How could this be explained to someone so sensible and respectable as Miss Atwell?

In hoping to avoid Snowden and Betsey I decided to steer us clear of all English society. If Miss Atwell guessed anything was afoot she said nothing, for she was perfectly happy to take in the surrounding courtside, tour the markets and view the beautiful papist churches that I suggested. She always encouraged me to take my sketching materials with me so I could draw the sights for her. It was her wish that one day I paint them so she may have a pleasing collection of the landmarks of Europe in her future parlour, wherever she chose to settle.

Towards the end of the week, when we returned from the market, Snowden's card awaited us and the land lady, Signora Ricci, said he would call tomorrow, claiming he knew me from Bath.

'Is that so?' Miss Atwell asked me.

I nodded. 'Yes. He…he is the half-brother of Lt Driscoll, who is a friend to Captain Parnell.'

'Indeed,' she smiled. 'Interesting that he should seek you out.'

'I suppose if he has just arrived he may want introductions.'

'Had you told him or Lt Driscoll you were here?'

I shook my head. 'But I suppose he must have heard from some common acquaintance.'

'Well he has invited himself so I suppose we must receive him. We must make haste now or we will be late for the opera.'

*

The clock struck three in the afternoon at last. The day had inched on, and my mood was one of growing dread and resignation. Would he make accusations against me and reveal my bad behaviour to Miss Atwell? Would he bring Betsey? Would he try and renew his advances to me? Every time I tried to think of telling Miss Atwell all I could think was that she would send me home, and I would have to make my way back across Europe unaccompanied and penniless. Or worse, supposing Miss Atwell liked him? Or suppose I told Miss Atwell that he was a fortune hunter, but she thought that I must have been part of engineering it?

Almost as soon as the clock struck three was a rapping at the door. We had been awaiting him in the parlour and Signora Ricci showed him in. He was as foppish as I remembered, perhaps more so. He was squeezed into a waistcoat, strangled with an emerald cravat and crammed into a plum cut away. The less said about his breeches the better.

Miss Atwell was dressed very nicely, perhaps too nicely for the occasion but her appreciation of fashion had grown with our travels so whilst she did not slavishly follow it she was often described as very stylish and elegant. Mostly I liked to secretly credit myself with this but today I wished I had no such success at all for Mr Snowden smiled toadishly when he laid eyes upon her, dressed in a russet silk dress, with a white chemise underneath and a few tasteful wild flowers in her hair which I had painstakingly arranged. I wore my plainest dress, a navy walking dress, and I wore neither flower nor ribbon in my own hair, in fact I styled it as severely as if I were Lydia.

'Please be seated,' Miss Atwell said.

He looked between us, still smiling. 'Miss Atwell how pleased I am to make your acquaintance, everyone speaks so well of you. And Miss Amelia, how do you fare these days?'

'Well enough, thank you.'

'I am well also,' he gave Miss Atwell a pointed look as if I was a rude child, but she did not return it as we sat down.

'And how do you find Europe, my dear lady?'

'I like it a great deal,' Miss Atwell said. 'There is so much to learn.'

'I suppose there is, as someone from a fledgling nation you must see much here that is awe inspiring and to envy.'

'Awe inspiring yes sir, but I am not sure that I envy it. There is much to learn in terms of history, what has been done right but there is also plenty which Europe does wrong in my view as well.'

He gave a nervous laugh.

'I shall fetch some tea,' I said, wishing to busy myself away from him, but as soon as I left the room I regretted it. He could easily speak out of turn without me present and then what? I clattered into the kitchen and prepared the tea as fast as I could. As I hurried to take it back I almost tripped on the way.

As I entered the parlour, the room was filled with laughter.

'Oh Miss Atwell,' he said. 'You are quite a wit.'

She smiled, her eyes bright. She really was very pretty for someone so near to thirty.

'So what is it you do, Mr Snowden?' she asked as poured the tea.

'I am a poet,' he looked about in a preening manner.

'Where might I find your writings, sir?'

'Well,' he tapped his head. 'I am in the process I writing my first collection.'

'Oh,' she said raising her eyebrows. 'And you are how old?'

'Miss Atwell, such a direct question!'

'Well I was simply wondering how long it takes one to write a volume of poetry.'

'It takes as long as it takes.'

'So how long have you been trying? Had you started writing it in Bath, when you met Miss Amelia?'

'He said he was, though I saw little evidence of that,' I said and instantly regretted my foolish sharpness for he shot me a deadly look.

'I hardly think little girls are qualified to answer such questions.'

I swallowed, thinking I had already spoken too freely and had no wish to antagonise him. 'I suppose I know little on the subject of how one writes a poetry volume.'

'I also know little of the subject,' Miss Atwell said. 'So please tell us your process.'

'It takes a lot of thinking and looking inspiration-'

'So how many poems do you say you write a month?'

'Well it really depends on the month, one has to wait for inspiration-'

'How about in a year?'

'Miss Atwell, I did not come here to bore you with discussions on the writing process of poetry.'

'Why did you come here then?'

He blinked at her. 'To make your acquaintance. I had heard of your wit and beauty spoken of far and wide. I could try and write you a poem, about your fiery beauty if you should like?'

'Fiery beauty? Please Mr Snowden, because of my hair? You shall try and romanticize my journey from a distant land into the bargain as well.'

He squirmed in his seat, and no one needed to say out loud she was starting to think him a fortune hunter.

'The true reason for my visit is of a very delicate nature.'

'I'll wager it is,' Miss Atwell said.

He glared at me and cold fear trickled over me, freezing me, leaving me powerless to watch him as he started to speak.

'Miss Amelia and I were very well known to each other Bath and Brighton, in fact it was I who paid for her lodging. I came to warn you that your companion is a thief.'

Miss Atwell's face did not flicker, and her lack of reaction caused Snowden to stumble. 'She is, I do declare. In her possession you will find a pearl necklace that has been in the Snowden family since the restoration.'

Holy Lord! I had not known it was that valuable!

'How did this come to be in its possession?'

'She stole it, or more she tricked it from me.'

My stomach dropped. Should I offer the necklace back or feign ignorance?

'Women are always tricking men, are they not?'

'Indeed, oh...'

Miss Atwell raised an eyebrow at him. He wrung his hands. 'You see, I thought I had gifted one of a lesser value and my mistake has only come to light recently.'

'Mr Snowden I must beg of you to leave immediately.'

'May we not-'

'I think not.'

'You ought thank me for revealing the viper in your nest.'

'I think you are the only viper in this nest, Mr Snowden and as such I am asking you to leave now. Do not dally, for Signora Ricci has some strapping sons who would doubtless be happy to see you from the premises.'

Mr Snowden stood up and stormed out. My relief was only momentary for Miss Atwell turned to me, eyes blazing. 'Amelia, would you please care to explain what just happened?'

I nodded and swallowed. 'Yes ma'am.'

Miss Atwell's stern expression did not change as I related the facts to her. I started at the beginning and left nothing out, I did not weep or exaggerate but told as truthfully as I could. When I finished she nodded. 'And does your Mama know of this?'

I shook my head. 'She knows a little of what became of Betsey, but she does not know about what happened between Mr Snowden and I.'

'Or rather what Mr Snowden presumed would happen.'

'I suppose, but I rather think I must bear some of the blame.'

'Just because you accepted presents does not mean he can presume to make you his mistress. The point of a courtship is to see if one likes a person enough to form an attachment. If you realise you do not like that person, you are under no obligation to carry on with it, especially if it transpires that person's motives were far from pure. He did not want to marry you, did he? It was always his design to make you his mistress, you were not to know that. He used you most ill and simply because he gave you gifts he sets himself up as the injured party. It is hardly a stain on you that you accepted gifts.'

She reached over and pressed my hand. 'I think perhaps if he was a competent predator we might have more to fear, but seeing as he is not I think we had best quit while we are ahead.'

'Quit?'

'Let us set a course for Spain!'

I smiled, relieved. It was as if a heavy weight was lifted from me. She had done more than just listen, she had accepted and found me more in the right than I had found myself.

Lydia

Mother was there, her voice was a constant. Sometimes I could make out her words, other times I could not. My body ached, my skin was on fire, it itched and felt as if it were being stretched. It was so tender and raw. Mostly I could not focus on the room, my mind floated away while Mother's voice sounded in the background but I could not see her, nor the room. Sometimes it was as if moved down a corridor. Mother spoke from behind one door and Father laughed from behind another. I moved between the doors but I did not open either, I did not even try. Another time I sat in a field, Mother's voice drifting down around me so I could not hear the birds and animals in the field just her voice and on a hilltop in the distance was the shape of a man, a man I knew to be father but I did not try to go to him. I just wanted to sleep, I just wanted to be alone.

I heard Ruby's name but not her voice, and my heart leaped. Where was Ruby? Was she ill also? Ruby's words in Mother's voice urged me to get better, to use all my strength to fight. I would try but I did not know how, everything was too heavy, it was as though I was drowning in scalding water.

Jessica
The rash turned into pustules, red and angry looking on her cheek, on her neck, on her hands and arms. She stopped vomiting and her fever went down but still she slept, tossing, turning and moaning. I stayed at her bedside, with the windows open and no fire in the grate as Mr Campbell had instructed. He visited every evening, looking grave, and letting blood, always saying only time would tell.

James paid for two more medical men to attend on Lydia; a ship surgeon named Mr Grimes who he had sailed with, who insisted that no fire should be lit in the grate, and a fully-fledged doctor from Clifton, Dr. Whitson. Lord knows what that cost him. Dr Whitson went further than insisting no fire should be lit in the grate he also demanded the window should be left open and that she should only have few bed sheets, no blankets or quilts.

I thanked James after the doctor had gone.
'It is the least I can do,' he said.
'Do you not think Mr Campbell is very good?'
'I do not think he is very sober,' he replied. I nodded and he pressed my hand. Sometimes James would sit with me, and I would rest against him, his arm around me whilst I held Lydia's hand. He wrote to our friends, found new accommodation for our guests and bought me up the letters that Ruby constantly sent as well as food and told me that I must not worry about anything, he would see to all matters so I could stay at Lydia's side. He said what Mr Campbell did not; that it seemed to him Lydia was making progress, that she was a

fighter, that she was strong. It seemed to me that she grew worse, her fever had not broken, and the girl I knew was lost behind the red swellings.

Reading to Lydia kept me busy, my mind occupied. When I stopped, grief rose up in me like a wave. I could not bear to see her in pain, but I would not leave her. She did not seem to heed my words or notice my presence. In my head I prayed constantly for her not to be taken from me. If she went it would be as if a limb had been severed from me. I did not think that I would ever recover from the loss of her.

Chapter 37

Lydia

The room was cold as my eyes fluttered open. Mother was sitting at my beside, a book open on her lap, dozing. I yawned, and felt the skin crack across my face as though I was covered entirely in a crust. Slowly, with sore hands I pushed myself up into a sitting position. Blinking was painful.

Mother stirred than her gaze fixed upon me. 'Lydia, darling!' She threw her arms about me and I cried out in pain. She drew back, tears falling, gently pressing my forehead. 'Your temperature has gone down. Oh my dear, how do you feel?'

'I have a headache, and I'm sore, but better than before.'

'The spots have started to scab, that's good isn't it?'

I nodded.

'I shall send Captain Parnell for Mr Campbell.' She darted out into the corridor. 'James! Lydia is awake! Will you go for Mr Campbell?'

There was the sound of footsteps as I sunk back among my pillows, then Mother came back to sit at my side.

'So Mr Campbell knows the truth?'

She nodded.

'Was he angry?'

'He was at first, but he wanted to treat you.'

'Maybe he will be angry now.'

She shrugged. 'Perhaps, but we can bear his wrath now you are on the mend, can we not?'

*

Mr Campbell treated me as if I were any other patient - perhaps with more courtesy than he treated them - but he did not treat me as Hugh Sommers.

'Your fever has broken, and these pustules will be going down now. I shall tell your mother to burn these bedsheets-'

'When can I come back to work, sir?'

He looked at me as he closed his medical case with something almost like pity. 'You cannot.'

'Why not?'

'We both know why not. I should never have taken you on in the first place.'

'But you did take me on, and I was good.'

'Yes but I cannot take you back knowing what I know.'

'Why?'

He frowned at me. 'I see being argumentative wasn't something you adopted for your role as Hugh Sommers.'

'No, it wasn't.'

'People will guess and we'd be a laughing stock, or worse face some kind of criminal charge. I will grant you, you are a remarkable girl but I cannot continue to have you as my apprentice. The best I could offer you was to be my housekeeper, but that would simply involve doing the tasks you did not like.'

'Well obviously I do not accept.'

'That is as I thought. Let us at least part in friendship, Miss Fitzwilliam. You had a good run of it.'

He extended his hand but I turned my head away.

'As you wish,' he said before heading off down the stairs. Once I heard the front door close, I let myself cry.

Jessica

I cooked as if I was an ancient making offerings to the gods to thank them for Lydia's survival. There was pease pottage, and a thick beef stew, fresh bread to make sandwiches with butter and cheese I sent James to get fresh from the market, and I stewed the fruit the Thomases sent down to make a crumble. I made more macaroni and cheese and tried one of the curries that James had written down, which was warm with spices.

He helped where he could, buying me ingredients, new books for Lydia, and sending messages to our friends. As he headed out once more, to buy new bedsheets for Lydia, I took his hand.

'Thank you,' I said, kissing his cheek.

'You do not need to thank me, Jessica. This is what families do, isn't it?'

I took Lydia up a tray of stew. I had been up to see her several times and found her drowsy or dozing which had worried me but when I woke her she just said she needed rest. This time as I opened the door I saw her trying to hide the fact that she had been crying. If it had been Amelia she would have been weeping for the pox scars that would likely stay on her cheeks

'Lydia, what is the matter? Do you feel unwell again, shall I send for Mr Campbell?'

'No, I never want to see him again!'

'Why ever not?'

'He has said I may not resume my apprenticeship.'

'I see.'

'He thinks it will expose him to too much scandal and he is scared, he is a coward.'

'Lydia, I think he is simply being practical. We ought be glad he hasn't tried to expose us.'

'At least if he did expose us people may see that a girl can be just a good apprentice as a boy. If I had never gotten ill he would never have known. I always put my waistcoat back on before he returns but I fainted. I fainted like a girl-'

'Lydia, you fainted because you were sick. What is done is done. I am very sorry for you, but it is not the end of you and it shall not be an end for your extraordinary talents. We will find you other opportunities, maybe not as a doctor but I will not see you wither and fade away to nothing, I will not see you marry into mediocrity. Do you understand me?'

I was surprised at the amount of passion which had risen in me during the speech. Lydia nodded, looking almost shame-faced and I drew her into an embrace.

After a while she sat back and started on her stew. 'I am famished,' she said.

'Good, there is plenty more food where that came from. I have been sending James out for all sorts of ingredients.'

'James, is it?' she asked with a smile, causing me to blush.

'Well I suppose it is to me at least, though I would not call him that in public.'

Lydia raised her eyebrows.

Lydia

Ruby wrote constantly, twice a day and professed that she was overjoyed to hear of my recovery. I could not write back directly as my hand was too swollen to hold a pen and my scabs were flaking off, but Mother took down what I wanted to say. Ruby begged that as soon as I was well enough I come and stay with her for a few days.

The invitation pleased me. I would have my own time back at least now I was not working for Mr Campbell, so I may see Ruby more and perhaps work again at Mr Syrett's. Whilst all that was appealing, I still felt a heavy weight in my chest at all that had been lost. If only I had not removed my waistcoat, if only I had stayed home that day and been honest with myself about my symptoms, if only I could still be Hugh Sommers.

In some ways it was as if he had died and as the scabs flaked off, I shed his skin like a snake, and with it went his bright future and all the possibilities that had been open to me. I was not sure that I could be the same person I was before; now that I knew I was good enough to be a surgeon, how could I be content to be a woman? But then there was some relief. I did not have to lie any more, to fear discovery, to live a double life. Was there not a way I could be both? Still be Lydia Fitzwilliam but be fulfilled and use my abilities? What was the point of being good at medicine if I could do nothing with it?

Over the next week, the scabs all fell off leaving me with marks all over my skin. My face was not so bad, but it made me realise I had been beautiful before and not realised it, now my cheeks, especially my lower left cheek was adorned with pock-marks, along with my hands, arms, neck and legs. They would fade more in time Mother said, and Captain Parnell rolled up his sleeves to prove her point. His smallpox scars there was very faint indeed.

Gradually my skin stopped hurting, and I could wear more than just loose night dresses. I wore an amber dress that Miss Atwell had left for me, and found I liked it well enough. Hugh's clothes had been burnt for fear of infection, and though I felt a flash of rage when I heard this I knew it had been medically the right course of action.

After a week and a half had passed, Mother said I must be healthy enough for a trip and she asked the Captain to drive us to the country. We drove out to the hamlet of Shirehampton and sat in the meadows for our picnic, near the river Avon, on the opposite banks to the village of Pill. It fortified me greatly. We encountered a few people, and since I was not wearing a veil to cover the scars they stared, but not so much as to cause a commotion.

Mama and Captain Parnell kept the conversation jovial and I was pleased to be out of the city and breathe the fresh air. It was very restorative. As we headed back to the city, I asked the Captain how much shore leave he had left. 'Not long I fear,' he said. 'Only a week.'

Even in the fading light I saw Mother's smile became more forced.

'I am sorry to hear that,' I said honestly. 'And I must apologise for taking up your time with my illness.'

'Do not apologise on that account, Miss Fitzwilliam,' he said. 'You are well now. That is all that matters.'

Mother put her arm around me.

*

The rest of the next week passed with short walks around the harbourside, and much cooking from Mother. She experimented with curries and pastas, made pies, stews, soups and all kinds of fancy desserts and cakes. I spent much time on the sofa in the parlour writing to Ruby and Amelia. I took on the task of telling Amelia of my illness as Mama had held back since there was little she could do about it from Europe until the outcome was known.

After assuring both Mother and the Captain I felt very well indeed, we took another drive to the country and visited the grounds of the Kings Weston and Blaise Castle estates. Such wonderful natural beauty was to be admired there! Both could boast magnificent views of Bristol, the River Avon and the surrounding countryside. Ruby would love to see all the variety of trees and flowers, and Amelia would be most jealous that the housekeeper of Kings Weston House granted us tour. It was a very grand place indeed.

Every evening, Captain Parnell dined with Mother and me. As ever, Mother would serve and fuss, even when we started to eat. The Captain would tell her fondly to sit down and enjoy the meal, then pour her a glass of wine first. After dinner, we would sit and he or myself would read aloud from the paper or from my pile of new books which everyone had seen fit to gift me with. We had started to behave as a family and I found I did not mind.

When Amelia returned I hoped she would not mind either. On what was Captain Parnell's last day of shore leave I was deemed well enough to go and visit Ruby for a couple of days. Mr Thomas came to pick me up in the evening in the family cart, and commented on how well and undiminished I looked. I thanked him for his words though I knew they were a kindly exaggeration.

Jessica

I came back in from bidding Lydia farewell and sat on the sofa next James.

'We have eaten so well these past few days I find myself at a loss as to what to cook,' I admitted. 'A salmagundi using some of our leftovers will serve, won't it?'

'Of course.'

'She will be fine, won't she?'

He put down his book and looked at me. 'She will be.'

I pressed his hand. 'And you…will you be fine when you return to duty?'

'I think we both know I would be foolish to promise that,' he said. 'However, I can promise I will do my best to be fine. The Aries is an excellent ship with a good crew - and if all else fails, I can swim.'

I laughed but playfully shoved him.

'I am looking for ways to resign or go to half pay. It is a lengthy processes but hopefully I'll find a way out, since I can be promoted no further I rather hope they will see my reasoning. It is said there are more captains than ships, which is good for me. But either way, the next time I have shore leave - I want to marry you.'

I pressed his hand. 'Was that a proposal?'

'Not quite,' he said.

'So I am just to tell people I have an understanding with a navy captain? Not many people would believe you would be steadfast.'

I was teasing, but while I believed him I knew others would not.

'No, what I mean is…I want you to know I did not install you in this house for this to happen, I did it respecting you, admittedly thinking you were very beautiful but I never did it for this.'

'I know you did it because you felt sorry for me.'

'Well yes,' he stroked my cheek. 'But it doesn't sound very complimentary like that, does it?'

'It sounds honest,' I said. 'I am glad you felt sorry for me. And I did not take this position expecting anything to happen, but I am glad it has, very glad. I have fallen in love with you, James.'

He got down on one knee. 'Jessica, will you become my wife? I have never loved anyone as I love you. It is as though I have waited so long to meet you I had begun to think I never would. I was foolish to think of waiting until the war was over just so everything could be perfect. If I can marry you, it will be perfect.' From his pocket he produced a ring and I gasped. It was silver, with a small, elegant diamond. 'I am not a rich man, but I am of means - which is a world away from where I started. If I can achieve that by myself imagine what we could achieve together, my dearest Jessica.'

I threw my arms around him. 'Yes, I will marry you,' I managed. 'Yes, oh yes!'

He slipped the ring onto my finger, a perfect fit. I drew him close for a kiss. He kissed me with more passion than we had before and our bodies pressed against each other.

'Oh Jessica,' he whispered. 'I love you.'

'I love you,' I said, then carried on kissing him.

*

I sat at the breakfast table, my cup of coffee warmed my fingers, my engagement ring glinting in the morning sun. On the table was a feast of porridge, stewed fruits, plum cake, and eggs. James sat opposite me, his uniform pressed and buttons gleaming. He cocked his head and smiled at me. 'This is how I shall think of you.'

I laughed, and told him he was being foolish, for my hair was uncombed, I was barefoot and still in my nightgown which slipped down over one shoulder. I was not entirely sure how I would think of him but I hoped it would not involve the navy uniform, dashing though it was, for it was the reason he must go away. I said this, aware of how it might sound but since I was engaged for the second time and my daughters were not in the house I fancied I could say what I pleased.

He grinned wickedly, then drew me into an embrace before kissing my cheeks, my neck and my shoulders.

'I shall miss you,' he said. 'I do not think a letter will be enough this time and they will take an age to get through.'

I nodded. 'I shall miss you too, while you are off fighting for king and country.'

'I flatter myself, but I would much rather imagine myself fighting for you. It makes the going strangely more bearable.'

We laughed, but I thought it was oddly true. If they lost, Britain would be invaded and Bristol could be one of the first places overrun. I drew him close again, breathed deeply enough to fill my lungs with his smell of soap and starch, clean linen.

'I will miss our conversations,' he said. 'And your quick wit-'

'I do not think I have ever been called quick witted. My daughters have more wit than I.'

'They both have wit enough, but you have intelligence, measured and considered. I shall miss your thoughtfulness and how nothing much phases you. Your laugh, your laugh is quite wonderful...'

'You see me for who I am,' I said. 'Selfish though it is, I will miss that. I like being Jessica with you, not Mama or Mrs Fitzwilliam.'

'How curious,' he said. 'I rather like being James with you, not Captain Parnell. You have given me the sort of home I always wanted, Jessica.'

'You make me feel safe,' I said quietly. 'As though I never had a truer friend.'

We kissed once more and held each other tightly. 'I shall come down to the dockside with you,' I said, fighting back tears. 'To say goodbye there. Then when I return I will write to girls to tell them the good news.'

Chapter 37

Lydia

When I disembarked from the cart I was greeted by Ruby, who threw her arms about me and guided me to the parlour. She smelled as pretty as ever; of spring flowers.

'You look well!' she said.

'Do not lie.'

'You do, I swear it. And the scarring isn't at all bad, if I may say.'

'You may.'

We sat together, her arm linked with mine and joy beat in my chest. I had missed her most painfully, without her my senses were quite dulled. The rest of the Thomas family came to sit down and spoke with me warmly.

Mrs Thomas mentioned that even George sent his best wishes. She said it as though she was a great compliment which I supposed it was, considering how distanced he was from his family.

'After dinner,' Mrs Thomas said, 'Fleur can play the piano for us, then you can sleep in with the girls. If you are feeling strong enough we might venture into Clifton for a spot of shopping on the morrow.'

I smiled; it felt so long since I had simply relaxed in the company of friends.

'That sounds delightful. I am sure I shall be well enough for shopping tomorrow, especially if we can find some book-shops.'

Fleur rolled her eyes but Ruby laughed gaily and gave my arm an extra squeeze, 'Of course we shall!'

I slept in the same room as Ruby, Fleur and Hyacinth. I was given Ruby's bed and she shared with her sisters. Fleur chatted excitedly about Ruby's forth coming wedding, the fabrics, the flowers and how lucky Ruby would be to have a house of her own. Ruby joined in with plans for her new garden. It did seem set that they would be moving to London, to a place called Summer's Town, and a have townhouse near a reformist church where Mr Bradley would preach. I nodded and smiled, whilst she insisted that I come and stay. 'You could stay for longer now.'
'Why now?' Fleur asked.
'Oh,' I said. 'I am not working as a housekeeper anymore,' the lie came smoothly.
'Why?' Hyacinth asked.
Ruby quickly changed the subject to wedding dresses and her sisters did not question it.

The next day, as promised, we went shopping in Clifton. It was a pleasant stroll from Cotham and once we arrived Mrs Thomas suggested we started looking for fabrics to help make Ruby's trousseau. Ruby smiled, before looking at me with an apology in her eyes while her mother was distracted by a window display. I forced a smile and saw the joy and relief spread over her features. She linked arms with me but inside my heart plummeted. The look of happiness and relief that she had tried to disguise on my behalf meant she truly did want to marry Mr Bradley, and that I was souring it for her. I did not want that, I wanted her to be happy above all things. I just wished I could have a bigger stake in her happiness.

The conversation turned to what sorts of fabrics and patterns Ruby should buy. A floral wedding muslin was desired. Ruby listed the flowers that she favoured whilst pondering their meanings. I had never been good at remembering which flowers symbolised what and told her she ought to just go for the ones she liked, that she would look beautiful in anything, but Fleur shook her head and said that people would comment if Ruby made some sort of blunder and chose an unlucky flower or a mourning one.

As we walked through the streets of Clifton, a gentleman strode passed us, followed by his black footman in livery. The footman shot

Ruby, Fleur and Hyacinth a look which they did not return. Ruby's arm was linked with mine while Fleur's and Hyacinth's were linked with their Mother's. I made no comment on it but felt his eyes, and the eyes of others, boring into our backs.

We entered a pretty fabric shop, which smelled of lavender and linen. The woman came from behind the counter to greet us with a bland smile. 'Good day to you madam, how may I be of service?'

'I am here to select some fabrics for my daughter's wedding.'

The woman turned her gaze to me, and before I could protest, she eyed the scars on my cheeks and said, 'I suppose you will be wanting a thick veil.'

I flushed. 'It's not-'

'This is my daughter,' Mrs Thomas said, moving Ruby forwards.

The woman raised her eyebrow. 'A thicker veil still then,' she said.

'I beg your pardon?' Mrs Thomas said.

'I do not think we have anything here to suit your daughter.' The woman opened the door.

Ruby took my arm, looking shamefaced as though she was the one at fault. All the excitement vanished from her sisters' faces.

Mrs Thomas strode towards the door. 'My money is just as good as the next person's.'

'And we are not without connections,' I said sharply, suddenly inspired. 'We shall ensure that our friends know of your rudeness. My sister is a companion to a very wealthy heiress. She will never spend so much as a penny in your shop.'

We left without waiting for her response. Mrs Thomas led us down the street in a bluster of indignation, but Ruby made no comment.

'Ruby-'

'It matters not,' she said.

In the next shop, we were not treated with as much open contempt, but Ruby was very obviously assumed to be the servant and even after her position was explained, the shop woman kept deferring to Mrs Thomas and I. The last shop, Ruby spoke first, in a rush before her mother or the shop keeper could get a word in. 'I am to be married. I need new fabrics.'

The shop keeper smiled and was all cordiality but while Ruby did relax and chose some fabrics for her trousseau, she could not settle on anything for her wedding gown.

'We do not have to decide today,' Mrs Thomas said. 'But I shall leave my address so the shop-keeper can notify me when they next get new fabrics.'

Mrs Thomas took us directly to a bookshop, where she said that pin money was no object today and the girls could choose what they wanted. Fleur and Hyacinth chose novels by Ann Radcliffe and Fanny Burney. Ruby poured over the botany books and selected three.

'I rather wish I could have a trousseau of books,' she confided with a smile.

'Now that is something which makes the idea of marriage sound appealing.'

She laughed, her ease returning though she was still not as talkative on the way home as Mrs Thomas and Fleur gossiped a little too merrily about their neighbours.

Matthew took me home in the cart.

'You are looking well,' he said awkwardly.

'Thank you,' I said, though I felt fatigued.

'What will happen now to our enterprise with Mr Campbell?'

'I do not know. I have not seen him since he said I could no longer be his apprentice.'

'You are lucky he did not notify the authorities about you.'

'Am I? Lucky is not exactly the word I would use.'

'I may call on Mr Campbell on my way home to see if anything can be done to salvage the enterprise.'

'Do as you will but he will not work with me again.'

When I reached home Mother sat me down.

'Lydia dear, I have something of a great import, and I hope joy, to acquaint you with.'

Her hands were folded on her lap and I saw on the finger which had been empty these past few months, which for so long had borne her wedding ring now had something else. A silver band with a diamond.

'You are engaged to Captain Parnell?' I said.

She followed my gaze and laughed. 'Indeed I am!'

'Well, my congratulations,' I said honestly and drew her into embrace, pushing away notions of how our lives might change and only focusing on the thought that I was happy to see her happy.

Jessica

After writing a letter to Amelia to tell her the news, I decided to next tell Mrs Webster, given that she had already made her views clear on my attachment. It was best to get this meeting out of the way, and if her reaction was more positive than I was expecting all the better for it.

On hearing that Mrs Webster may be less than pleased at the news of my engagement Lydia looked vaguely amused.

'What concern is it of hers?' she asked with a grin. 'It is hardly as if her own family is famed for behaving with propriety.'

'Well no, but she did offer us a roof over our head when we had none, we must not forget that.'

'So did Captain Parnell,' Lydia pointed out.

Mrs Webster arrived, driven by Edward. He presented me with a letter.

'What is this?'

'It is from Captain Parnell,' he said with a faint frown. 'And if I may be so bold I advised him against it.' Without waiting, he took his leave.

I tore the seal and saw a note and a legal document. Lydia appeared at my shoulder as I unfolded the paper whilst Mrs Webster watched keenly. I read it, trying to take it in.

'He has signed the house over to you,' Lydia gasped. 'You own this place!'

'Oh my goodness,' Mrs Webster said.

'But he is not a rich man,' I said, sitting down, my heart pounding, my mind racing. I looked at the date. He had done it before he had proposed to me.

'Read the note before I do!' Lydia said.

Dearest Jessica,

I have signed the house over to in order to keep my promise to you that you shall be well provided for in the event of my death. It is my hope that you feel secure. I have asked that this be given to you by Mr Edward Webster, as I did not want to put you under any pressure in my presence especially in light of a question which I hope to ask you before I go.

With all my love,

Captain J G Parnell

'Well?' demanded Mrs Webster.

'It relates very much to the reason that I wanted you here today,' I said, passing the note to Lydia. 'I am engaged to Captain Parnell.'

'For how long?'

'Two days since,' I said. 'Before he went back to his ship.'

Lydia rose to go and make tea.

Mrs Webster frowned. 'Do you not think it all a bit hasty?'

'How can it be hasty? I have known him for over two years.'

'But you have the house now.'

I blinked at Mrs Webster. 'You think I was marrying him for the house? For security?'

'Come now, Mrs Fitzwilliam-' her use of my name, my old name, Peter's name, set my teeth on edge. 'You cannot be so foolish as to tell me you are marrying for love?'

'Why on earth not?'

'As I have said to you before, it will make your life remarkably difficult to be married to a Catholic. People will not trust you, if you have more children-'

'I love him, and he is financially secure. It is a good match.'

'You would have a good life if you just kept the house,' she said. 'If you want to wed again in time, I am sure we can find someone more suitable.'

I stared at her, rage growing.

'For example, John is not ten years younger than you. He is a good, sensible worker and has been most devout since the death of his wife.'

I stood up. 'You want me to consider your eldest son?' I bit my tongue to avoid from saying the only thing John Webster did devoutly was drink.

'It is not so terrible a match,' Mrs Webster looked offended.

'I have no wish to have a husband that is ten years younger than me, and no wish to sign Captain Parnell's house, my house, over to that husband. This house is for me, my girls and the Captain. No one else.'

Mrs Webster flushed. 'I was only thinking you might consider it.'

Lydia came in with the tea. 'Odd what we can consider now,' she said suddenly. 'When two years ago you told Edward very definitely he was not to consider me.'

Mrs Webster flushed deeper. 'How did you…?'

'I have excellent hearing.'

A tension filled the room.

'I had rather hoped you might be happy for my mother,' Lydia said.

I folded my arms. Was this likely to be the reaction I would get from everyone?

'It is Miss Fitzwilliam and Miss Amelia I worry for. What will having a Catholic as a step-father do for their marriage prospects?'

'Probably no worse than having a gambler and bankrupt for a father did.'

Mrs Webster's eyes rounded at Lydia's bluntness making me feel a rush of pride, before she turned to me.

'Since Mr Fitzwilliam's death you spend time with the Thomases, and Captain Parnell, all these unsuitable, dissenting types. I do not think Mr Fitzwilliam would have approved. Mr Webster does not and he and Mr Fitzwilliam were such friends.'

'With all due respect, it does not matter to me that your husband disproves of me, and it certainly does not matter to me if Peter would have approved. I did not approve of him leaving me penniless. All my life I did as I was told and acted as was right and proper. I do not think I am even doing anything so very rebellious. I simply ask for your good wishes, as a friend, since I have reason to be happy after such a period of upheaval.'

Mrs Webster sighed, but did look shamefaced. She swallowed

'We have long been friends, have we not?' she said. 'I remember when you were a young wife first come to Bristol and you stood so nervously between your mother and your husband at the trader's ball, barely more than a little girl yet already carrying this one. Such a fragile looking thing you were.' She reached her hands out. 'Since Mrs Hughes is sure to disapprove when she hears of it, I must surely approve then, must I not? Or at least, since I cannot honestly manage that I will say that I don't disapprove, that will have to suit. Though you will have to allow me that your life will not be easy.'

I took her hands. 'Life never is,' I said.

She chuckled. 'No, indeed. Now come, what church will it be at? God preserve us, that at least will be one of ours, and hopefully not the one you frequented with poor Mr Fitzwilliam.'

Amelia

We travelled through Spain; fitting in the very beautiful Madrid and Barcelona. We did it rather quickly for the spectre of war hung over the continent, and we knew that even going past France could be dangerous. Miss Atwell was hopeful she could secure us passage on a non-English ship, so it would not be captured by the French navy. A Spanish ship should serve us.

As to our travels we saw many more grand papist churches in Seville, some Moorish buildings as well. I rather liked the Spanish habit of sleeping during the day and since Miss Atwell had visited Texas in America, she was well versed in the Spanish tongue. Having spent so long among the Italians I flattered myself that I could at least make sense of some of the Spanish language on the words that were similar, of which there were several.

A letter reached us in Madrid which to my horror detailed the grave news about Lydia - she had smallpox! The primary purpose of the letter was to assure me of her survival, but still I was beset with a great wave of sadness. When I relayed the events to Miss Atwell she asked after Lydia's wellbeing.

I swallowed. 'She survived, thank god. But to think what could have happened!'

'She is not blinded or any such thing?'

'I do not think so, I suppose there may be scars, but that hardly matters does it?'

I stood up and started to pace, my mind unable to be quiet. All that could have passed in my absence! All that might have been lost. I could hardly believe it. A sickness and great uneasiness took hold of me.

'I think that decides it then,' Miss Atwell said.

'Decides what?'

'We have been away long enough, and with troubles growing in France I do not want us to be trapped here. I am sure your Mama would be most grieved. We shall stay on a few more weeks and then embark on our journey homewards.'

I nodded, greatly gladdened at the thought of going home. Travel was indeed such a marvellous thing, but so was going home.

Chapter 38

Lydia

Ruby's wedding approached like a charging bull. The date was set, the house selected in London, the trousseau paid for and the dress made. Now that I did not work with Mr Campbell I was asked up to their house often and watched with growing sadness as Ruby's new life as Mrs Bradley was constructed before my eyes.

I could see that she had grown very fond of Mr Bradley, he adored her and the match delighted her family, yet I could not be happy about it as much as I tried. I think I put up a passable front though, for Mother stopped asking me if all was well. Mrs Thomas and Fleur spoke as excitedly to me about it as if I was in league with them. Ruby herself even started to speak happily to me about it, whereas before she had been cautious in her approach to discussing it. Even Mr Bradley spoke with me as if we were old friends.

Why could I not be happy about it? Was it because she would move away? The thought of visiting her in her marital home made me anxious. She was desperate for me to stay with her, indeed it would give me excuse to see in London, so then why did I mind that she would be married to a perfectly nice man whom she liked? It caused a dull ache in my stomach, a tightening in my back, a whirling pit of misery in my chest. In the morning I would wake for a few moments and believe all was well, then something would remind me that it was not.

It could not simply be that I did not approve of Mr Bradley, for there was nothing exactly wrong with him, and when I tried to think of another man I would rather she marry – one of the Websters, some of the younger abolitionists, even in fantasy the heroes from some of the

Gothic Romances that Amelia enjoyed – I could find none that would satisfy me as a decent match for Ruby.

*

The day of Ruby's wedding arrived and I waited in the church with Mother. She smiled and commented on the pretty flower arrangements and fretted over the chicken pies she had bought with her for the wedding breakfast.

Mr Bradley stood at the front of the church, nervously smiling and I found myself wishing that Ruby would not arrive, that he would be jilted. I stood up, tears of anger rising in me and an overwhelming thought that I could not be here thinking wicked thoughts on a day that was supposed to be happy, yet I could not bear to see Ruby wed to this man. Mother lay her hand on my arm. 'Sit down my dear, I am sure we will get a good enough view from here.'

She waved to Mrs Thomas and Matthew as they entered, George followed close behind. Then as Mrs Thomas and her sons sat down the organ started.

Mother nudged to me. 'How lovely she looks.'

Mr Thomas smiled proudly, and beneath a bonnet and a veil, holding a bunch of pink roses, Ruby was on his arm. Her dress was forget-me-not blue with a delicate floral print and her veil was not too heavy to obscure the pure joy on her beautiful face as she smiled widely, looking passed everyone and directly at Mr Bradley.

I regarded her, unable to look away. I love you, Ruby Thomas. The love I had for her was daunting, overwhelming, repulsive, joyous – but I knew in my bones that right or wrong I could not alter that. I just had to be glad I knew her. I swallowed the heavy sadness in my throat, did not cry but smiled, because though she could not be mine she would be happy, and I could not make her so, but she did love me in her own way. It could be a thousand times worse, I could have never known her or never have her friendship. Something was better than nothing, but knowing I wanted what I could never ever have was like a sharp twist of a knife.

At the wedding breakfast I did not get much of a chance to speak with Ruby, only snatched moments with Mr Bradley next to her, to wish them my happy regards of the day.

'Should you like this for yourself, Miss Lydia?' Matthew asked, plonking himself next to me at the dining table.

'Like what?'

'A wedding day? A marriage?'

I sighed. 'I think not.'

'Suppose you had a husband who thought your mind was an asset?' He cleared his throat. 'Who wanted to carry on making medicinal remedies, let us say?'

I looked at Matthew. There was no love or longing in his eyes but calculation. It was an odd way to be proposed to, and in a strange way would bring me closer to Ruby. There was a fairly strong resemblance between them, but she was far prettier than he was handsome.

I sighed. 'I think not,' I said, standing. 'I think we have had our day with medicinal remedies.'

I headed out alone into the garden, not looking back.

Jessica

I sent a letter to Amelia detailing my engagement, but received one back only a few days later to say she would be leaving Spain so any other correspondence was unlikely to get through. The thought of telling her in person cheered me a great deal, though it was not without a cloud since I worried she may rear up with loyalty at her father's memory – though I daresay if she widowed she would marry again.

Miss Thomas, Mrs Bradley now, had set off on her honeymoon to the Peak District and Lydia was subdued without her, so I took care to prepare her favourite meals of game birds and salads to try and bring her cheer. I had never been so far north as the Peak District and wondered if perhaps James might consider it for our honeymoon, though I should like to see the sea again. There was no reason why we could not see both - oh what happy thoughts! I tried to restrain my wedding talk around Lydia who probably needed no more talk of weddings since marriage had so recently deprived her of a friend so I kept my musings to myself.

She started to work for Mr Syrett again without complaint and he was happy to have her. I could not help feel that this would only add to her discontent for it must seem like a step backwards. If only some liberal-minded young scholar or doctor would visit the shop and take a fancy to her! She would do well as the head of her own household, or helping to run a business and I would be so happy to think of her contented and safe. It seems life is difficult for her whatever she tries. I cannot help but take slight umbrage at fate on her behalf, surely, she is owed some good fortune at last?

The next few weeks passed slowly, and I alternated between

feverishly reading newspaper reports for news of the HMS Aries and avoiding all hints of the Navy all together. With the news about the engagement at Boulogne Harbour, I was fraught, but it seemed despite losses the British came out of it and the HMS Aries had survived – there were no newspaper reports stating otherwise.

After Mrs Webster's initial misgivings about my engagement she had returned to ease and friendliness, although I noted I had not seen her husband nor been invited to dine and their orders for meat pies had diminished. Their oldest son John took and made the deliveries and he made no mention of my engagement either, neither to congratulate or chastise. I mentioned it to him and got a nod and a grunt.

Mr Syrett congratulated me on having secured such a well-read fiancé, and the Thomases were joyous. Mrs Thomas took me aside and, while insisting she was happy for me said she expected I knew that being married to be a Catholic would be very different to being married to an old country protestant. I laughed at her description of Peter, and she said she meant in terms of people's attitude. I was sure it would be nothing to what she had faced with Mr Thomas, which she confirmed was the truth but she said I must learn develop a thick skin nonetheless, and perhaps decide sooner rather than later what religion I intended our children to be.

I confided that I was not holding out much hope of children at all. I had carried four children, and lost the eldest and the youngest before they were properly formed. All of my pregnancies had been between the ages of sixteen and twenty-three, so I was not expecting to fall pregnant again.

Mrs Thomas smiled at this and tapped her nose. 'Well you never know. You are a very handsome couple, are you not!?' She chuckled wickedly and I indulged her with a tap and a giggle, though secretly thought that if the day of our engagement was anything to go by the trying for children at least was likely to be a very enjoyable aspect of our wedded life.

Amelia

As we neared Bristol I stood on deck. My seasickness was no better, but it was raining and I was glad for English rain is like no other. I can say that now I am well-travelled. The air gets a certain way of heaviness, it smells of moss and sod even if you can see neither of those things – at sea of course there is a dank addition of a heavy saltness – but mixed with such dampness it can only be British. What an odd, glorious thing to be proud of!

I watched Bristol grow in size from a small dot to the welcoming harbour port as we jostled for position with navy ships and slavers, merchant vessels bringing tobacco, cotton and spices, pleasures ships. The nearer we got among the roar of the sailors voices from the harbourside became distinguishable with the warming burring Rs and the Ss pronounced as Zs - the West Country way but all spoken quicker than the rural tongue – the Bristol way as I myself spoke! What a thrill it was to be home. I felt as I had betrayed the traveller in me, but Miss Atwell came and stood on deck me.

'We can only appreciate our home once we have been away from it,' she said with a smile. I smiled back at her. She had spoken of returning to America and settling in the north, but she was to travel to Wales before that to meet with a friend of hers who had married a Welsh man who made his fortune in her land and returned to his.

We had not broached the subject of whether she would want me to accompany her back as her companion in America. I felt in my heart that if she asked me, I would go. I had only seen Europe, what a small fraction of the world! I would of course miss Mama and Lydia terribly, that would be the only thing that could change my decision however…maybe Lydia could be persuaded to come since if I read her letter right, she was no longer Mr Campbell's 'housekeeper', but would Miss Atwell want another companion? And what about Mama? Perhaps there could be some way that we could all go…

*

'Hello?' I called as I entered the house.

Mama hurried from the kitchen, apron covered in flour. As she drew me into a crushing embrace, which I heartily returned, I processed the two changes in her appearance. She was out of black and wearing her old blue dress, alerted to fit the latest fashion, and on the finger which had once borne her wedding ring, was a pretty little diamond ring.

'You are engaged?' I said as she drew back. She nodded, a mixture of joy and apprehension in her eyes.

'Yes,' she said. 'Captain Parnell asked me on his last visit here. I sent a letter to you but then yours arrived to say you were coming home.'

I nodded. Strangely, I was not at all surprised but it was excessively odd to think she would no longer be Mrs Fitzwilliam, that she might have a whole new, different life, that she may even have more children now and I would no longer be the youngest, that he could try to impose some strict laws upon us or convert us to Catholicism.

I realised I had not spoken, but was staring at her ring, thinking it much smaller than the one Papa had given her. Supposing Papa had won it at cards and not told us, now I could never be able to ask him. Raising my eyes, the apprehension in hers had grown. If I said I was not happy about the match, she might put it off or even abandon it but then despite all my misgivings I was not unhappy. I should not sit about mourning a husband who had bankrupted me even if he had been as wonderful as Papa, and if she truly did love Captain Parnell I could not be the villain of the piece and prevent their match no matter how much I might feel slighted on Papa's behalf; Papa was not here to feel slighted himself.

'You love the Captain?'

'I do.'

'More than Papa?' I blurted and she blushed.

'Differently,' she said quietly. 'Every love is different.'

'I am happy for you then,' I said pressing her hand. 'And I must insist upon being bridesmaid.'

'But of course!' she laughed.

'And will you have to become a Catholic?'

She shook her head. 'We have to marry in the Church of England,' she said.

'Ah, that is good!'

Another realisation hit me. Lt Driscoll may also attend the wedding, and if Captain Parnell was to be my step-father – that did indeed sound queer, I did not think I would be using that title just yet – there would also be other ample opportunities to meet Lt Driscoll. A pleasing thought indeed.

Mama moved to greet Miss Atwell, who had finished settling with the coach drive who had carried our luggage in, and Lydia came down the stairs. I rushed to embrace her.

'Hello Millie,' she said fondly.

'I am so pleased to see you up and about!' I said. 'You look so well!'

I had feared her languishing in bed like an invalid, her face riddled with scars – and while she was not without blemishes she looked a deal better than my horrid fantasies.

The pox marks were only on her cheeks and mostly on the left one. In time they would fade, and they are not such an uncommon sight. Perhaps if I could persuade her to use powder they could be concealed altogether.

She moved to help me carry my cases upstairs but I waved her away.

'I am hardly invalided,' she retorted.

I rolled my eyes and we lugged my cases up together.

'I bought you back some lace, though I am sure you shall scorn it,' I said. 'But I chose the plainest I could find, though you will note it is still very fine.'

I handed it to her and was pleased to see her smile.

'Yes,' she said. 'It is very fine, thank you. I suppose I shall have more need of it now I am confined to dresses once more.'

'You are no longer Hugh Sommers?' I asked tentatively.

She shook her head. 'I came down with the smallpox whilst working,' she said. 'Mr Campbell treated me. My secret is out.'

'Was he angry?'

She shook her head. 'Surprisingly not, but he has refused to have me back as Hugh Sommers. He did offer me the position of being his housekeeper,' she laughed wryly. 'But that would involve all the duties I did not like and none of the ones I did. I am back where I started, at Mr Syrett's.'

'Well he was always was a kind sort,' I said, seeing her sorrow.

She nodded.

'Do we have any lodgers at present?'

'Mother was saving a room for Miss Atwell, and we have a retired Commodore and his wife come for the spa. They are pleasant enough, oh and – of course you do not know. Captain Parnell-'

'And Mama are engaged? I saw the ring-'

'He has given her the house.'

'What? Mama owns this house?'

'In case he dies at sea before they are married, she – we- are protected.'

'That is rather romantic, even if it is rather practical sounding when you describe it,' I said. 'If we own the house, we need not take lodgers in at all.'

Lydia laughed. 'The mortgage still must be paid,' she pointed out. 'And we still must live.'

I sat on the bed. 'What do you think of him?'

'I like him.'

'Even though he was angry with you?'

'I was looking through his accounts.'

'You think it is a good match, then? That he loves her?'

Lydia nodded. 'I do not doubt it. Anyway, I am sure you shall be married and I shall be the old maid so you will not have to live with them for the rest of your days. It ought not concern you as much.'

'Lydia how can you talk so! Does Mr Bradley not have any handsome friends for you?'

'I think not.'

She opened my trunk and started to unpack my dresses. As she unrolled my finest ballgown I lunged forward. There I had hidden my treasures from Mr Snowden. I was not quick enough for the ruby pendent, diamond brooch and pearl necklace clunked to the floor. Her eyebrows shot up.

'Amelia, did Miss Atwell buy you these?'

I could easily have lied but I stopped myself. 'No, they are from Charles Snowden.'

'Who is that?'

'Lt Driscioll's half-brother. I met him in Brighton.'

'All that time ago?'

'Yes.'

'Are you engaged to him or—'

'No Lydia, certainly not. He is quite a rogue. He wanted me to be his mistress.'

'Heavens!'

'You sound an old maid, which you are not yet despite your designs upon the role.'

'You did not—'

'No! I repelled his advances.'

'But you kept his gifts?'

'Yes.'

Lydia gave me a long, hard look. 'Very well. I suppose you were under the charge of Betsey Webster.'

I nodded, thinking of the sad, desperate figure I had last seen. Her baby was likely born by now. I wondered if she and it had survived, if Mr Snowden had taken her home or abandoned her in Europe. The latter seemed more likely. Poor Betsey.

Lydia handled the pieces. 'What will you do with them? They must be worth a pretty penny.'

I sat down on the floor next to her, thinking she was ever a Sommers mercenary but since I had taken them I supposed I was as well.

'The pearl necklace is a family piece, so I was thinking I might return it to Lt. Driscoll.'

'When?'

I shrugged. 'At a time of my choosing. Lt Driscoll is illegitimate, so unlikely to inherit anything from his father's estate. If I give him this he will be in my debt.'

Lydia nodded. 'What of the pendent and the broach?'

I picked them up. 'I never intended to keep them...' Looking between it and Lydia an idea struck me. 'I could invest it in a business venture.'

'What do you know of business ventures?'

'You will wish you had stopped your tongue before you heard what I had to say,' I said. 'While you are right I know little of such matters, I know someone who does.'

'Who?'

'You.'

'What do you mean?'

'You know all about accounts and running a shop from Old Mr Syrett, you probably learnt a few things from Mr Campbell and your enterprise with the tinctures.'

'I suppose book-keeping is not so hard at all-'

'Well then, let us open a shop.'

'A shop?' Lydia blinked a few times.

'I shall not insist you sell ribbons and lace or any such thing, in fact I intend to have as little to do with the running the business as possible. You can sell books or tinctures or whatever you chose.' I hesitated as Lydia's face lit up. 'Women can own shops, can they not?'

'I believe so.'

'Well, if we cannot we can use the Captain's name. If he insists upon marrying our mama it really is the least he can do.'

Lydia laughed, loudly and properly. 'Indeed! Ah, Ruby once talked of opening a shop with me, but now she is wed...Oh Amelia this will be perfect!'

Chapter 39

Lydia

Amelia had only been home a few weeks when I was invited up to London with Mrs Thomas and Fleur, to visit Ruby and Mr Bradley in their house in London.

We took a coach to London, and Amelia gave me a list of recommendations of places to see. What I was most excited about was the British Museum. Ruby promised she would not visit the British Museum until I was at her side, so we might experience the wonders it held together for the first time. Amelia loftily said that was all well and good, but the ruins on display there hardly compared to the grandeur of Rome. I gladly forgave her this snobbery as the thoughts of our owning a shop pleased me greatly, and when thinking of all the different things we might sell I felt a lightness and joy that had eluded me for months.

When we pulled up outside Ruby's town house, the curtain twitched and she dashed out into the street to meet us. Her curls were hidden beneath her married woman's cap but she still looked as pretty as ever.

'Mrs Bradley, what a pleasure to see you!' Mrs Thomas laughed. Ruby embraced me tightly, her brown eyes shining. 'I am so glad you have come!' she said. 'Please do come inside.'

The terraced house was pleasant and clean, and Ruby had hung botanical paintings and pressed flowers all about the place. Mrs Thomas and Fleur were to share a room and I was given my own small but very pretty room in which Ruby had left a pile of books upon the table for me.

'I hope you like it,' she said, pressing my hand. I nodded.

'I do and what a pleasure it is to have my own room.'

We took tea in her small garden, which she had already started to tend to and had a patch set aside for the kitchen and another set aside for flowers.

They had a young runaway slave called Jupiter who Mr Bradley had taken pity upon and was training to become a footman, as well as a London cook who had come from some home for destitute women along with her daughter who was their maid.

Ruby confessed that staff had been harder to find than she would have hoped, since several candidates, even among the destitute women had refused to work for a mulatto mistress, but Mrs Morris and Eliza had taken to their positions with great enthusiasm. Mrs Thomas commented that it was a very enviable set up. Ruby beamed with pride and said she was glad they had their servants in place now for she would need all the help she could get, then pointedly touched her stomach.

She was carrying Mr Bradley's child. After such a pleasant introduction the news shocked me, momentarily repelled me. If she was so fertile how would she get time to continue to devote to her garden and all the cultural pursuits London offered? She had been so looking forward to that. She could be condemned to child bed for the next ten or twenty years, I realised with horror unless it killed her or Mr Bradley showed some consideration. Pushing these thoughts down I smiled along with the rest of the party and offered what I hoped was a sincere show of congratulations.

Jessica

Miss Atwell left to visit her friend near Cardiff. Mrs Nutall returned to take her room and Commodore and Mrs Collins had the other. Amelia was grieved at this as she had the idea that now I owned the house we ought have our own bedrooms, but money still must be made.

'Are we all to still share a room once you are married?'

'I imagine we may move to a bigger house when we are married. Perhaps we will still have an area for lodgers, but we could also have a separate area for family where maybe you might have your own room, but for now we will stay as we are.' I pressed my lips together and paused from baking, not sure how Amelia would take this news but knowing I could not start a new life and leave my girls behind. 'The Captain and I have considered emigrating. I would want you to come as well of course, but it is all yet to be decided.'

Amelia smiled. 'I have been thinking of that lately,' she said slowly. 'If Miss Atwell requires a companion to return home with, and you are also of a mind to emigrate, then I believe that should fit together rather neatly.'

'That is good to hear,' I confessed as a great weight lifted from my mind. She eyed me cautiously, and I could not help shake the feeling she held the future of my happiness in her hands. If she chose to object she could make life very unpleasant for all of us. But she was not the same girl she had been before Peter died, nor was she one she had been in the months after his death. She was a young woman now. Hopefully she would find love soon enough and have no need to concern herself too closely with my second marriage.

'Mrs Fitzwilliam,' came Commodore Collins' cry as he came in through the front door. I went to greet him and saw, as was his habit, he was holding a pile of newspapers and gathering up the letters sent for him. Though he was as good as retired at nearly eighty years old, he liked to keep up to date on the naval news. He was mightily impressed that I was engaged to Captain Parnell, as he had heard of him by reputation but not met him. ('One of the war ships named after a God, isn't it? HMS Apollo or some such? Came up through the ranks, terribly good at heads and guns when he gets the chance I've heard.')

The Commodore sat himself on the sofa and spread his newspapers about himself whilst Amelia fetched him tea with his usual shot of brandy. He set about scouring the papers and taking notes on all the navy battles and activities mentioned.

I returned to the kitchen to finish hand raising the pastry for the pies, whilst Amelia stewed the fillings. As we worked Amelia hummed a merry tune, the cats played at our feet and for a while all was calm.

'Mrs Fitzwilliam!'

'Yes sir?'

'The Gazette Extraordinary reports that peace proceedings are beginning with the French!'

My heart leapt and Amelia beamed.

'But my dear madam…'

I tensed. I did not like the tone of his voice: not his usual cheerful bluster but one of concern.

'This is a very confusing story, The Times has listed the HMS Aries as sunk. It came into difficulties, in a storm.'

For a few moments the words caused my head to swim. No. No. Amelia was at my arm. No, not again, not when we had barely started. James was lost to me, dead and such a hollowness overtook my insides as a great sob rose in my chest. The future had been so bright, so –

'The Times may say it,' Amelia snapped. 'But what do the other papers say?'

'The other papers? But it is The Times, m'dear.'

'So then why do you read the others? Give me one, and let me see if it is reported there.'

Amelia snatched up one of the other papers and started to scan it, while Commodore Collins did the other. My heart pounded, please God, please, please let them have made a mistake.

'It isn't in this one,' Amelia said carefully. 'They report the HMS *Mars* as being sunk however.'

The admiral set his down. 'This reports neither the Aries nor the Mars.' A heavy silence fell, it seemed no one knew what they were reporting. 'How are we to know what is correct?'

'I could write to my contacts at the admiralty.'

'That could take weeks!' burst Amelia. The Commodore raised his eyebrows, but I could hardly ask Amelia to be calm at a time like this.

'If peace is being negotiated, the fleet should come home. Do you know where the fleet will come in?' I asked. 'Will it be Bristol?'

'It should come in at the end of the week, into Portsmouth,' he replied with a lowered voice. 'I had that in a coded letter.'

I looked at Amelia, whose eyes were wide.

'We're going to Portsmouth,' I said. 'I shall pack, can you write and tell Lydia?'

She nodded and we dashed upstairs.

Lydia

Mr Bradley did not disturb us as much as I had feared, for he did much work with the abolitionists and other charitable causes. Ruby and I visited the British Museum as she had promised. We were awed by all we saw; there were great statues of antiquity, all so aged, but in such a good state of repair. How lucky we were to move among such history. It was there I told Ruby of the plans for a shop. I do know why I chose to confide I, but Amelia's generosity and my own ideas suddenly slipped out – somethings would never change between Ruby and I. I would always be compelled to tell her everything.

'I mean to sell books of a medical and scientific nature as well as tinctures, for I fancy I could mix some myself.'

She pressed my arm. 'I fancy you could. How glad I am for you.' I flattered myself that I saw a brief moment of regret in her eyes but then it was gone and we moved on, arm in arm, to other antiquities.

*

The next few weeks passed with visits to botanical gardens and many walks in the fine parks. We also managed to visit the theatre and went to a couple of abolitionist meetings. I received a steady stream of letters from Mother and Amelia to keep me up to date on all that was happening at home.

After a day of shopping, as I readied for bed there was a great hammering on the door. A messenger had been sent express from Bristol. I opened the note which Amelia had scrawled in a very untidy hand.

'What is it?' Ruby asked.

I read aloud. 'One of the papers has reported that Captain Parnell's ship has been sunk whilst the others do not. Mother and Amelia are to go to Portsmouth when the fleet arrives to discover the truth.'

'Oh my goodness! How agonising for them!'

'I must go to Portsmouth to be with them.'

'Are you sure?'

'My Mother will be heartbroken if this is true,' I said. 'I must be with her…and I fancy Amelia wishes for an attachment with a lieutenant from the same ship. I must be there for both of them.'

I wrote a letter to be sent back express to say I would meet them there. They hoped to stay at a hotel called The Dolphin, which Mother had heard the Captain speak of before. I hoped I would be able to find them there.

Amelia

As expected, our coach ride to Portsmouth was arduous and uncomfortable. Mama was quiet and distracted, wringing her hands, her brow furrowed in worry. The fate of Lt Driscoll weighed upon my mind. I had not given much thought to the danger that he would be in, and any regard I held for him had all been in abstract until the damnable Commodore said his boat was lost. It was as if I had been struck, any girlish ideals of a reconciling crushed.

It had only been in panic that I had demanded to check the other newspapers to see a confirmation. I fully expected it to be there but it was not. But then as Commodore Collins said, could The Times of London truly be wrong? I would hold out hope that it was, as we journeyed down. I wore the family Snowden pearls and a scarf embroidered oak leaves in the hope I would have him there to show them off to when we arrived.

When we arrived at the hotel, it was Lydia who was waiting for us. To her annoyance and apparent surprise Mr Bradley had insisted upon driving her down, and now had gone to call upon some old friends. She had secured us a large, clean room with a view of the street and the harbour.

'The fleet has not arrived yet,' she told us. 'But is expected any moment.'

We called for some tea and Mother stood at the window, clutching her cup, watching the street.

'Do sit down,' I said, stopping myself from adding she was like some sad figure in a ghost story. She had no sooner done so then she leapt up again, foghorns sounded and a commotion came from the street below. The ships were coming in.

Jessica
For the past few days my emotions had swung between dread and misery. I had devoured every newspaper I could get my hands upon. Most spoke of victories, of the forth-coming peace agreement, no other mentioned the Aries' demise, but The Times had not issued a correction or an apology. How could we truly know until all the ships were safely in port? Commodore Collins seemed sure they would not make a mistake.

Please not now. We had such plans, such happiness. I loved him. He loved me. There could not now be a life without him, the thought of it seemed so lonely, so bleak when it had suddenly, briefly, been so bright. Physical pain gripped me, my back ached with tension, my stomach felt bruised and I could not eat or drink much. I swallowed but I would have to be strong, there was still the girls to think of, the house, the business…

We hurried along the harbour arms linked. Others emerged from their houses, waving flags and cheering, some anxiously looking through the crowd as I was. The sailors started to disembark, making the streets swarm with hundreds of men. The sea was clogged with more boats waiting to dock. How could anyone be found?

'There,' Lydia said suddenly. 'There is the HMS Aries.'

I gasped aloud and blinked away tears of relief while Amelia cheered. It was over the other side of the harbour through crowds.

'It looks as though they have disembarked already,' Lydia squinted, as the crowd jostled us.

Amelia released her hold on my arm and handed me the scarf she had around her neck. 'We shall only slow you, go find the Captain then we can meet back at the hotel.'

'I can hardly leave you among all these rowdy sailors!'

'We are not far from the hotel,' Lydia said, while Amelia's face suddenly glowed with a smile. I followed her gaze through the crowd, to where Lt Driscoll was pushing towards us, returning her expression.

'You see, Mother,' Lydia whispered. 'We shall be well taken care of. Now, go and find the Captain.'

Amelia
Before I had given Mama the oak leaf scarf I had seen Lt Driscoll pushing through the crowd. His eyes widened at the sight of us and stayed fixed on me. Suddenly I was embarrassed that he would see through me, forget me or worse think I was more in love with him than I was. That was why I gave Mama the scarf. I did not want him to know it had been done in his honour. Its removal had also revealed the pearls making his eyes widen more and ensuring I had his full attention. He pushed towards us as Mama vanished.

'Hello Lt Driscoll,' Lydia said.

'Miss Fitzwilliam, Miss Amelia, what are you doing here?'

'We heard the HMS Aries had sunk,' Lydia said.

'Slanderous lies! It was the Mars and we came to their aid!'

'Mama wanted to see about your Captain.'

'Indeed? Perhaps I could escort you back to your lodgings, this street is likely to become dangerous.'

'That would be most kind of you,' I said as Lydia and I took an arm each. Once we were back at the inn Lydia gave me a quick grin and darted inside. The streets had been too busy for much conversation aside from his boasts that they had caught a ship so would do well on prize money. Well better and better, he would not be so very poor. Standing in the doorway of the inn his eyes were on the pearl necklace again.

'Is that what I think it is?'

I touched the crest in the middle – the ugliest yet most easily identifiable part. 'It is.'

'Are you engaged to Charles?'

I shook my head. 'Not at all. He gave me this in Bath and has since accused me of stealing it - but I have no intention of returning it to him or his branch of the family.'

Lt Driscoll raised his eyebrows. 'So you may return it to another branch of the family?'

'I may be persuaded.'

He laughed and I smiled at him.

'May you permit me to ask…did an attachment grow between you and he?'

I looked at Lt. Driscoll. 'You were right to warn me about him and I ought have listened. He wanted me for his mistress and I refused. One night he was quite forceful about it, but I managed to escape and fled back to Bristol.'

'I am sorry to hear that.'

'You tried to warn me.'

'Yes, but I also presumed too much of an attachment on my own behalf. I expected to be obeyed, and why you should obey and listen to someone who was little more than an acquaintance? You had every right to refuse my letters, I ought not have behaved in so ungentlemanly a manner when you did.'

I extended a hand. 'May we start again then?'

He took my hand and kissed it. 'With pleasure. Allow me to introduce myself. I am Lt. Driscoll, at your service, Irish Bastard and hero of the navy.'

I jokingly rolled my eyes. 'And I am Miss Amelia Fitzwilliam, daughter of a bankrupt, and am not impressed at all by heroes.'

Jessica

I pushed through the crowds. At last I came to a gap and against all propriety, seeing my chance, I broke into a run, a few more people parted for me, some men cheered but I cared not. I felt my bonnet slip, my blood pump, my lungs gasp but I could not stop, I had to know that he was well.

Within the crowd I lost sight of the ship, then found it again. I saw a knot of sailors standing before it as I neared, and then there he was. I stopped, panting for breath. His back was to me, his hat under his arm – he was in conversation with other officers, then one of them paused and pointed. He turned and beamed at the sight of me, broke away from his group without any apology and ran towards me. I ran into his arms, felt him lift me. We kissed and then came the cheers of the sailors and a blush and a giggle rose up in me.

'I thought you had died,' I said. 'The Times reported the Aries as lost.'

He cocked an eyebrow. 'The Times indeed! No, we are not lost at all. We took another ship at Boulogne, a great beauty she was, and aided the Mars after a storm.'

I smiled, taking his face in my hands. 'And you are back, safe and sound.'

'I am,' he said. 'I am sorry for any worry, but I must confess to being so glad to see you here.'

I smiled, we were still holding each. I never wanted to let him go.

'They are saying the war might be over, that they may let some of the officers and ships go. I will request for that Jessica, so we may always be together, start our life our adventures, properly.'

I nodded blissfully happy, and arm in arm we walked back through the crowds together, towards the hotel.

Epilogue: Ten Years Later

From a large townhouse on a modern street, a girl emerged with long, flyaway black plaits. She was skinny, with green eyes and a Roman nose. She was followed by a blonde, fashionably dressed young woman whose stomach was rounded with an unborn child. Both woman and girl wore aprons flecked with paint.

'I shall bring your landscape over tomorrow, Madeline,' the young blonde woman said. 'I was planning on calling upon Mama anyway. It should be dry but you applied the paint so thickly we will have see.'

'Amelia,' the girl said, twisting a black plait. 'Do you suppose Mama and Papa will like it?'

'I am sure they shall,' the young woman said before adding with a wicked grin. 'Not that it means the painting has any merit for they are always most biased where you are concerned.'

The girl gave the woman a soft, playful shove and they laughed – a resemblance passing across their features which had not been there before.

As the woman removed the child's apron she told her to take care on the journey home, then ruffled the dark hair, a contrast to her own blonde and said, 'Summer's Coal.' The little girl poked her tongue out, then ran to the trough where a fine bay house was tied up. She mounted with ease, not sitting side saddle, revealing riding breeches beneath her skirts which the woman rolled her eyes at as she waved the girl off.

The girl rode down the road, all around her houses and stores were being built, cobbles being laid and fences being painted. Some of those busy at work waved or tipped their hats.

'Evenin' Miss Parnell!'

'Hello Maddie!'

'Miss Parnell, you tell your pa I'm going be over to look at that grey colt tomorrow.'

The girl waved and greeted everyone and to the last request she stopped her horse. 'Well sir, I think I better tell you Papa has had a lot of interest in that particular colt so

you'd better come with a good price.'

The man chuckled. 'Thank you for tip, missy!'

The girl, Madeline Parnell, dismounted at a shop, which bore the sign 'Medical Supplies and Apothecary.' She dashed inside. A while later she emerged holding hands with a handsome woman, whose brown hair was neatly pinned.

'But Mama said we were to picnic tonight Lydia, you ought come.'

'I have told you I have promised to dine with friends-'

'Any particular friends?' Madeline asked, affecting a grown-up tone.

'Did Amelia tell you to ask that?'

Madeline laughed.

The woman handed the girl some books.

'You ought read this first, because this won't make sense otherwise-'

The girl nodded. 'Amelia lent me *Romance of The Forest*.'

'I'll bet she did. Well, read these first-'

'Mr Jones, you know my school master-'

'Yes.'

'He said I read too many books and all of them are most unsuitable for a girl.'

Lydia laughed. 'There is no such thing as reading too much, do not pay him heed.'

Madeline smiled. 'I was not intending to.'

They embraced and Lydia waved as Madeline rode off.

Once Madeline was out of the developing town, she got the horse to gallop but slowed it as she came to two buildings set back from the road. One was called Summer's Lodge Hotel, the other was a comfortably sized house, surrounded by a vegetable garden.

A middle aged blonde woman, walking between the two buildings, hailed the girl who stopped and smiled.

'Mama, my sisters send their best wishes.'

The woman reached up and kissed her daughter's cheek. 'I have some nice sandwiches for our picnic.'

The woman went into the house and came out with a basket then mounted the horse side-saddle behind the girl. They rode off into the fields in lively conversation, stopping when they neared pens and a riding range, where a tall man, his black hair flecked with grey, was training a horse.

The man helped the woman down, before giving the girl the reins to the horse he'd been training. Whilst on her own horse, she led the other to the stable. In a moment of solitude, the man and the woman laughed and kissed, spoke happily together until the girl ran back from the stables into the man's arms. He picked her up and swung her about as she shrieked with laughter. Her long black hair mostly escaped from the plaits and she spoke excitedly to the man while holding hands with the woman.

'So, Papa, he should give you a fine price for the colt-'

'That's my girl.'

Together they set off for an evening picnic.

Glossary

Abolitionist – Anti-Slavery campaigner

Ann Radcliffe – Writer of Gothic fiction set on the continent

Bibi – Indian mistress

Beau Monde – Fashionable Society

Blue Stocking – Female Intellectual

Breached – Both little boys and girls wore long gowns until they were six or seven, when the boys were 'breached', that is put into breeches (or britches)

Cabriolet- A small two seat carriage which requires only one horse, with a hood that can go up and down.

Catholic relief laws- Catholic Relief laws were passed in the late 1700s, allowing Catholics more freedom especially in public life and rights in property ownership.

Dance card – young ladies wrote names of men requesting to dance with them on their dance cards. It was considered improper to refuse a man, or to dance more than two dances with him

Dandy – Fashionable, vain young man

Dissenter – Radical, often liberal thinker, writer or philosopher

Entail – This was a clause written into the deeds of a property which meant it had to be left to the oldest male relative, which if there was no son would involve it being passed to the next male relative even if they were outside of the immediate family, such as a cousin or nephew. However, not all properties had this clause so it wasn't unusual for widows to inherit ahead of male relatives if this clause wasn't in place

Heads and Guns – A navy term for the prize money awarded for catching an enemy ship. Navy officers were not especially well paid so were incentivised into catching enemy ships which could then be used by the British fleet by large amounts of prize money.

Ignatius Sancho - Mr Thomas is inspired by the real-life abolitionist Ignatius Sancho who was a shop keeper with a wide ranging social circle, and whose published collection of letters became a best seller.

Link boy – Paid by pedestrians at night-time to light the way for them by carrying a torch

Middle Passage – Part of the Transatlantic Slave Trade. The Middle Passage was the journey between Africa and the Americas, transporting enslaved people in overcrowded and inhumane conditions which many did not survive. It was infamously cruel and was used by anti-slavery campaigns to illustrate the wrongs of slavery.

Mulatto – Term for a mixed-race person with one black parent and one white parent.

Navy – to become an officer in the army, one paid for the commission (the cavalry was more expensive than the infantry). This meant that generally only middle and upper class men were army officers. The navy was different – possibly due to the technical nature of sailing. An ambitious young man could either work his way up or pay to go to naval college; both paths allowed entry into the officer class of the navy. Naval officer positions could not be bought and were based on merit, though of course , as with everything , friends in high places could lend a hand when it came to promotions. This meant that navy officers tended to come from the lower middle class and trade, as well as, in theory, the working class. As well as this, the navy had sailors from all over the British Empire including from Asia and Africa, making a relatively multicultural institution for the time.

Oak – Oaks had long been a symbol of the navy. Heart of Oak was the navy's anthem and ladies (including Jane Austen) wore dresses with oak leaves to show their support for the navy

Quadroon – Term for a person of mixed heritage with one black grandparent and three white grandparents

Rake – Boisterous young man, often wealthy, interested in gambling, drinking and womanising

Reach Down Shop -Second hand clothes shop

Sahib - Polite way to address a man in India, during the Raj and British rule was often used to refer to white men

Sambo – Term for a person of mixed heritage with three black grandparents and one white grandparent, but sometimes used colloquially and offensively to describe a person of colour

Spencer – Short jacket

Surgeon – A medical professional, not unlike a GP who qualified by an apprenticeship rather than study. They tended various ills in the community and were cheaper than doctors

Syllabub – A sweet yogurt, posset like dessert

Tawny – A way of describing a black or mixed-race person, sometimes forming a nickname. Tawny Bess was a real-life waitress in Covent Garden who is featured in Hogarth's engravings. This is who the minor character of Alice, referred to by Amelia as Tawny Alice, is named after.

Trade – To be 'in trade' as the Fitzwilliams and many of their friends were meant to work for a living, managing your own business (examples in the book include hoteliers, shop keepers, grocers, butchers and cobblers). This put you above the working class, and equated to the lowest sort of middle class. Being in trade meant that you were not a 'gentleman' as you had to work for a living. Professions in the clergy, law or military were among the few one could pursue and still be gentleman.

Trousseau – New clothes for a young woman getting married, ready for her to wear as a wife

Printed in Great Britain
by Amazon